Clarence™

Chicken Phantom

ROSS RICHIE CEO & Founder • MATT GAGNON Editor-in-Chief • FILIP SABLIK President of Publishing & Marketing • STEPHEN CHRISTY President of Development • LANCE KREITER VP of Licensing & Merchandising • PHIL BARBARO VP of Finance • BRYCE CARLSON Managing Editor • MEL CAYLO Marketing Manager • SCOTT NEWMAN Production Design Manager • IRENE BRADISH Operations Manager • CHRISTINE DINH Brand Communications Manager • SIERRA HAHN Senior Editor • DAFNA PLEBAN Editor • SHANNON WATTERS Editor • ERIC HARBURN Editor • WHITNEY LEOPARD Associate Editor • JASMINE AMIRI Associate Editor • CHRIS ROSA Associate Editor • ALEX GALER Assistant Editor • CAMERON CHITTOCK Assistant Editor • MARY GUMPORT Assistant Editor • MATTHEW LEVINE Assistant Editor • KELSEY DIETERICH Production Designer • JILLIAN CRAB Production Designer • MICHELLE ANKLEY Production Design Assistant • GRACE PARK Production Design Assistant • AARON FERRARA Operations Coordinator • ELIZABETH LOUGHRIDGE Accounting Coordinator • JOSÉ MEZA Sales Assistant • JAMES ARRIOLA Mailroom Assistant • HOLLY AITCHISON Operations Assistant • STEPHANIE HOCUTT Marketing Assistant • SAM KUSEK Direct Market Representative

For information regarding the CPSIA on this printed material, call: (203) 595-3636 and provide reference #RICH - 663308. A catalog record of this book is available from OCLC and from the KaBOOM! website, www.kaboom-studios.com, on the Librarians Page..

BOOM! Studios, 5670 Wilshire Boulevard, Suite 450, Los Angeles, CA 90036-5679. Printed in USA. First Printing.
ISBN: 978-1-60886-792-9, eISBN: 978-1-61398-463-5

Written by
Derek Fridolfs

Illustrated by
JJ Harrison
& **Cara McGee**
with **Matt Smigel**

Colors by
Joie Brown

Lettered by
Warren Montgomery

Cover by
JJ Harrison

Designer
Kara Leopard

Associate Editor
Whitney Leopard

Editor
Shannon Watters

With Special Thanks to Marisa Marionakis, Rick Blanco, Curtis
Lelash, Conrad Montgomery, Meghan Bradley, Keith Mack, Eric
Cookmeyer and the wonderful folks at Cartoon Network.

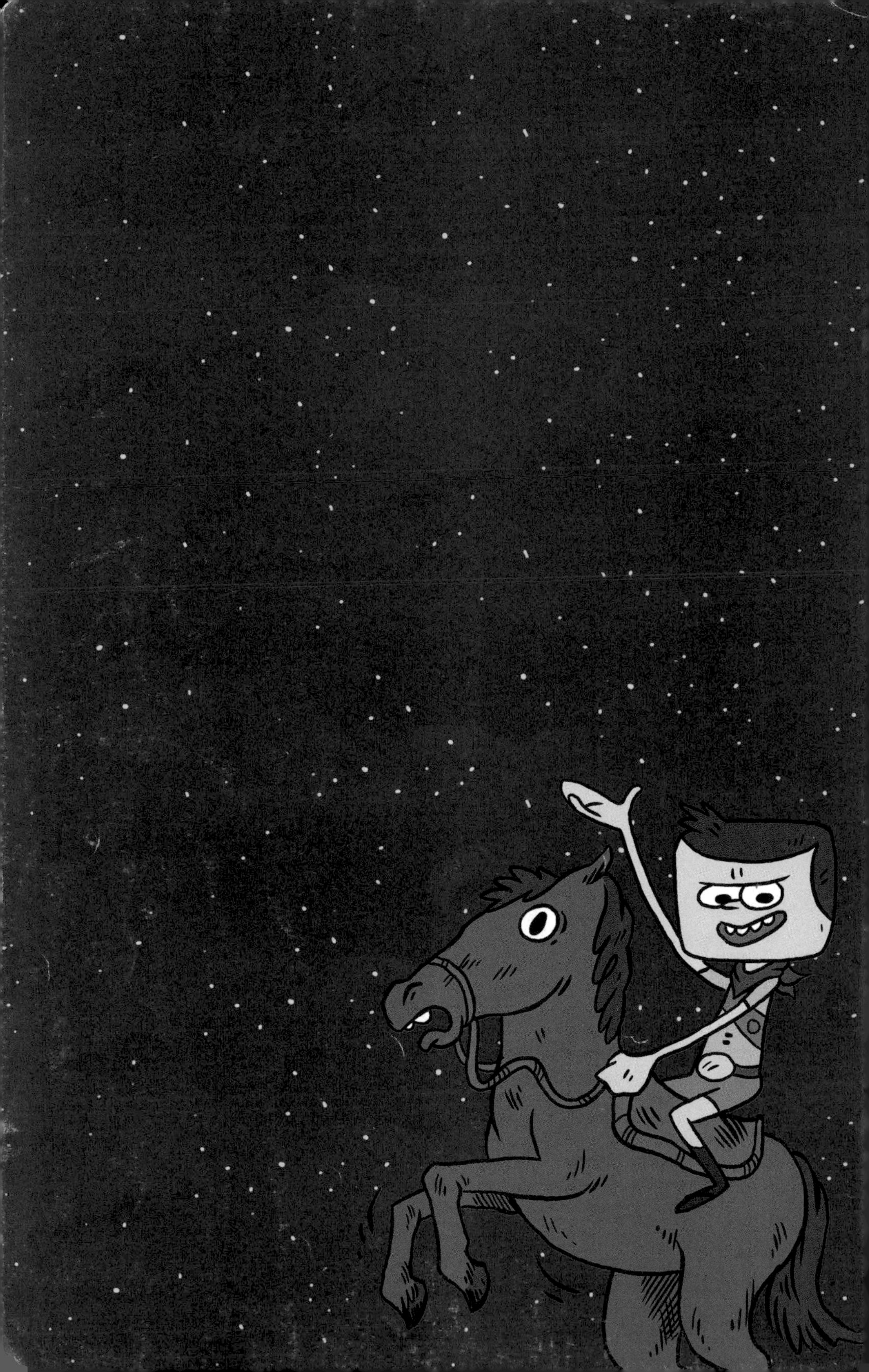

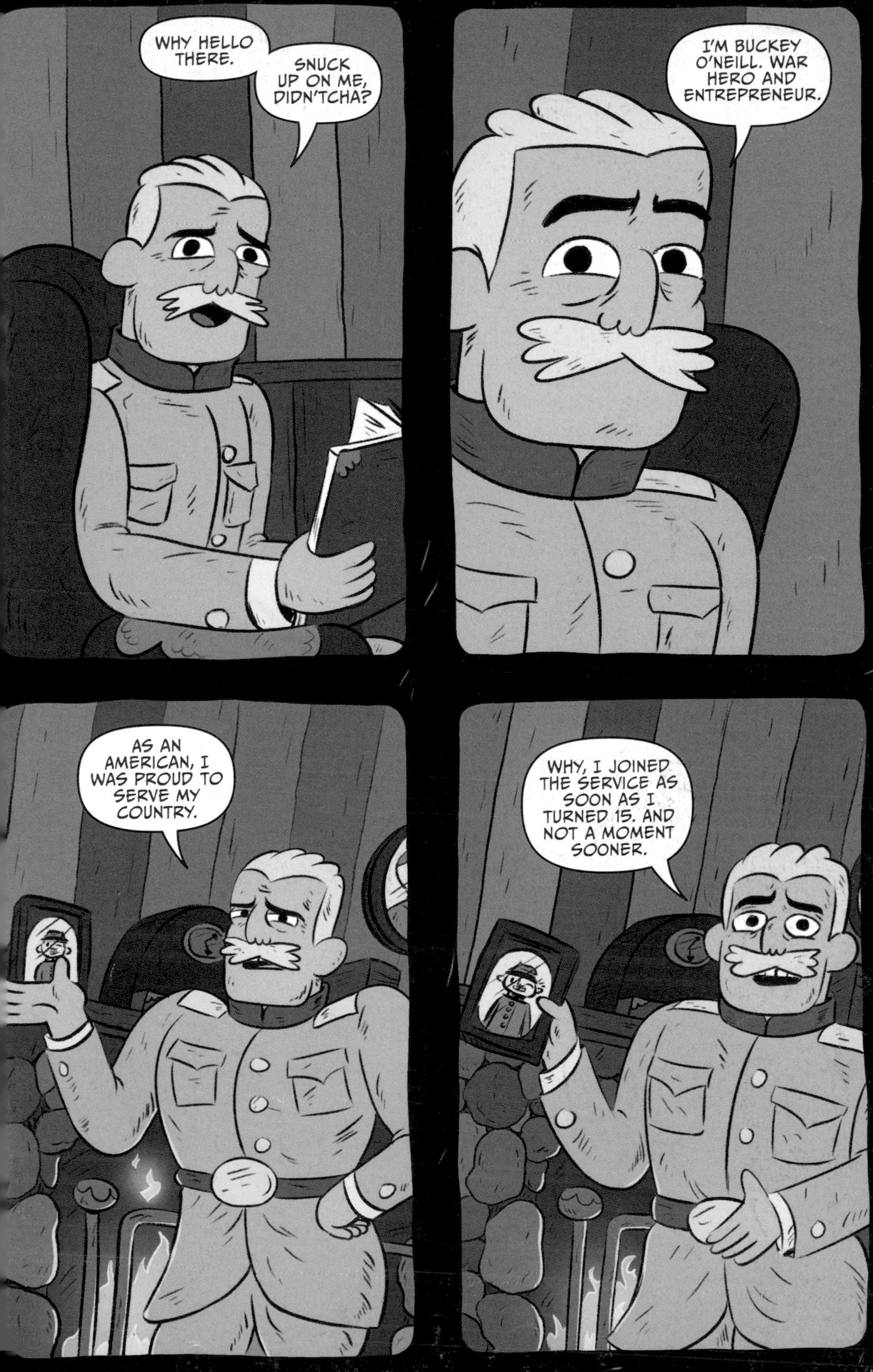
WHY HELLO THERE.
SNUCK UP ON ME, DIDN'TCHA?
I'M BUCKEY O'NEILL. WAR HERO AND ENTREPRENEUR.
AS AN AMERICAN, I WAS PROUD TO SERVE MY COUNTRY.
WHY, I JOINED THE SERVICE AS SOON AS I TURNED 15. AND NOT A MOMENT SOONER.

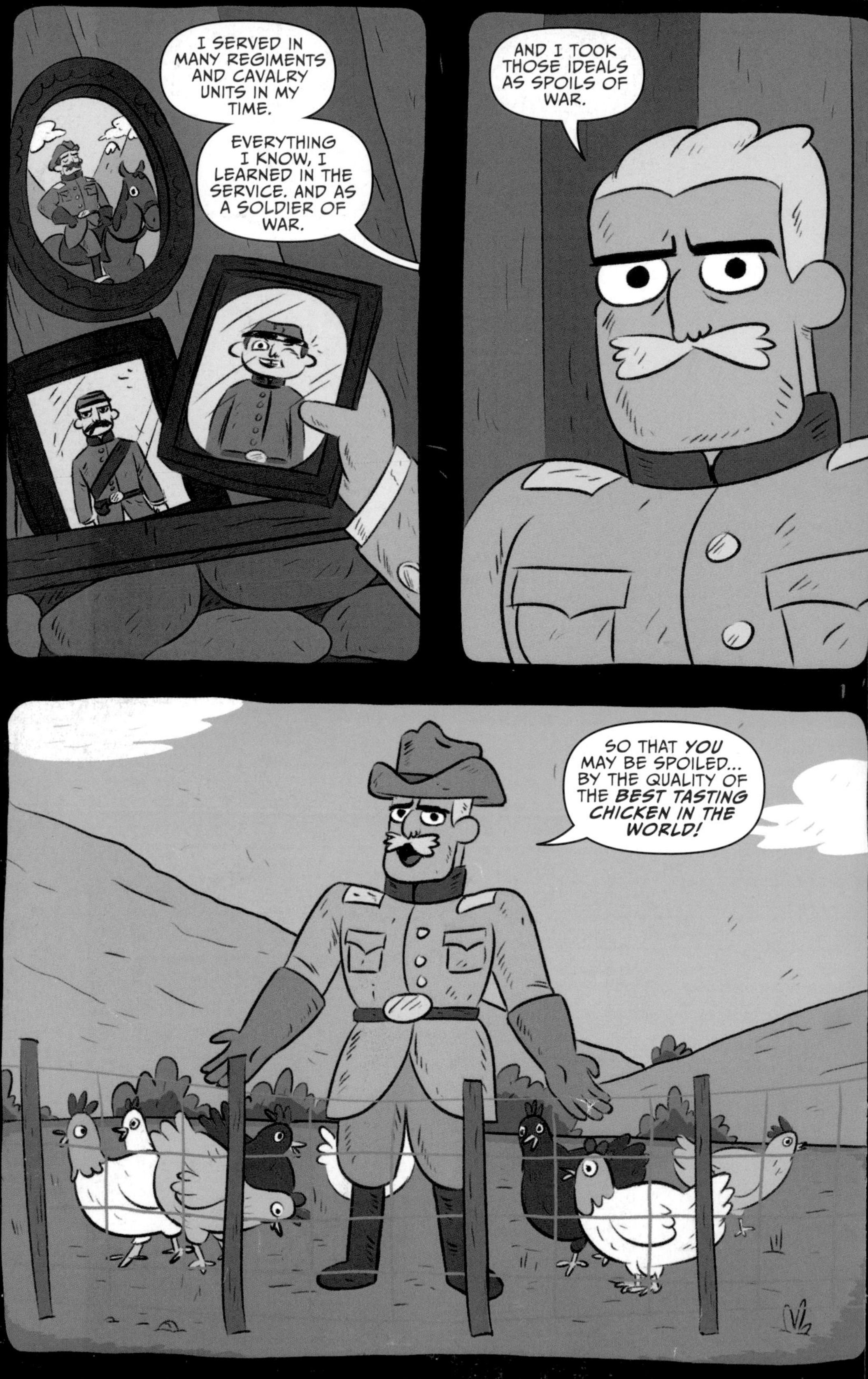
I SERVED IN MANY REGIMENTS AND CAVALRY UNITS IN MY TIME.
EVERYTHING I KNOW, I LEARNED IN THE SERVICE. AND AS A SOLDIER OF WAR.
AND I TOOK THOSE IDEALS AS SPOILS OF WAR.
SO THAT *YOU* MAY BE SPOILED... BY THE QUALITY OF THE ***BEST TASTING CHICKEN IN THE WORLD!***

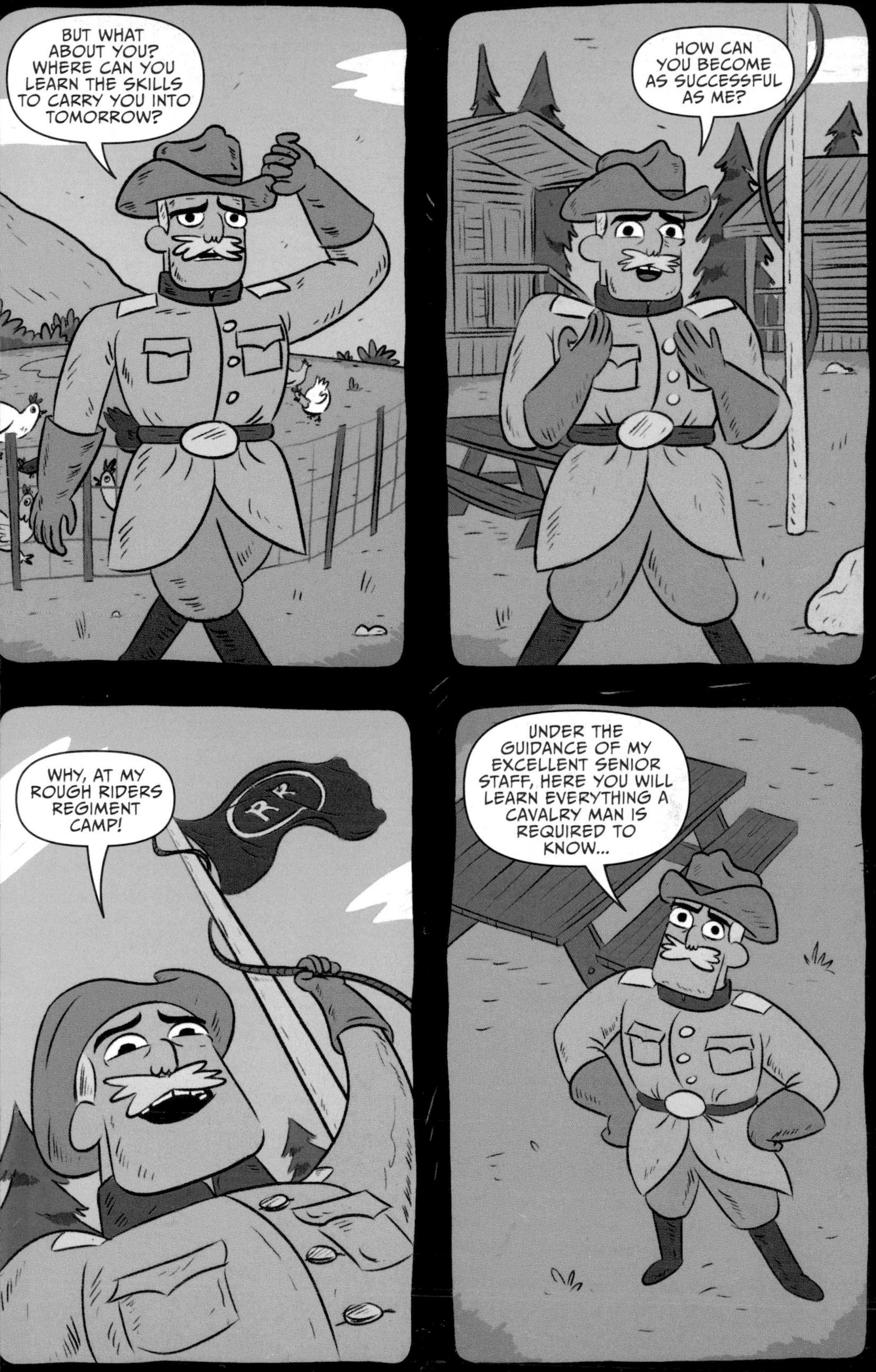
BUT WHAT ABOUT YOU? WHERE CAN YOU LEARN THE SKILLS TO CARRY YOU INTO TOMORROW?
HOW CAN YOU BECOME AS SUCCESSFUL AS ME?
WHY, AT MY ROUGH RIDERS REGIMENT CAMP!
RR
UNDER THE GUIDANCE OF MY EXCELLENT SENIOR STAFF, HERE YOU WILL LEARN EVERYTHING A CAVALRY MAN IS REQUIRED TO KNOW...

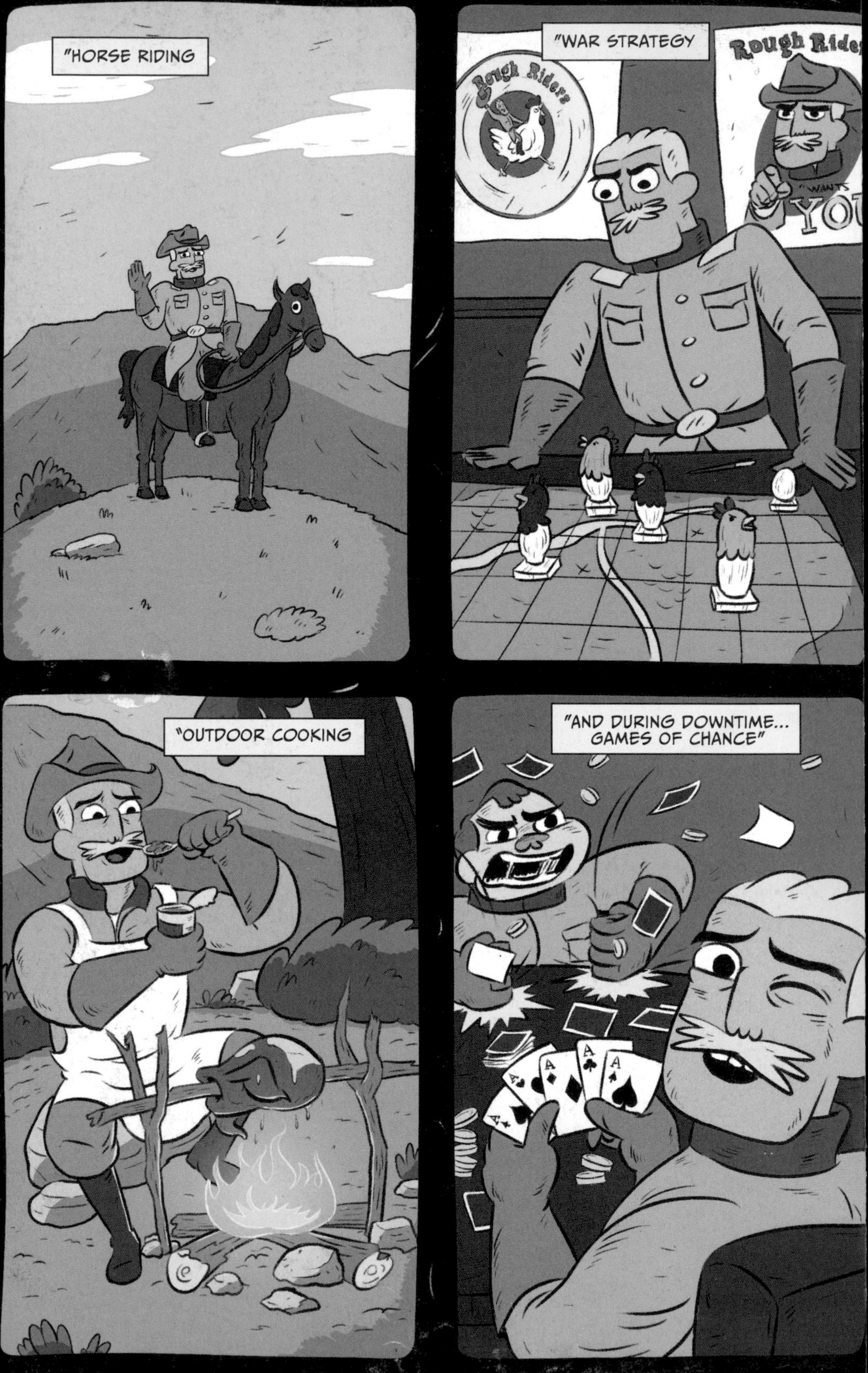
"HORSE RIDING
"WAR STRATEGY
Rough Riders
"OUTDOOR COOKING
"AND DURING DOWNTIME... GAMES OF CHANCE"

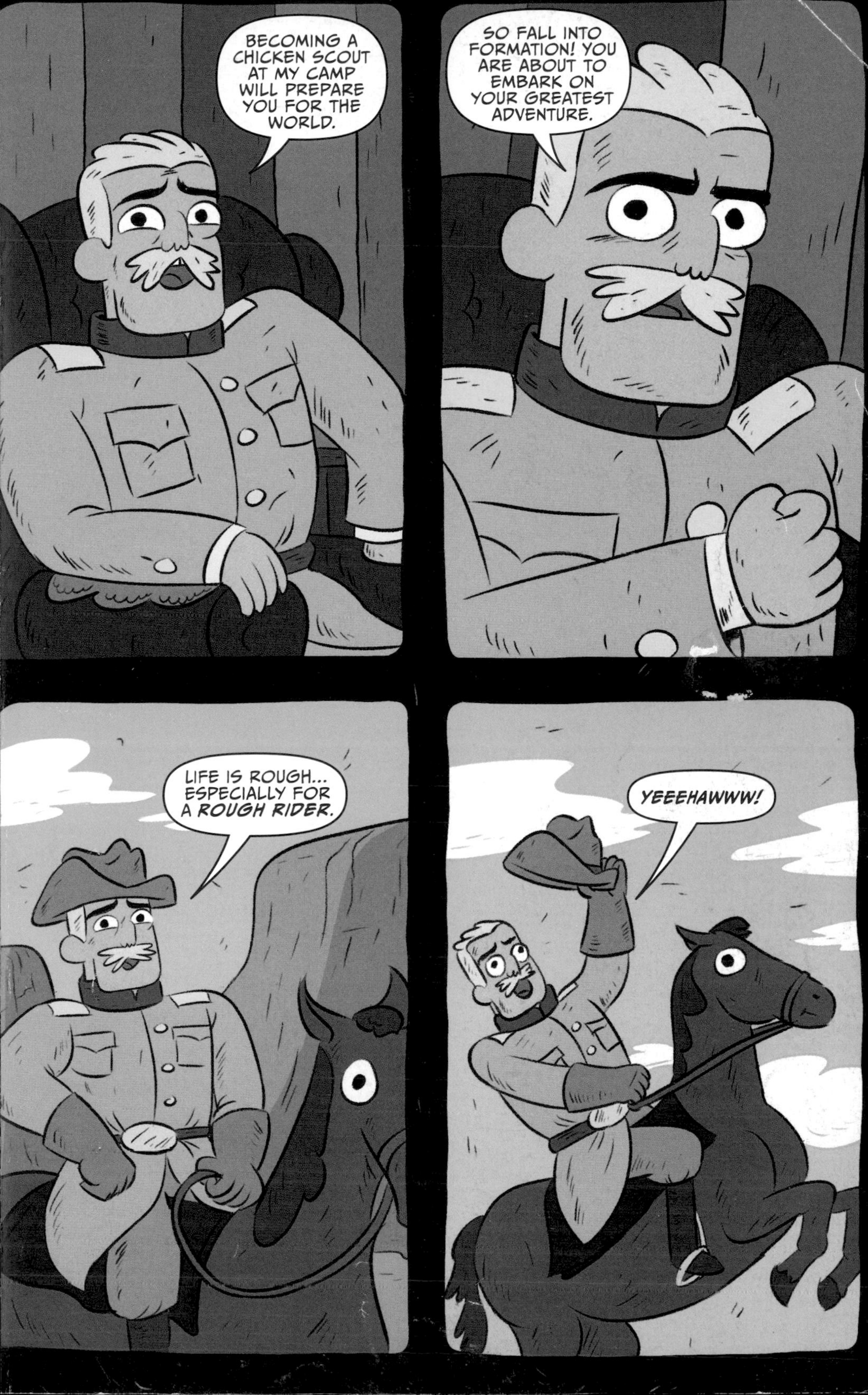
BECOMING A CHICKEN SCOUT AT MY CAMP WILL PREPARE YOU FOR THE WORLD.
SO FALL INTO FORMATION! YOU ARE ABOUT TO EMBARK ON YOUR GREATEST ADVENTURE.
LIFE IS ROUGH... ESPECIALLY FOR A *ROUGH RIDER*.
YEEEHAWWW!

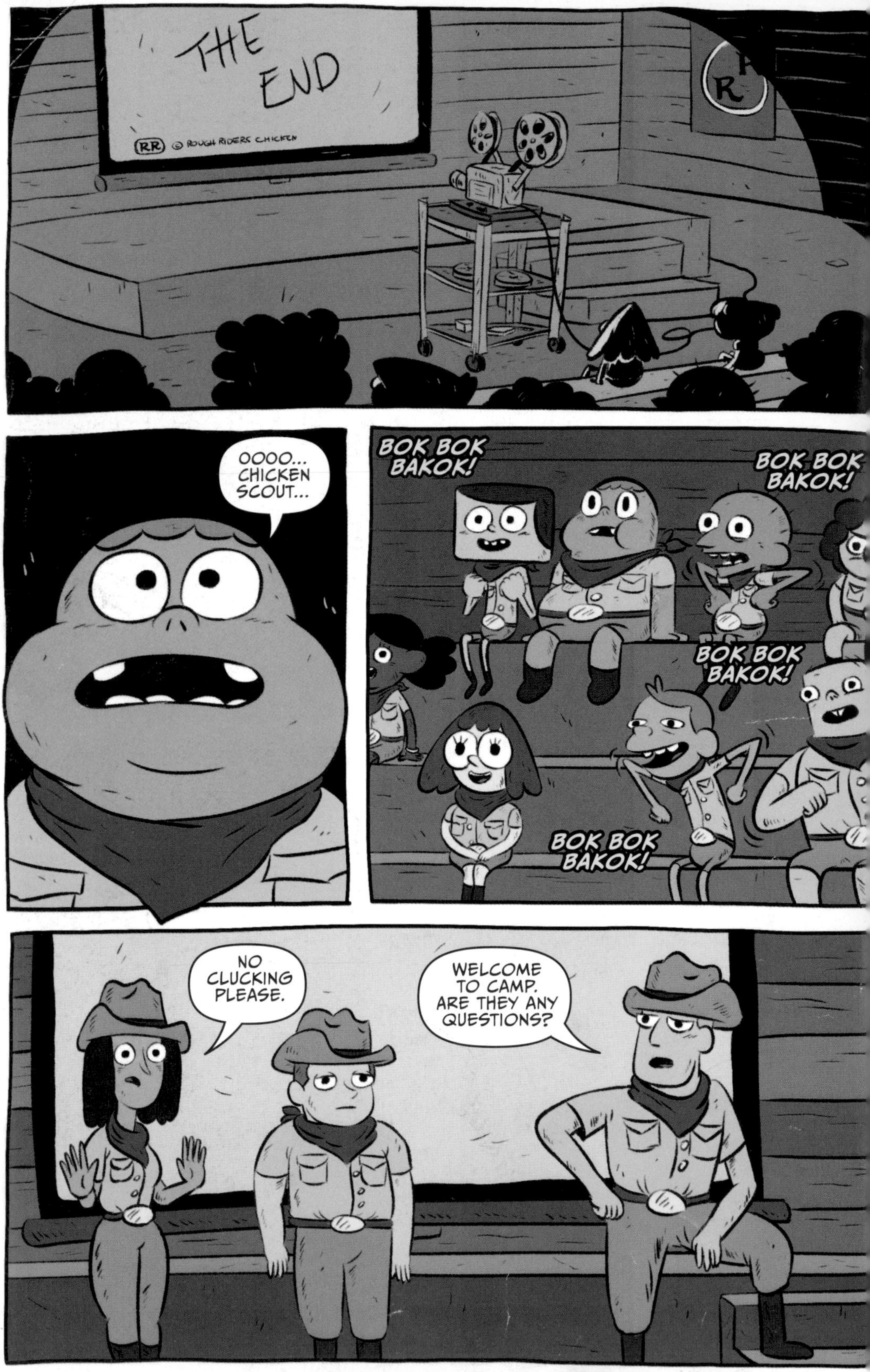
THE END
RR © ROUGH RIDERS CHICKEN
OOOO... CHICKEN SCOUT...
BOK BOK BAKOK!
BOK BOK BAKOK!
BOK BOK BAKOK!
BOK BOK BAKOK!
NO CLUCKING PLEASE.
WELCOME TO CAMP. ARE THEY ANY QUESTIONS?

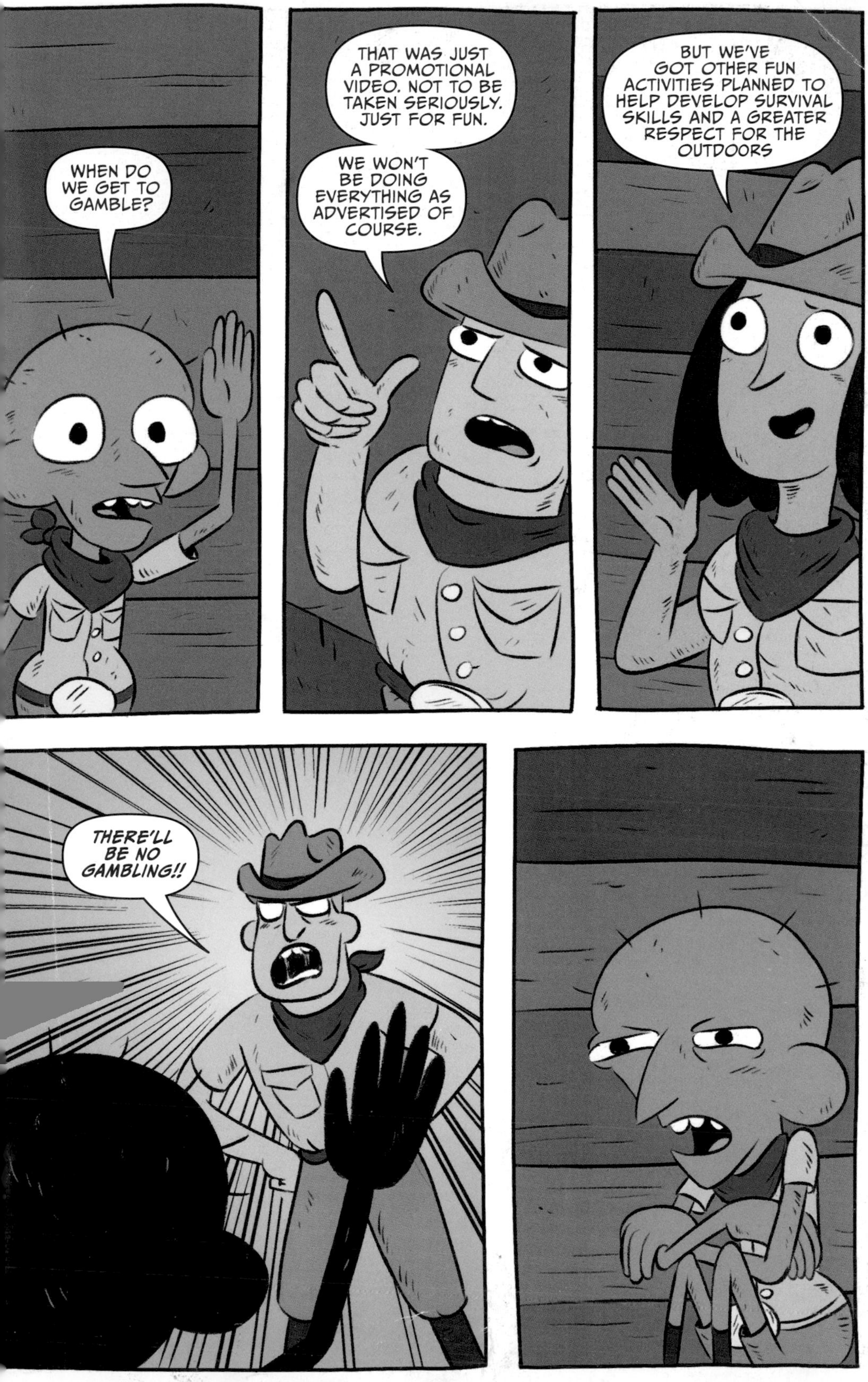
WHEN DO WE GET TO GAMBLE?
THAT WAS JUST A PROMOTIONAL VIDEO. NOT TO BE TAKEN SERIOUSLY. JUST FOR FUN.
WE WON'T BE DOING EVERYTHING AS ADVERTISED OF COURSE.
BUT WE'VE GOT OTHER FUN ACTIVITIES PLANNED TO HELP DEVELOP SURVIVAL SKILLS AND A GREATER RESPECT FOR THE OUTDOORS
THERE'LL BE NO GAMBLING!!

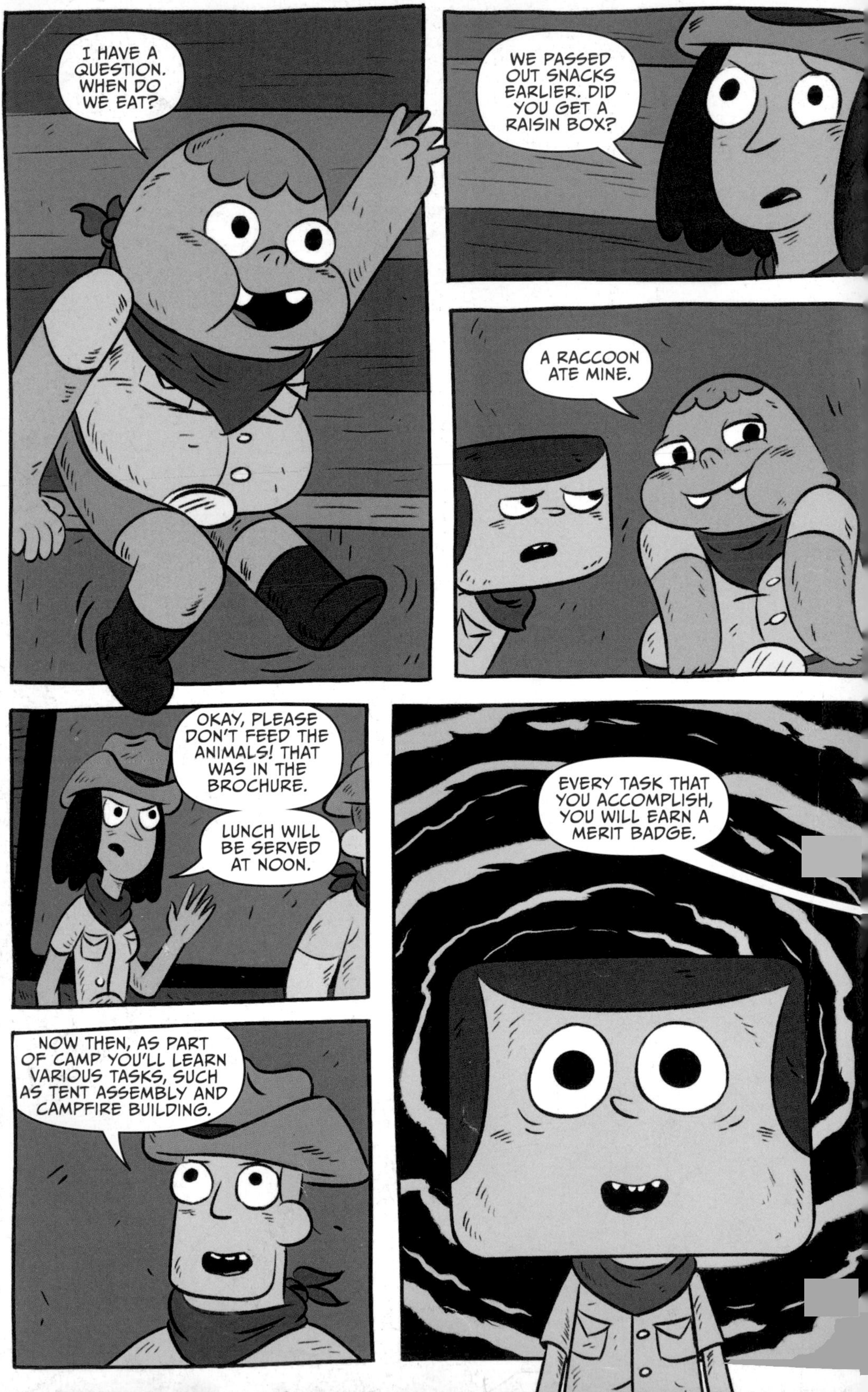
I HAVE A QUESTION. WHEN DO WE EAT?
WE PASSED OUT SNACKS EARLIER. DID YOU GET A RAISIN BOX?
A RACCOON ATE MINE.
OKAY, PLEASE DON'T FEED THE ANIMALS! THAT WAS IN THE BROCHURE.
LUNCH WILL BE SERVED AT NOON.
NOW THEN, AS PART OF CAMP YOU'LL LEARN VARIOUS TASKS, SUCH AS TENT ASSEMBLY AND CAMPFIRE BUILDING.
EVERY TASK THAT YOU ACCOMPLISH, YOU WILL EARN A MERIT BADGE.

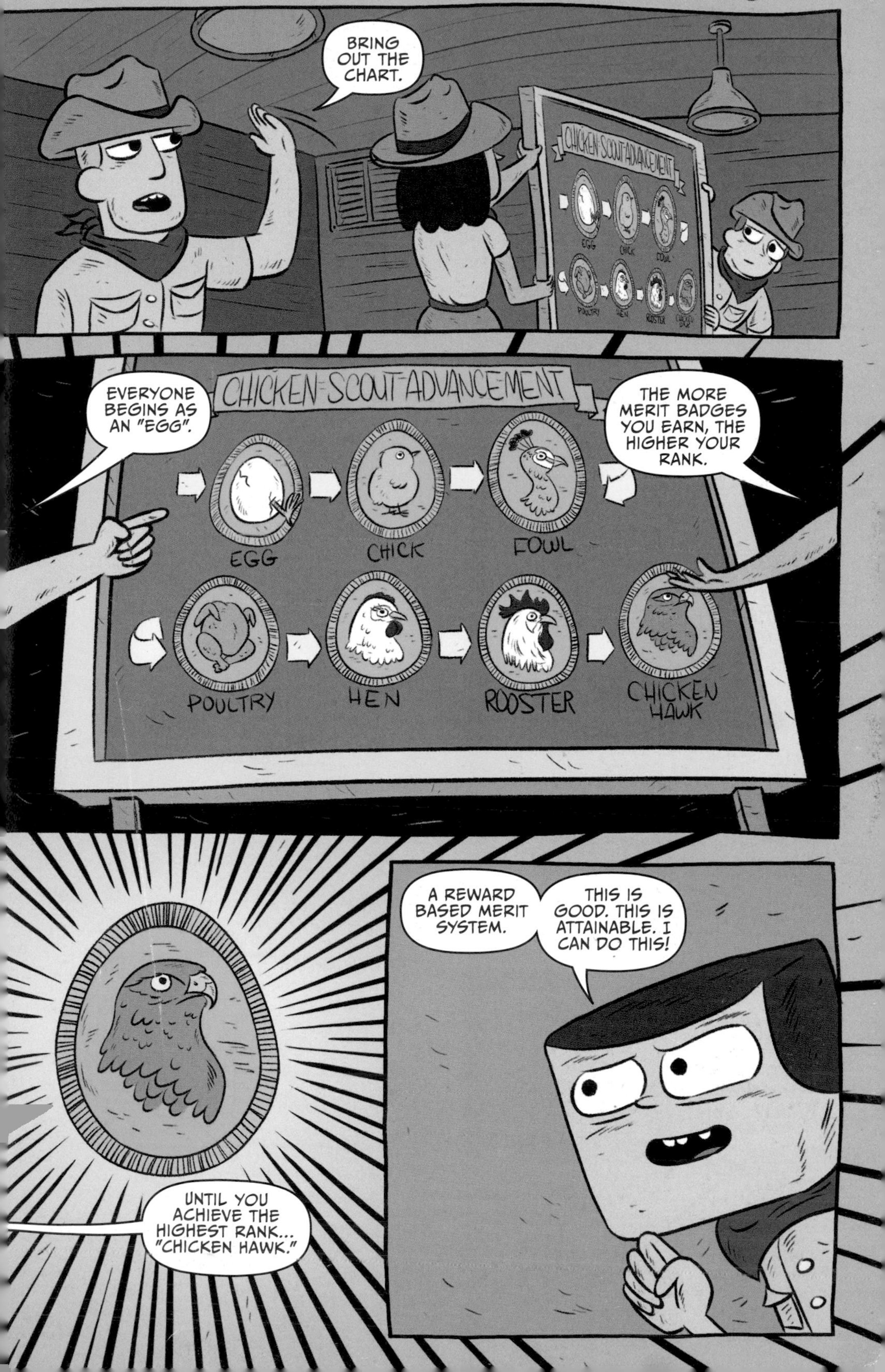
BRING OUT THE CHART.
CHICKEN-SCOUT-ADVANCEMENT
EVERYONE BEGINS AS AN "EGG".
THE MORE MERIT BADGES YOU EARN, THE HIGHER YOUR RANK.
EGG
CHICK
FOWL
POULTRY
HEN
ROOSTER
CHICKEN HAWK
UNTIL YOU ACHIEVE THE HIGHEST RANK... "CHICKEN HAWK."
A REWARD BASED MERIT SYSTEM.
THIS IS GOOD. THIS IS ATTAINABLE. I CAN DO THIS!

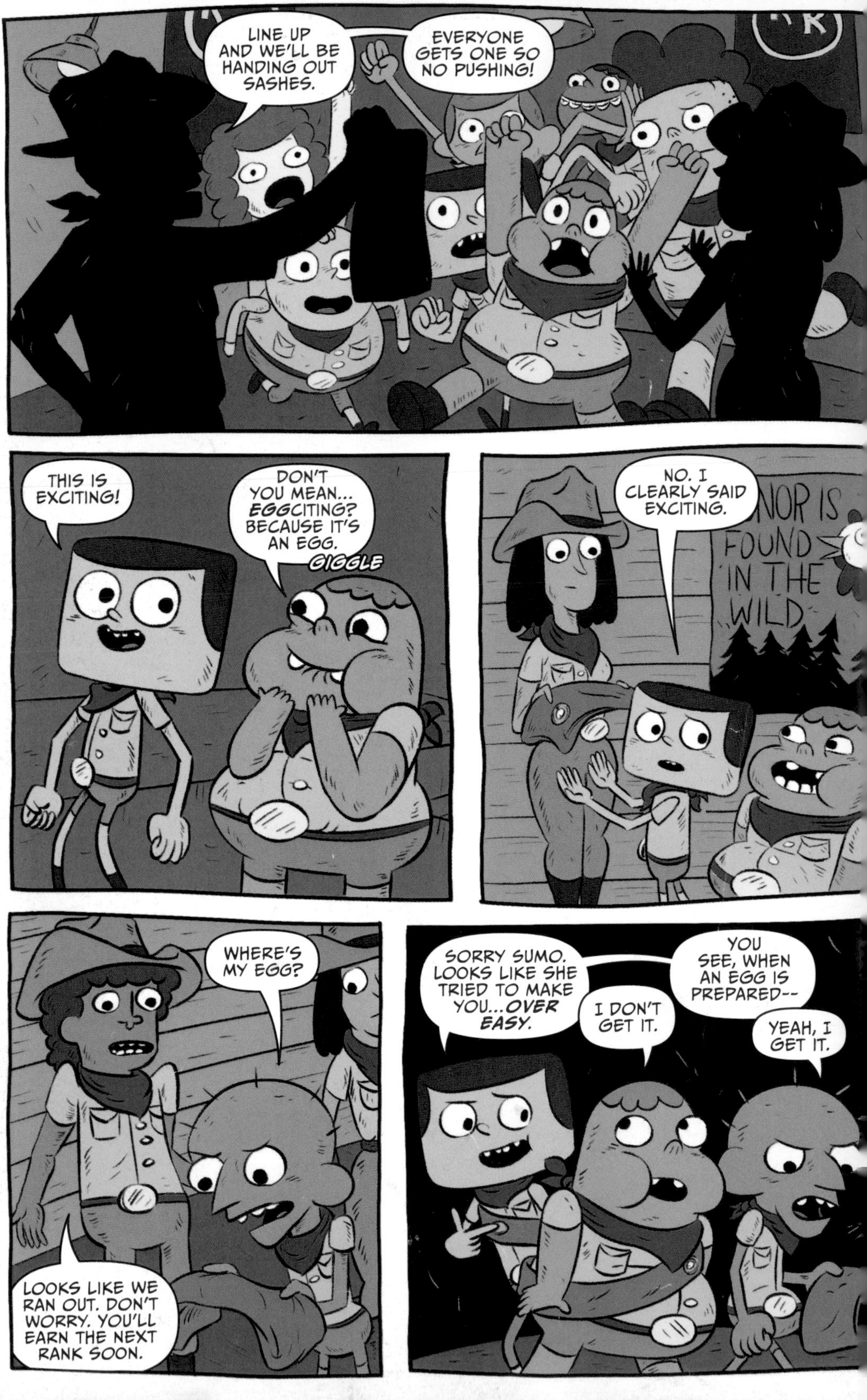

LINE UP AND WE'LL BE HANDING OUT SASHES.
EVERYONE GETS ONE SO NO PUSHING!
THIS IS EXCITING!
DON'T YOU MEAN... EGGCITING? BECAUSE IT'S AN EGG.
GIGGLE
NO. I CLEARLY SAID EXCITING.
NOR IS FOUND IN THE WILD
WHERE'S MY EGG?
LOOKS LIKE WE RAN OUT. DON'T WORRY. YOU'LL EARN THE NEXT RANK SOON.
SORRY SUMO. LOOKS LIKE SHE TRIED TO MAKE YOU...OVER EASY.
YOU SEE, WHEN AN EGG IS PREPARED--
I DON'T GET IT.
YEAH, I GET IT.

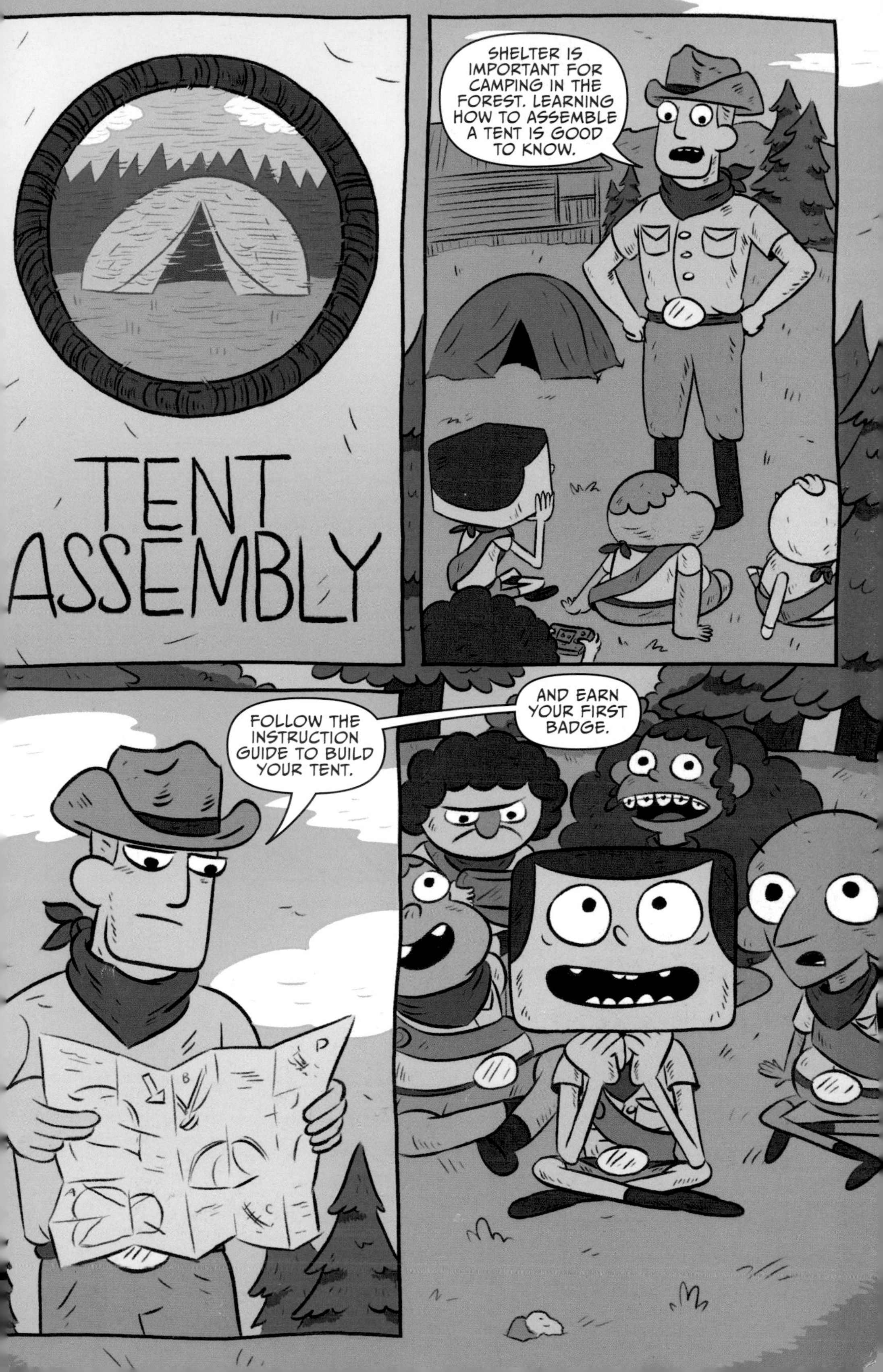
TENT ASSEMBLY
SHELTER IS IMPORTANT FOR CAMPING IN THE FOREST. LEARNING HOW TO ASSEMBLE A TENT IS GOOD TO KNOW.
FOLLOW THE INSTRUCTION GUIDE TO BUILD YOUR TENT.
AND EARN YOUR FIRST BADGE.

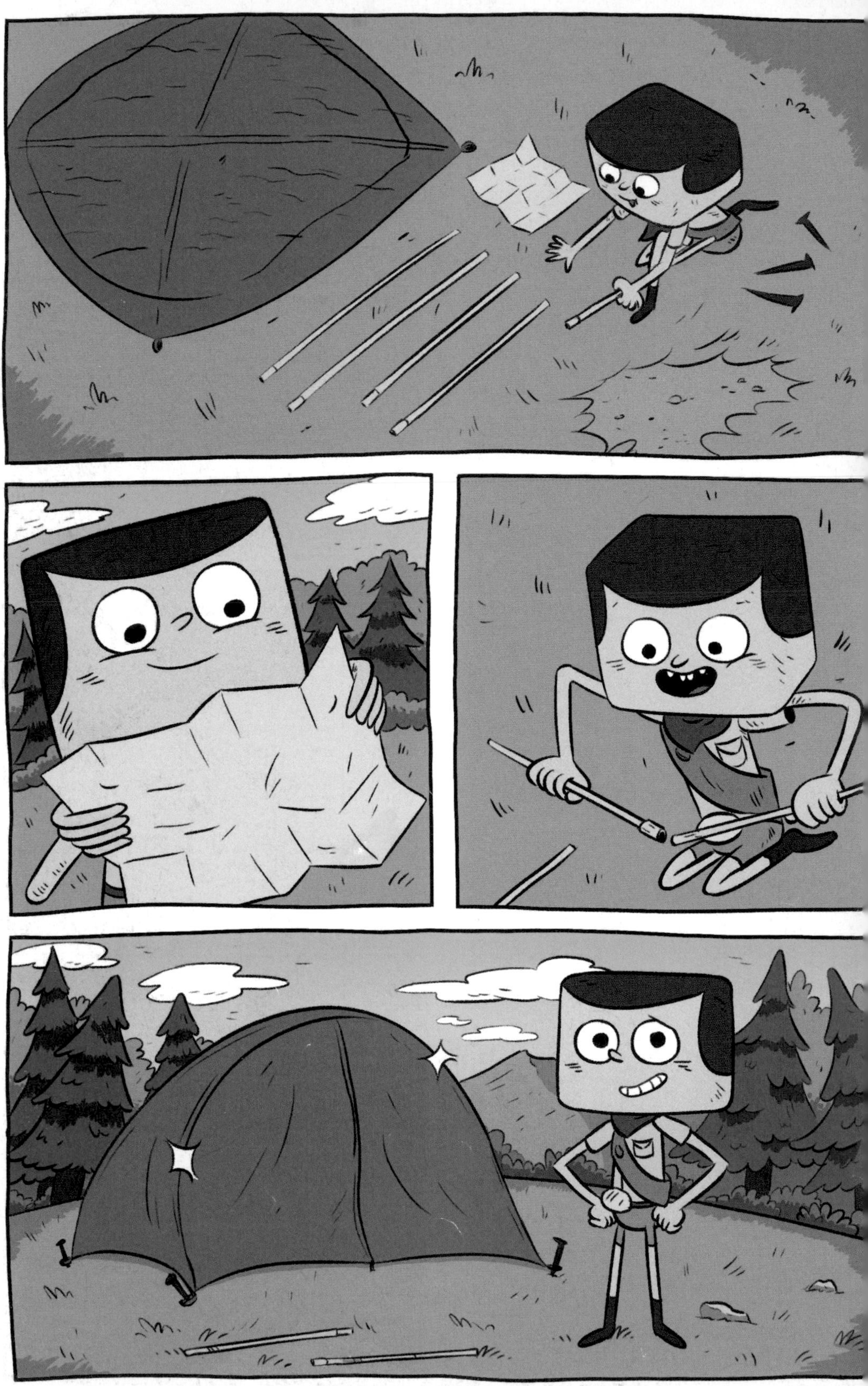

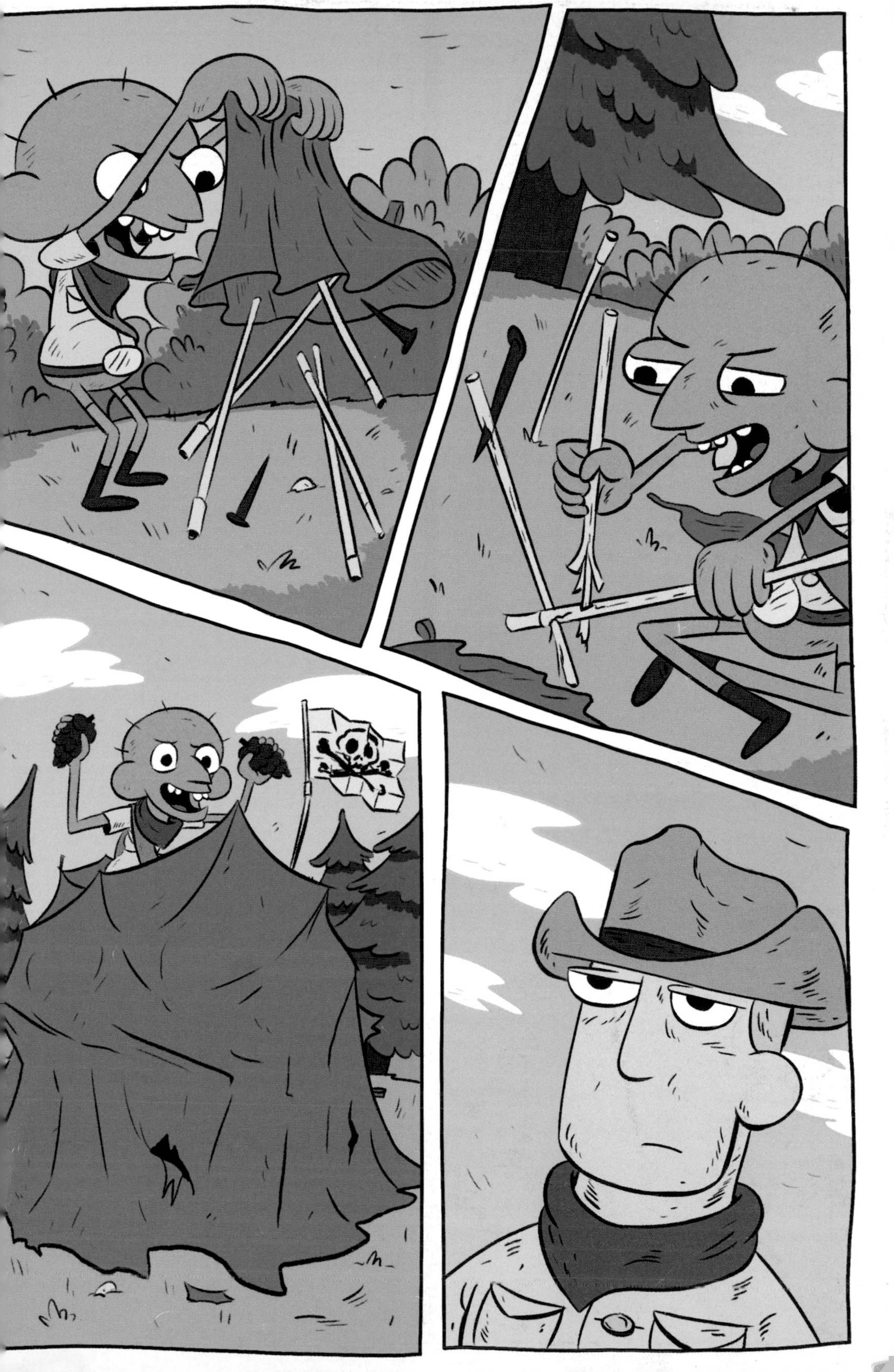

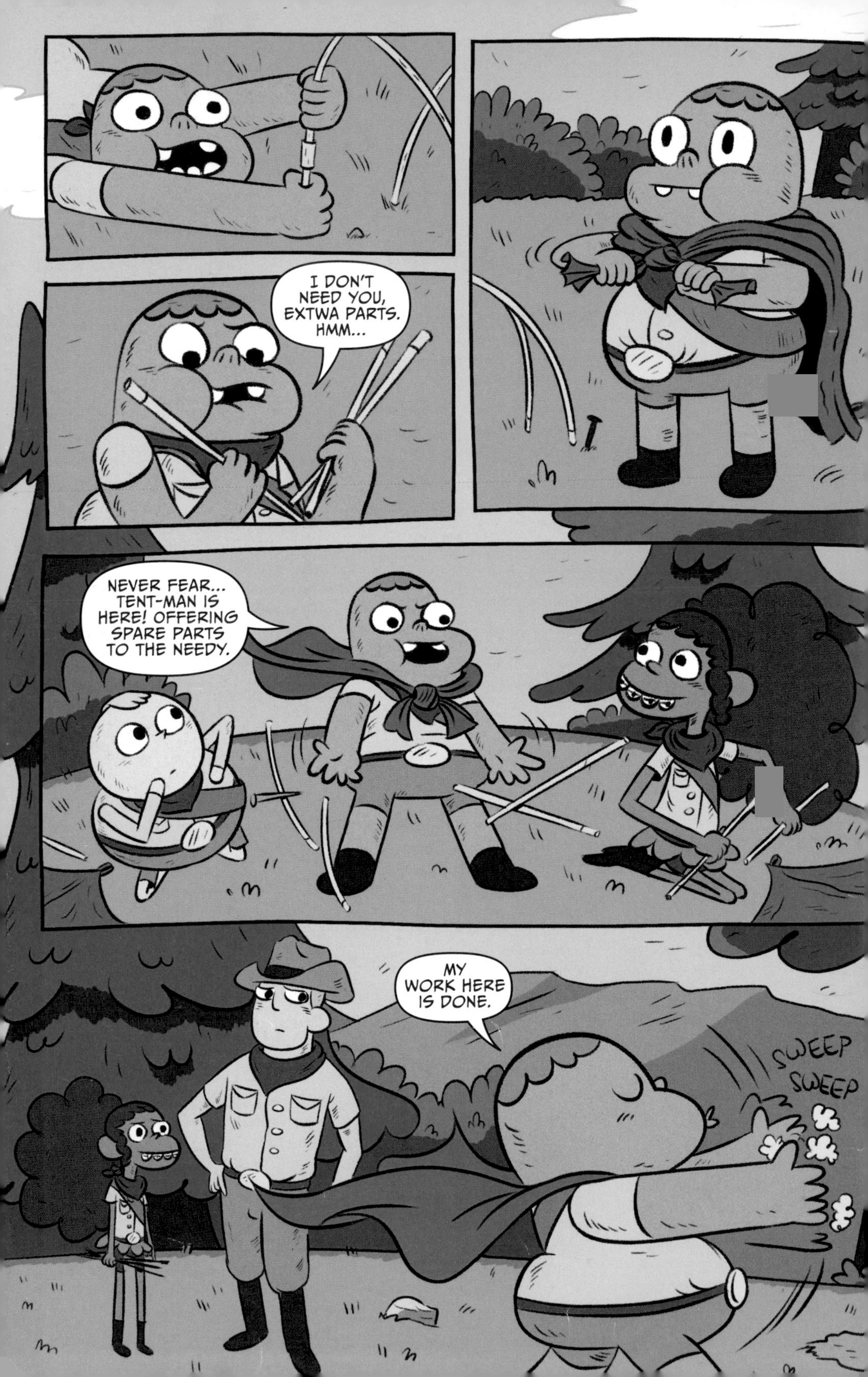
I DON'T NEED YOU, EXTWA PARTS. HMM...
NEVER FEAR... TENT-MAN IS HERE! OFFERING SPARE PARTS TO THE NEEDY.
MY WORK HERE IS DONE.
SWEEP
SWEEP

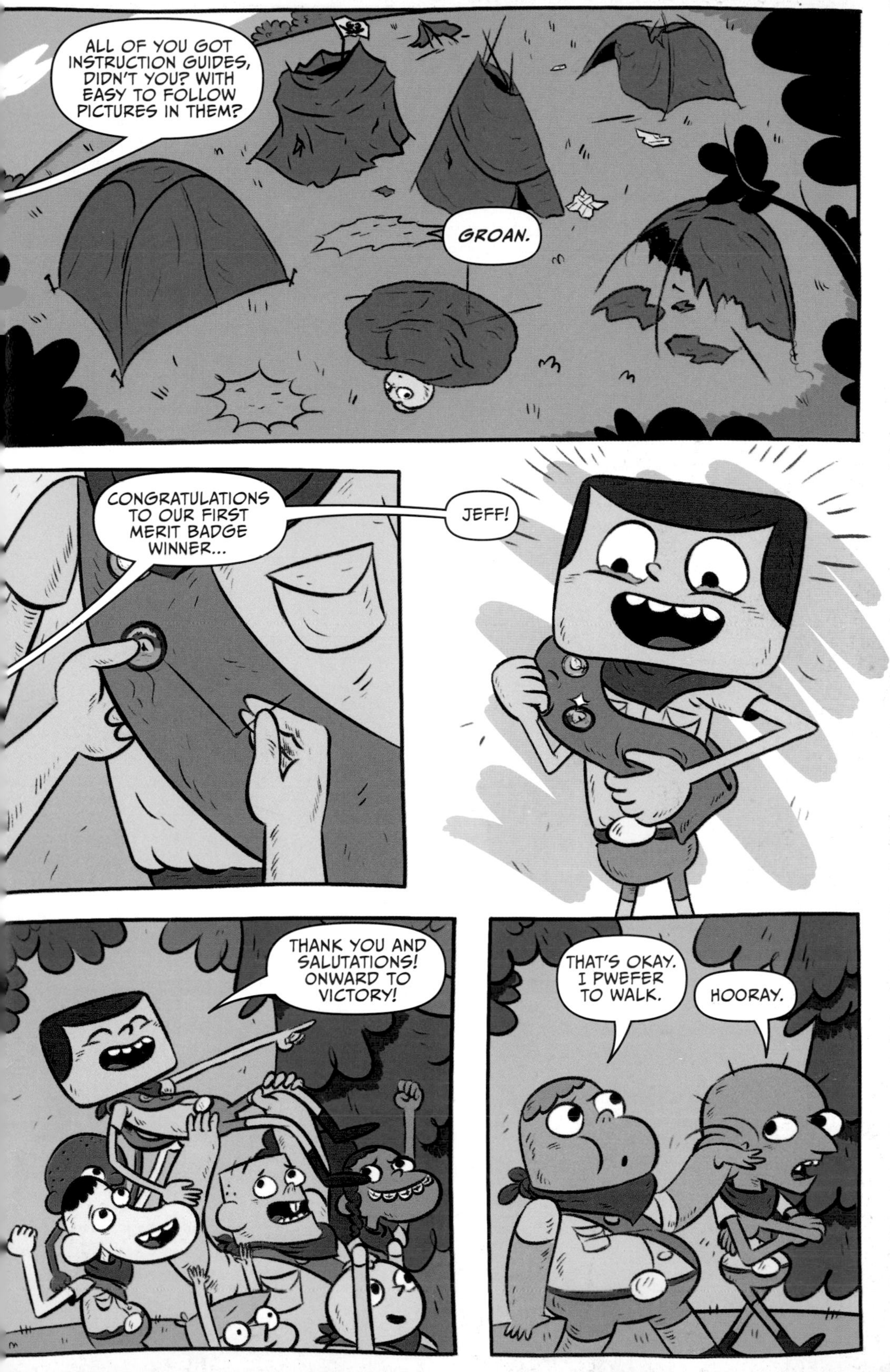
ALL OF YOU GOT INSTRUCTION GUIDES, DIDN'T YOU? WITH EASY TO FOLLOW PICTURES IN THEM?
GROAN.
CONGRATULATIONS TO OUR FIRST MERIT BADGE WINNER...
JEFF!
THANK YOU AND SALUTATIONS! ONWARD TO VICTORY!
THAT'S OKAY. I PWEFER TO WALK.
HOORAY.

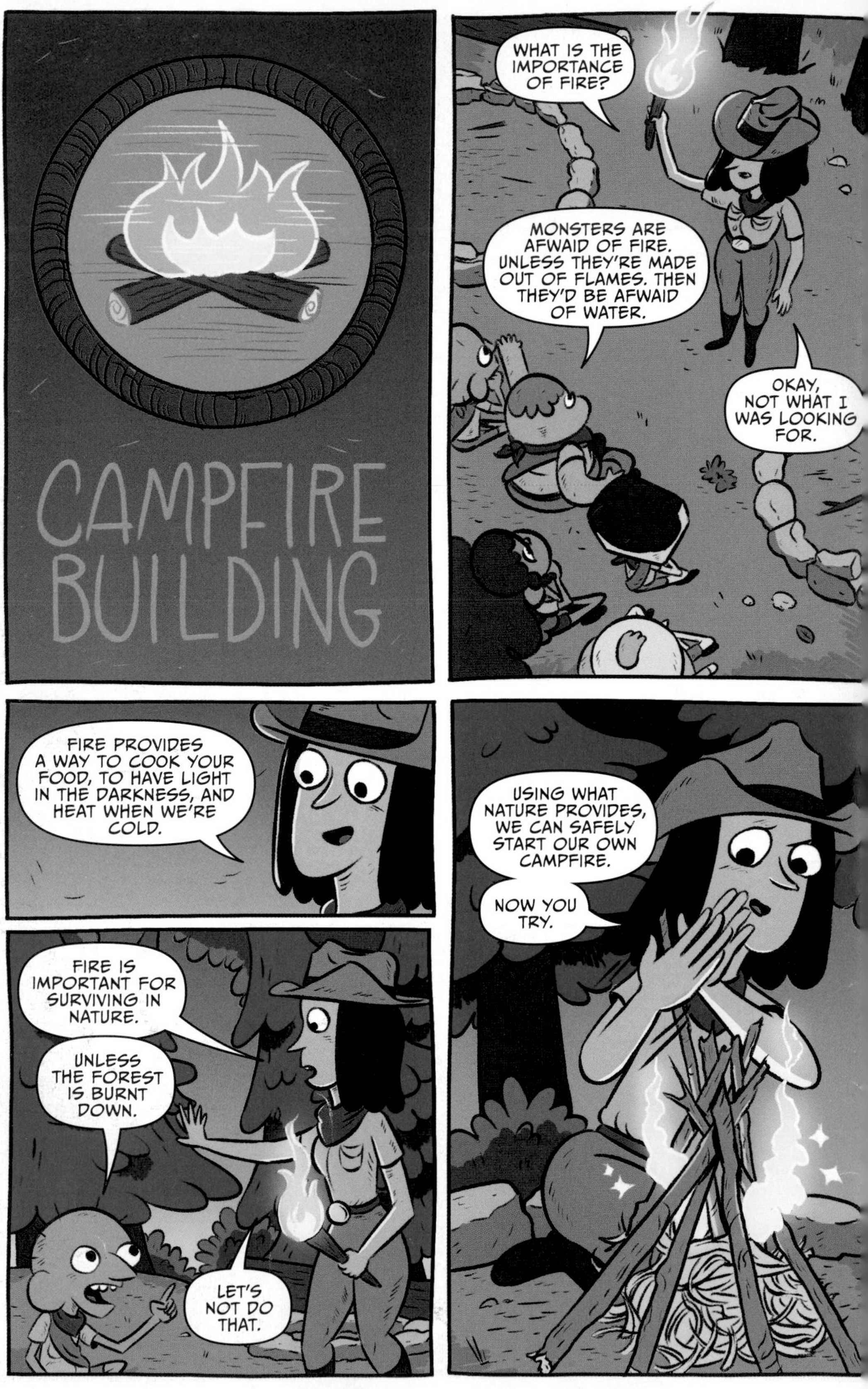
CAMPFIRE BUILDING
WHAT IS THE IMPORTANCE OF FIRE?
MONSTERS ARE AFWAID OF FIRE. UNLESS THEY'RE MADE OUT OF FLAMES. THEN THEY'D BE AFWAID OF WATER.
OKAY, NOT WHAT I WAS LOOKING FOR.
FIRE PROVIDES A WAY TO COOK YOUR FOOD, TO HAVE LIGHT IN THE DARKNESS, AND HEAT WHEN WE'RE COLD.
FIRE IS IMPORTANT FOR SURVIVING IN NATURE.
UNLESS THE FOREST IS BURNT DOWN.
LET'S NOT DO THAT.
USING WHAT NATURE PROVIDES, WE CAN SAFELY START OUR OWN CAMPFIRE.
NOW YOU TRY.

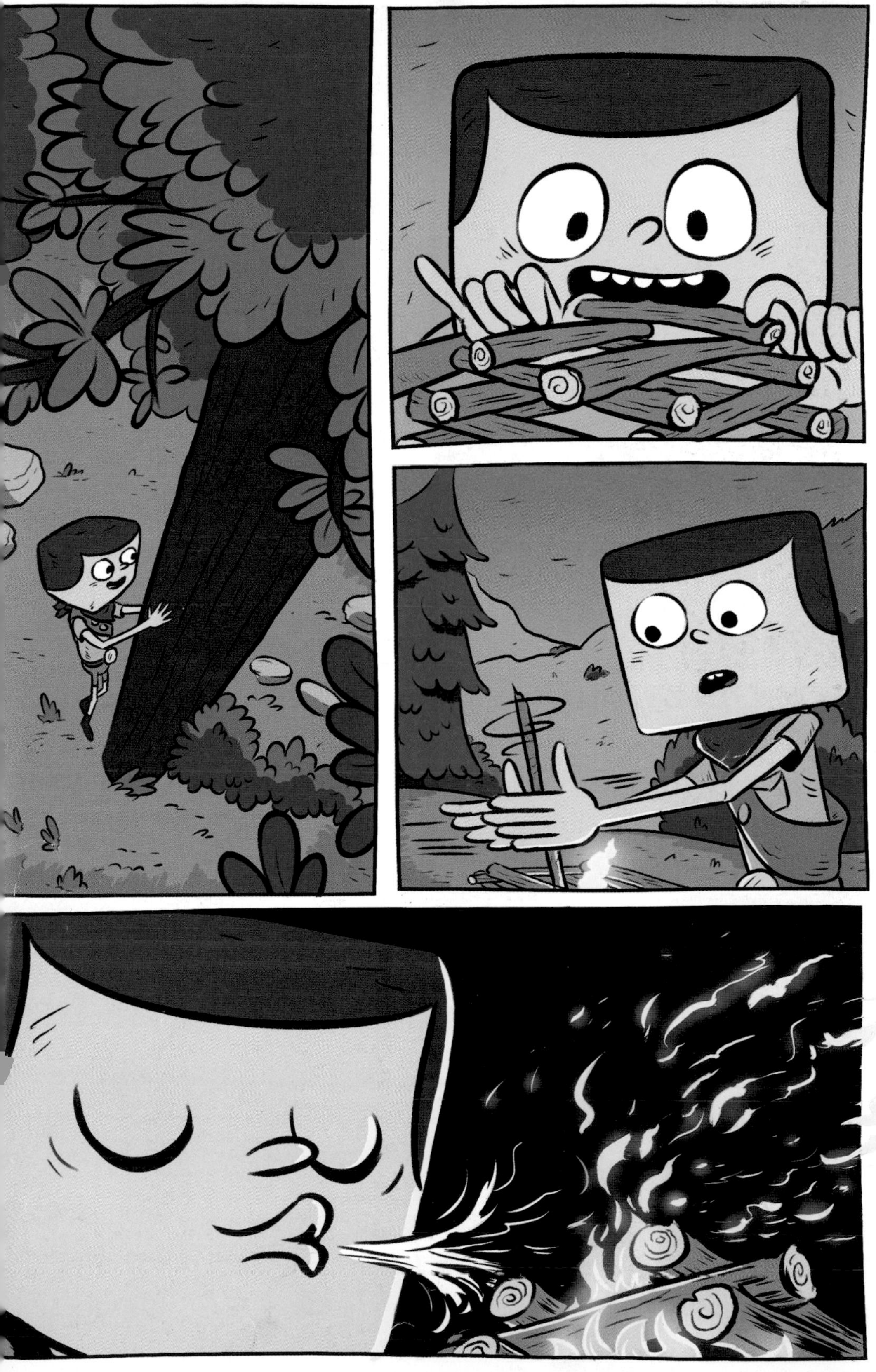

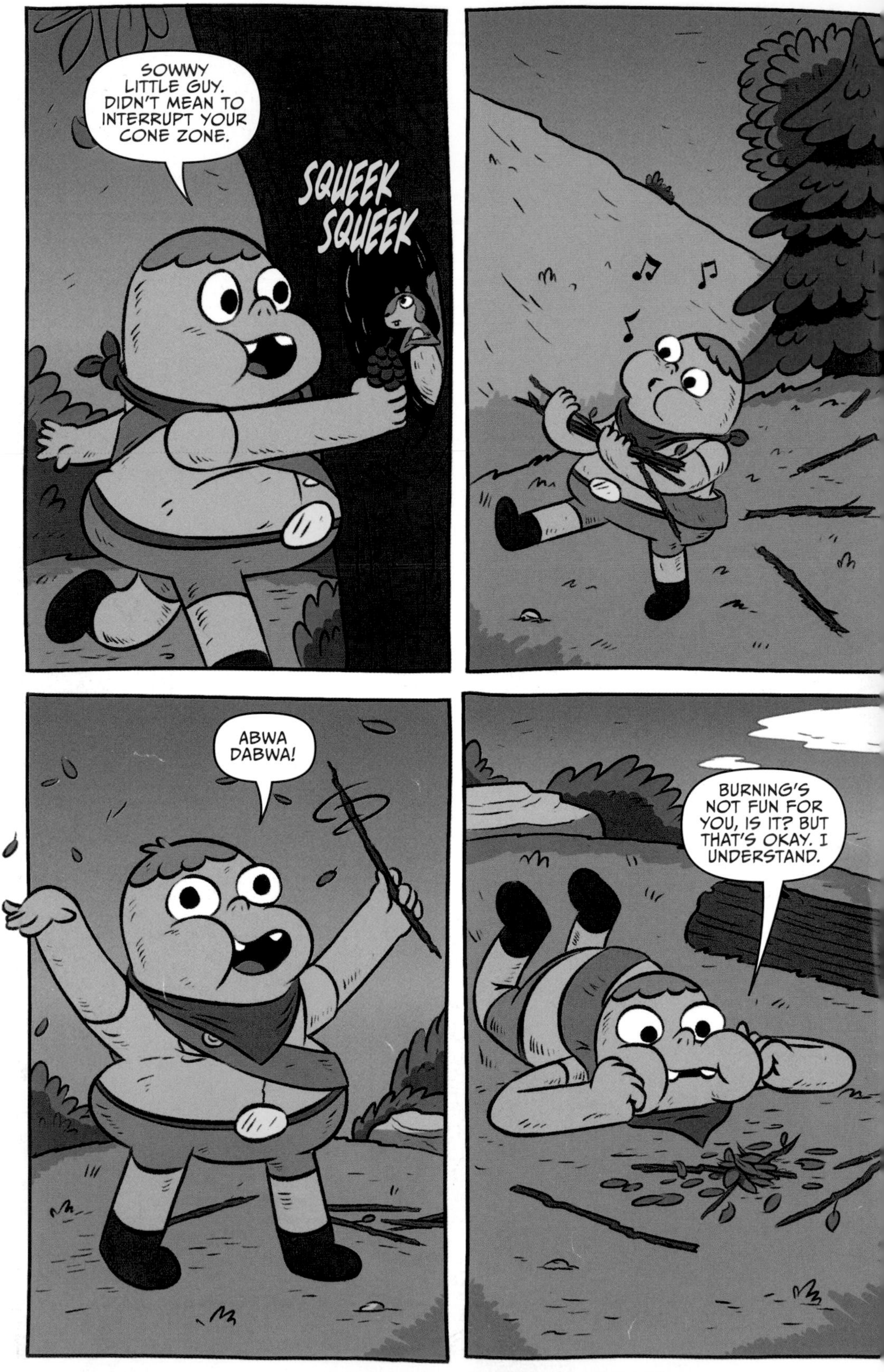
SOWWY LITTLE GUY. DIDN'T MEAN TO INTERRUPT YOUR CONE ZONE.
SQUEEK SQUEEK
ABWA DABWA!
BURNING'S NOT FUN FOR YOU, IS IT? BUT THAT'S OKAY. I UNDERSTAND.

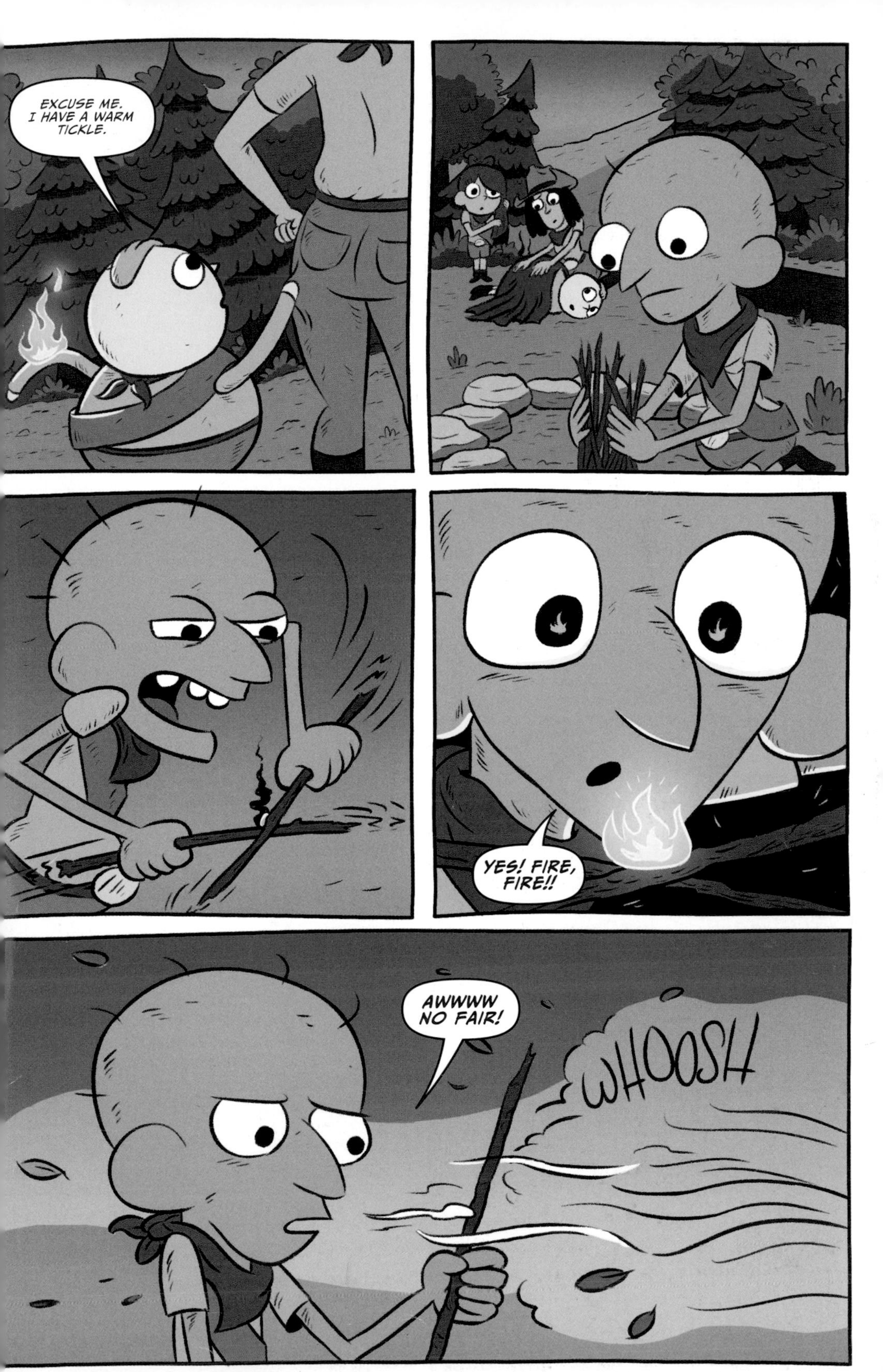
EXCUSE ME. I HAVE A WARM TICKLE.
YES! FIRE, FIRE!!
AWWWW NO FAIR!
WHOOSH

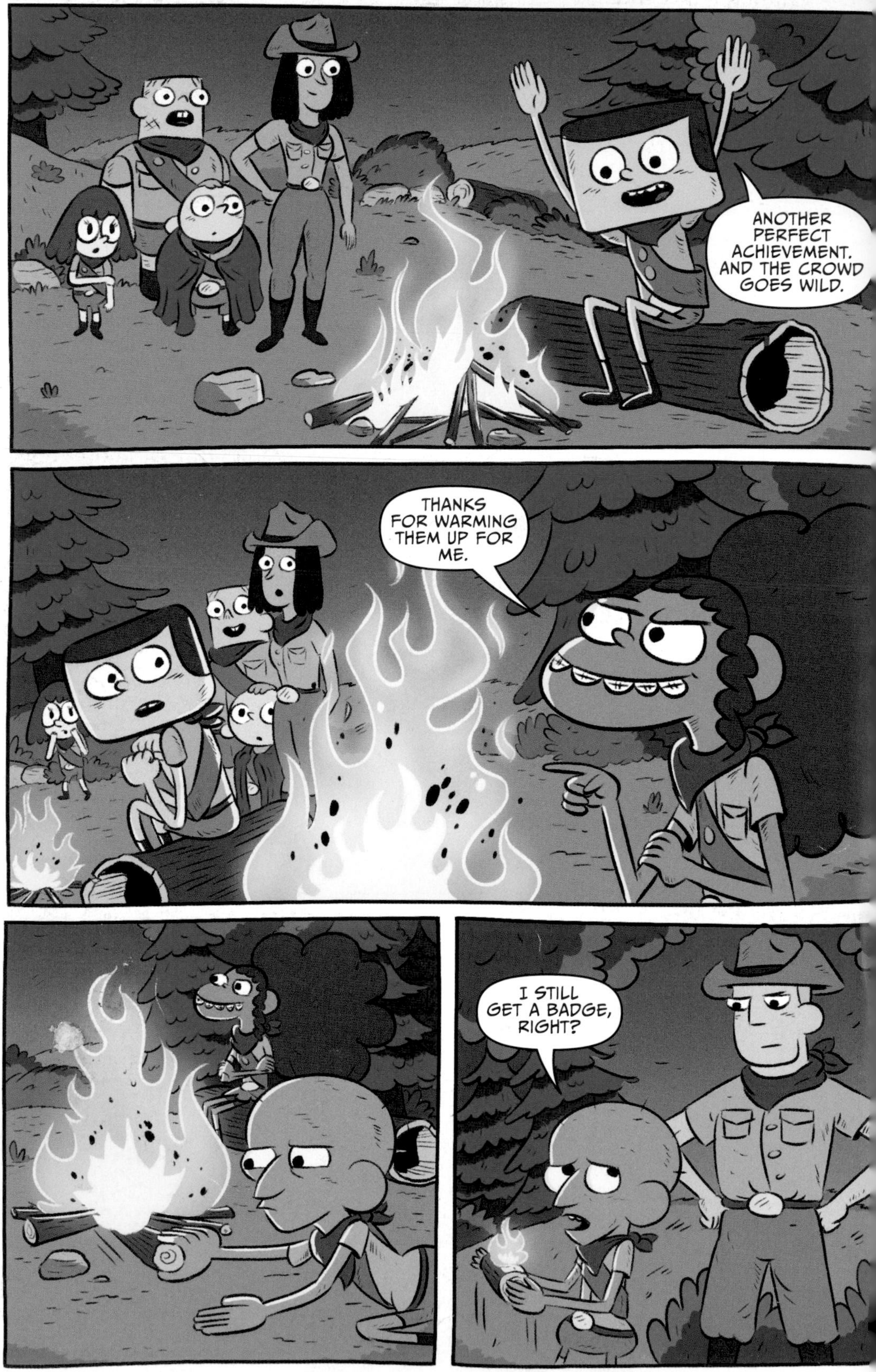
ANOTHER PERFECT ACHIEVEMENT. AND THE CROWD GOES WILD.
THANKS FOR WARMING THEM UP FOR ME.
I STILL GET A BADGE, RIGHT?

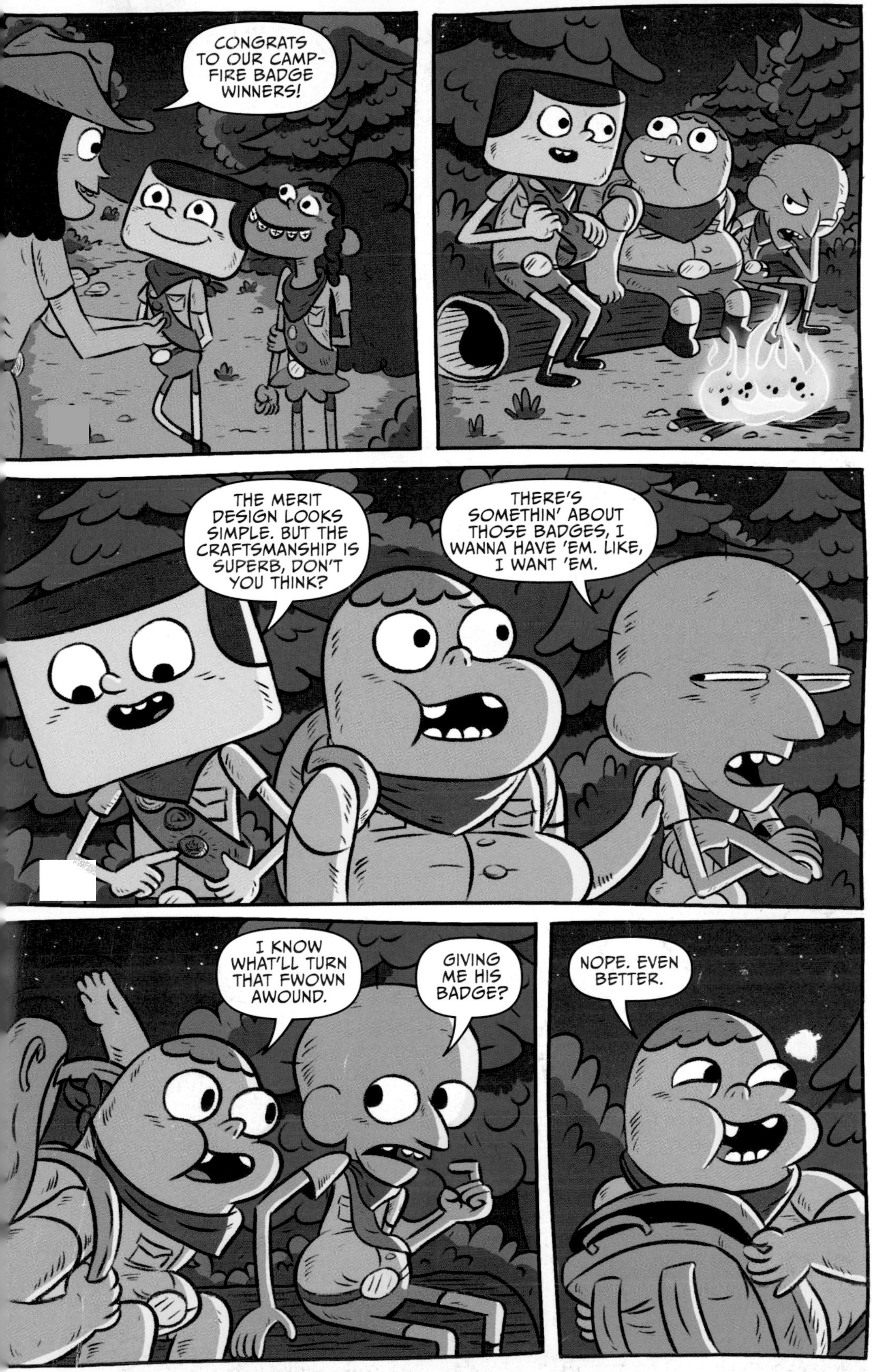
CONGRATS TO OUR CAMP-FIRE BADGE WINNERS!
THE MERIT DESIGN LOOKS SIMPLE. BUT THE CRAFTSMANSHIP IS SUPERB, DON'T YOU THINK?
THERE'S SOMETHIN' ABOUT THOSE BADGES, I WANNA HAVE 'EM. LIKE, I WANT 'EM.
I KNOW WHAT'LL TURN THAT FWOWN AWOUND.
GIVING ME HIS BADGE?
NOPE. EVEN BETTER.

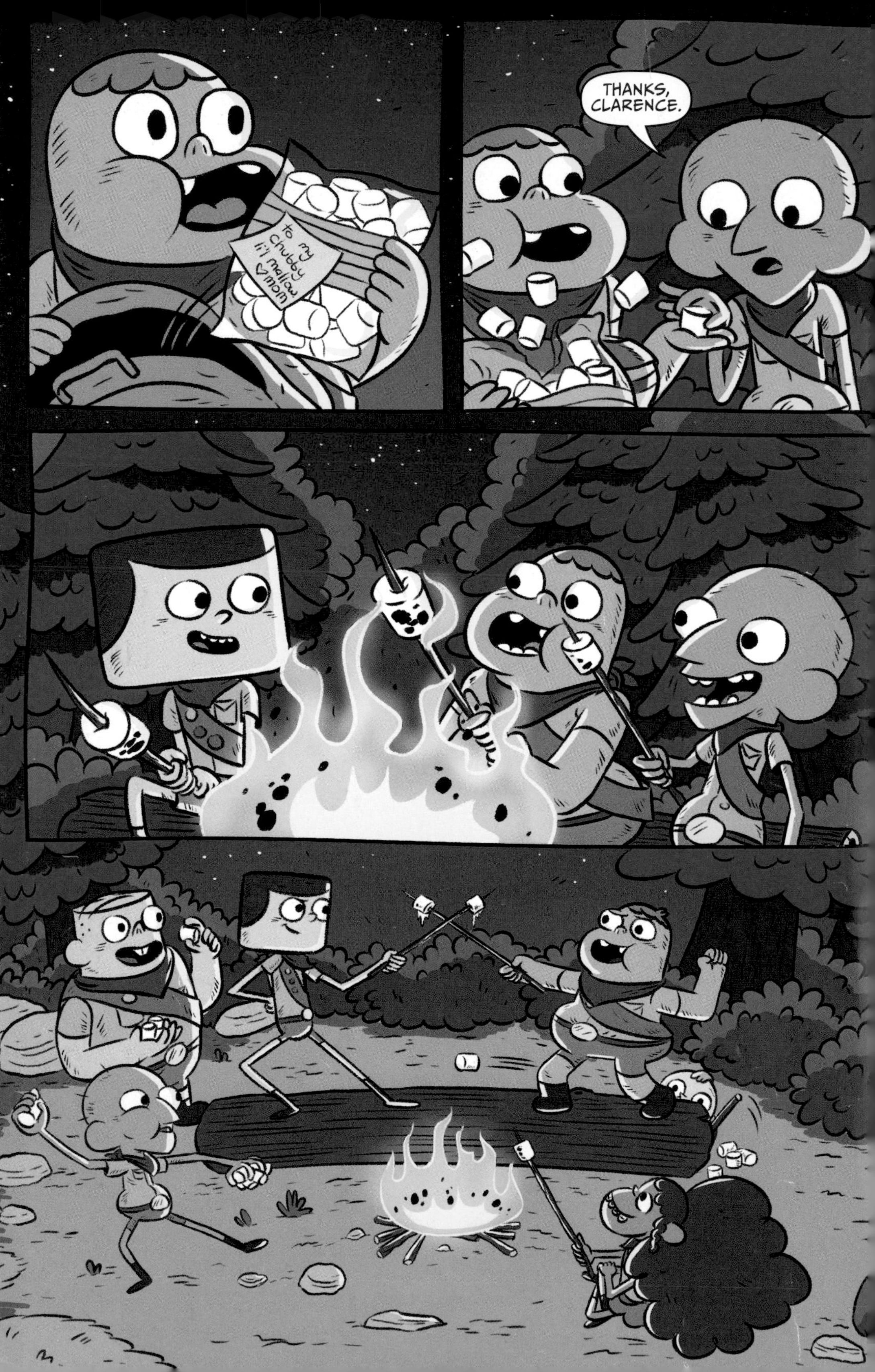
to my
chubby
li'l mallow
♡mom
THANKS, CLARENCE.

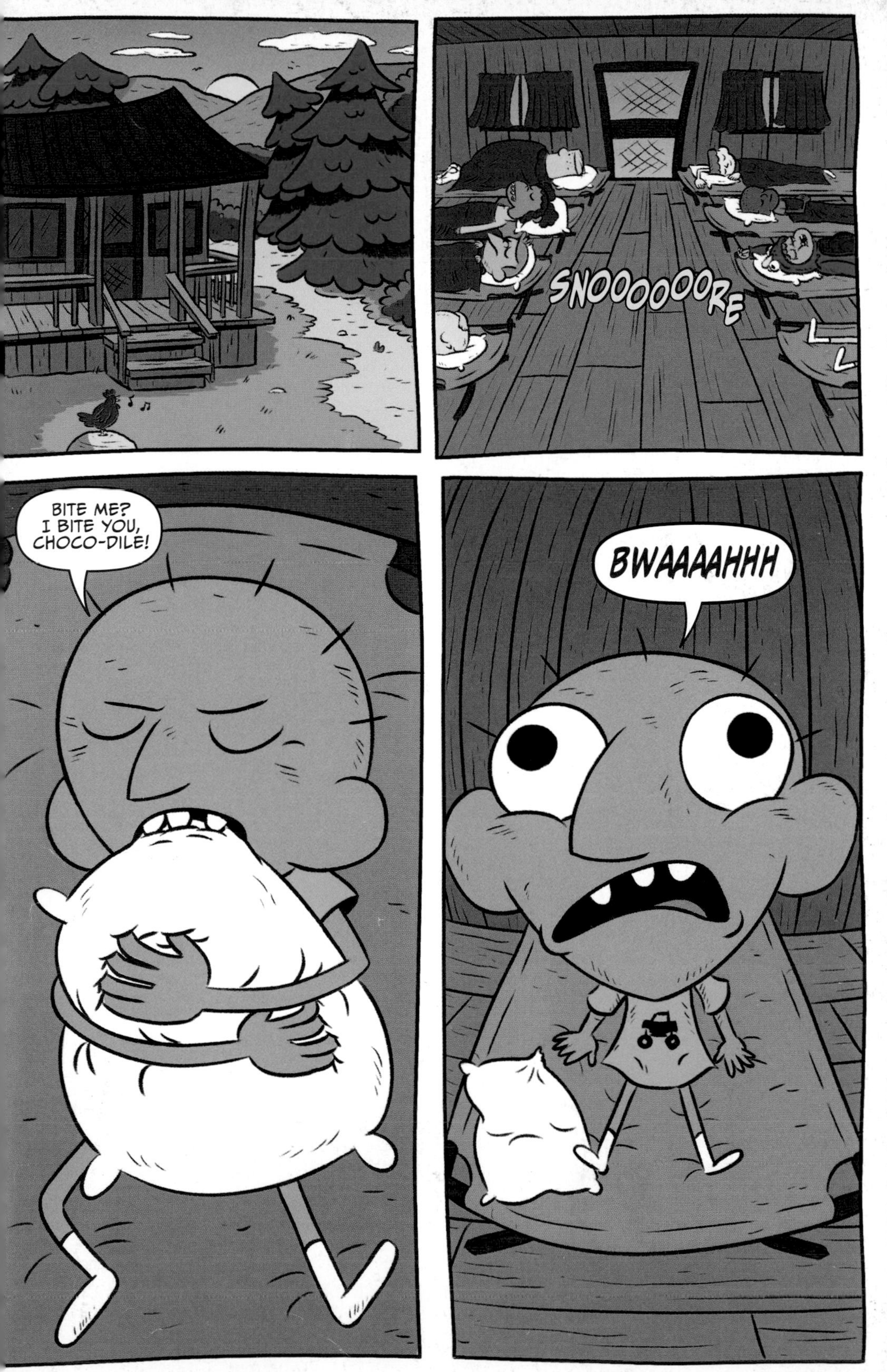
SNOOOOOORE
BITE ME? I BITE YOU, CHOCO-DILE!
BWAAAAHHH

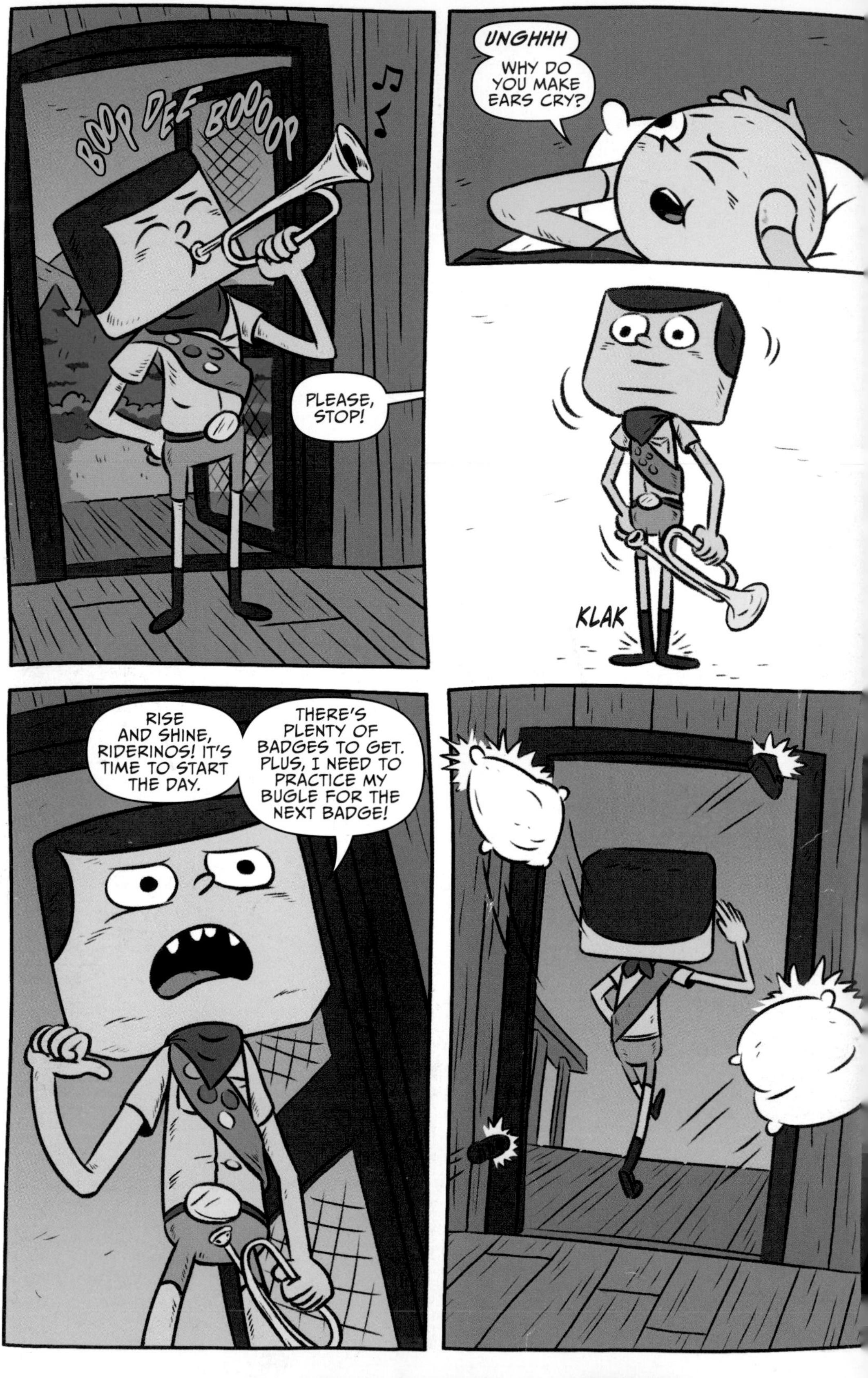
BOOP DEE BOOOOP
PLEASE, STOP!
UNGHHH
WHY DO YOU MAKE EARS CRY?
KLAK
RISE AND SHINE, RIDERINOS! IT'S TIME TO START THE DAY.
THERE'S PLENTY OF BADGES TO GET. PLUS, I NEED TO PRACTICE MY BUGLE FOR THE NEXT BADGE!

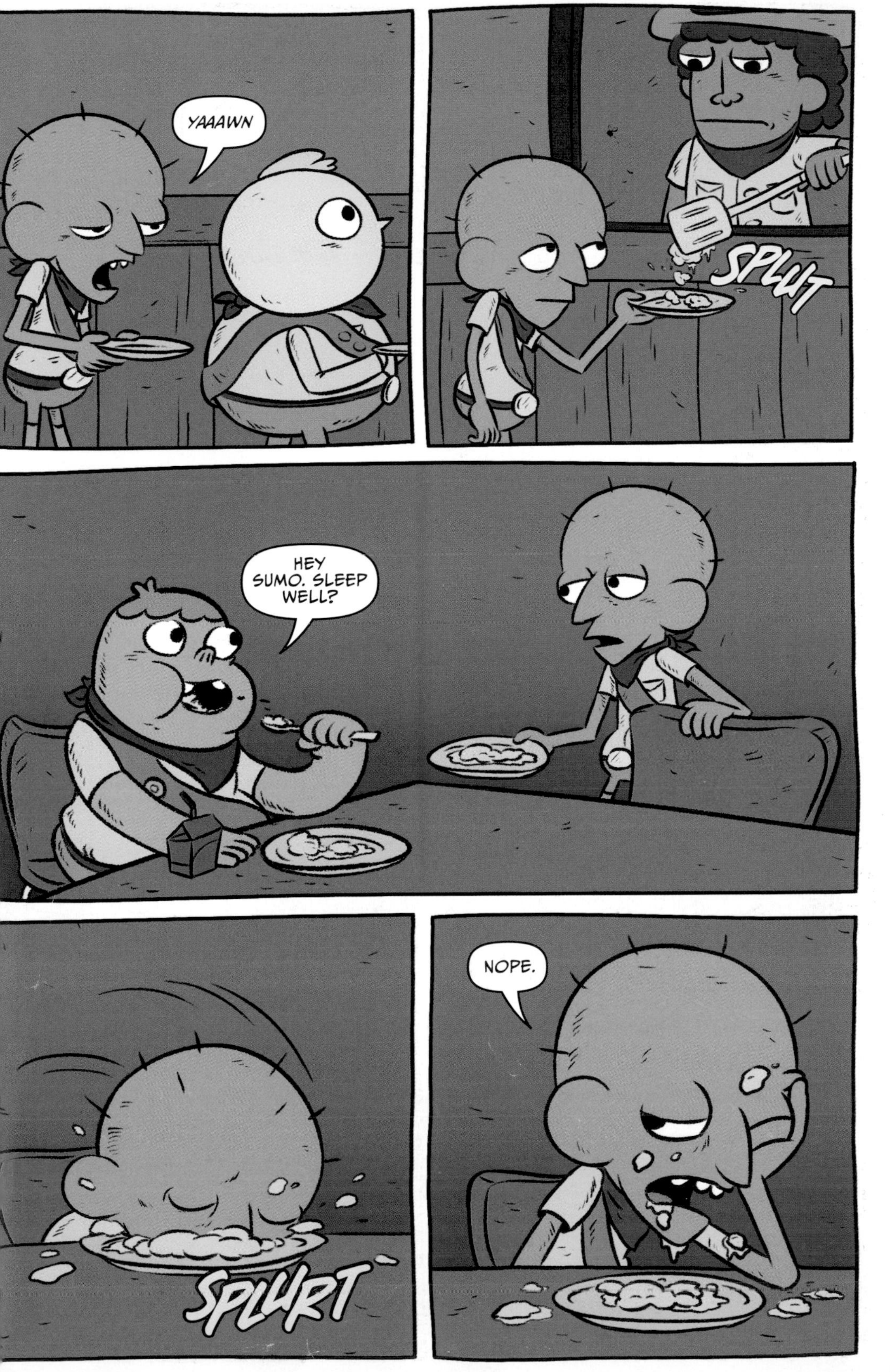
YAAAWN
SPLUT
HEY SUMO. SLEEP WELL?
SPLURT
NOPE.

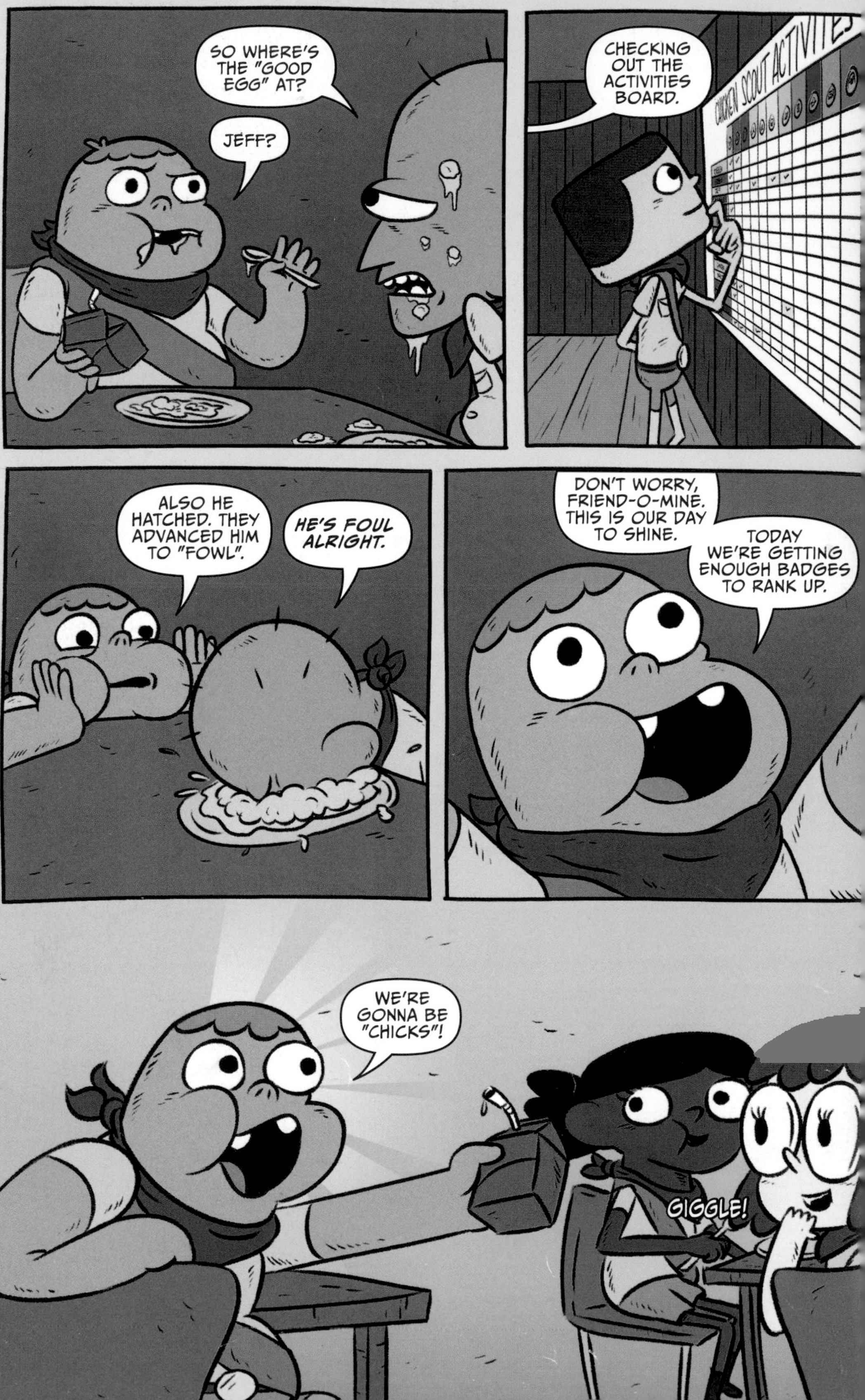

SO WHERE'S THE "GOOD EGG" AT?
JEFF?
CHECKING OUT THE ACTIVITIES BOARD.
CHICKEN SCOUT ACTIVITIES
ALSO HE HATCHED. THEY ADVANCED HIM TO "FOWL".
HE'S FOUL ALRIGHT.
DON'T WORRY, FRIEND-O-MINE. THIS IS OUR DAY TO SHINE.
TODAY WE'RE GETTING ENOUGH BADGES TO RANK UP.
WE'RE GONNA BE "CHICKS"!
GIGGLE!

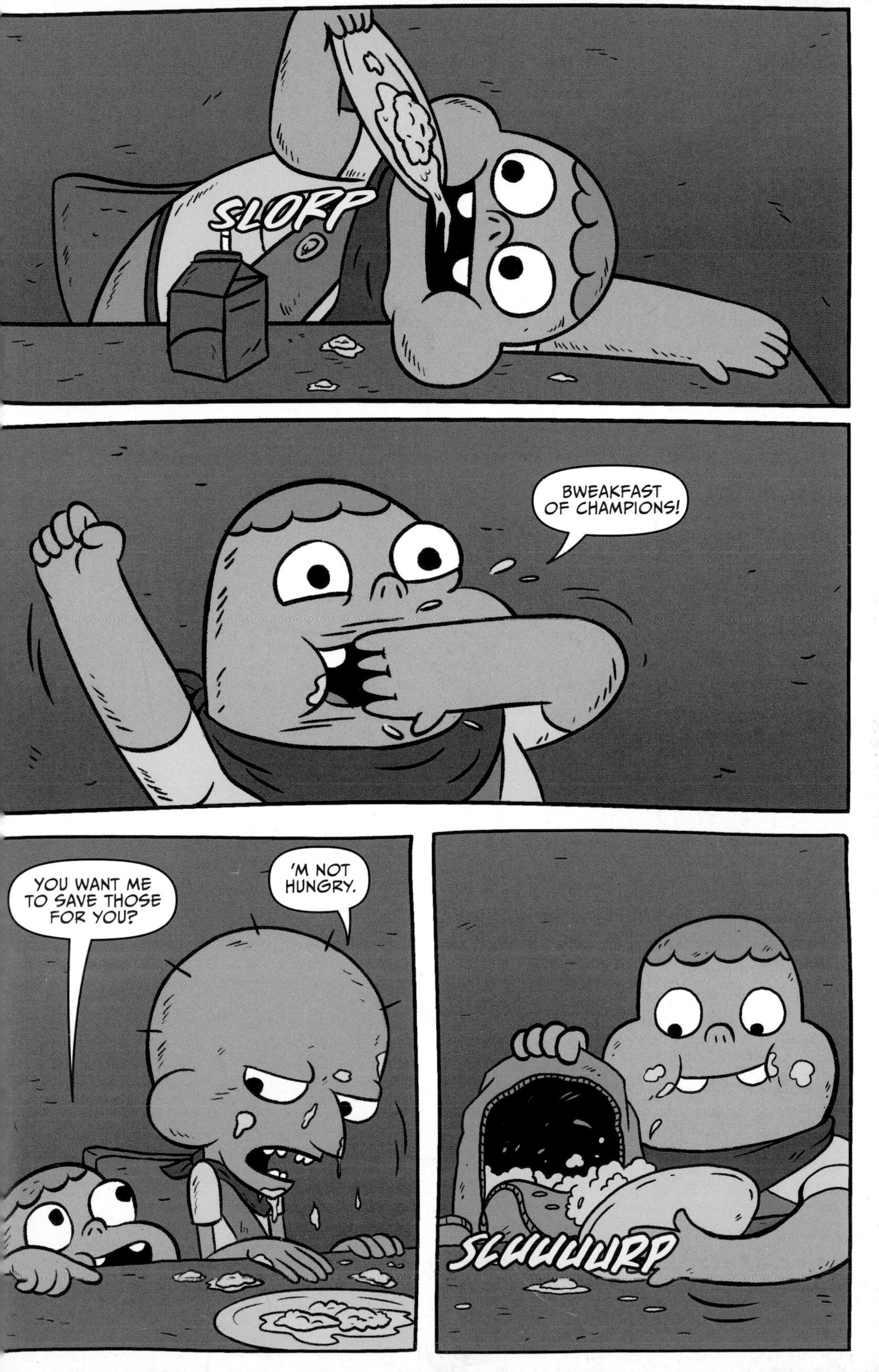
SLORP
BWEAKFAST OF CHAMPIONS!
YOU WANT ME TO SAVE THOSE FOR YOU?
'M NOT HUNGRY.
SLUUUURP

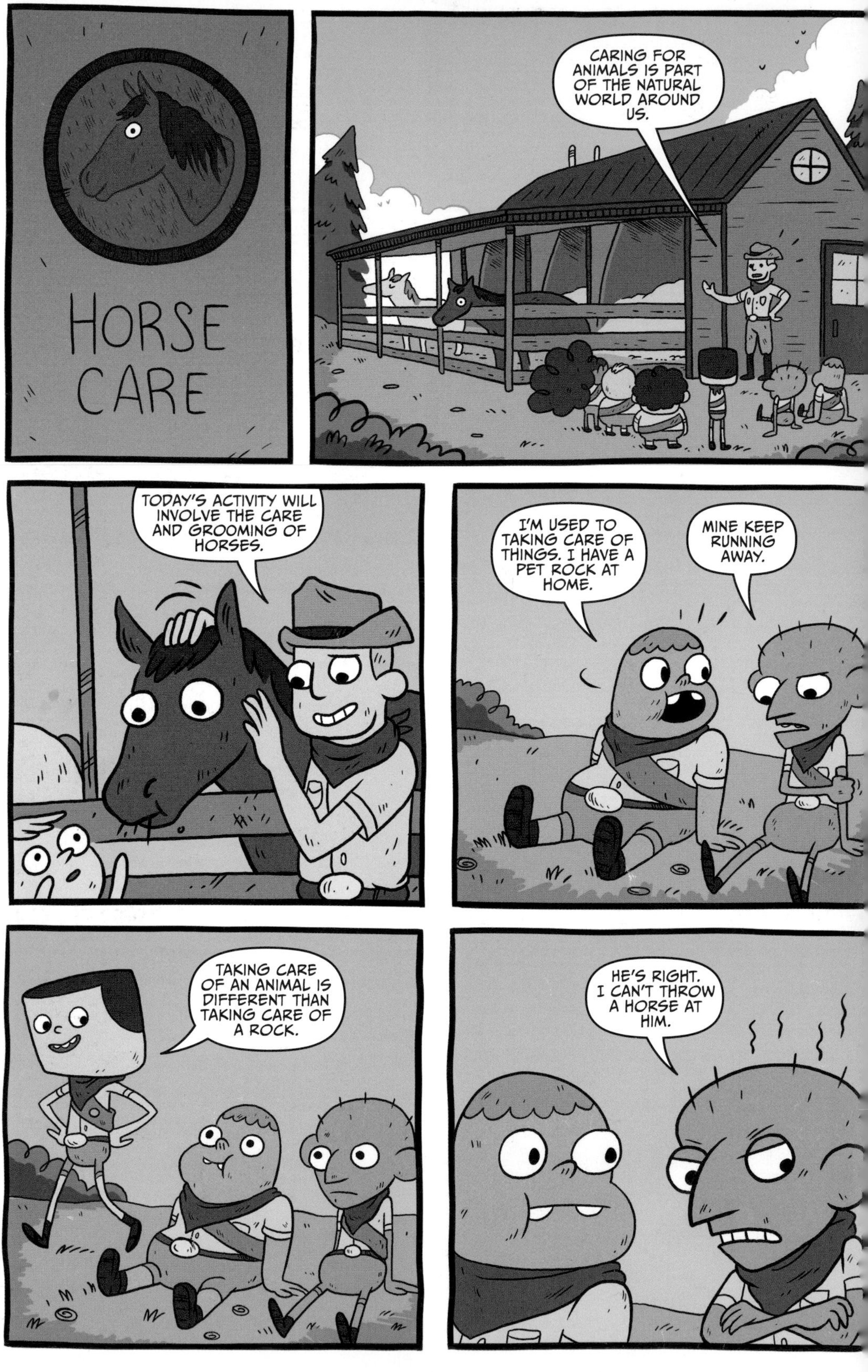
HORSE CARE
CARING FOR ANIMALS IS PART OF THE NATURAL WORLD AROUND US.
TODAY'S ACTIVITY WILL INVOLVE THE CARE AND GROOMING OF HORSES.
I'M USED TO TAKING CARE OF THINGS. I HAVE A PET ROCK AT HOME.
MINE KEEP RUNNING AWAY.
TAKING CARE OF AN ANIMAL IS DIFFERENT THAN TAKING CARE OF A ROCK.
HE'S RIGHT. I CAN'T THROW A HORSE AT HIM.

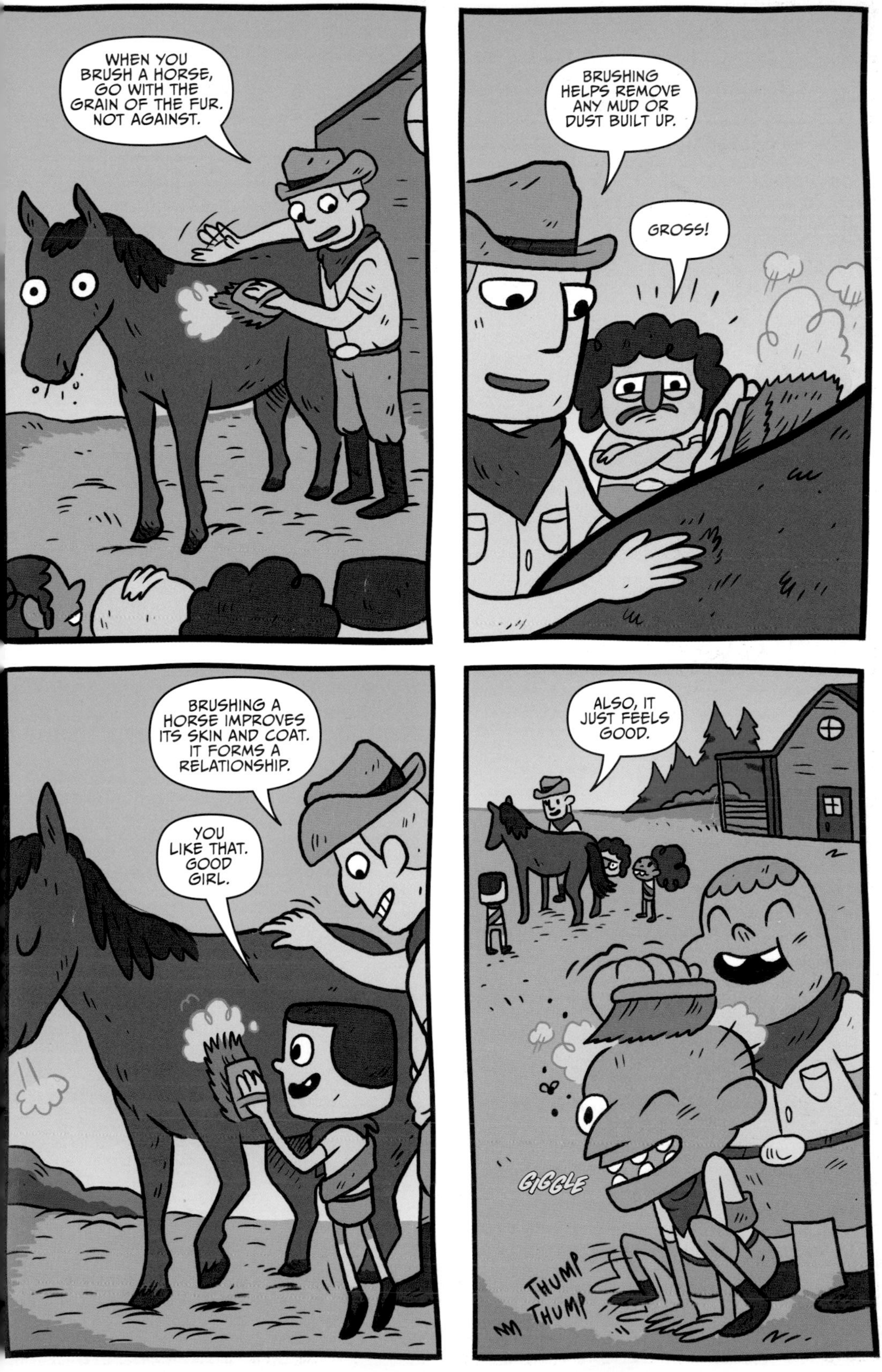
WHEN YOU BRUSH A HORSE, GO WITH THE GRAIN OF THE FUR. NOT AGAINST.
BRUSHING HELPS REMOVE ANY MUD OR DUST BUILT UP.
GROSS!
BRUSHING A HORSE IMPROVES ITS SKIN AND COAT. IT FORMS A RELATIONSHIP.
YOU LIKE THAT. GOOD GIRL.
ALSO, IT JUST FEELS GOOD.
GIGGLE
THUMP THUMP

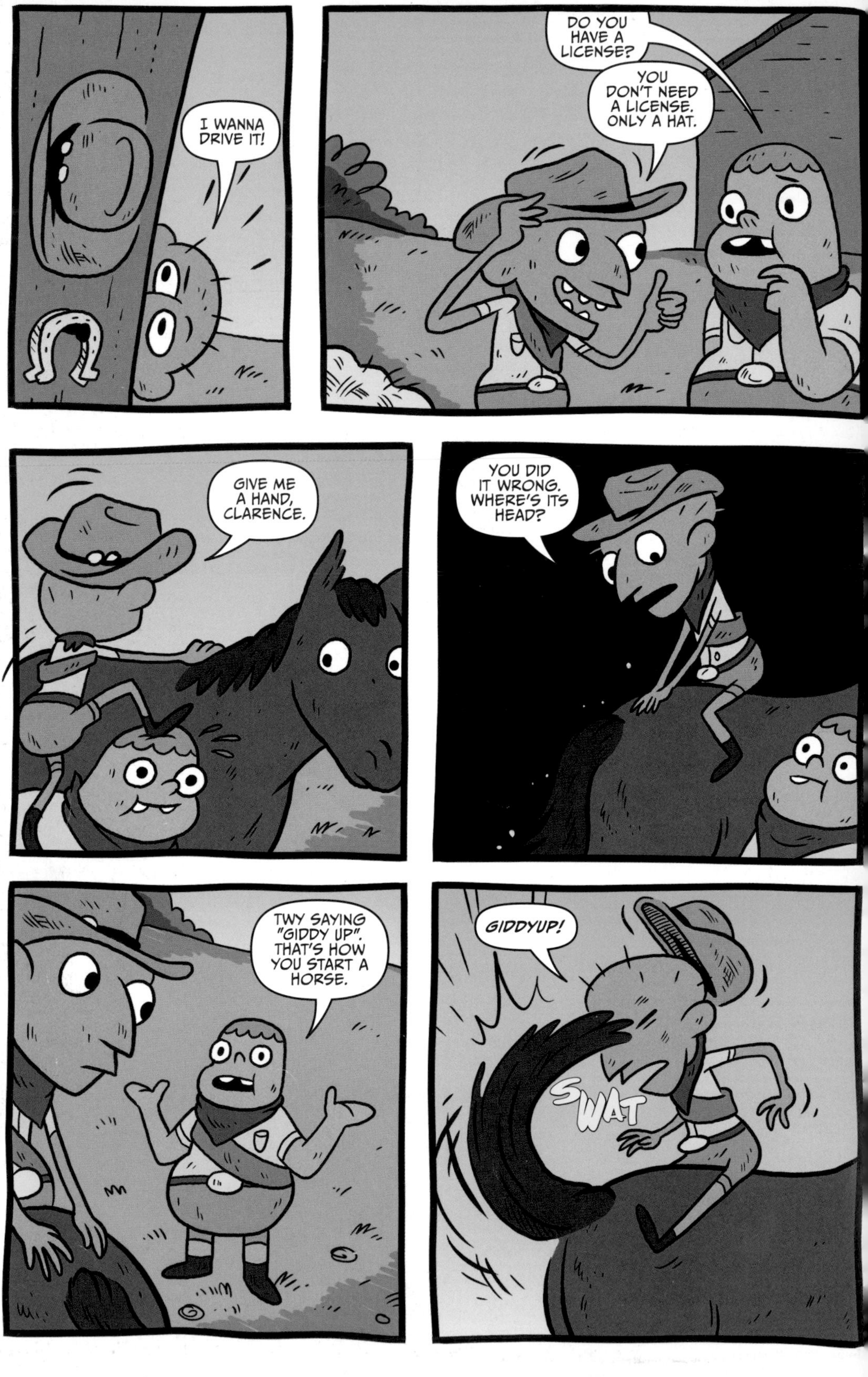

I WANNA DRIVE IT!
DO YOU HAVE A LICENSE?
YOU DON'T NEED A LICENSE. ONLY A HAT.
GIVE ME A HAND, CLARENCE.
YOU DID IT WRONG. WHERE'S ITS HEAD?
TWY SAYING "GIDDY UP". THAT'S HOW YOU START A HORSE.
GIDDYUP!
SWAT

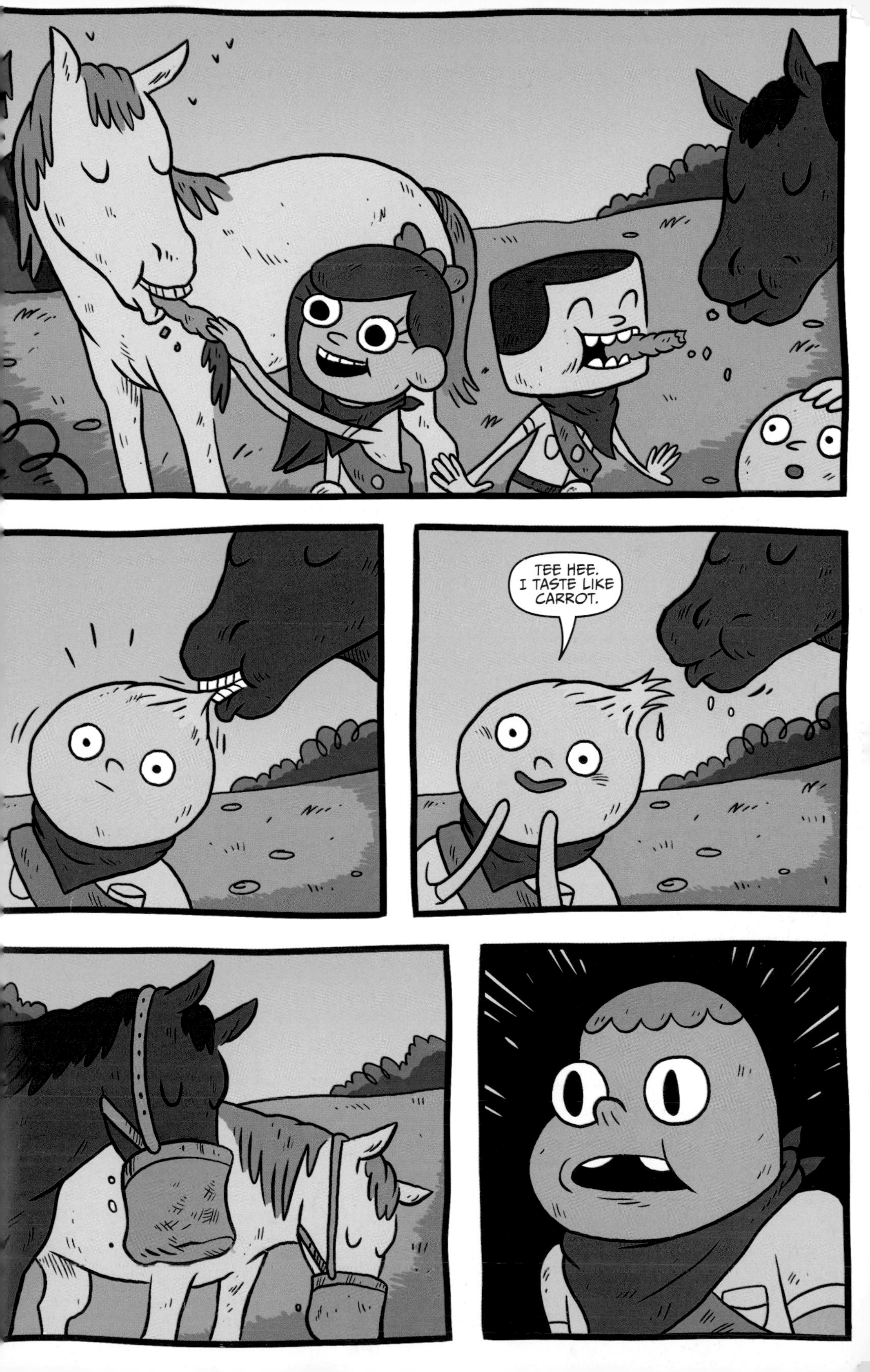
TEE HEE. I TASTE LIKE CARROT.

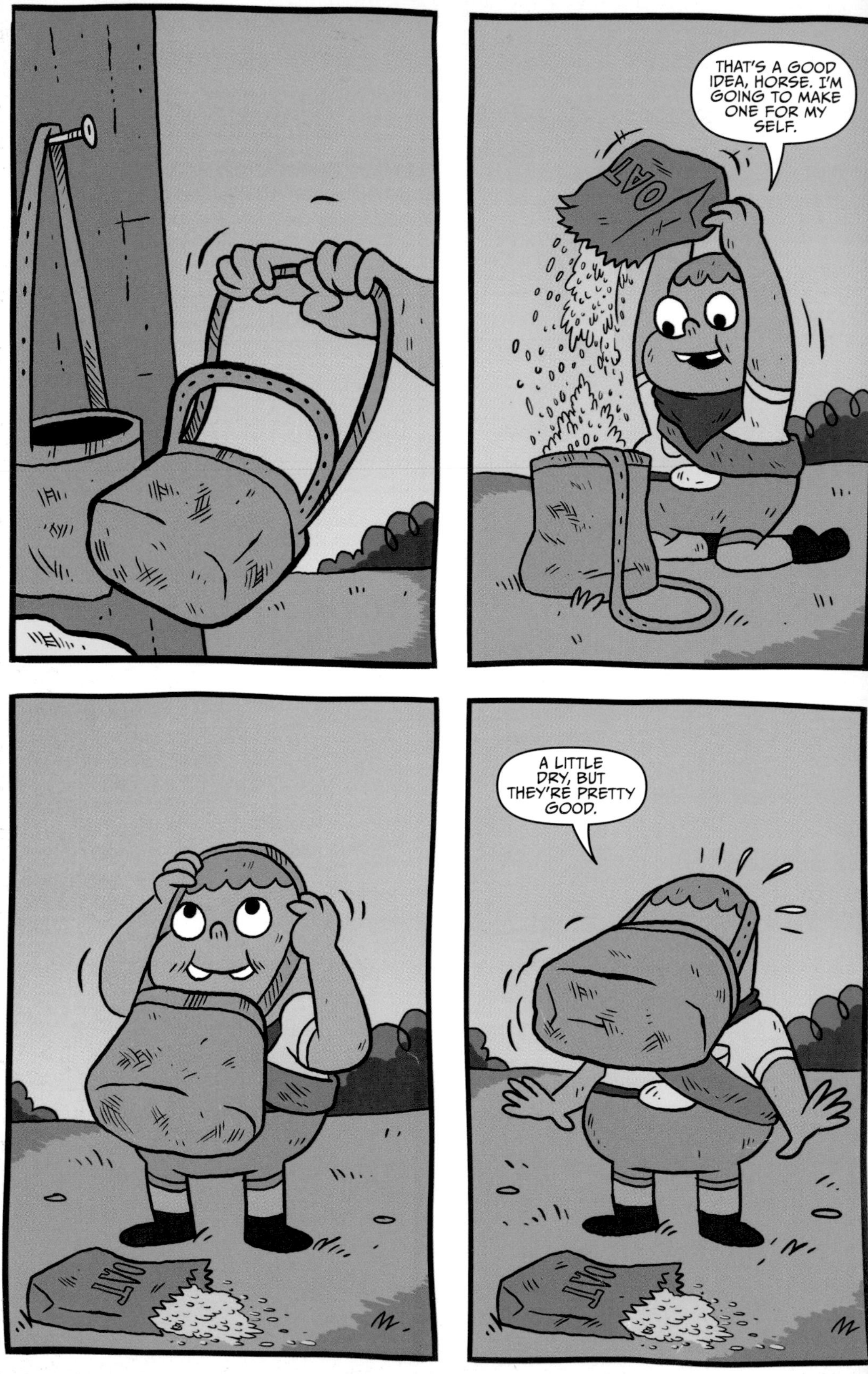
THAT'S A GOOD IDEA, HORSE. I'M GOING TO MAKE ONE FOR MY SELF.
OAT
OAT
A LITTLE DRY, BUT THEY'RE PRETTY GOOD.
OAT

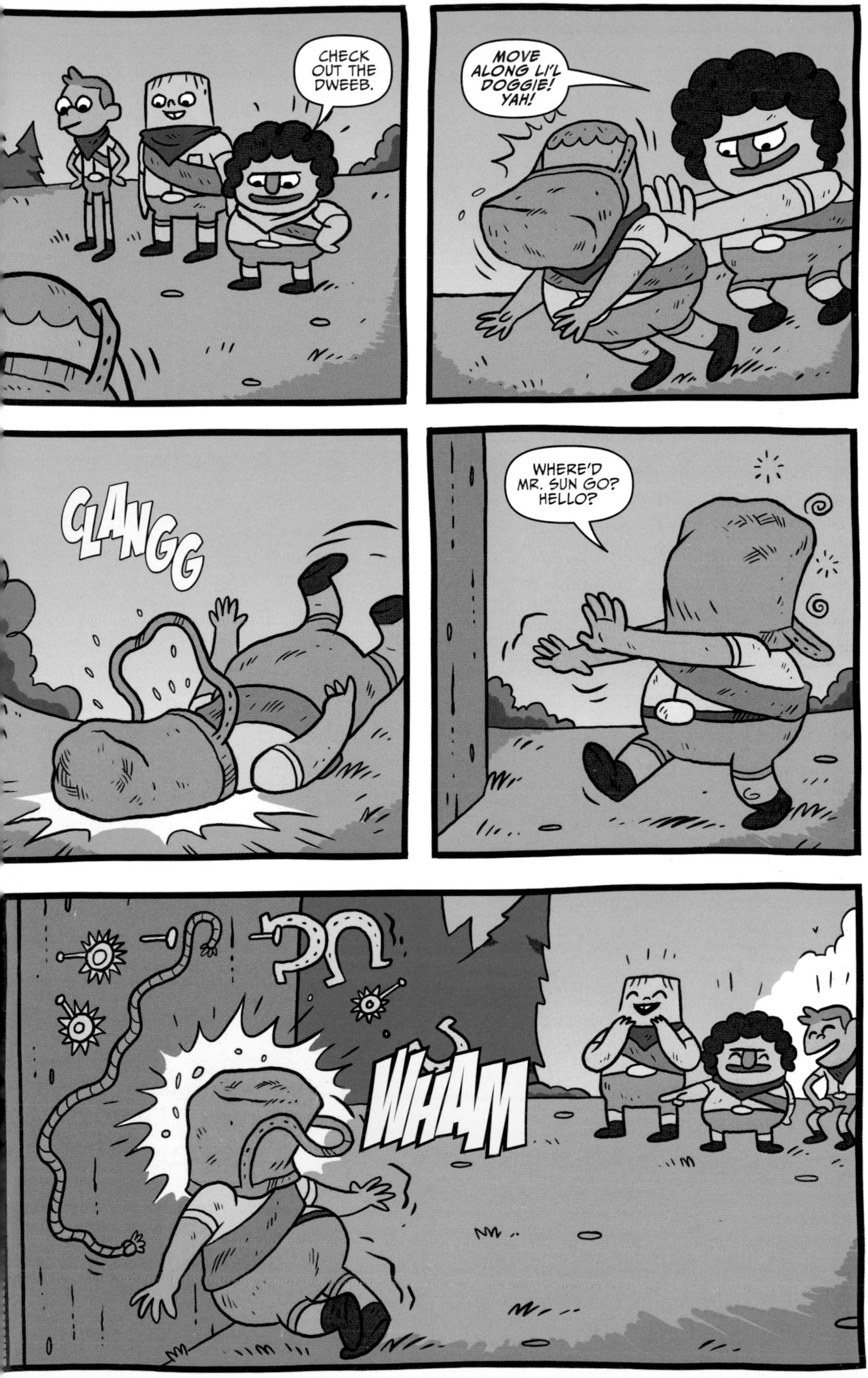
CHECK OUT THE DWEEB.
MOVE ALONG LI'L DOGGIE! YAH!
CLANGG
WHERE'D MR. SUN GO? HELLO?
WHAM

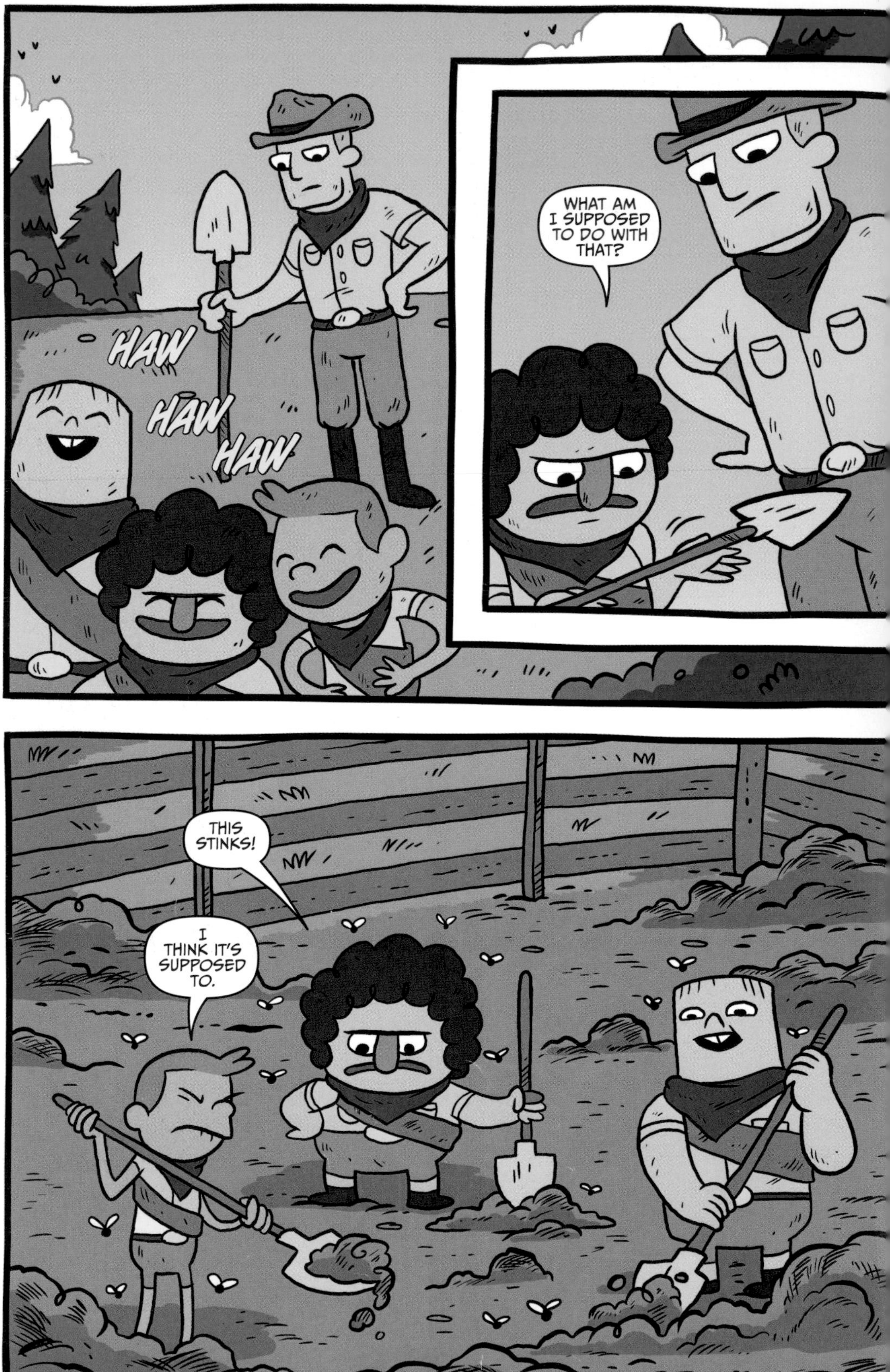
HAW
HAW
HAW
WHAT AM I SUPPOSED TO DO WITH THAT?
THIS STINKS!
I THINK IT'S SUPPOSED TO.

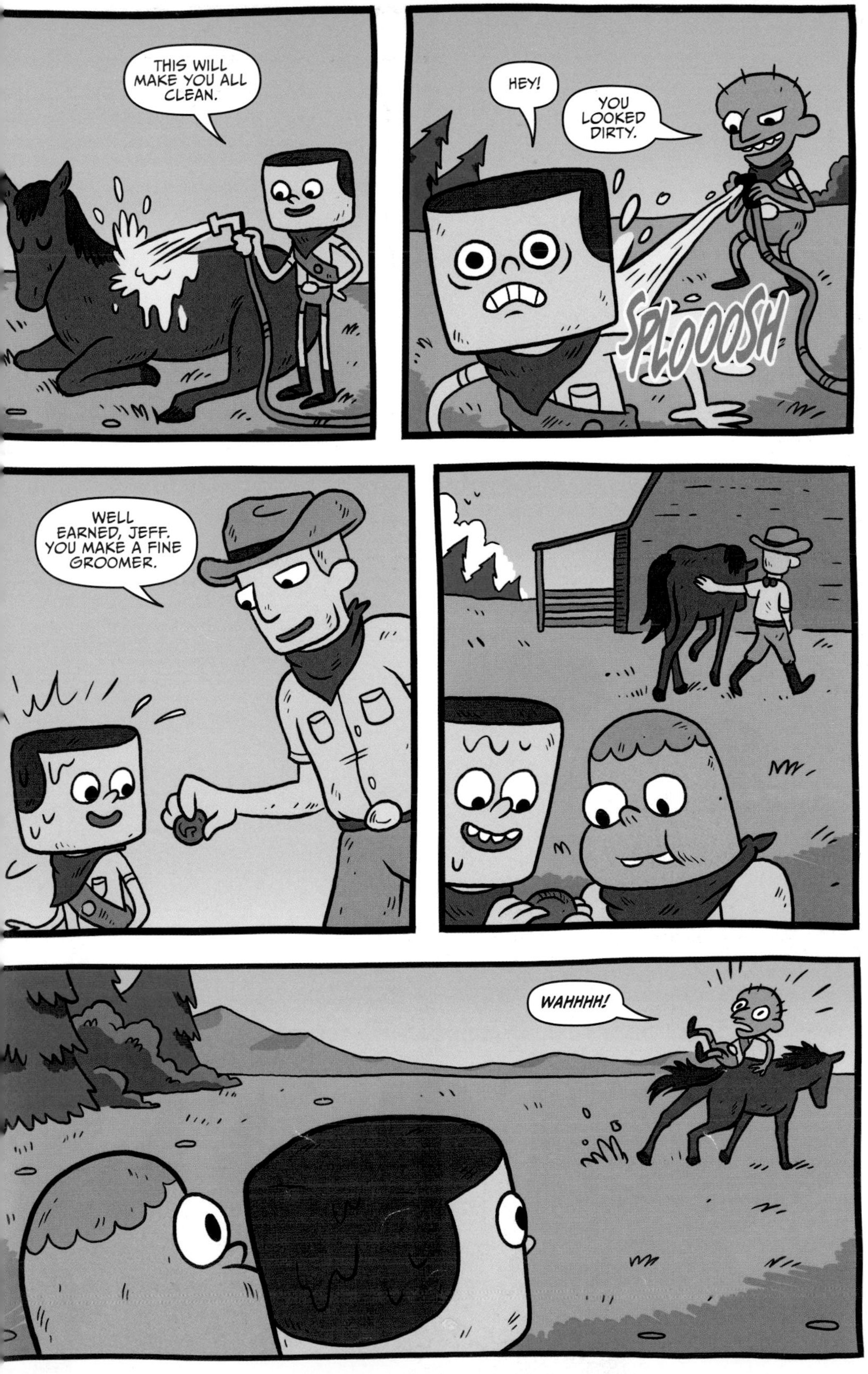
THIS WILL MAKE YOU ALL CLEAN.
HEY!
YOU LOOKED DIRTY.
SPLOOOSH
WELL EARNED, JEFF. YOU MAKE A FINE GROOMER.
WAHHHH!

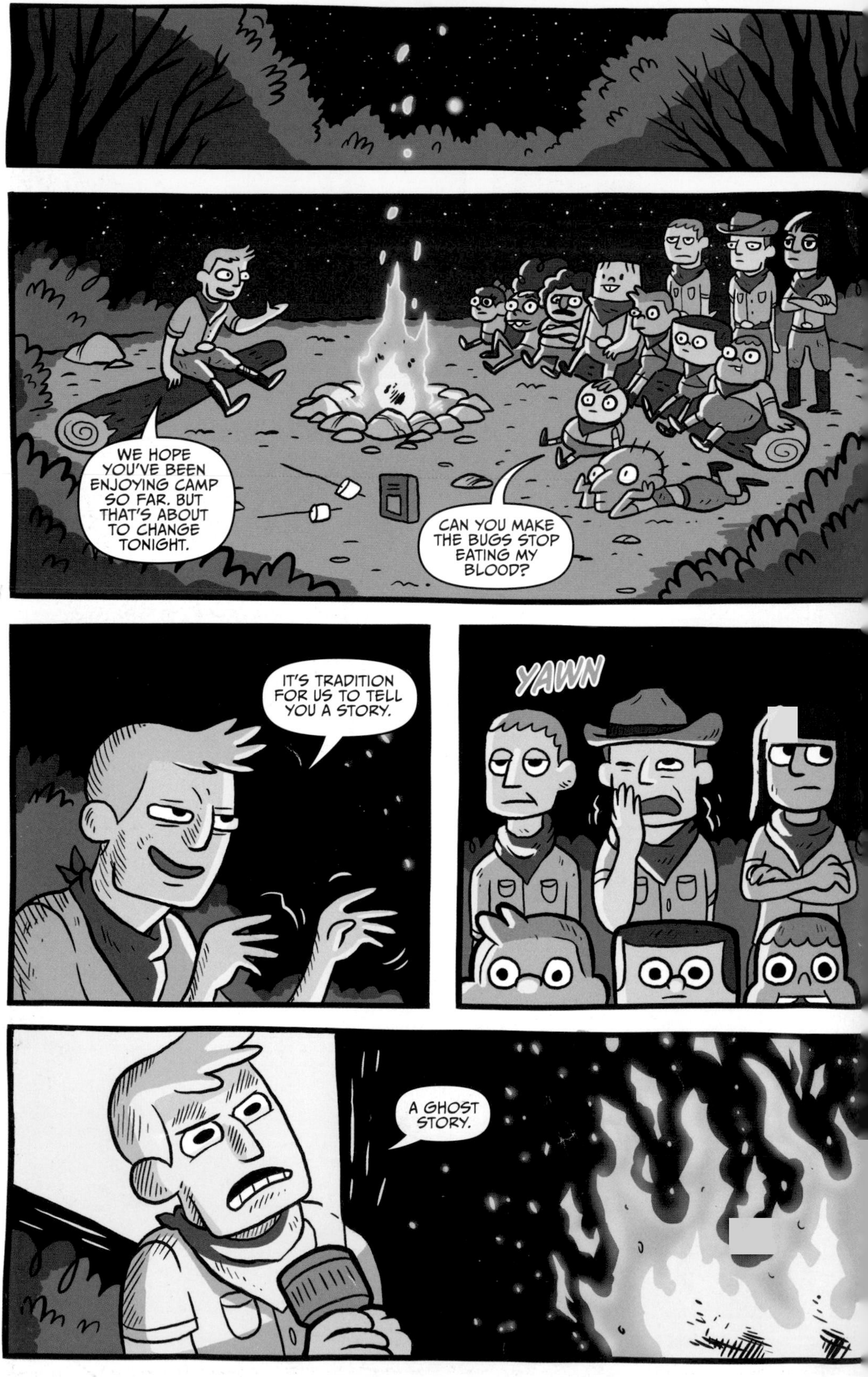

WE HOPE YOU'VE BEEN ENJOYING CAMP SO FAR. BUT THAT'S ABOUT TO CHANGE TONIGHT.
CAN YOU MAKE THE BUGS STOP EATING MY BLOOD?
IT'S TRADITION FOR US TO TELL YOU A STORY.
YAWN
A GHOST STORY.

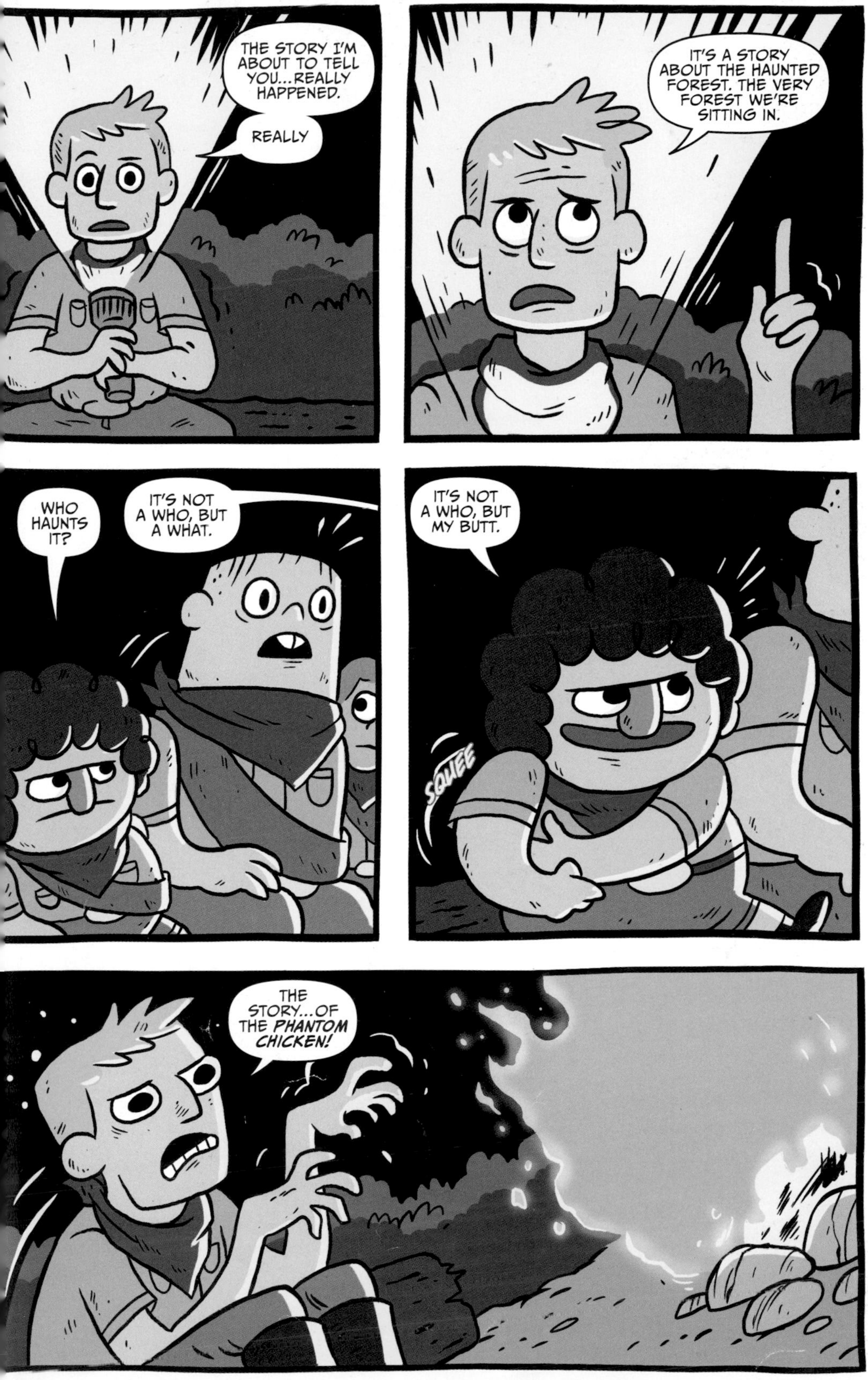
THE STORY I'M ABOUT TO TELL YOU...REALLY HAPPENED.
REALLY
IT'S A STORY ABOUT THE HAUNTED FOREST. THE VERY FOREST WE'RE SITTING IN.
WHO HAUNTS IT?
IT'S NOT A WHO, BUT A WHAT.
IT'S NOT A WHO, BUT MY BUTT.
SQUEE
THE STORY...OF THE *PHANTOM CHICKEN!*

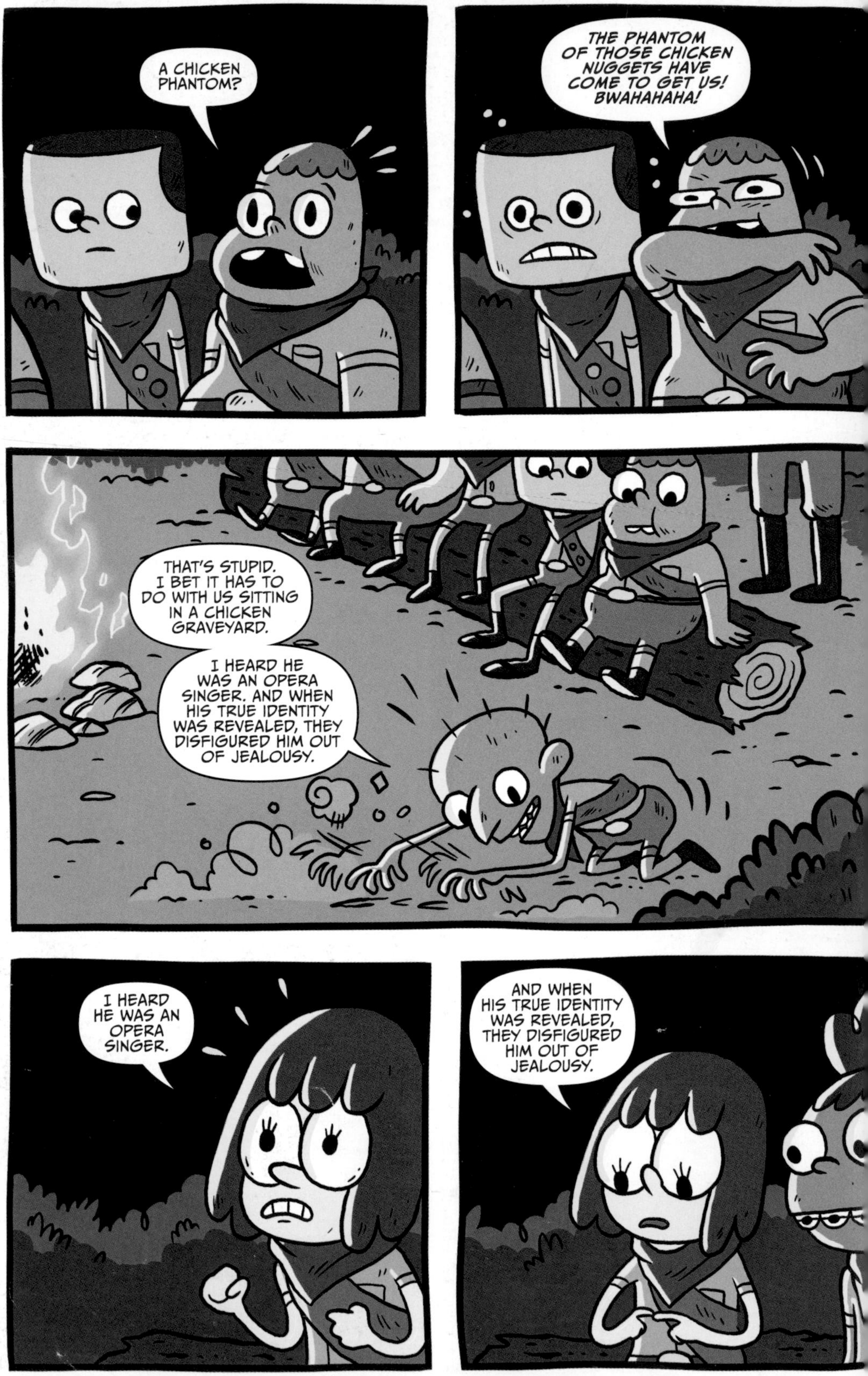
A CHICKEN PHANTOM?
THE PHANTOM OF THOSE CHICKEN NUGGETS HAVE COME TO GET US! BWAHAHAHA!
THAT'S STUPID. I BET IT HAS TO DO WITH US SITTING IN A CHICKEN GRAVEYARD.
I HEARD HE WAS AN OPERA SINGER. AND WHEN HIS TRUE IDENTITY WAS REVEALED, THEY DISFIGURED HIM OUT OF JEALOUSY.
I HEARD HE WAS AN OPERA SINGER.
AND WHEN HIS TRUE IDENTITY WAS REVEALED, THEY DISFIGURED HIM OUT OF JEALOUSY.

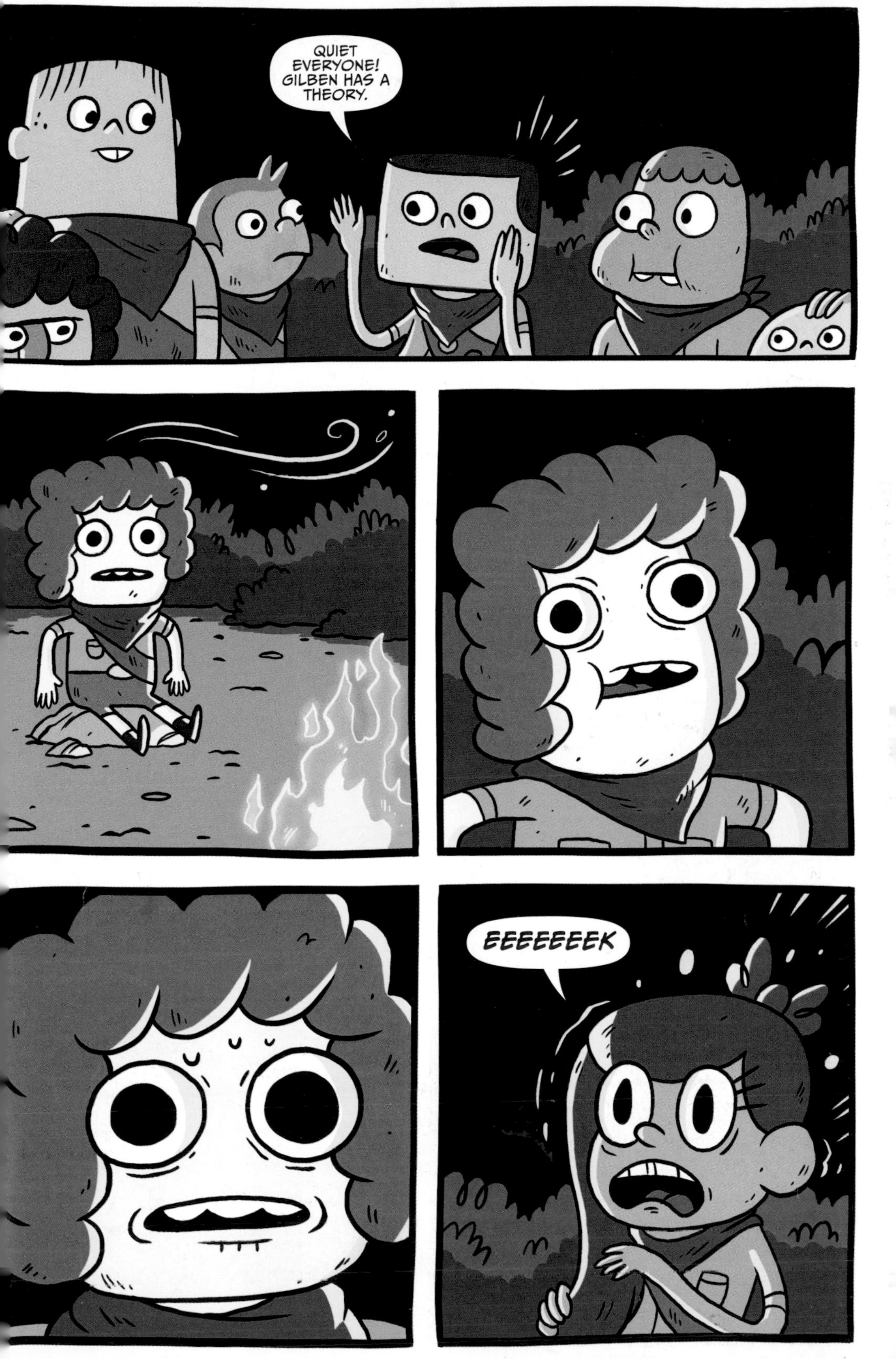
QUIET EVERYONE! GILBEN HAS A THEORY.
EEEEEEEK

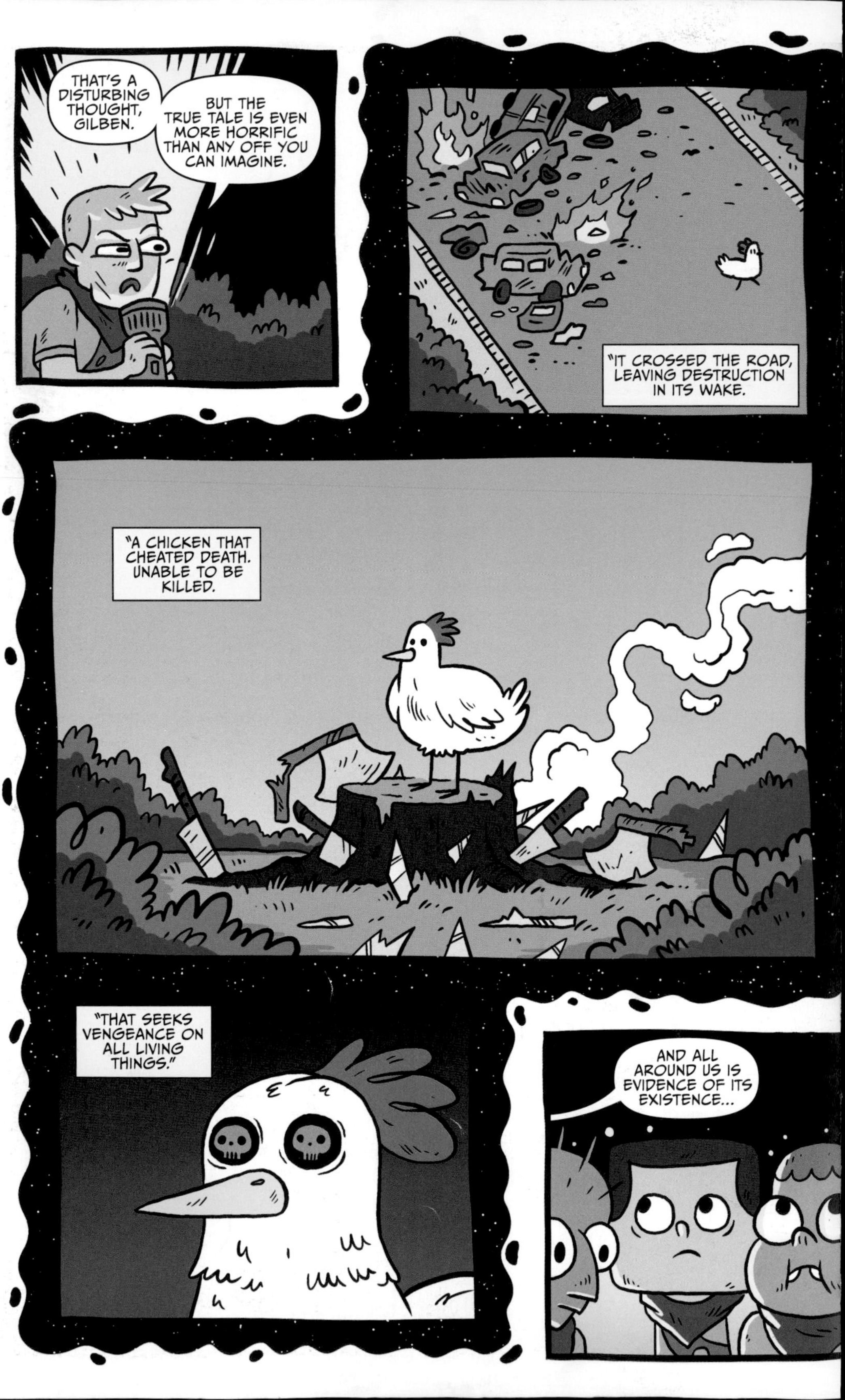

THAT'S A DISTURBING THOUGHT, GILBEN.
BUT THE TRUE TALE IS EVEN MORE HORRIFIC THAN ANY OFF YOU CAN IMAGINE.
"IT CROSSED THE ROAD, LEAVING DESTRUCTION IN ITS WAKE.
"A CHICKEN THAT CHEATED DEATH. UNABLE TO BE KILLED.
"THAT SEEKS VENGEANCE ON ALL LIVING THINGS."
AND ALL AROUND US IS EVIDENCE OF ITS EXISTENCE...

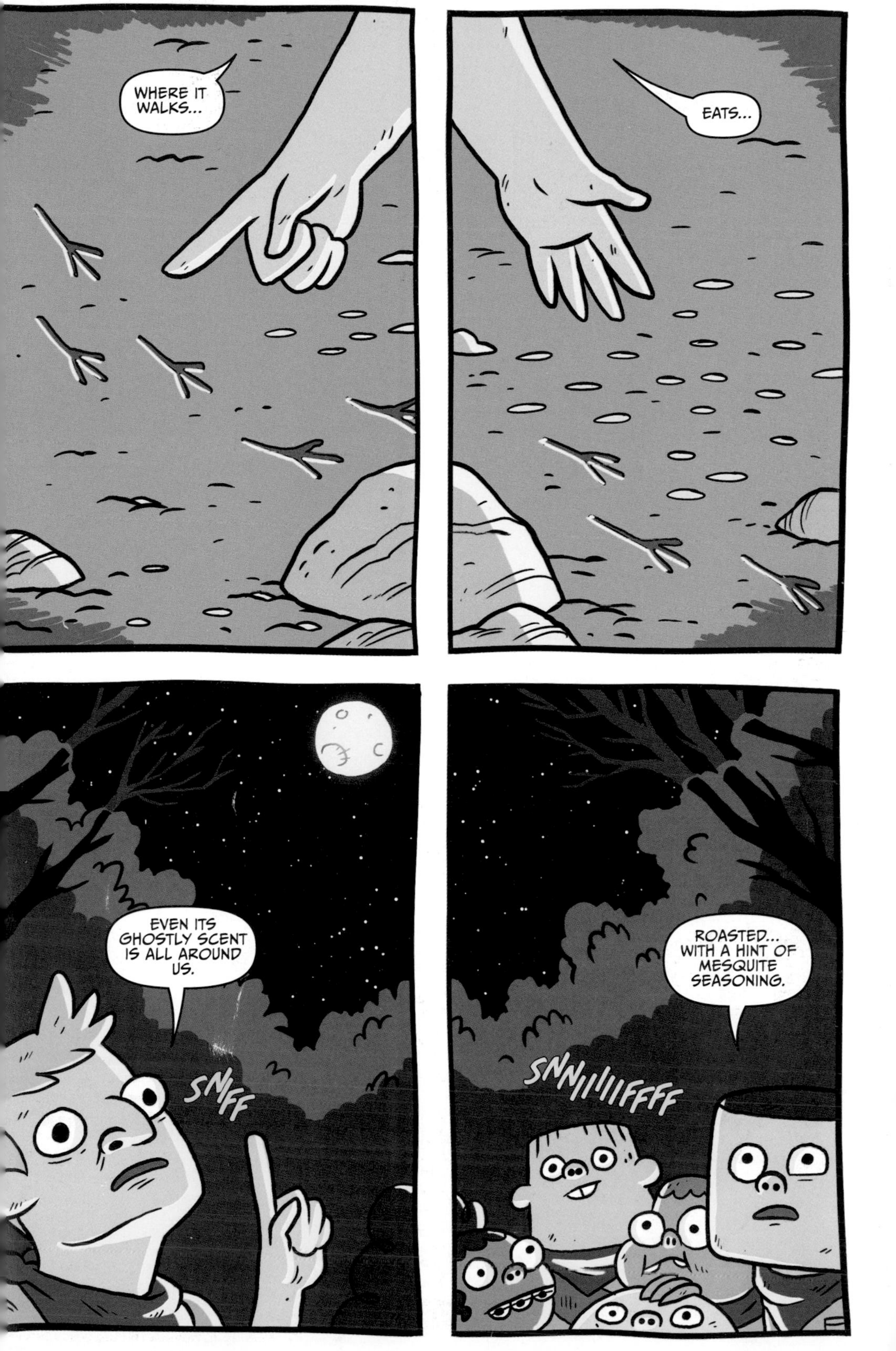
WHERE IT WALKS...
EATS...
EVEN ITS GHOSTLY SCENT IS ALL AROUND US.
SNIFF
ROASTED... WITH A HINT OF MESQUITE SEASONING.
SNNIIIIIIIFFFF

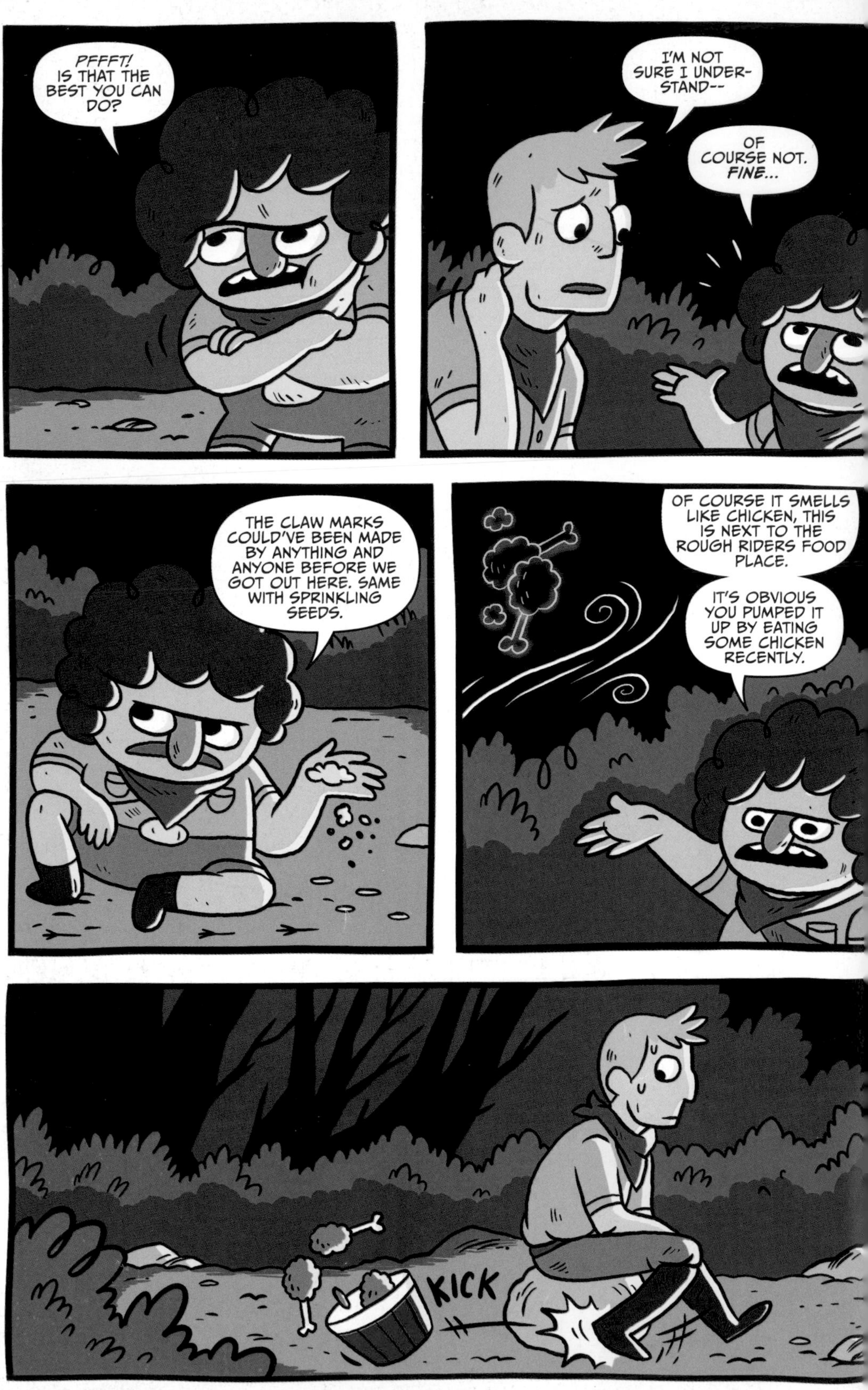
PFFFT! IS THAT THE BEST YOU CAN DO?
I'M NOT SURE I UNDER-STAND--
OF COURSE NOT. FINE...
THE CLAW MARKS COULD'VE BEEN MADE BY ANYTHING AND ANYONE BEFORE WE GOT OUT HERE. SAME WITH SPRINKLING SEEDS.
OF COURSE IT SMELLS LIKE CHICKEN, THIS IS NEXT TO THE ROUGH RIDERS FOOD PLACE.
IT'S OBVIOUS YOU PUMPED IT UP BY EATING SOME CHICKEN RECENTLY.
KICK

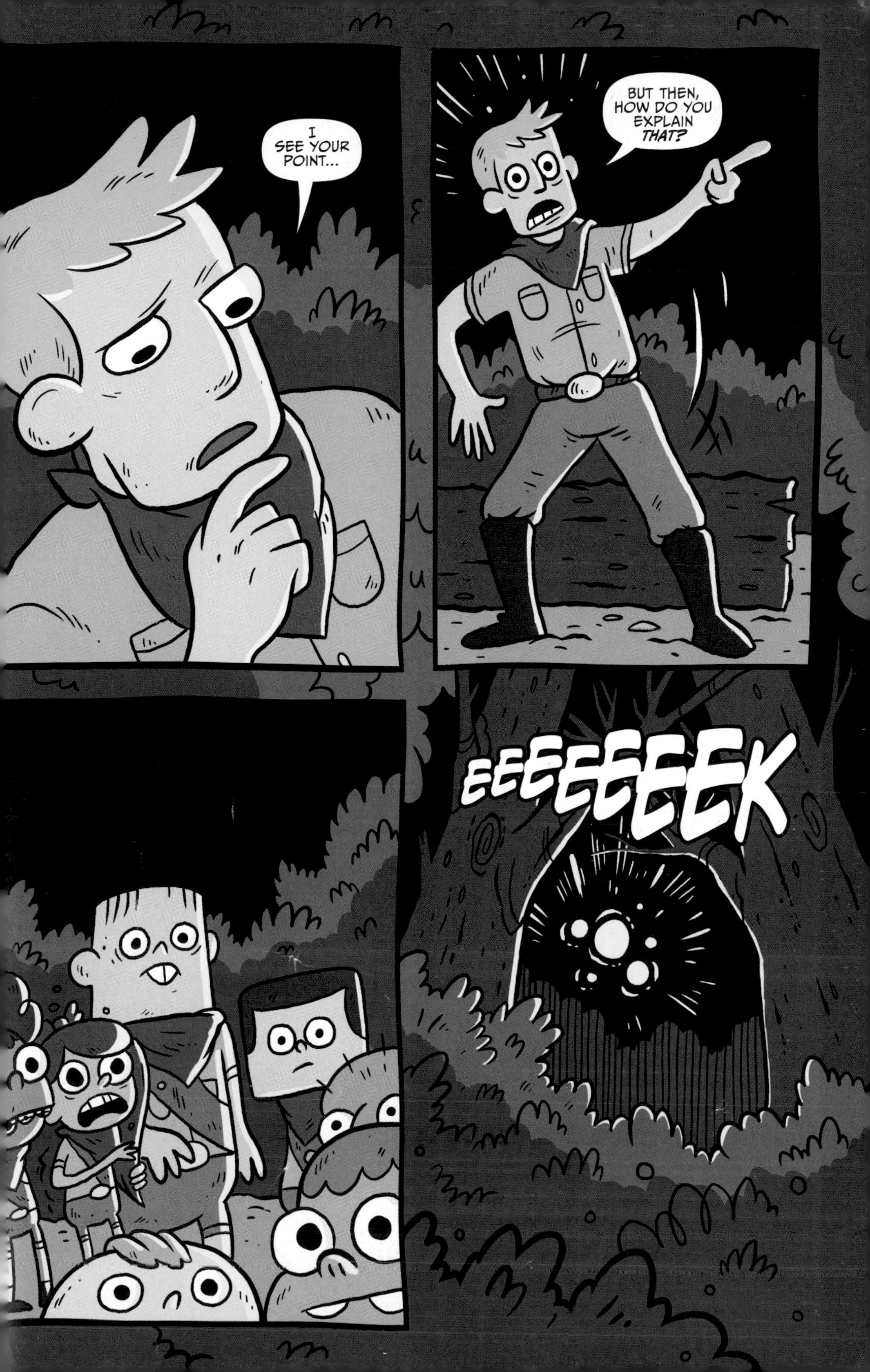
I SEE YOUR POINT...
BUT THEN, HOW DO YOU EXPLAIN THAT?
EEEEEEEEEK

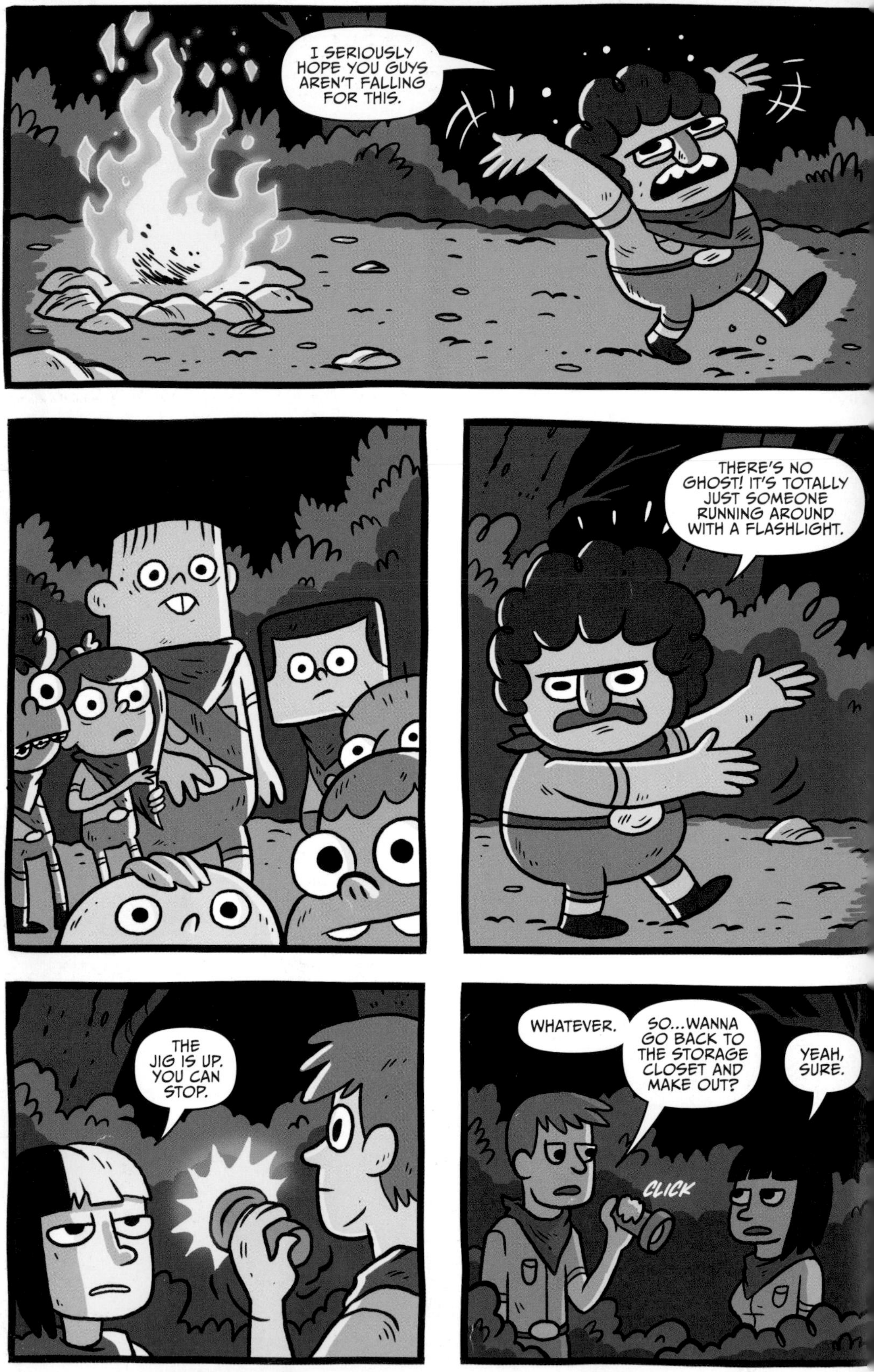
I SERIOUSLY HOPE YOU GUYS AREN'T FALLING FOR THIS.
THERE'S NO GHOST! IT'S TOTALLY JUST SOMEONE RUNNING AROUND WITH A FLASHLIGHT.
THE JIG IS UP. YOU CAN STOP.
WHATEVER.
SO...WANNA GO BACK TO THE STORAGE CLOSET AND MAKE OUT?
CLICK
YEAH, SURE.

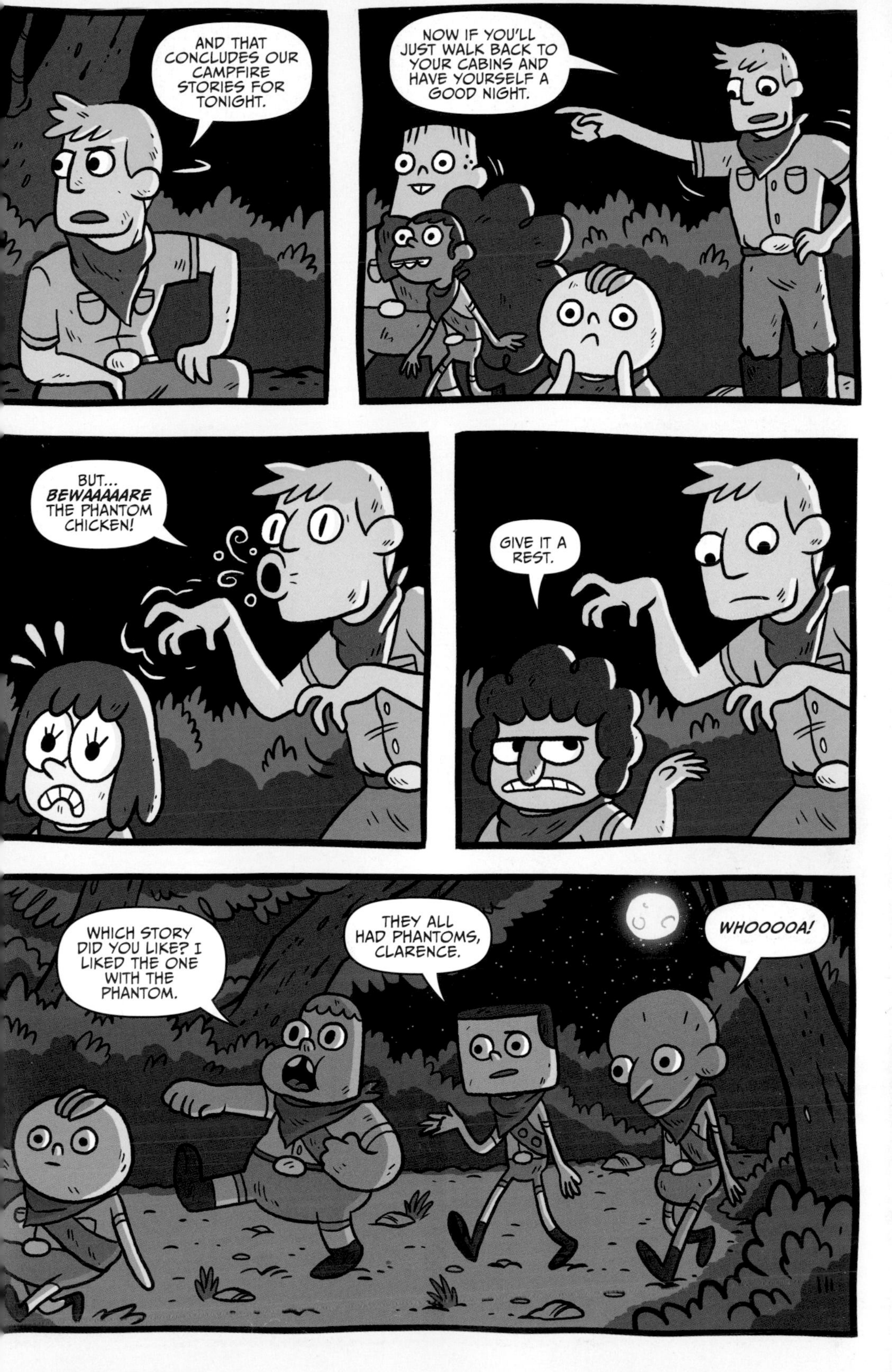
AND THAT CONCLUDES OUR CAMPFIRE STORIES FOR TONIGHT.
NOW IF YOU'LL JUST WALK BACK TO YOUR CABINS AND HAVE YOURSELF A GOOD NIGHT.
BUT... *BEWAAAAARE* THE PHANTOM CHICKEN!
GIVE IT A REST.
WHICH STORY DID YOU LIKE? I LIKED THE ONE WITH THE PHANTOM.
THEY ALL HAD PHANTOMS, CLARENCE.
WHOOOOA!

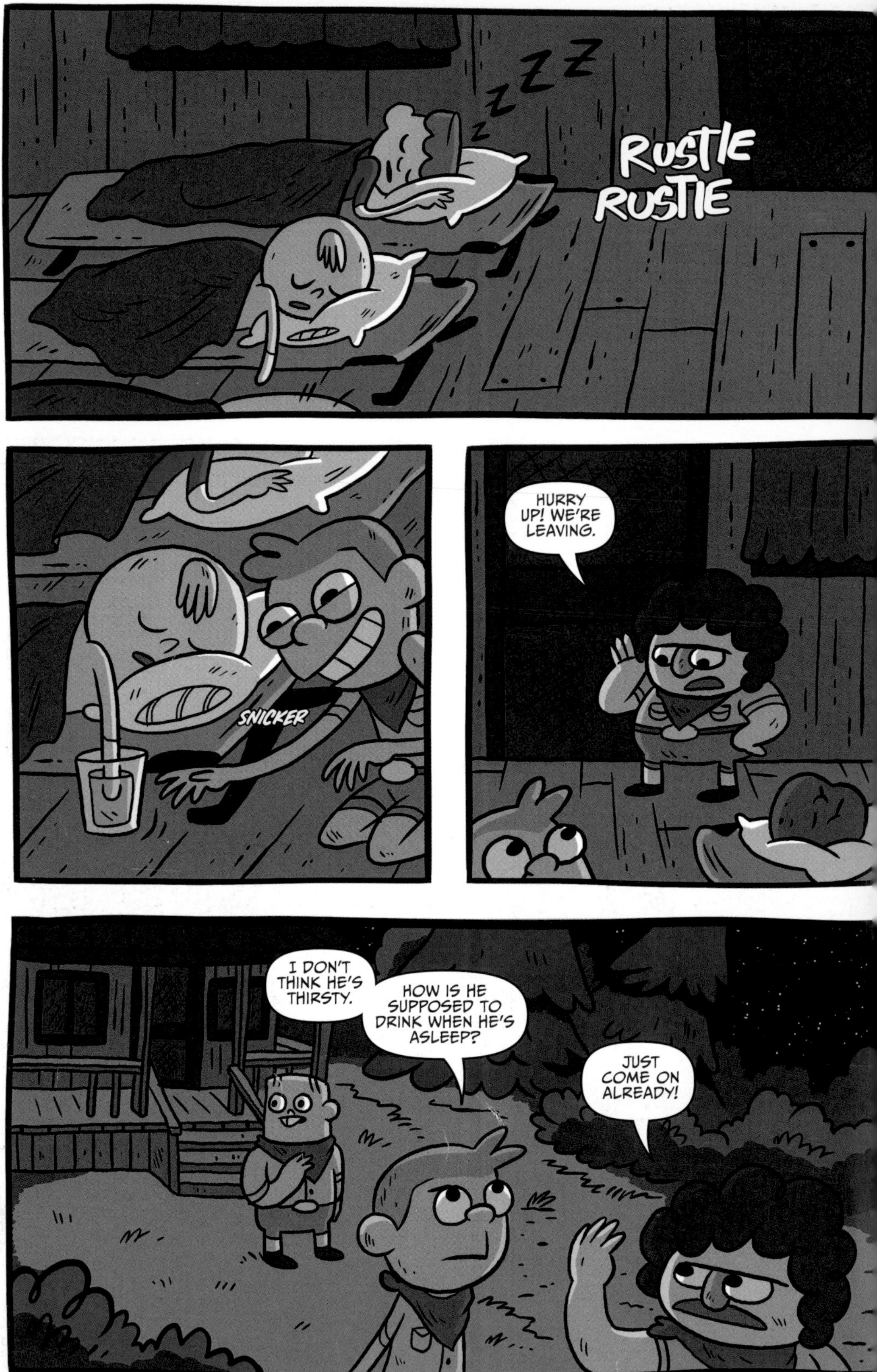

ZZZZ
RUSTLE RUSTLE
SNICKER
HURRY UP! WE'RE LEAVING.
I DON'T THINK HE'S THIRSTY.
HOW IS HE SUPPOSED TO DRINK WHEN HE'S ASLEEP?
JUST COME ON ALREADY!

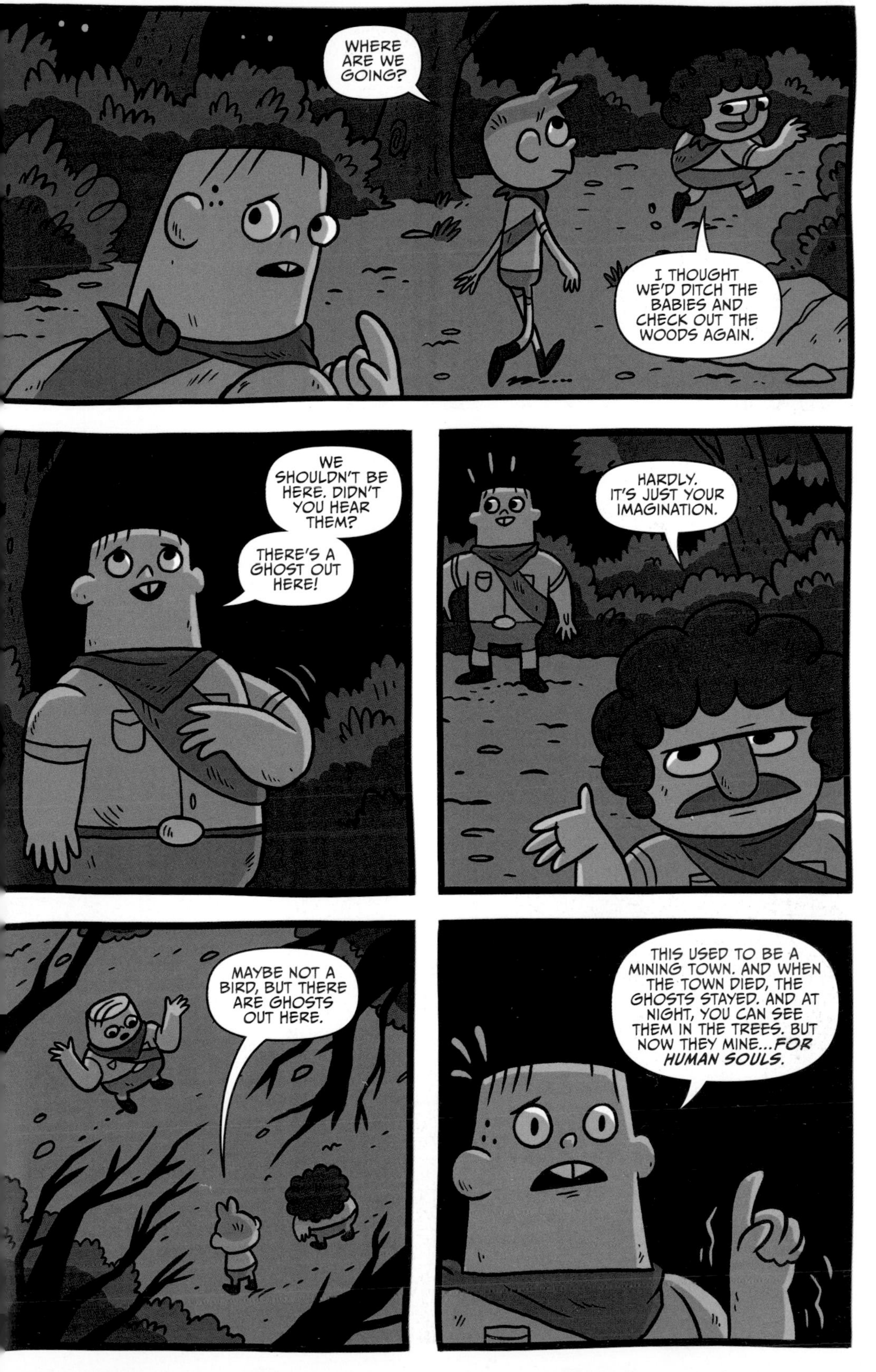
WHERE ARE WE GOING?
I THOUGHT WE'D DITCH THE BABIES AND CHECK OUT THE WOODS AGAIN.
WE SHOULDN'T BE HERE. DIDN'T YOU HEAR THEM?
THERE'S A GHOST OUT HERE!
HARDLY. IT'S JUST YOUR IMAGINATION.
MAYBE NOT A BIRD, BUT THERE ARE GHOSTS OUT HERE.
THIS USED TO BE A MINING TOWN. AND WHEN THE TOWN DIED, THE GHOSTS STAYED. AND AT NIGHT, YOU CAN SEE THEM IN THE TREES. BUT NOW THEY MINE... *FOR HUMAN SOULS*.

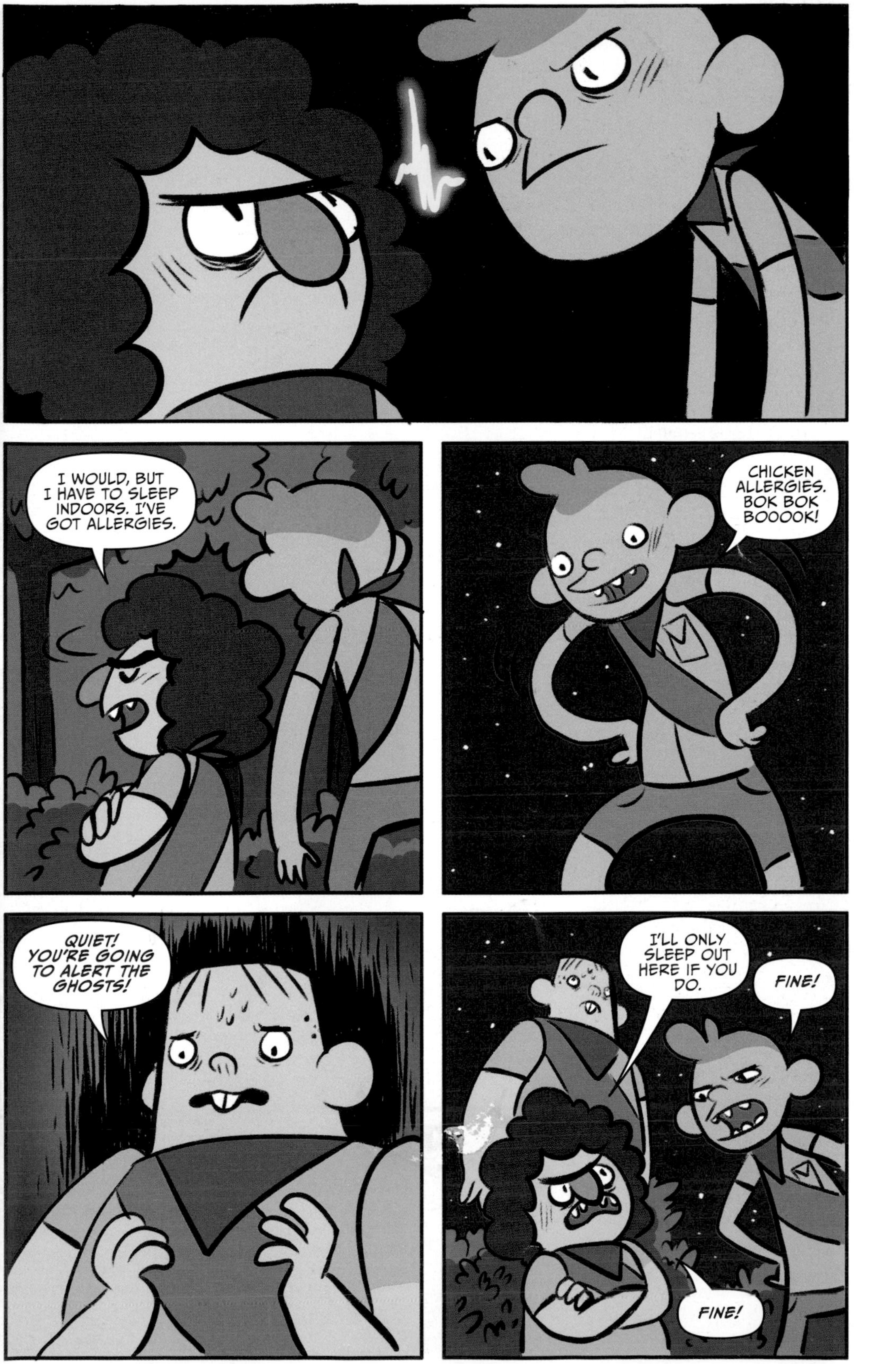
I WOULD, BUT I HAVE TO SLEEP INDOORS. I'VE GOT ALLERGIES.
CHICKEN ALLERGIES. BOK BOK BOOOOK!
QUIET! YOU'RE GOING TO ALERT THE GHOSTS!
I'LL ONLY SLEEP OUT HERE IF YOU DO.
FINE!
FINE!

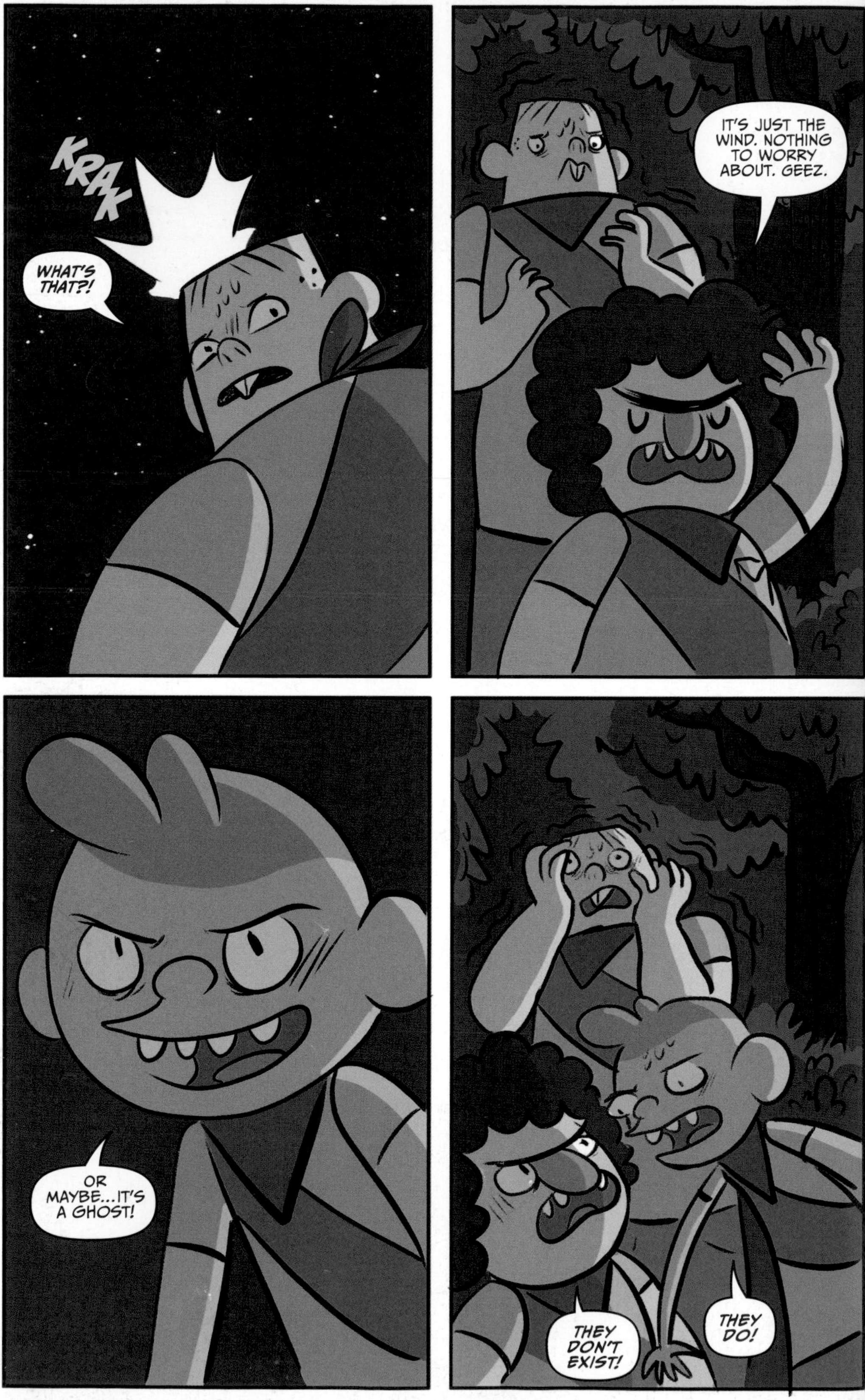
KRAK
WHAT'S THAT?!
IT'S JUST THE WIND. NOTHING TO WORRY ABOUT. GEEZ.
OR MAYBE...IT'S A GHOST!
THEY DON'T EXIST!
THEY DO!

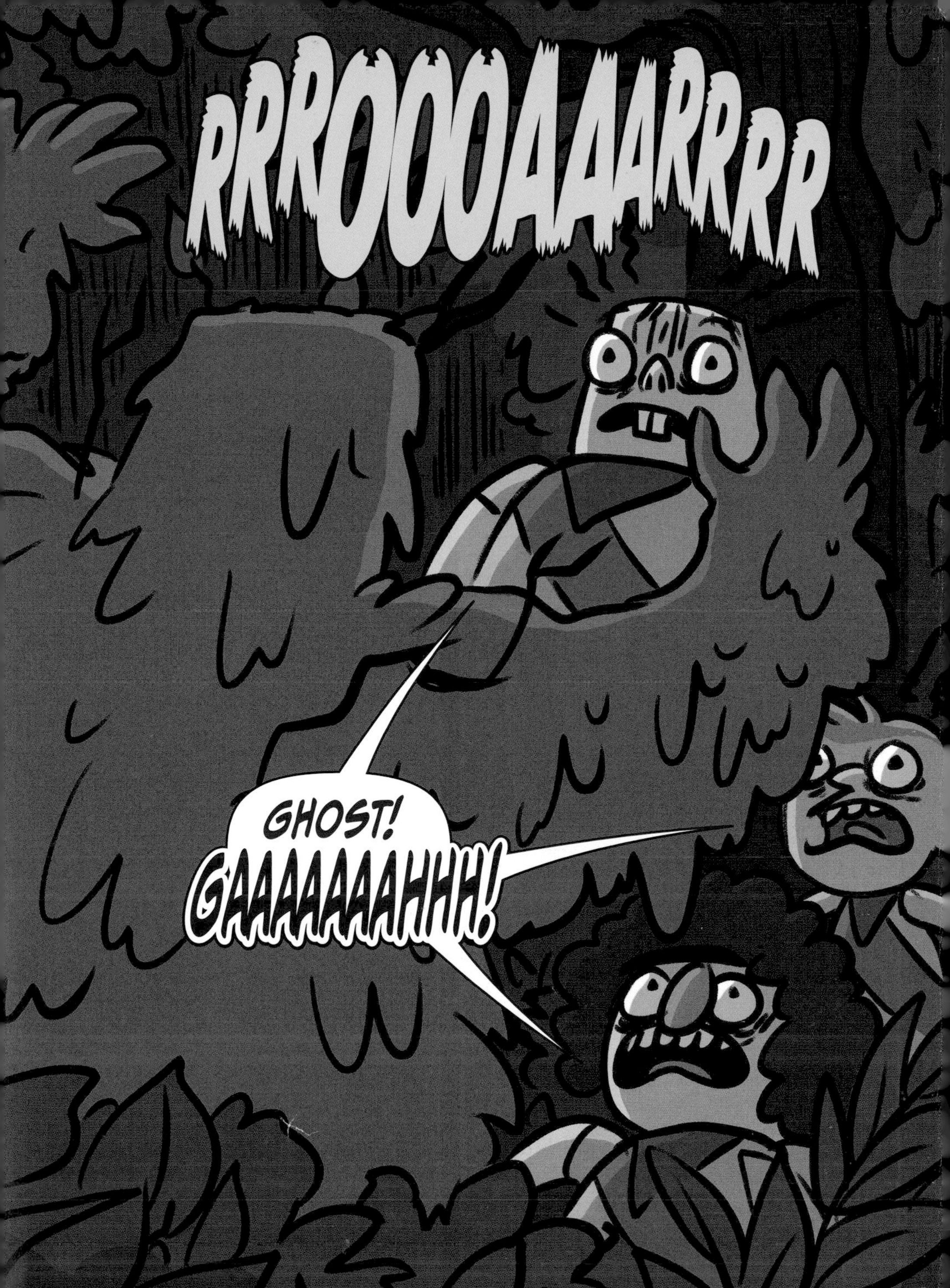
RRROOOAAARRRR
GHOST!
GAAAAAAAHHH!

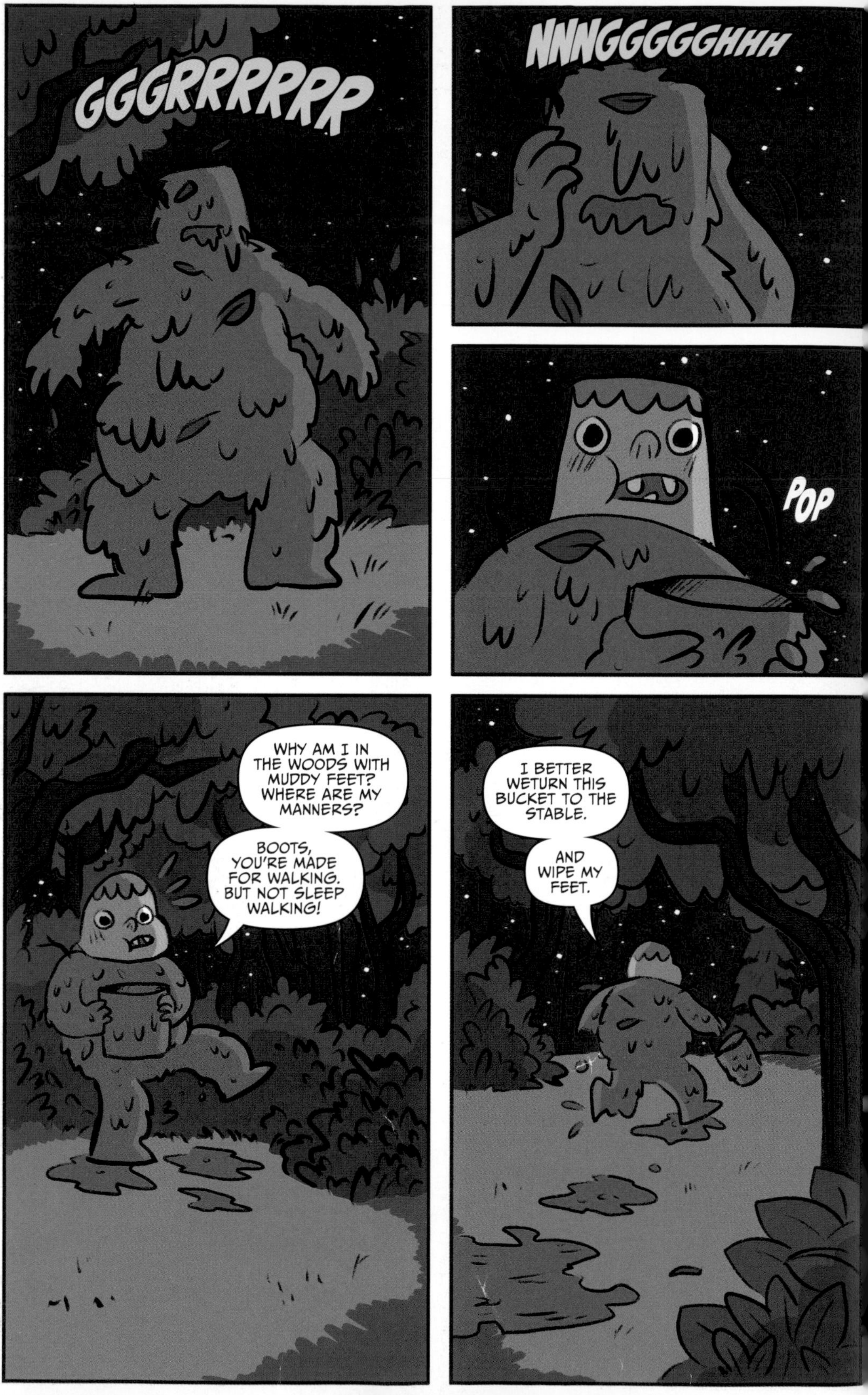
GGGRRRRRRR
NNNGGGGGHHH
POP
WHY AM I IN THE WOODS WITH MUDDY FEET? WHERE ARE MY MANNERS?
BOOTS, YOU'RE MADE FOR WALKING. BUT NOT SLEEP WALKING!
I BETTER WETURN THIS BUCKET TO THE STABLE.
AND WIPE MY FEET.

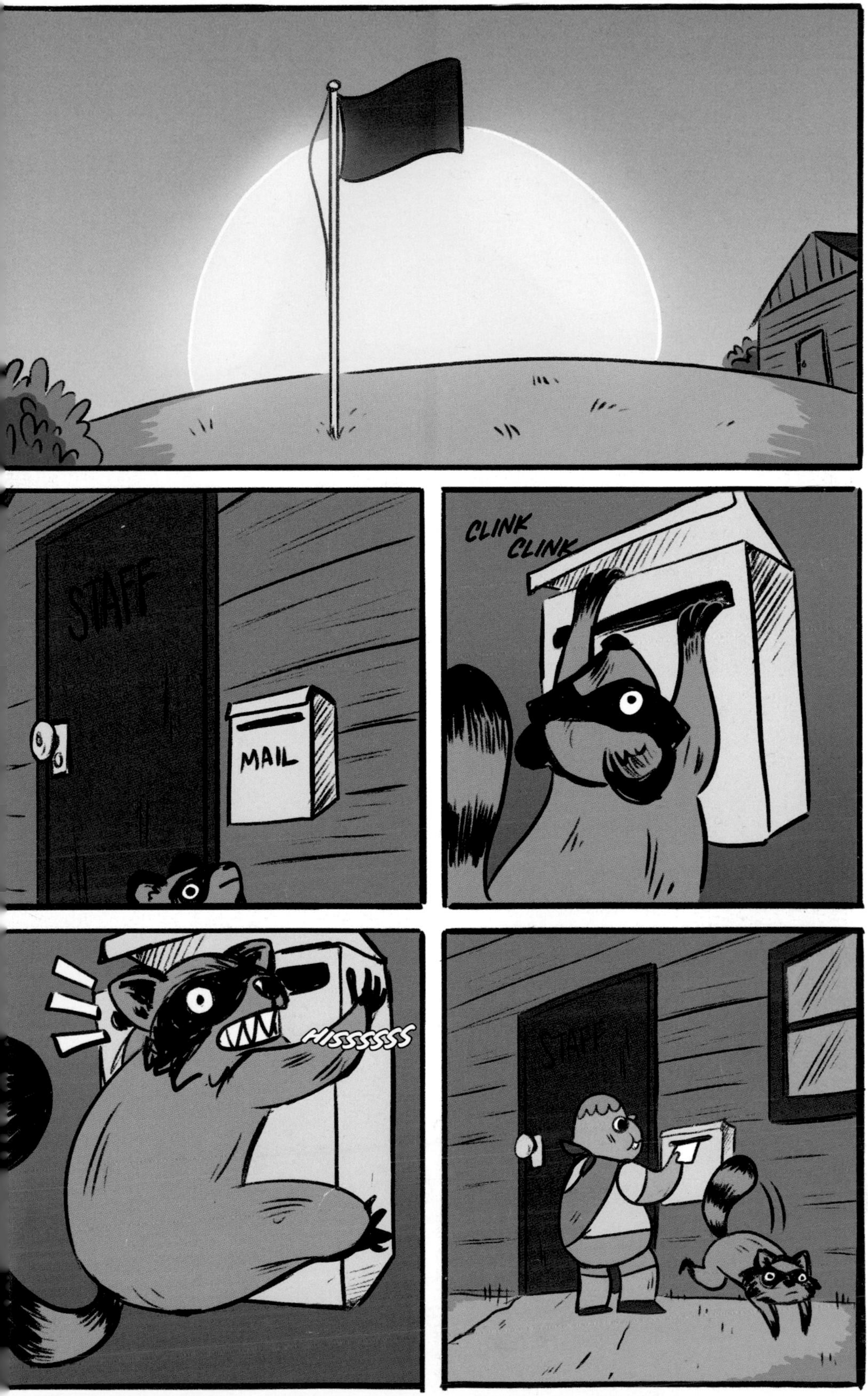
STAFF
MAIL
CLINK
CLINK
HISSSSSS
STAFF

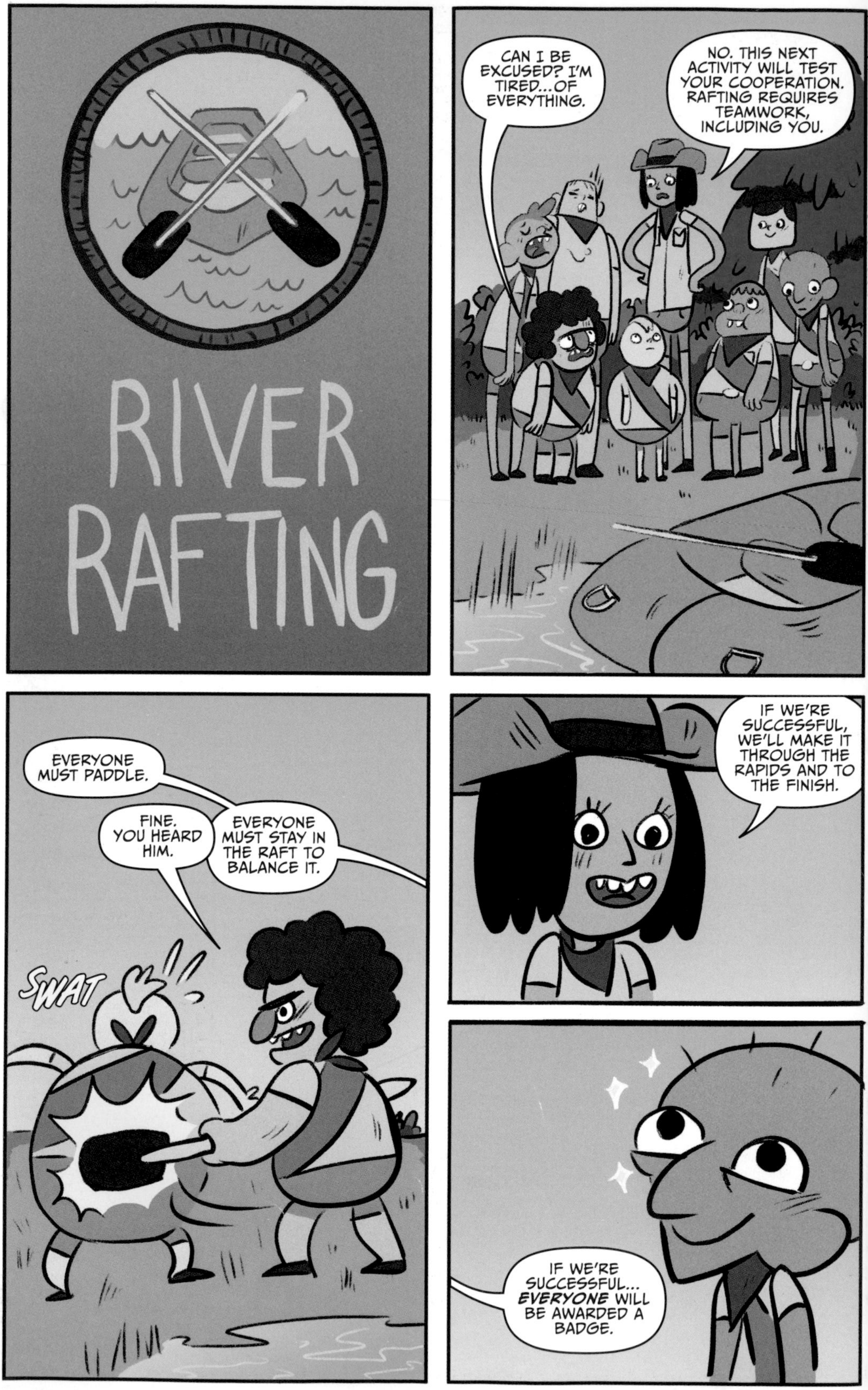
RIVER RAFTING
CAN I BE EXCUSED? I'M TIRED...OF EVERYTHING.
NO. THIS NEXT ACTIVITY WILL TEST YOUR COOPERATION. RAFTING REQUIRES TEAMWORK, INCLUDING YOU.
EVERYONE MUST PADDLE.
EVERYONE MUST STAY IN THE RAFT TO BALANCE IT.
FINE. YOU HEARD HIM.
SWAT
IF WE'RE SUCCESSFUL, WE'LL MAKE IT THROUGH THE RAPIDS AND TO THE FINISH.
IF WE'RE SUCCESSFUL... *EVERYONE* WILL BE AWARDED A BADGE.

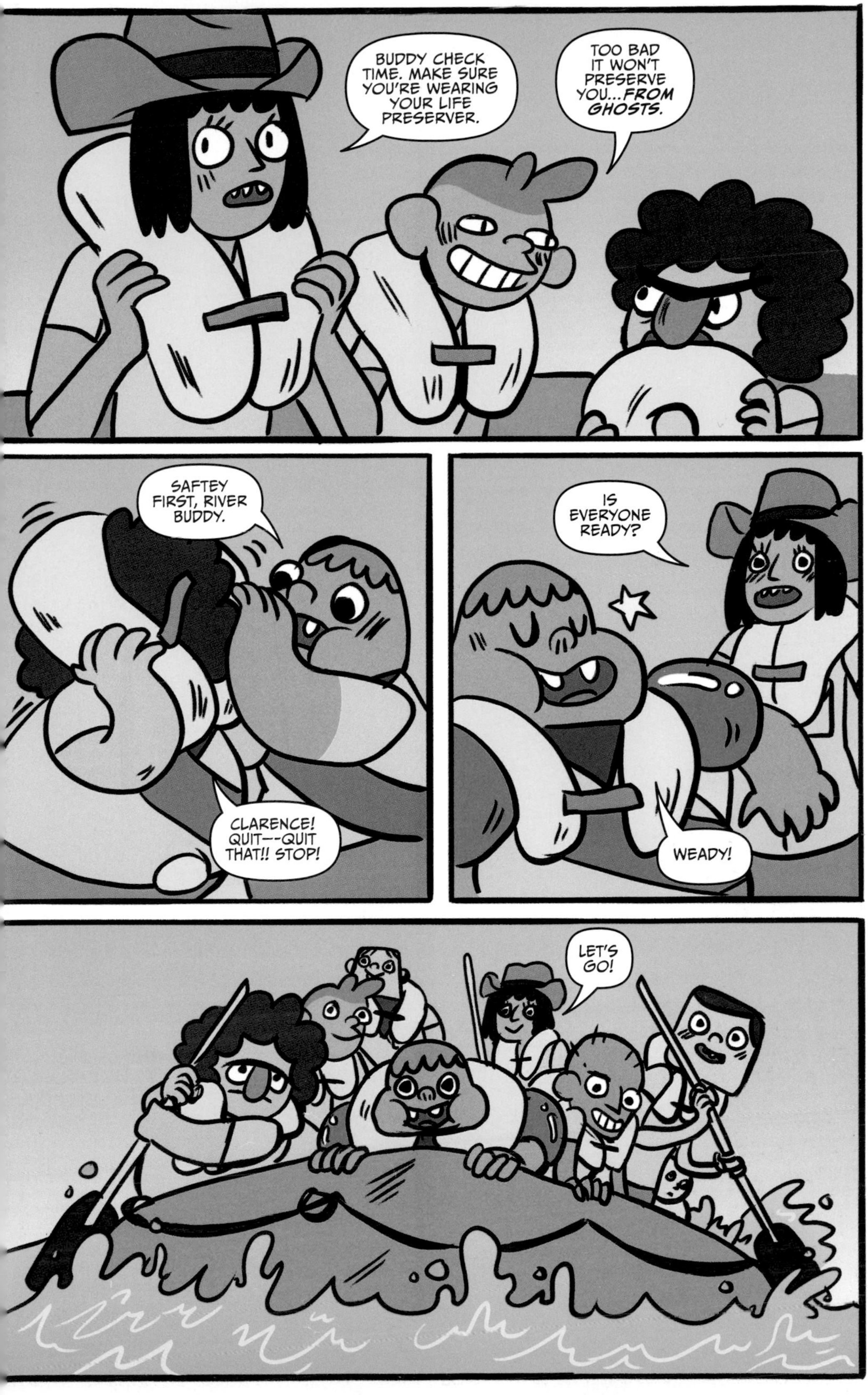
BUDDY CHECK TIME. MAKE SURE YOU'RE WEARING YOUR LIFE PRESERVER.
TOO BAD IT WON'T PRESERVE YOU...FROM GHOSTS.
SAFTEY FIRST, RIVER BUDDY.
CLARENCE! QUIT--QUIT THAT!! STOP!
IS EVERYONE READY?
WEADY!
LET'S GO!

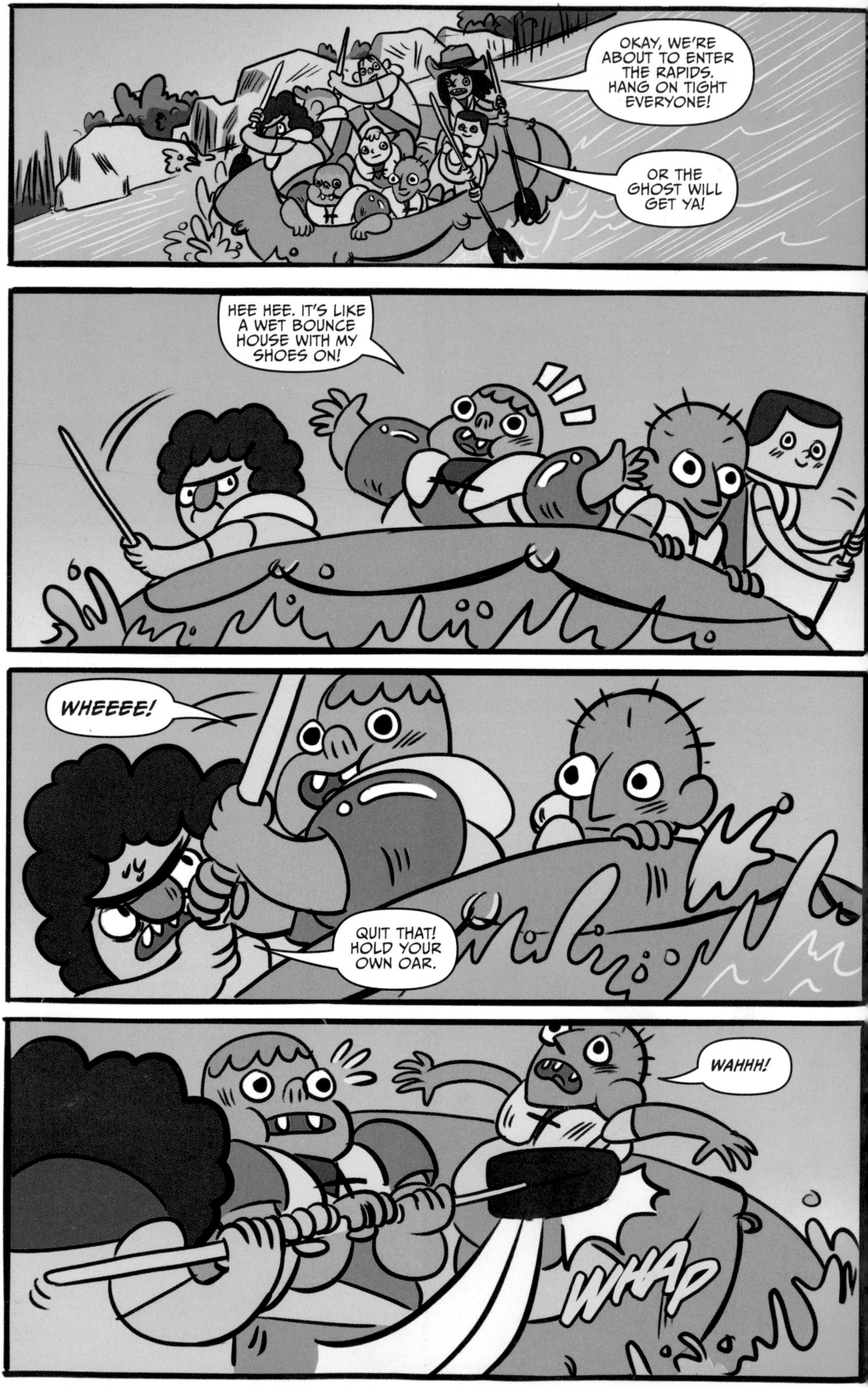
OKAY, WE'RE ABOUT TO ENTER THE RAPIDS. HANG ON TIGHT EVERYONE!
OR THE GHOST WILL GET YA!
HEE HEE. IT'S LIKE A WET BOUNCE HOUSE WITH MY SHOES ON!
WHEEEE!
QUIT THAT! HOLD YOUR OWN OAR.
WAHHH!
WHAP

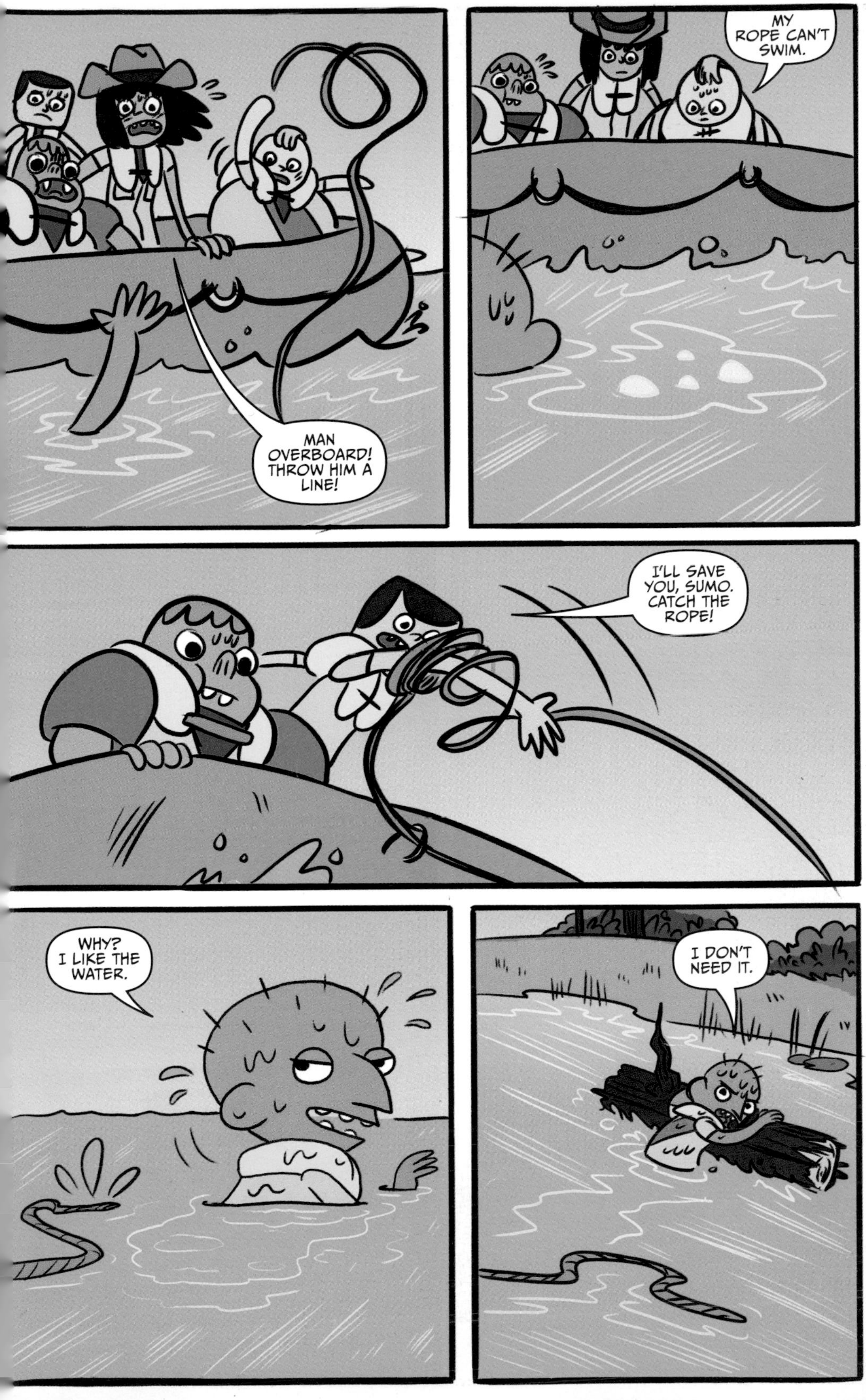
MAN OVERBOARD! THROW HIM A LINE!
MY ROPE CAN'T SWIM.
I'LL SAVE YOU, SUMO. CATCH THE ROPE!
WHY? I LIKE THE WATER.
I DON'T NEED IT.

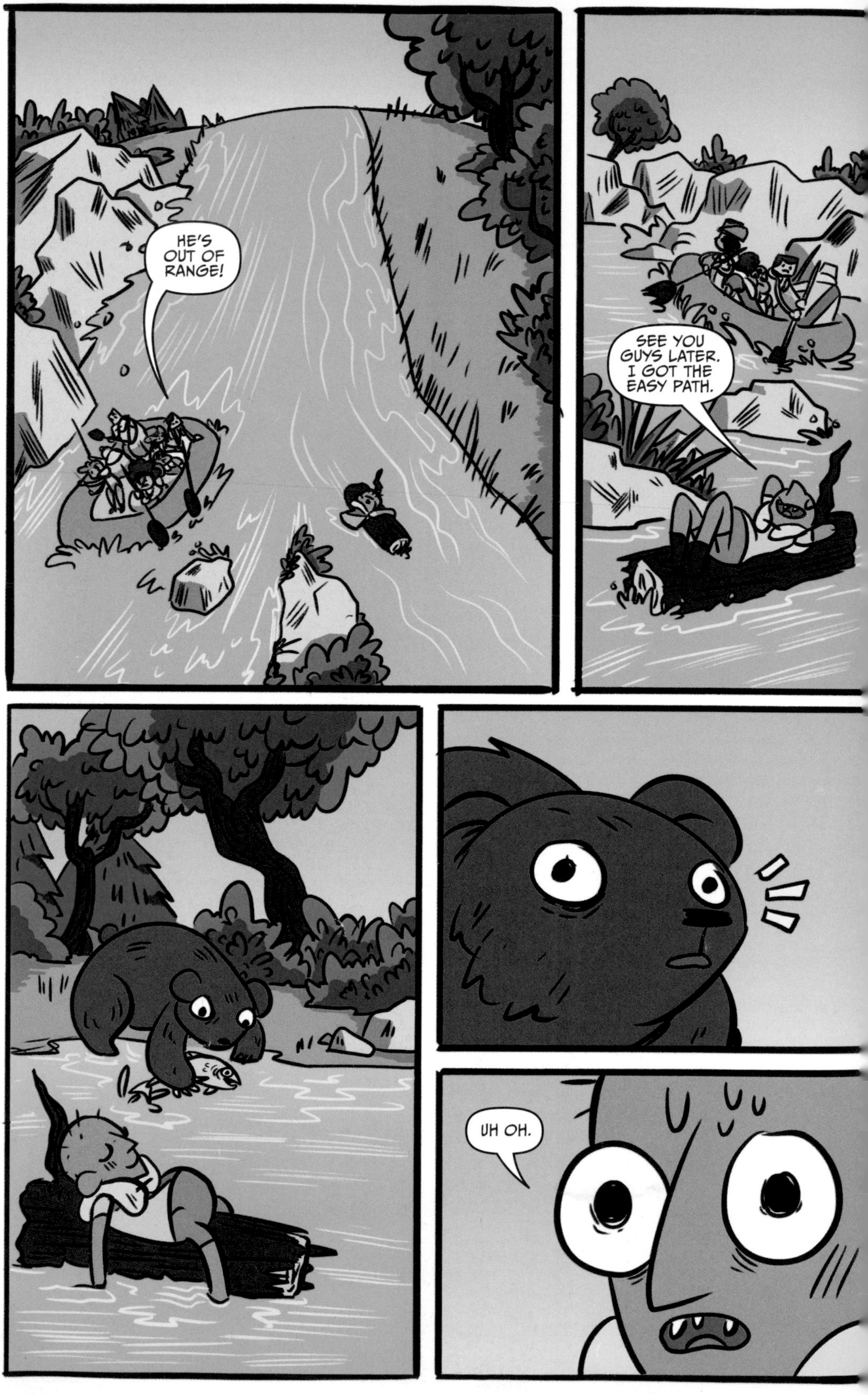
HE'S OUT OF RANGE!
SEE YOU GUYS LATER. I GOT THE EASY PATH.
UH OH.

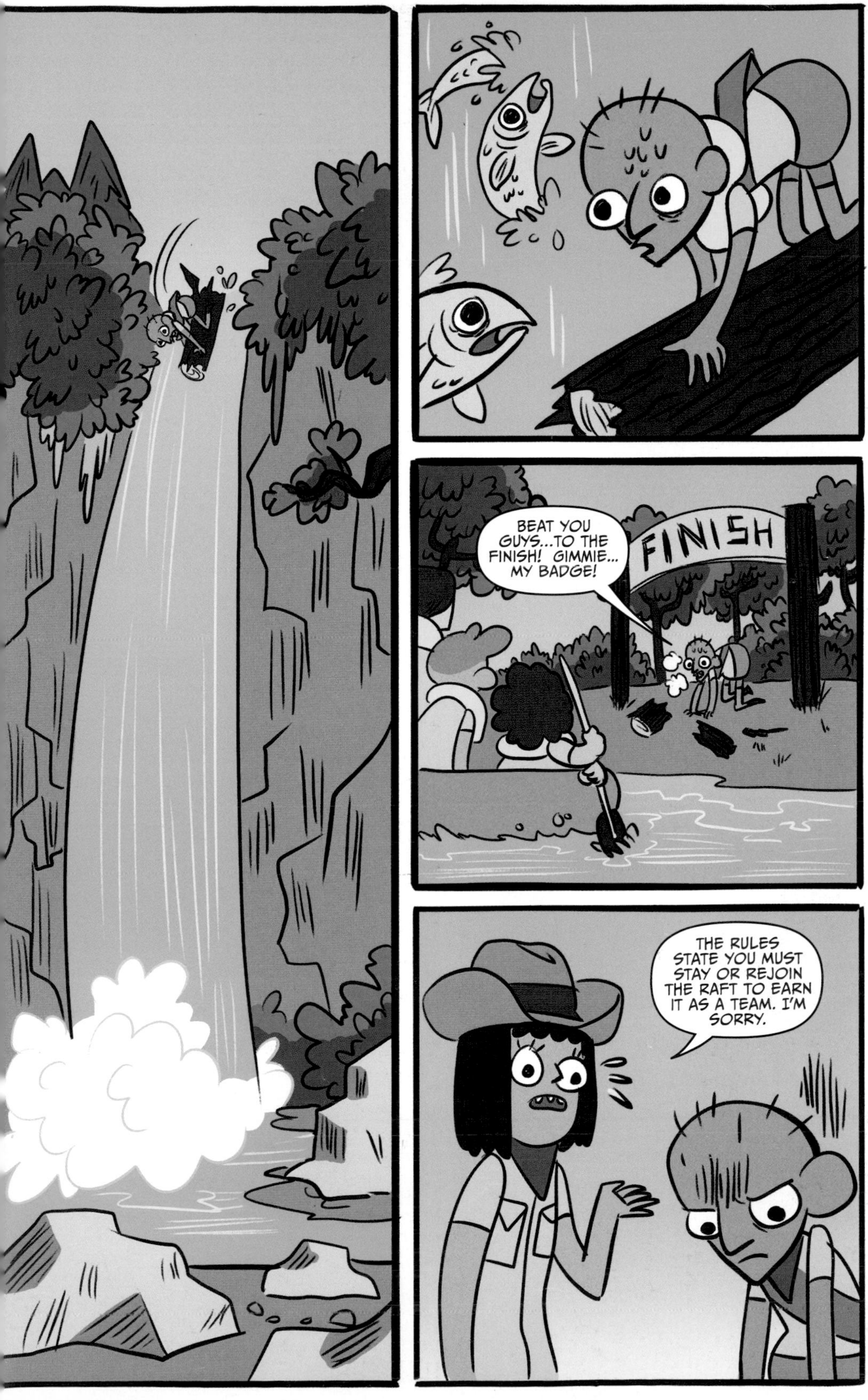

BEAT YOU GUYS...TO THE FINISH! GIMMIE... MY BADGE!
FINISH
THE RULES STATE YOU MUST STAY OR REJOIN THE RAFT TO EARN IT AS A TEAM. I'M SORRY.

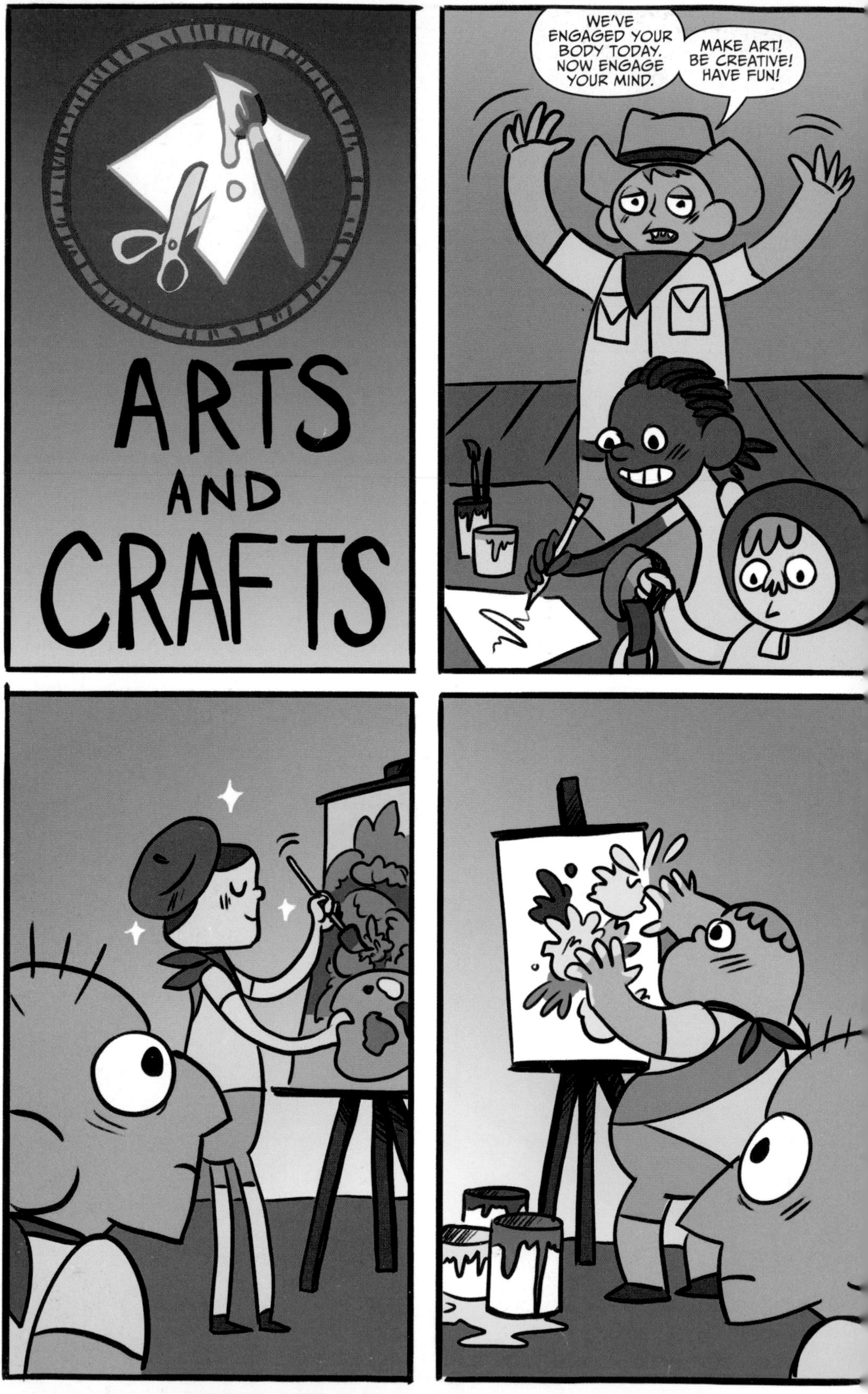
ARTS AND CRAFTS
WE'VE ENGAGED YOUR BODY TODAY. NOW ENGAGE YOUR MIND.
MAKE ART! BE CREATIVE! HAVE FUN!

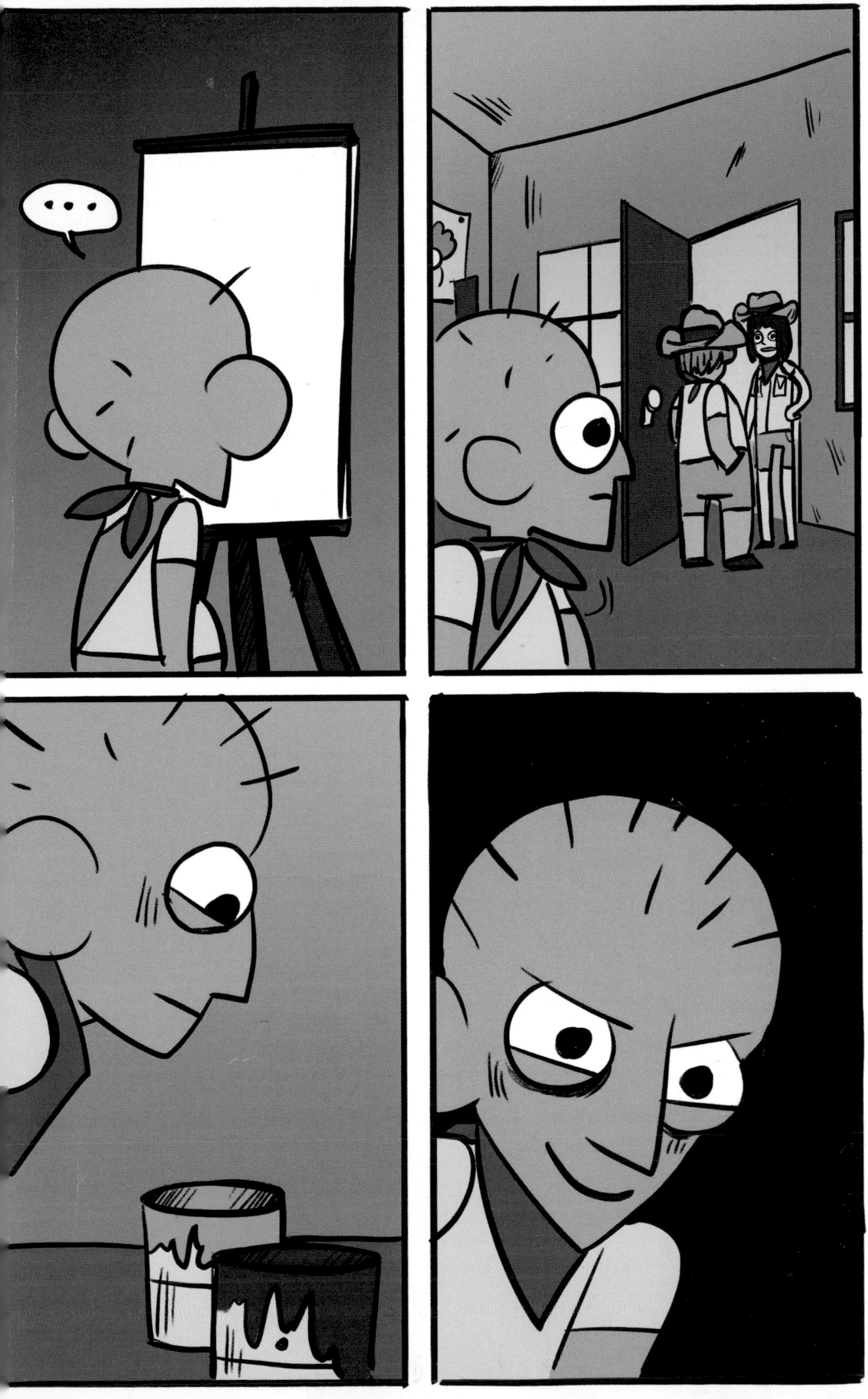
...

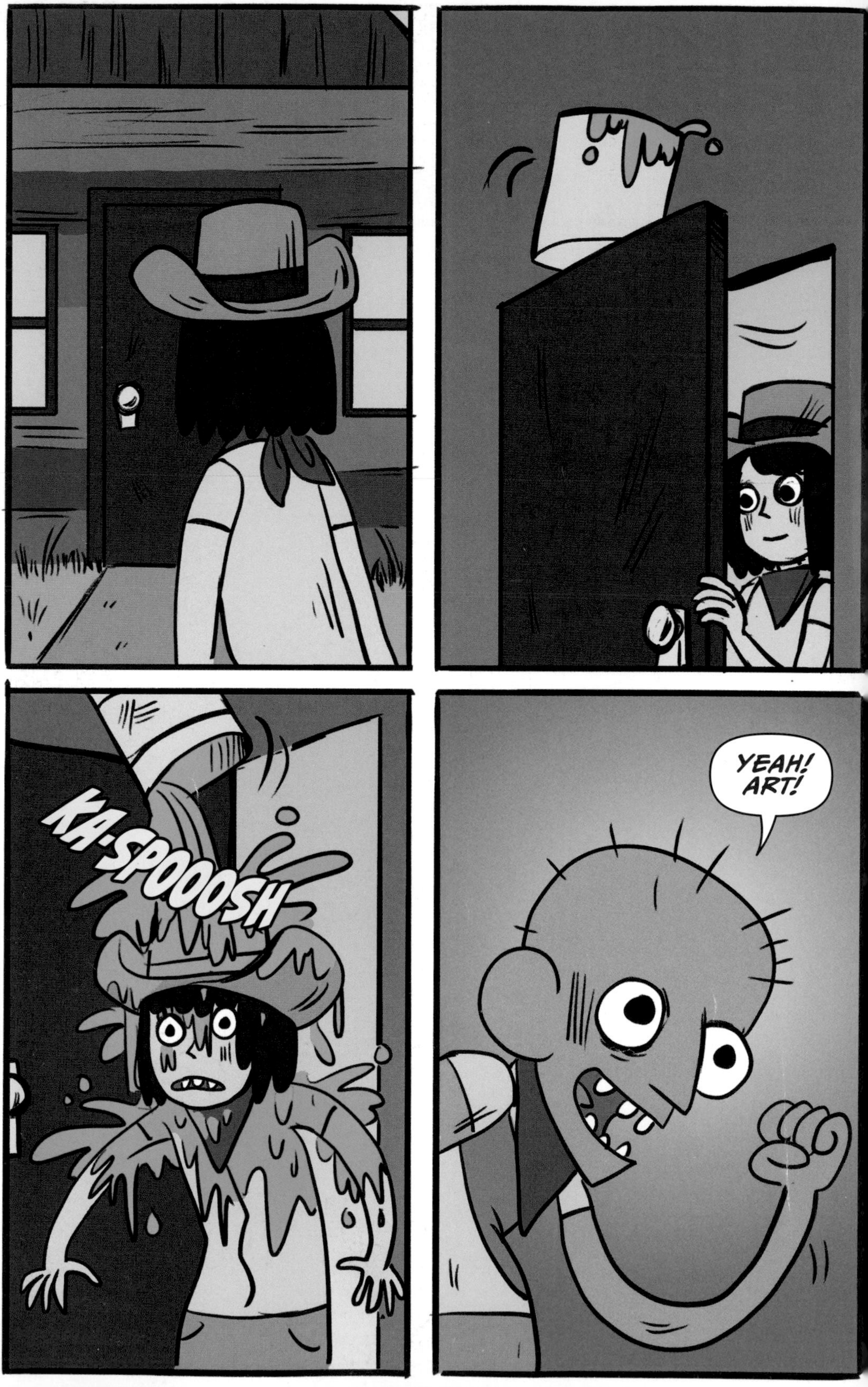
KA-SPOOOOSH
YEAH! ART!

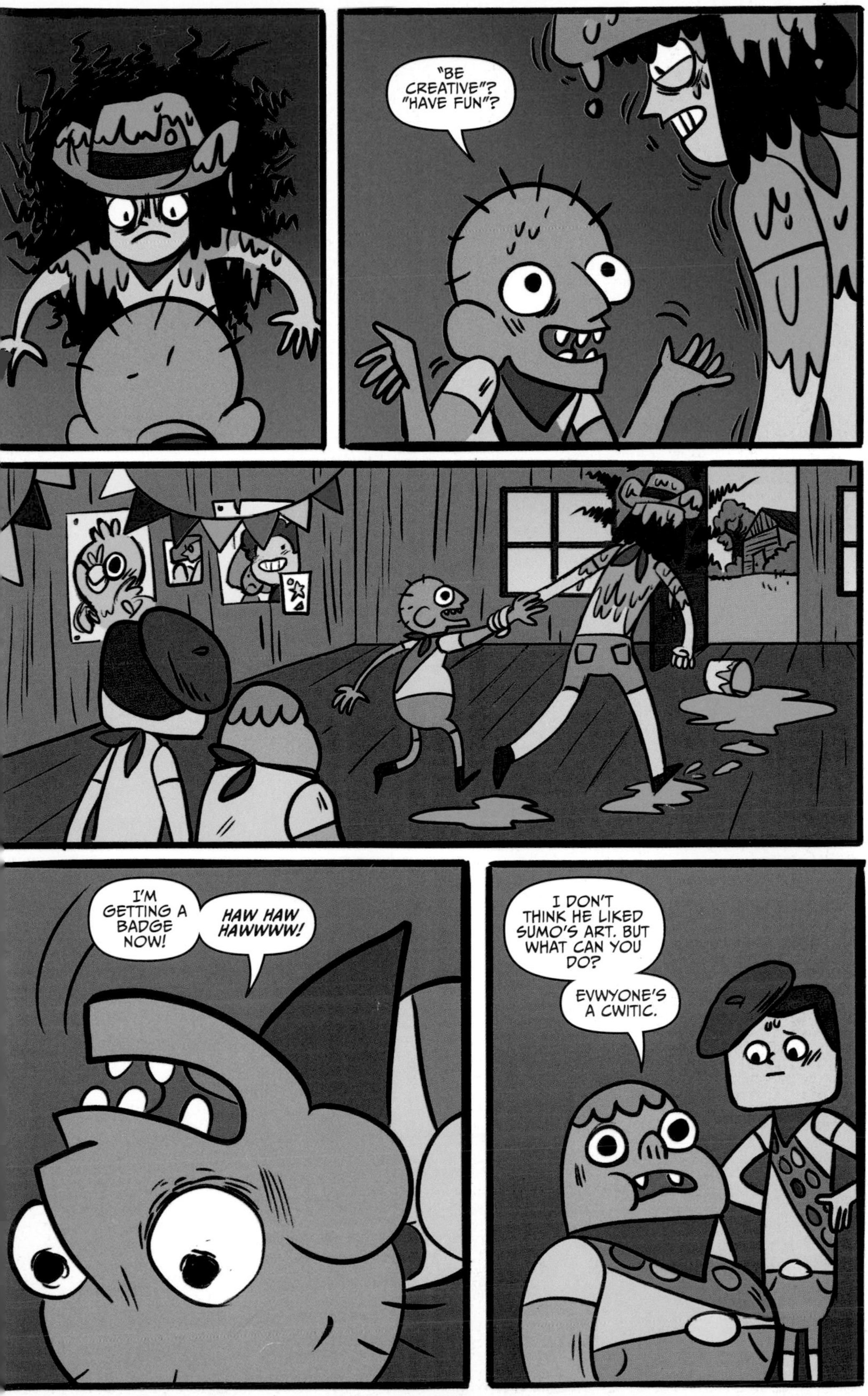
"BE CREATIVE"? "HAVE FUN"?
I'M GETTING A BADGE NOW!
HAW HAW HAWWWW!
I DON'T THINK HE LIKED SUMO'S ART. BUT WHAT CAN YOU DO?
EVWYONE'S A CWITIC.

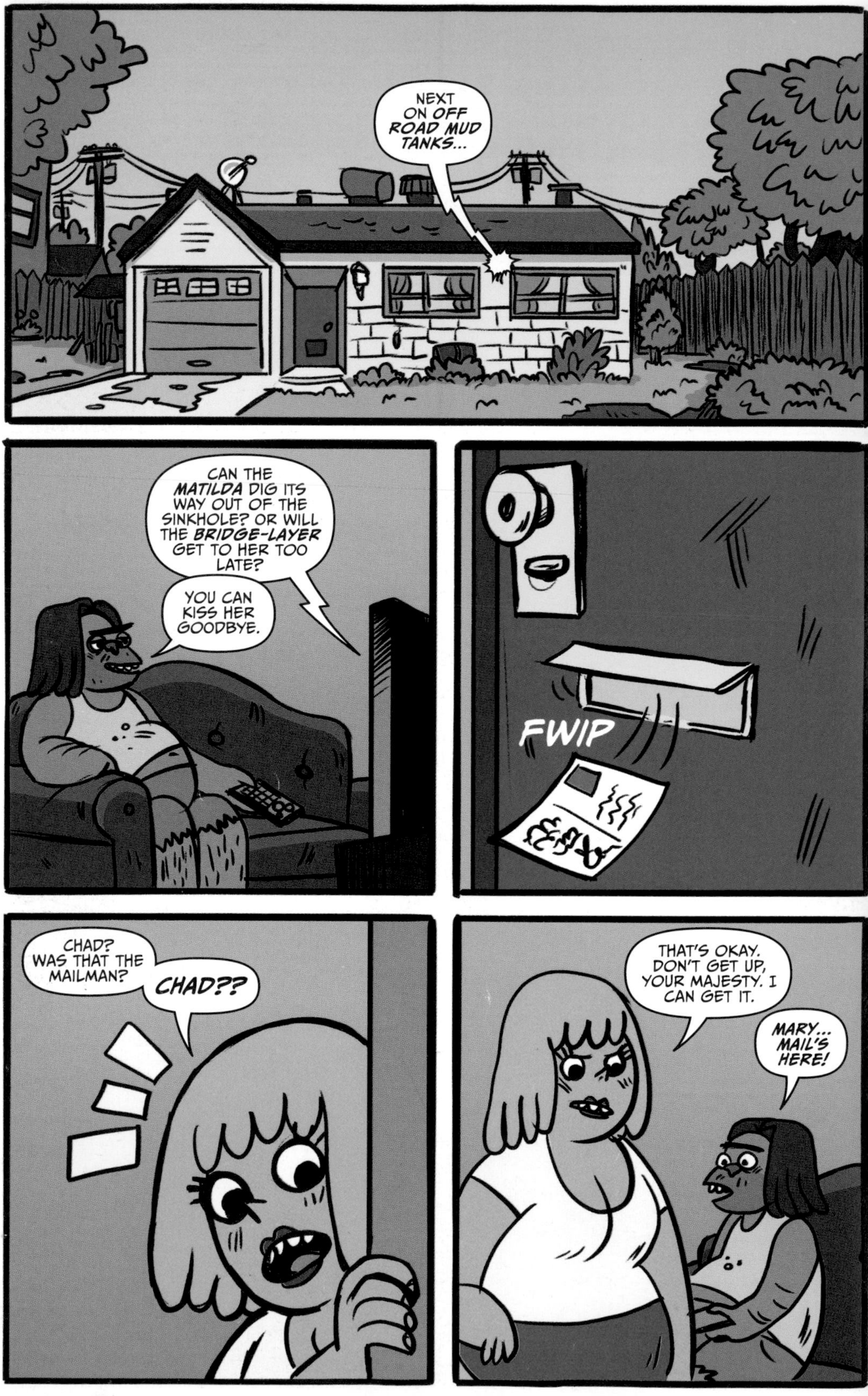
NEXT ON OFF ROAD MUD TANKS...
CAN THE MATILDA DIG ITS WAY OUT OF THE SINKHOLE? OR WILL THE BRIDGE-LAYER GET TO HER TOO LATE?
YOU CAN KISS HER GOODBYE.
FWIP
CHAD? WAS THAT THE MAILMAN?
CHAD??
THAT'S OKAY. DON'T GET UP, YOUR MAJESTY. I CAN GET IT.
MARY... MAIL'S HERE!

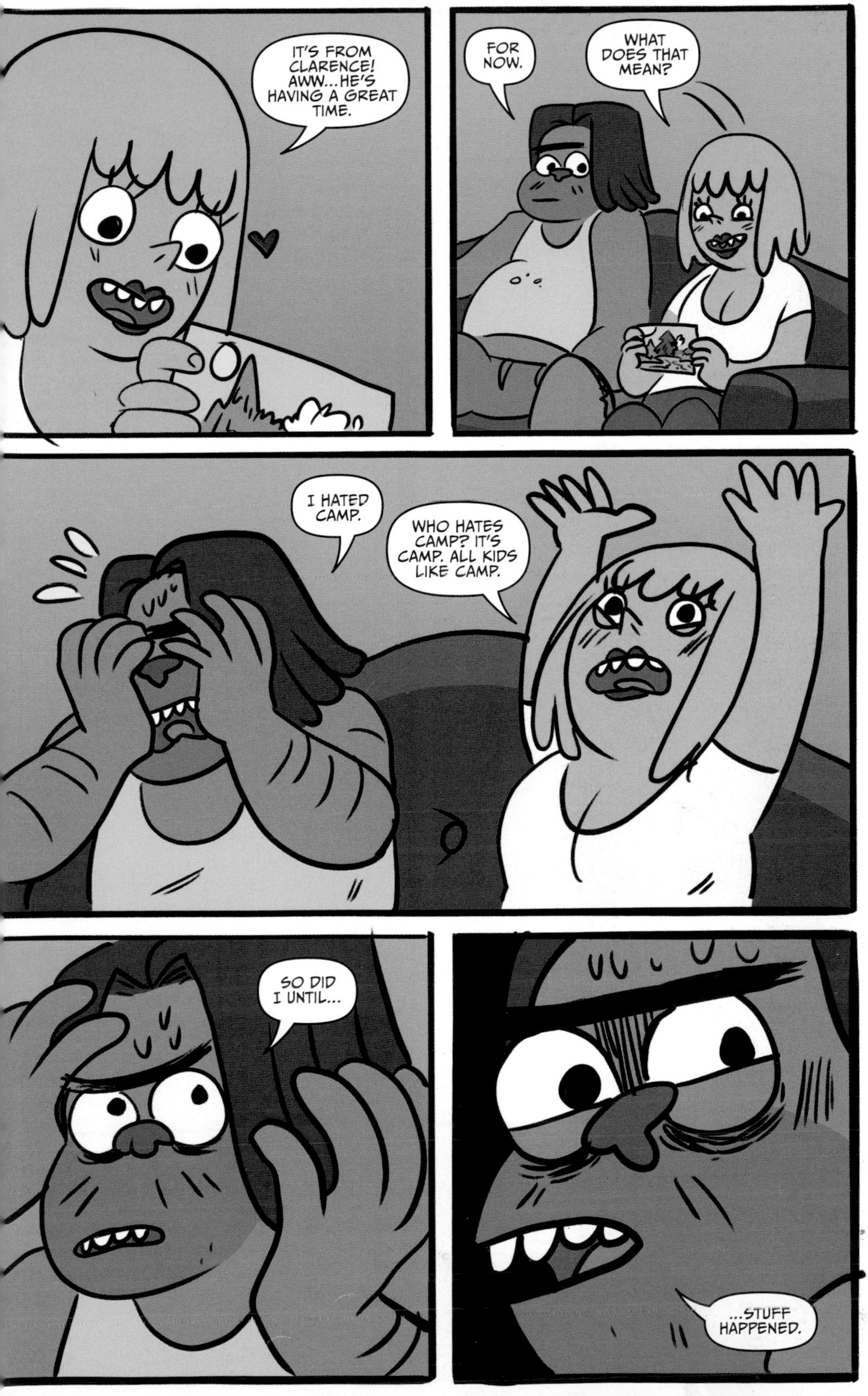
IT'S FROM CLARENCE! AWW...HE'S HAVING A GREAT TIME.
FOR NOW.
WHAT DOES THAT MEAN?
I HATED CAMP.
WHO HATES CAMP? IT'S CAMP. ALL KIDS LIKE CAMP.
SO DID I UNTIL...
...STUFF HAPPENED.

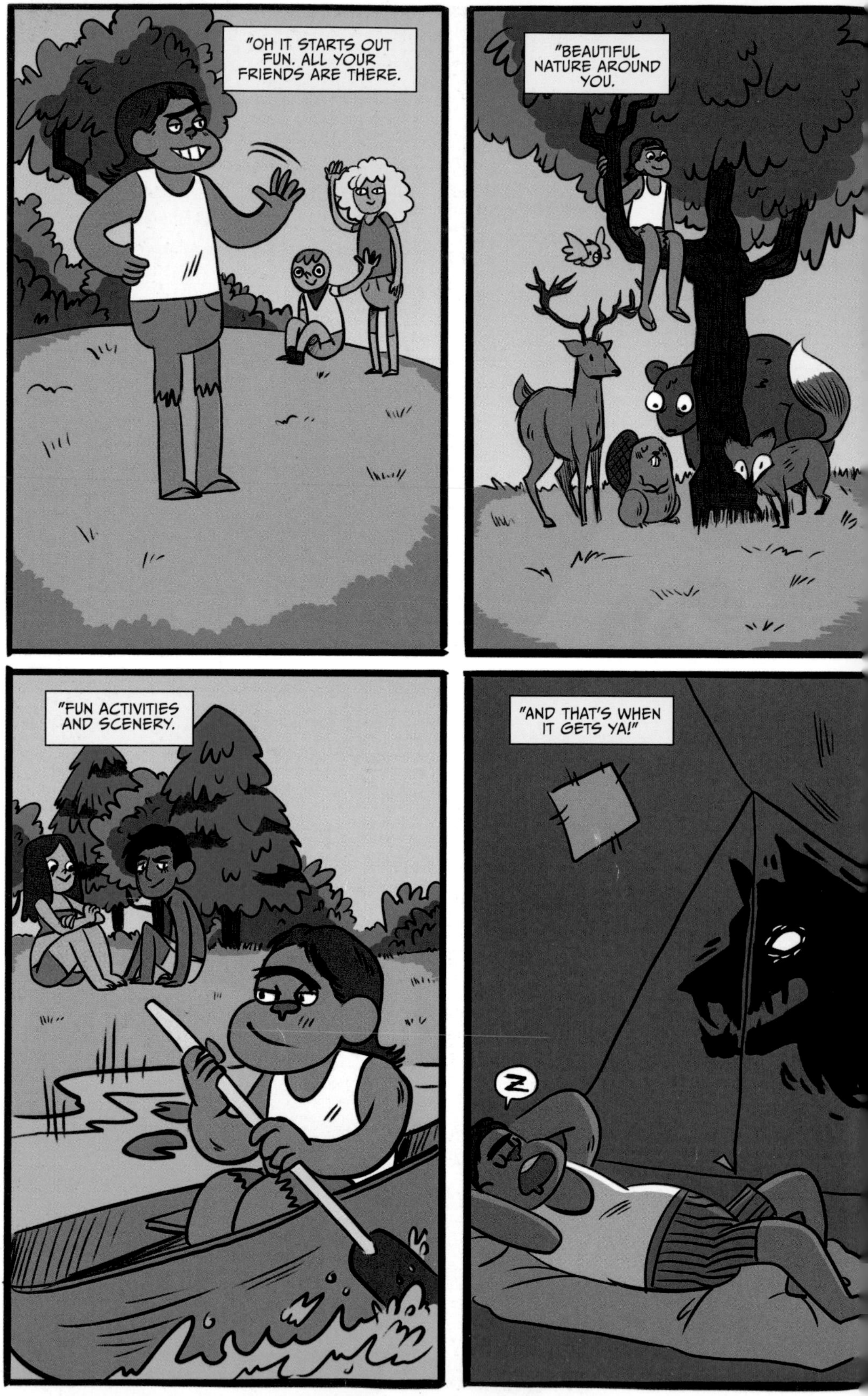
"OH IT STARTS OUT FUN. ALL YOUR FRIENDS ARE THERE.
"BEAUTIFUL NATURE AROUND YOU.
"FUN ACTIVITIES AND SCENERY.
"AND THAT'S WHEN IT GETS YA!"
Z

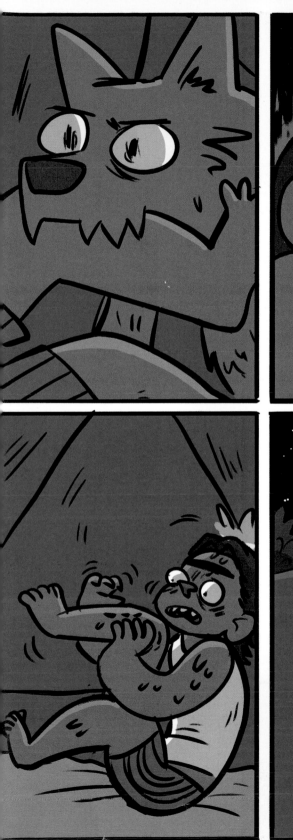

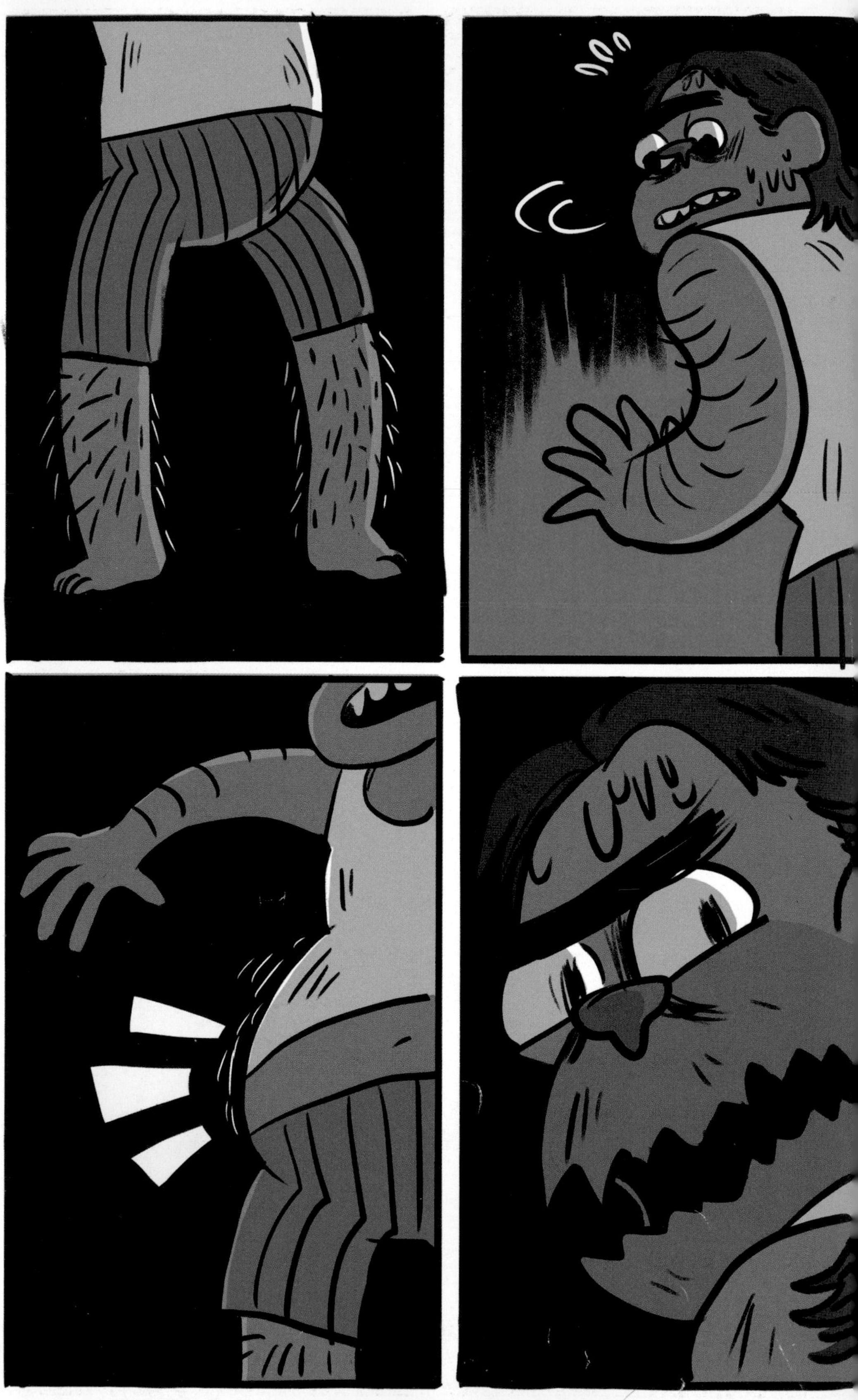

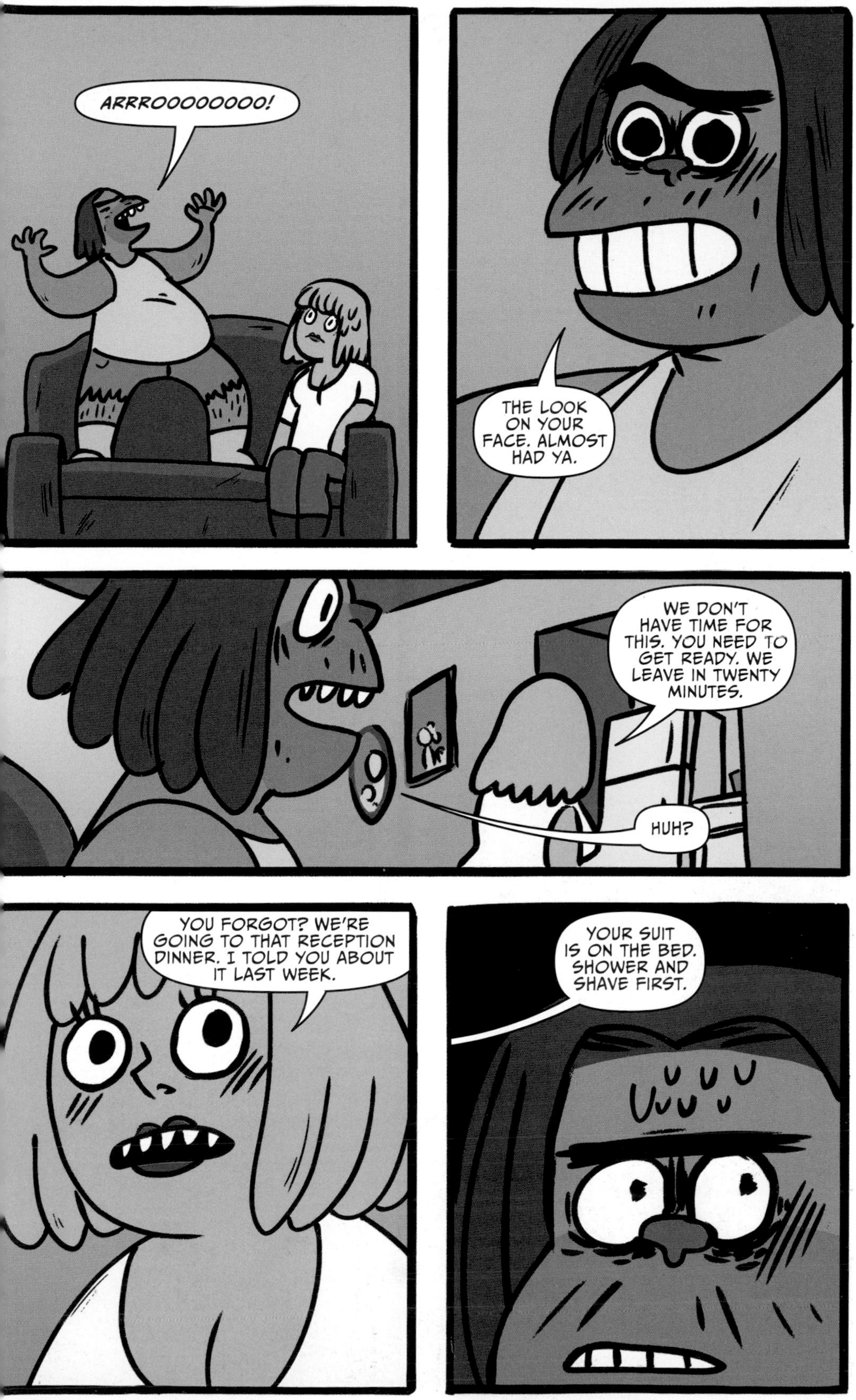
ARRROOOOOOOO!
THE LOOK ON YOUR FACE. ALMOST HAD YA.
WE DON'T HAVE TIME FOR THIS. YOU NEED TO GET READY. WE LEAVE IN TWENTY MINUTES.
HUH?
YOU FORGOT? WE'RE GOING TO THAT RECEPTION DINNER. I TOLD YOU ABOUT IT LAST WEEK.
YOUR SUIT IS ON THE BED. SHOWER AND SHAVE FIRST.

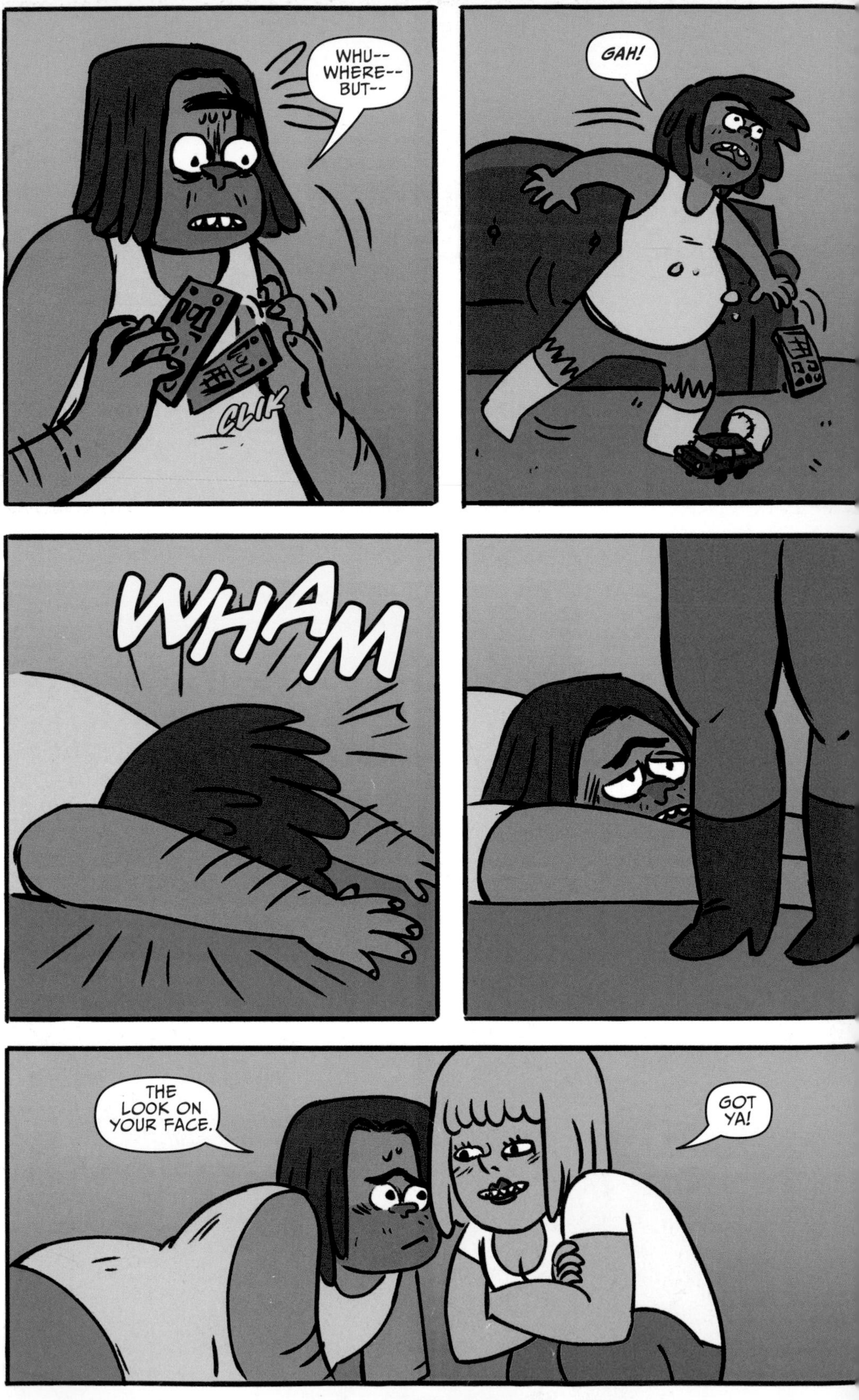
WHU-- WHERE-- BUT--
CLIK
GAH!
WHAM
THE LOOK ON YOUR FACE.
GOT YA!

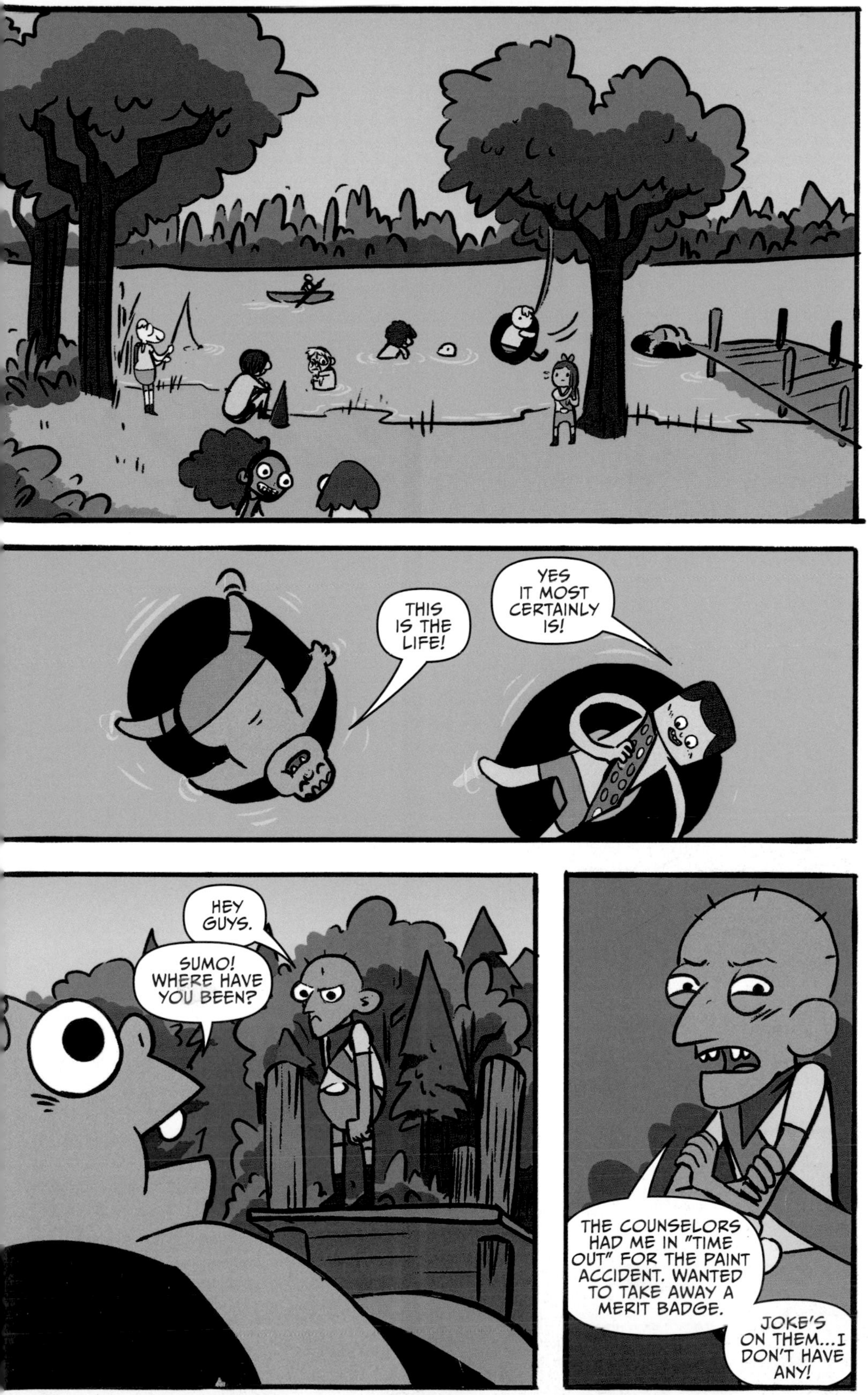
THIS IS THE LIFE!
YES IT MOST CERTAINLY IS!
HEY GUYS.
SUMO! WHERE HAVE YOU BEEN?
THE COUNSELORS HAD ME IN "TIME OUT" FOR THE PAINT ACCIDENT. WANTED TO TAKE AWAY A MERIT BADGE.
JOKE'S ON THEM...I DON'T HAVE ANY!

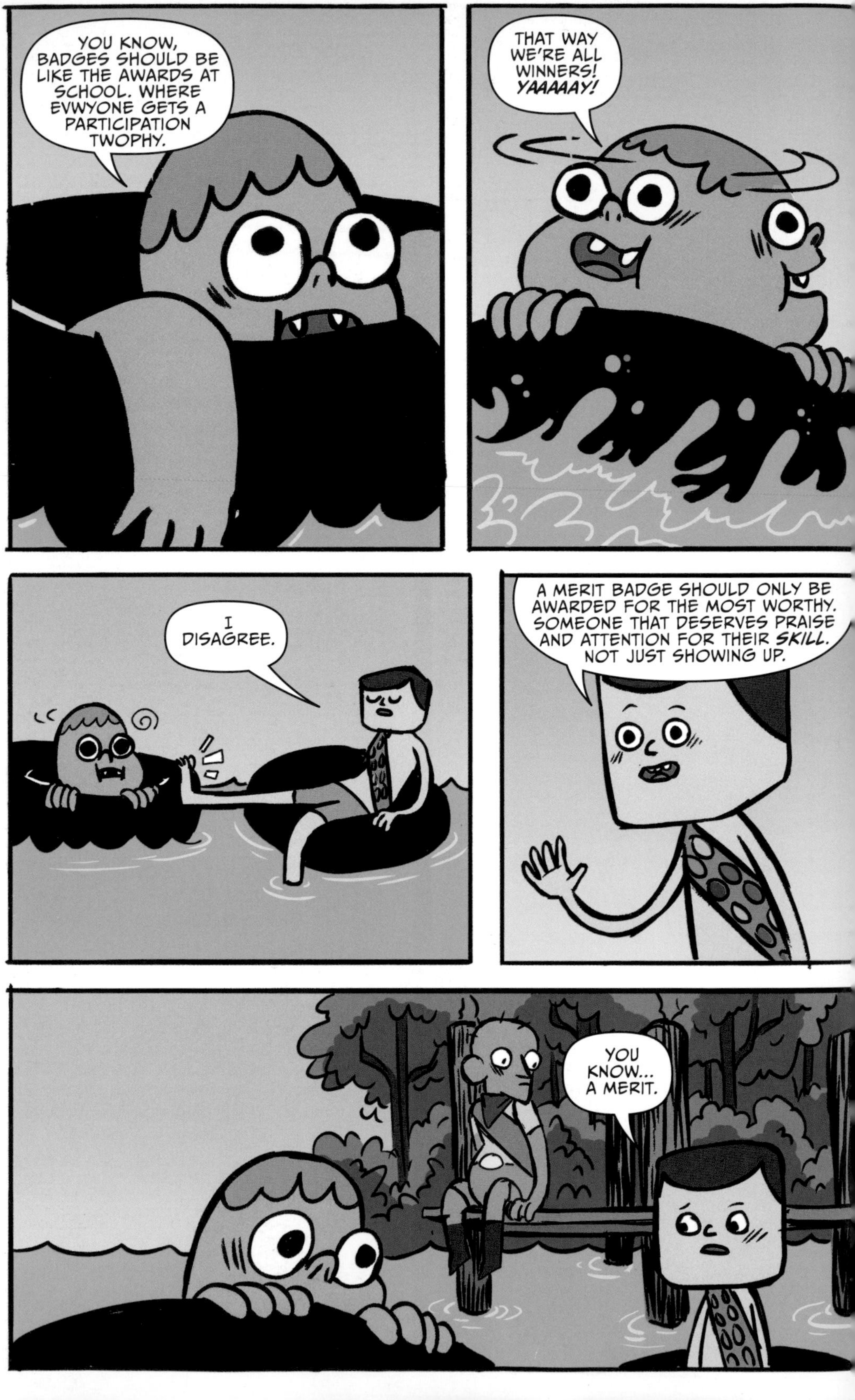
YOU KNOW, BADGES SHOULD BE LIKE THE AWARDS AT SCHOOL. WHERE EVWYONE GETS A PARTICIPATION TWOPHY.
THAT WAY WE'RE ALL WINNERS! *YAAAAAY!*
I DISAGREE.
A MERIT BADGE SHOULD ONLY BE AWARDED FOR THE MOST WORTHY. SOMEONE THAT DESERVES PRAISE AND ATTENTION FOR THEIR *SKILL*. NOT JUST SHOWING UP.
YOU KNOW... A MERIT.

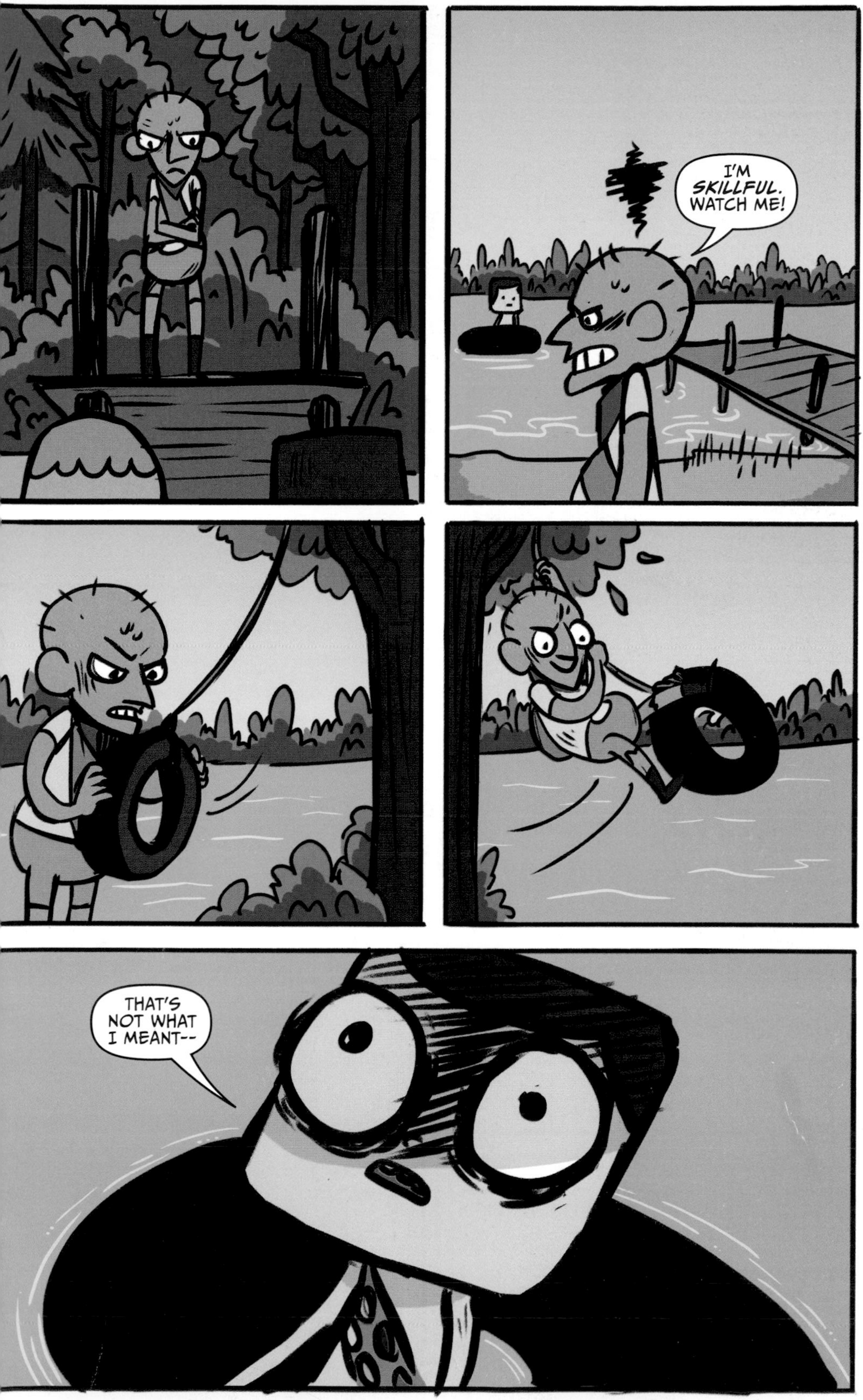
I'M SKILLFUL. WATCH ME!
THAT'S NOT WHAT I MEANT--

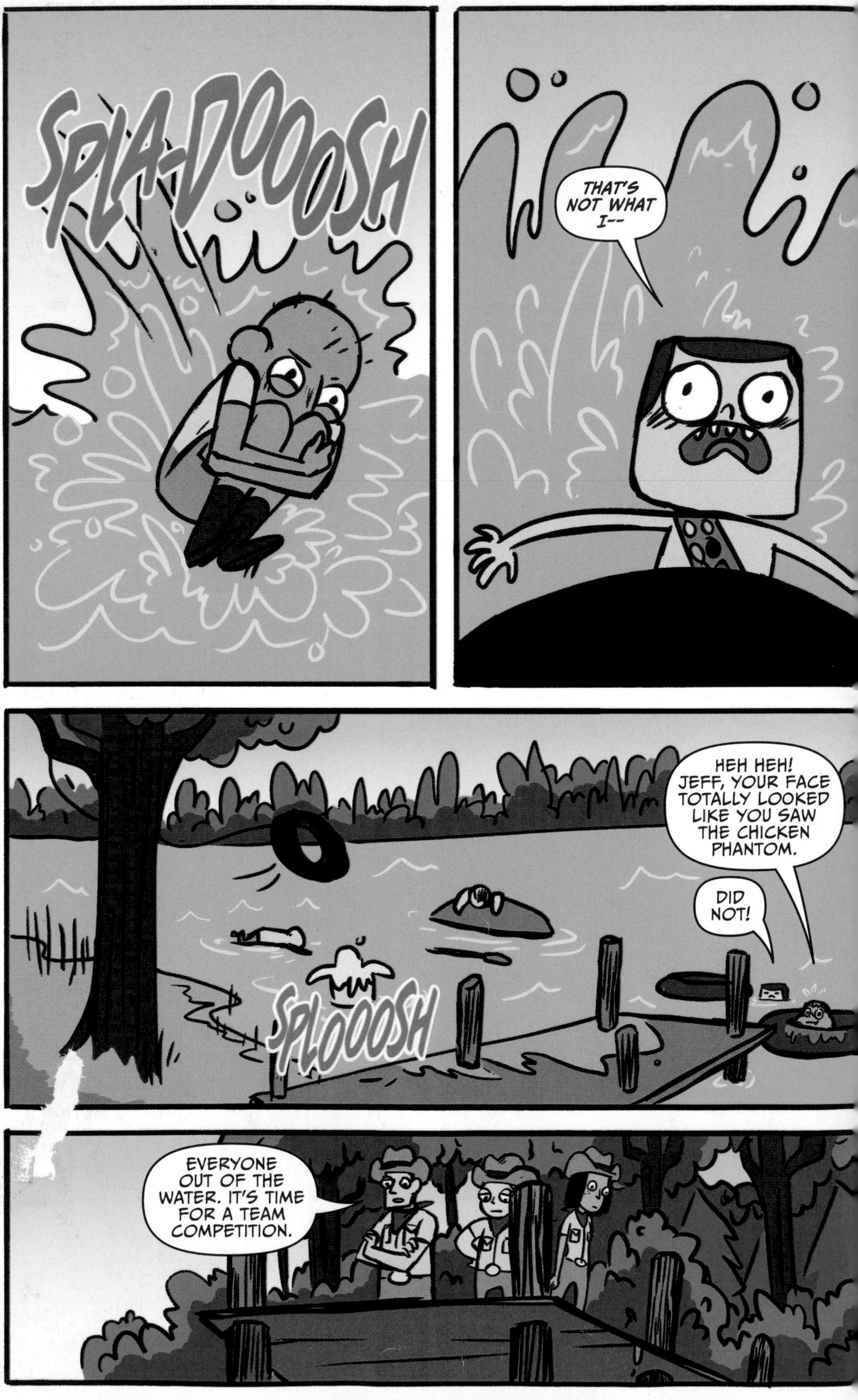
SPLA-DOOOOSH
THAT'S NOT WHAT I--
HEH HEH! JEFF, YOUR FACE TOTALLY LOOKED LIKE YOU SAW THE CHICKEN PHANTOM.
DID NOT!
SPLOOOSH
EVERYONE OUT OF THE WATER. IT'S TIME FOR A TEAM COMPETITION.

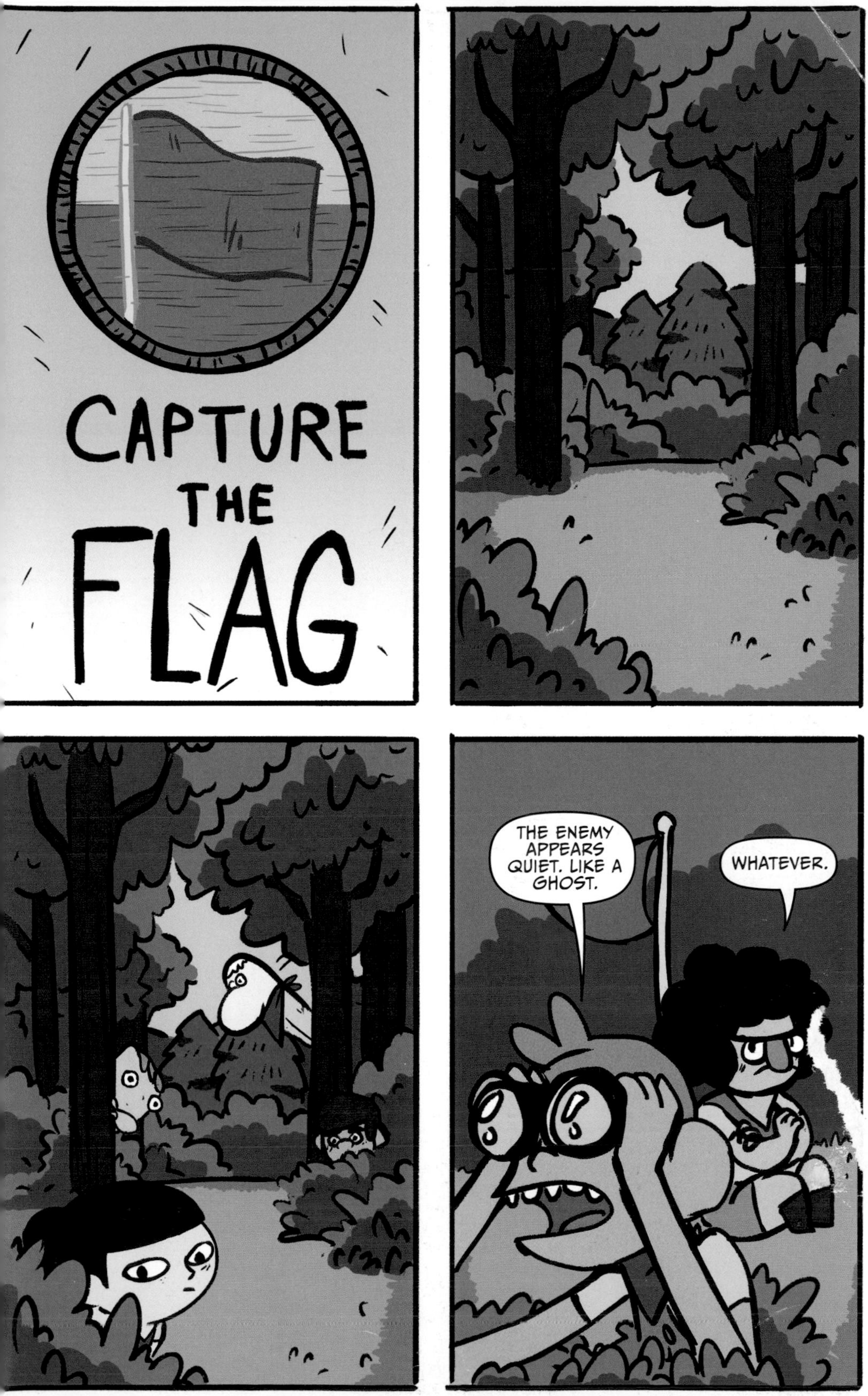
CAPTURE THE FLAG
THE ENEMY APPEARS QUIET. LIKE A GHOST.
WHATEVER.

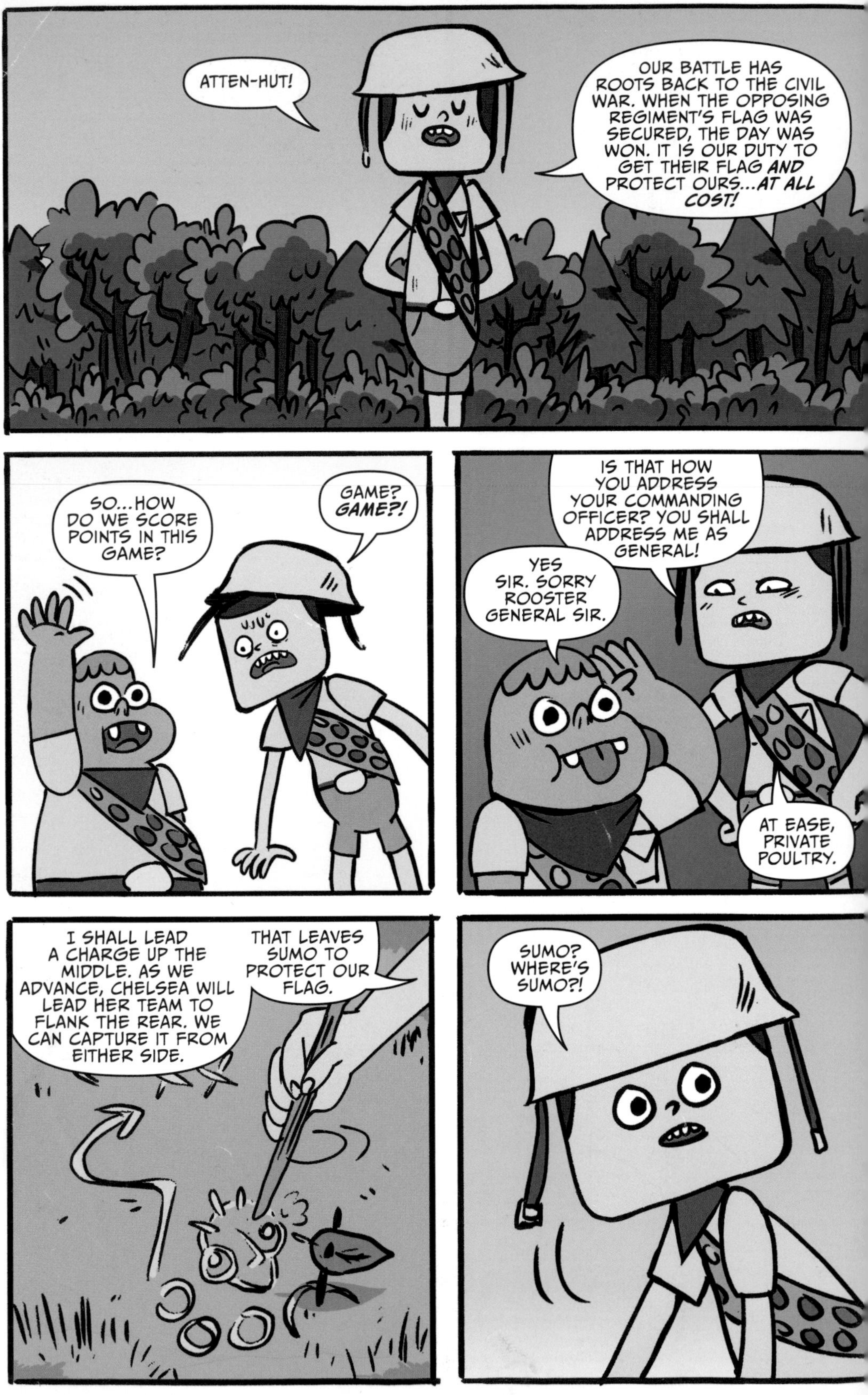
ATTEN-HUT!
OUR BATTLE HAS ROOTS BACK TO THE CIVIL WAR. WHEN THE OPPOSING REGIMENT'S FLAG WAS SECURED, THE DAY WAS WON. IT IS OUR DUTY TO GET THEIR FLAG AND PROTECT OURS...AT ALL COST!
SO...HOW DO WE SCORE POINTS IN THIS GAME?
GAME? GAME?!
IS THAT HOW YOU ADDRESS YOUR COMMANDING OFFICER? YOU SHALL ADDRESS ME AS GENERAL!
YES SIR. SORRY ROOSTER GENERAL SIR.
AT EASE, PRIVATE POULTRY.
I SHALL LEAD A CHARGE UP THE MIDDLE. AS WE ADVANCE, CHELSEA WILL LEAD HER TEAM TO FLANK THE REAR. WE CAN CAPTURE IT FROM EITHER SIDE.
THAT LEAVES SUMO TO PROTECT OUR FLAG.
SUMO? WHERE'S SUMO?!

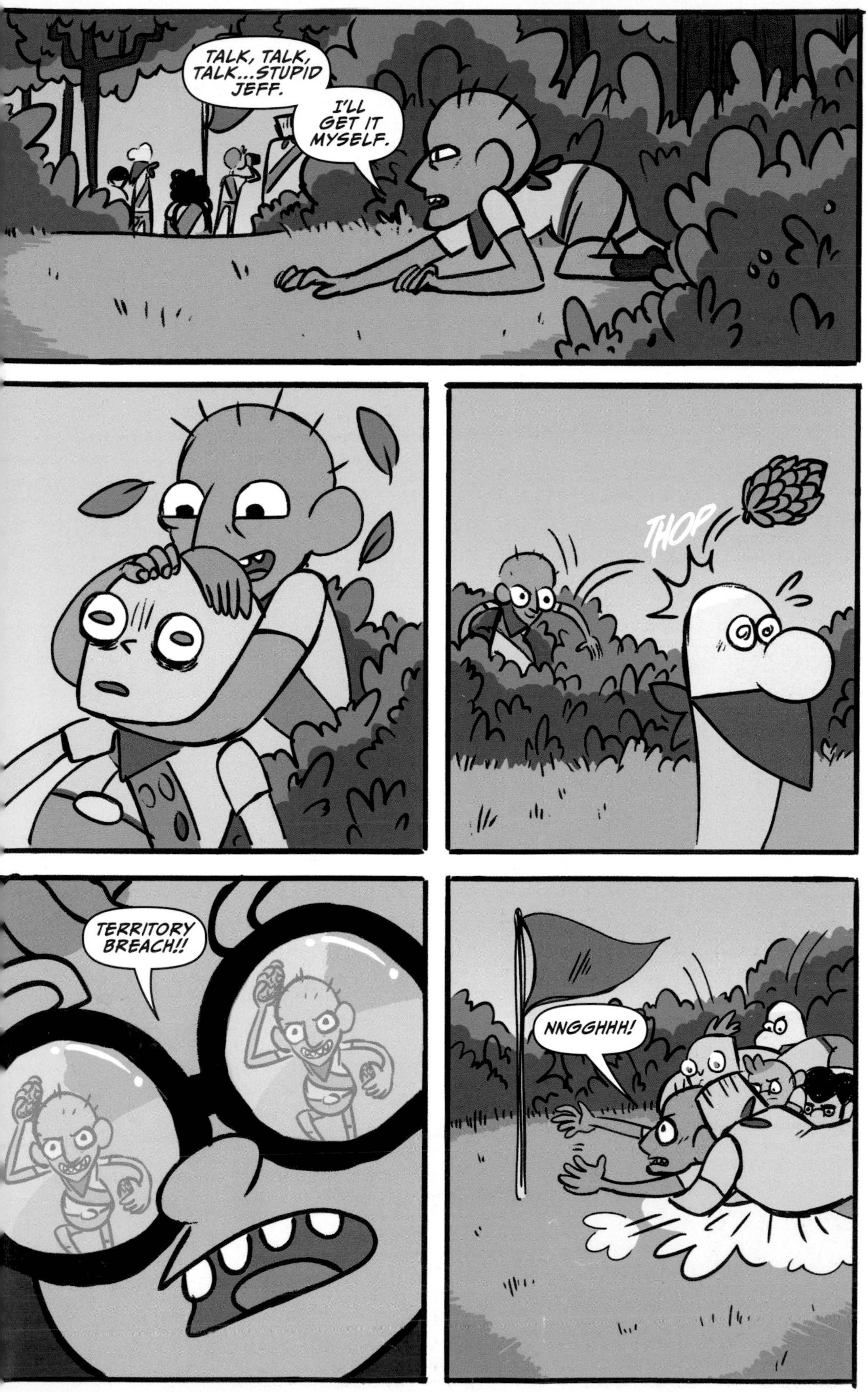
TALK, TALK, TALK...STUPID JEFF.
I'LL GET IT MYSELF.
THOP
TERRITORY BREACH!!
NNGGHHH!

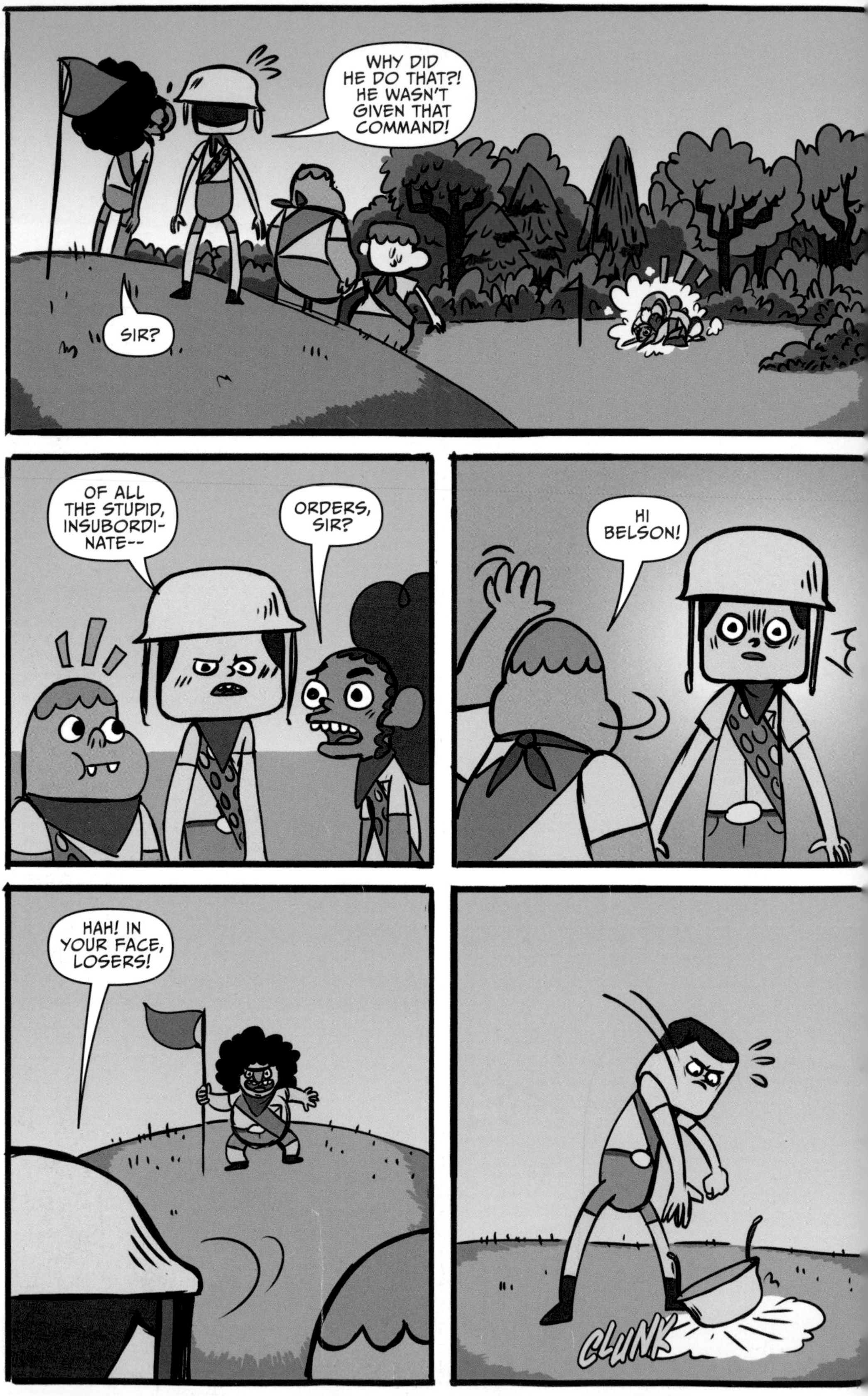
WHY DID HE DO THAT?! HE WASN'T GIVEN THAT COMMAND!
SIR?
OF ALL THE STUPID, INSUBORDI-NATE--
ORDERS, SIR?
HI BELSON!
HAH! IN YOUR FACE, LOSERS!
CLUNK

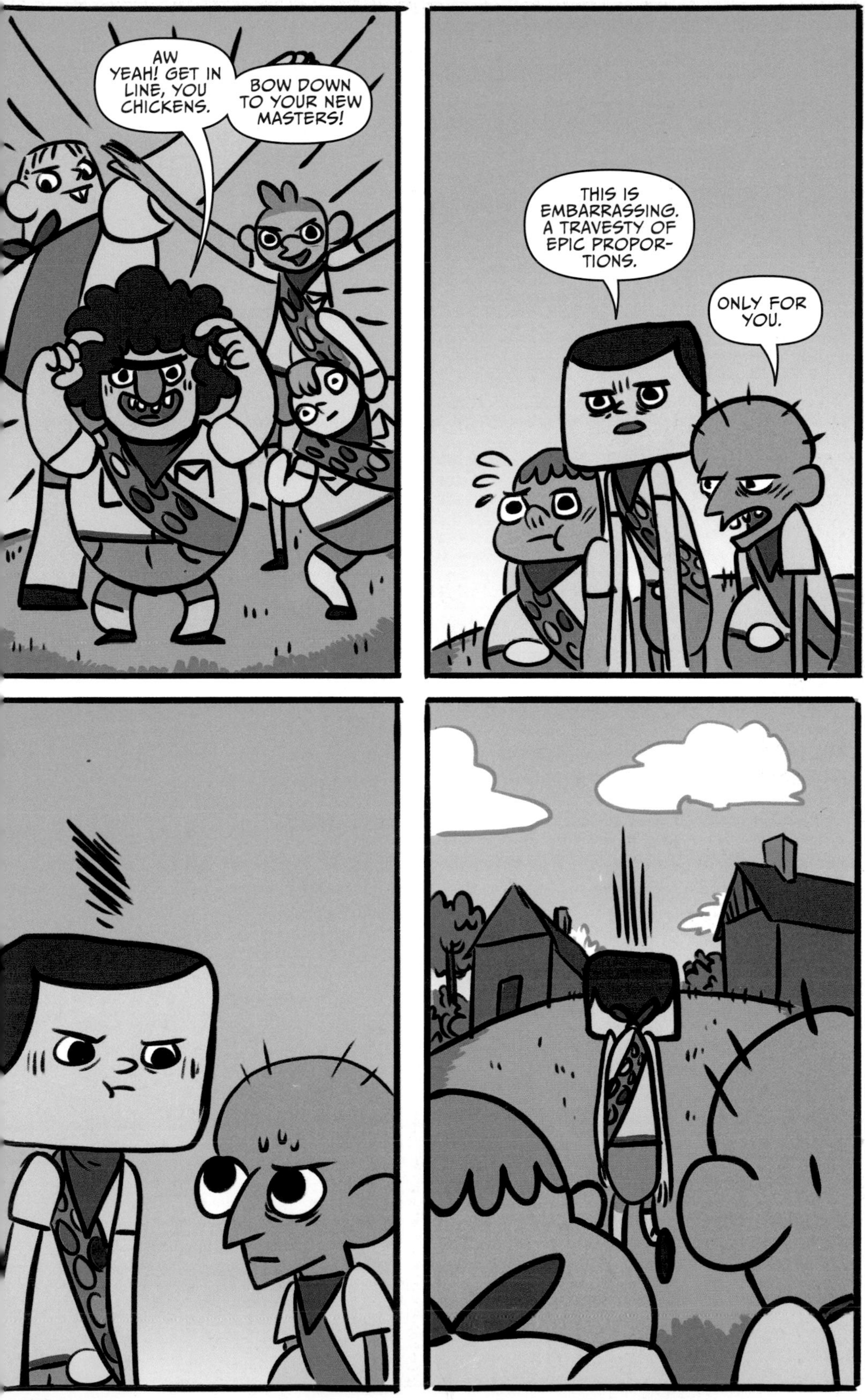
AW YEAH! GET IN LINE, YOU CHICKENS.
BOW DOWN TO YOUR NEW MASTERS!
THIS IS EMBARRASSING. A TRAVESTY OF EPIC PROPORTIONS.
ONLY FOR YOU.

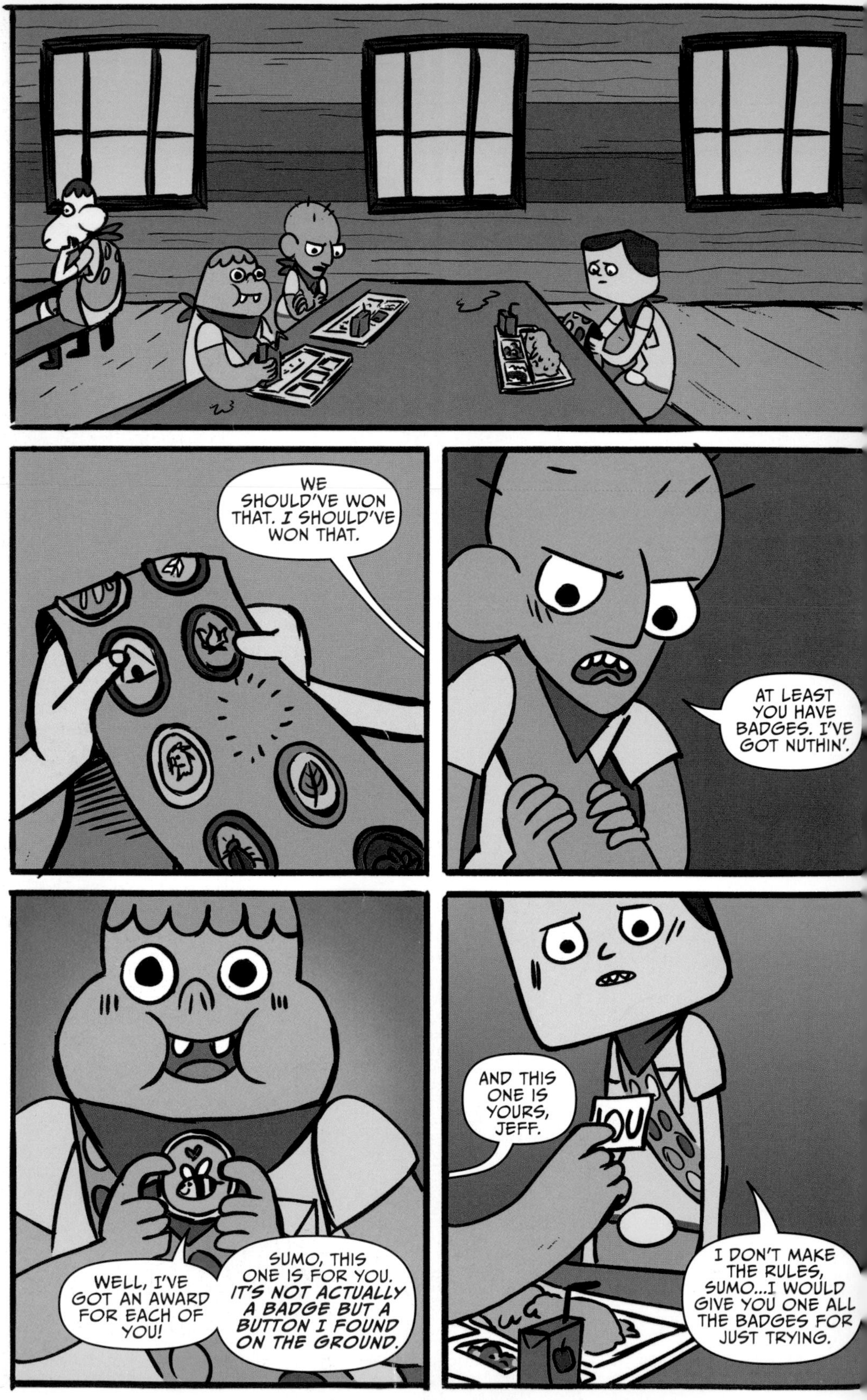
WE SHOULD'VE WON THAT. I SHOULD'VE WON THAT.
AT LEAST YOU HAVE BADGES. I'VE GOT NUTHIN'.
WELL, I'VE GOT AN AWARD FOR EACH OF YOU!
SUMO, THIS ONE IS FOR YOU. IT'S NOT ACTUALLY A BADGE BUT A BUTTON I FOUND ON THE GROUND.
AND THIS ONE IS YOURS, JEFF.
IOU
I DON'T MAKE THE RULES, SUMO...I WOULD GIVE YOU ONE ALL THE BADGES FOR JUST TRYING.

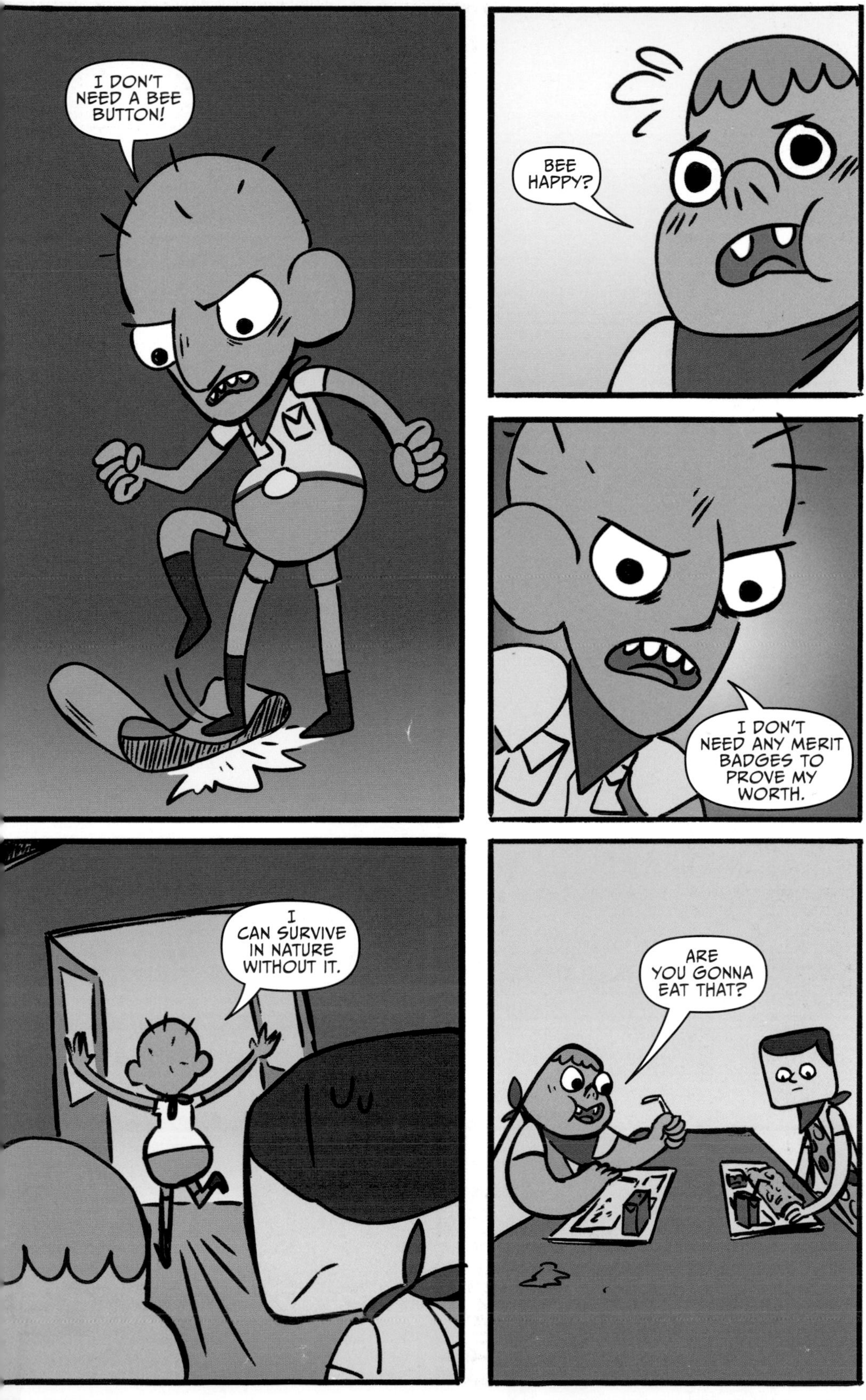
I DON'T NEED A BEE BUTTON!
BEE HAPPY?
I DON'T NEED ANY MERIT BADGES TO PROVE MY WORTH.
I CAN SURVIVE IN NATURE WITHOUT IT.
ARE YOU GONNA EAT THAT?

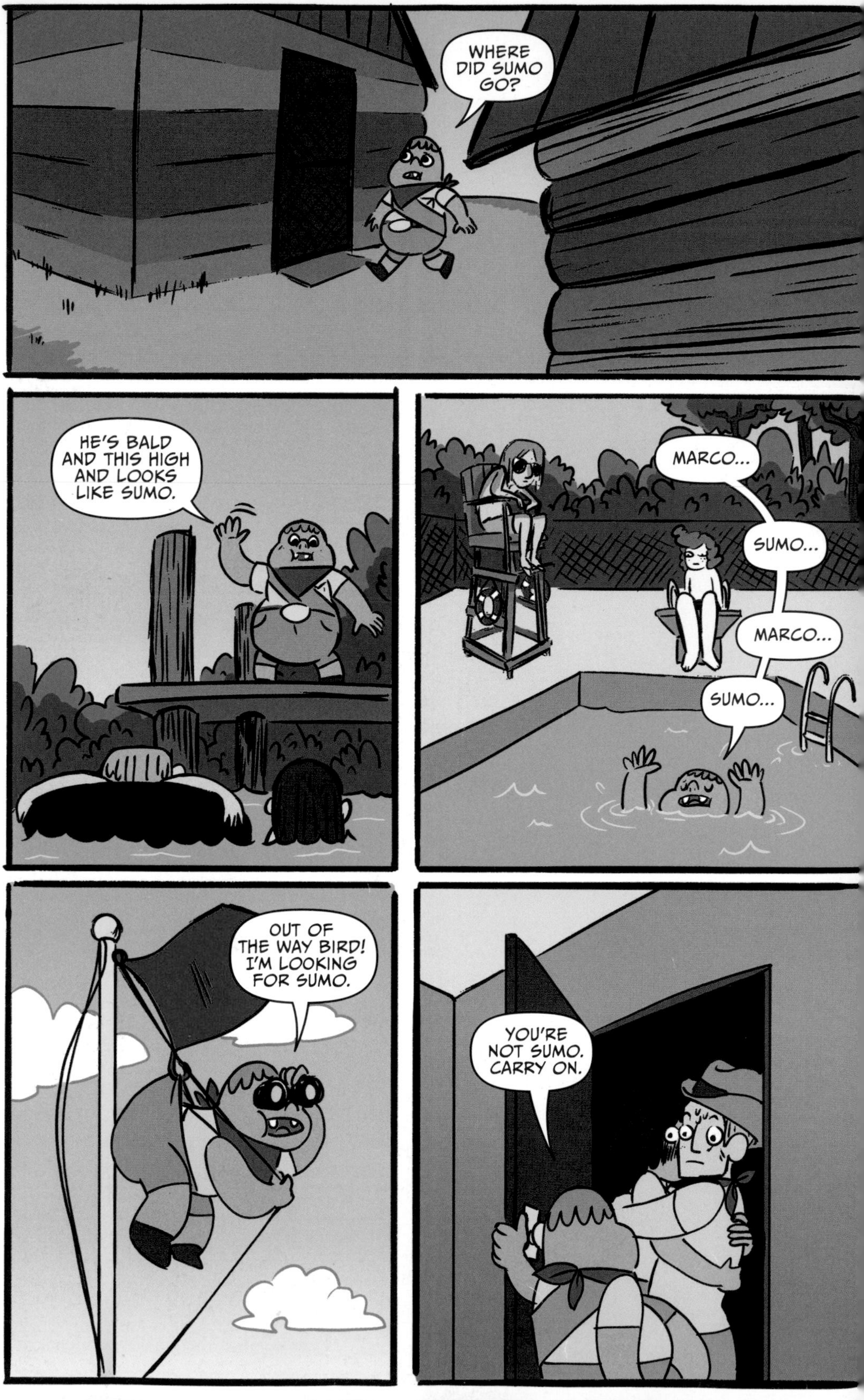
WHERE DID SUMO GO?
HE'S BALD AND THIS HIGH AND LOOKS LIKE SUMO.
MARCO...
SUMO...
MARCO...
SUMO...
OUT OF THE WAY BIRD! I'M LOOKING FOR SUMO.
YOU'RE NOT SUMO. CARRY ON.

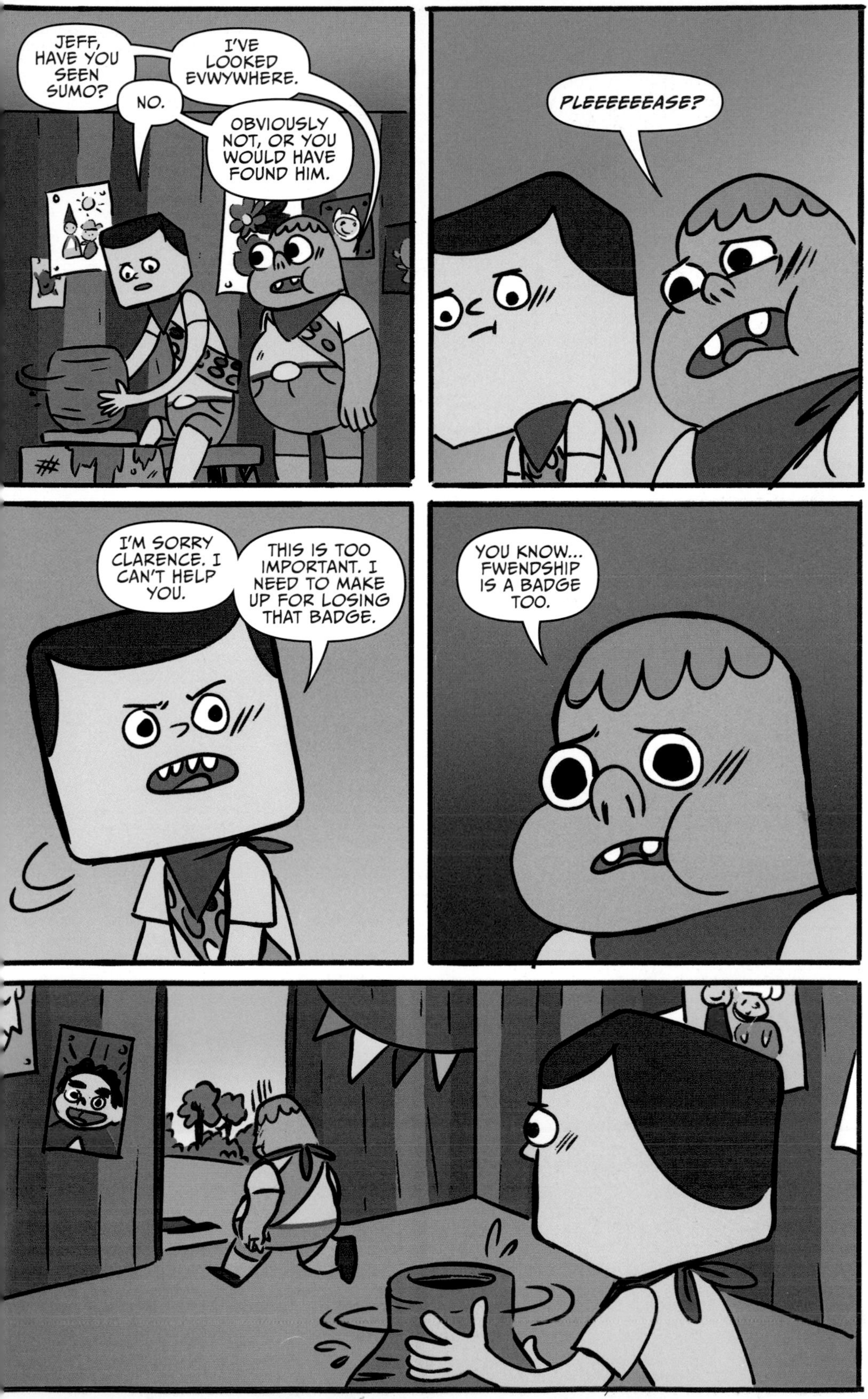
JEFF, HAVE YOU SEEN SUMO?
NO.
I'VE LOOKED EVWYWHERE.
OBVIOUSLY NOT, OR YOU WOULD HAVE FOUND HIM.
PLEEEEEEEASE?
I'M SORRY CLARENCE. I CAN'T HELP YOU.
THIS IS TOO IMPORTANT. I NEED TO MAKE UP FOR LOSING THAT BADGE.
YOU KNOW... FWENDSHIP IS A BADGE TOO.

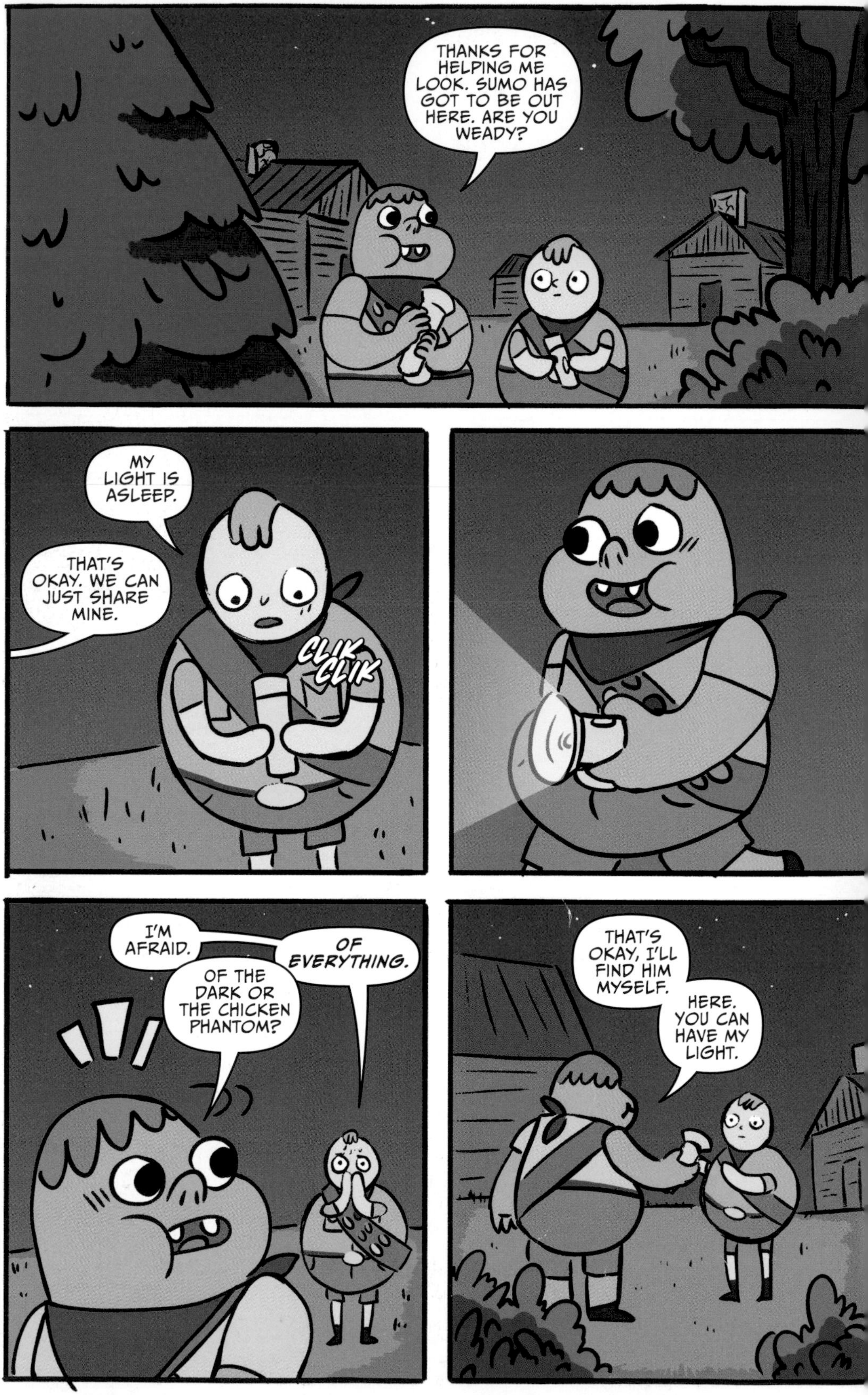
THANKS FOR HELPING ME LOOK. SUMO HAS GOT TO BE OUT HERE. ARE YOU WEADY?
MY LIGHT IS ASLEEP.
THAT'S OKAY. WE CAN JUST SHARE MINE.
CLIK CLIK
I'M AFRAID.
OF THE DARK OR THE CHICKEN PHANTOM?
OF EVERYTHING.
THAT'S OKAY, I'LL FIND HIM MYSELF.
HERE. YOU CAN HAVE MY LIGHT.

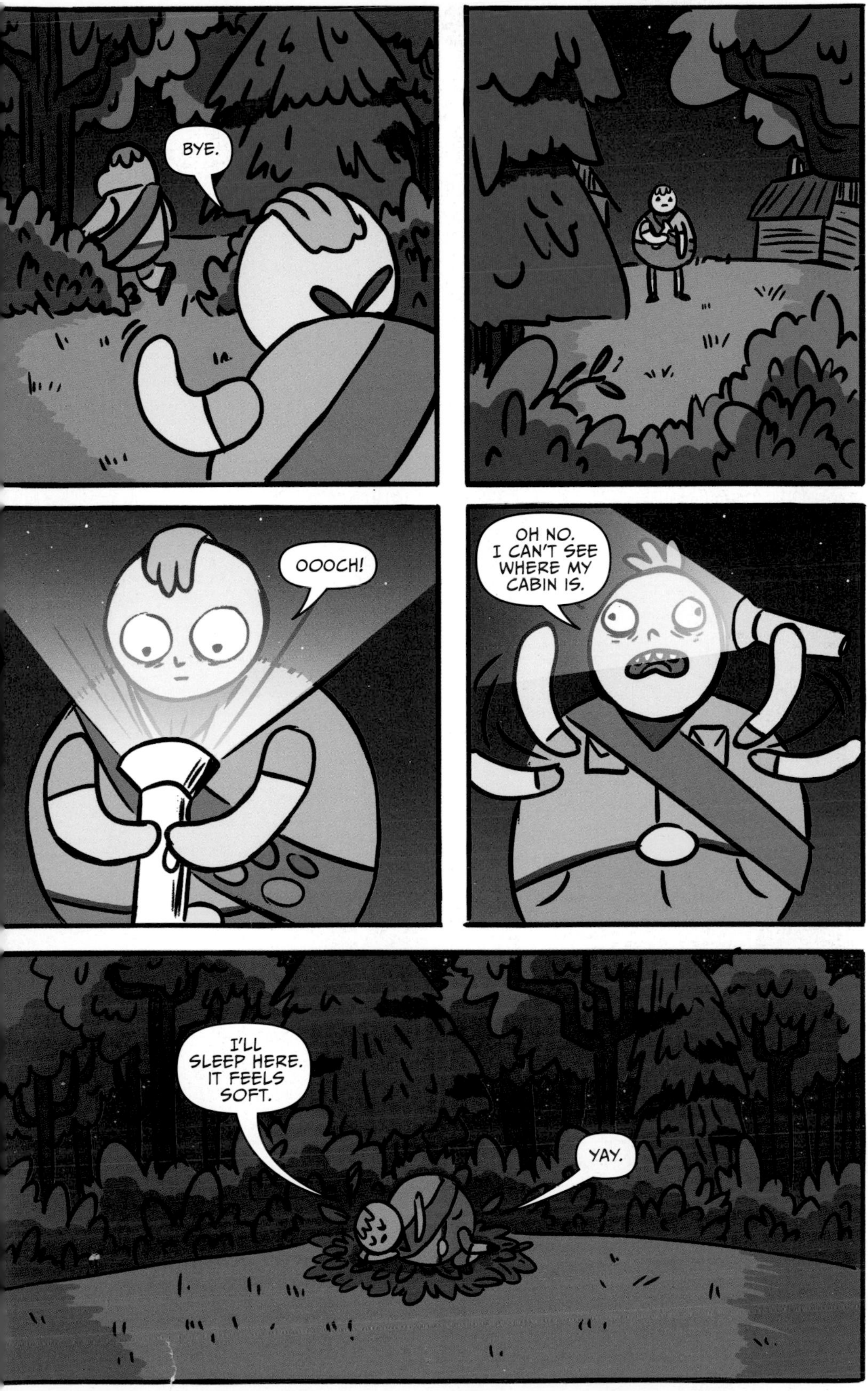
BYE.
OOOCH!
OH NO. I CAN'T SEE WHERE MY CABIN IS.
I'LL SLEEP HERE. IT FEELS SOFT.
YAY.

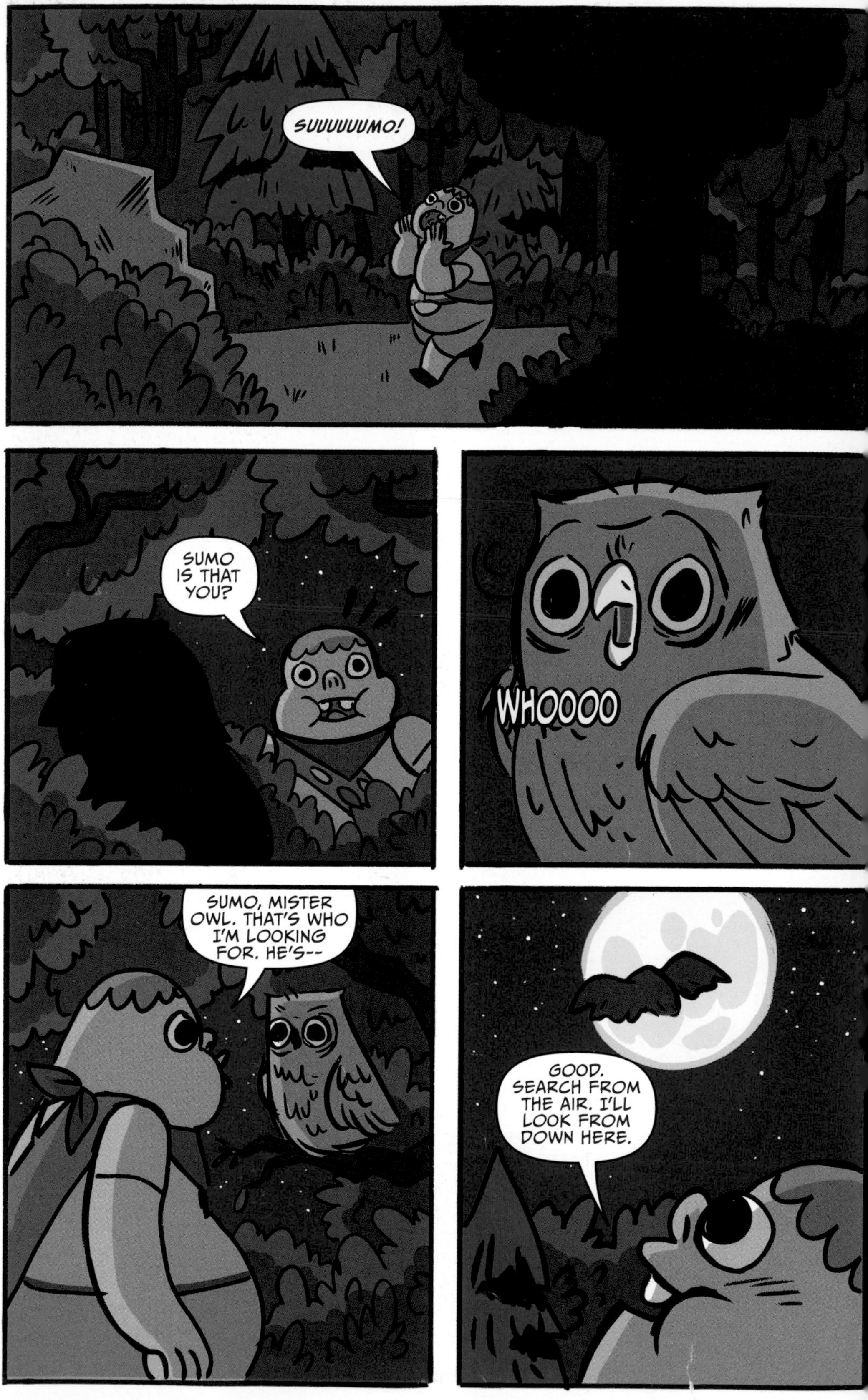
SUUUUUUMO!
SUMO IS THAT YOU?
WHOOOO
SUMO, MISTER OWL. THAT'S WHO I'M LOOKING FOR. HE'S--
GOOD. SEARCH FROM THE AIR. I'LL LOOK FROM DOWN HERE.

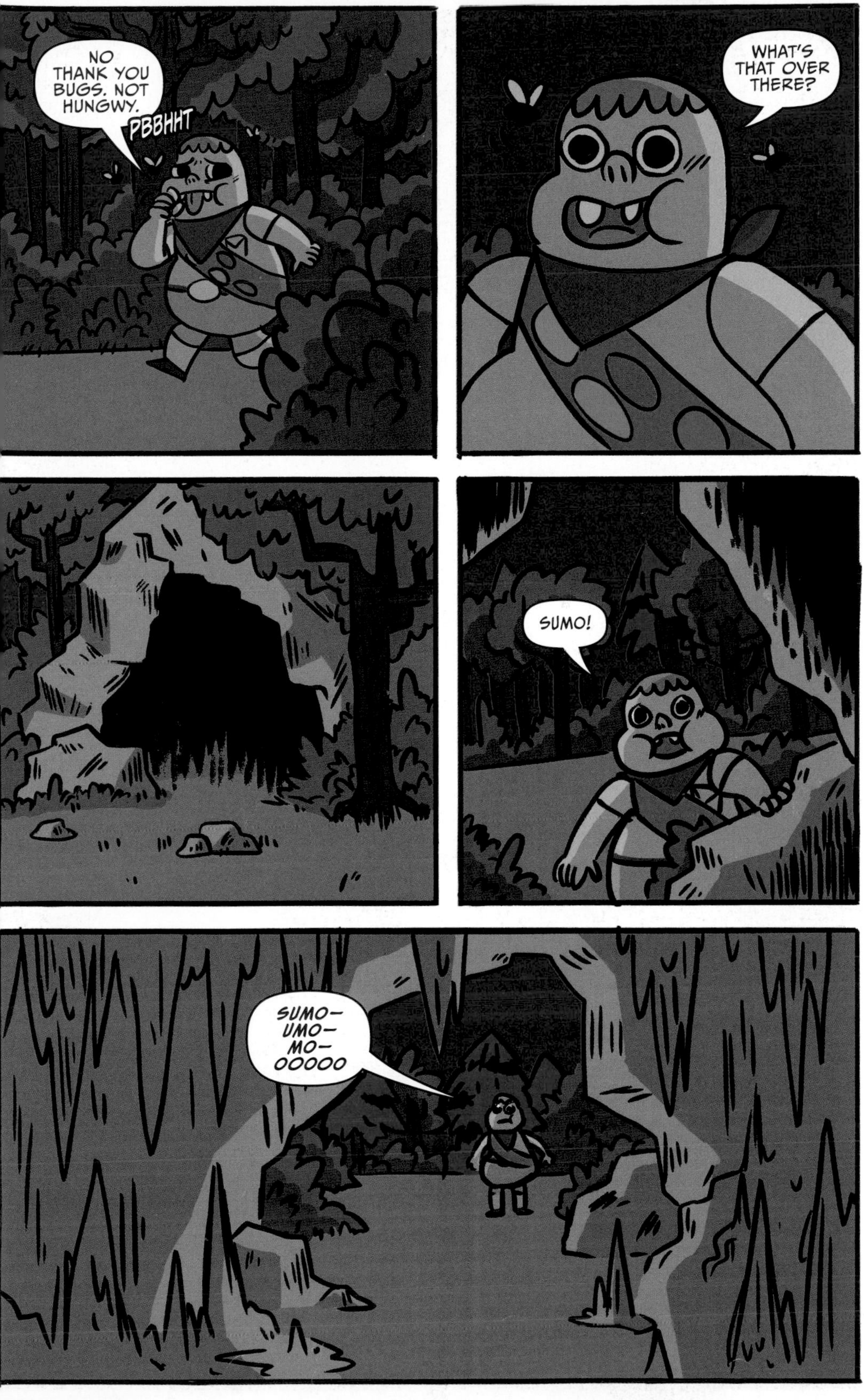
NO THANK YOU BUGS. NOT HUNGWY.
PBBHHT
WHAT'S THAT OVER THERE?
SUMO!
SUMO- UMO- MO- OOOOO

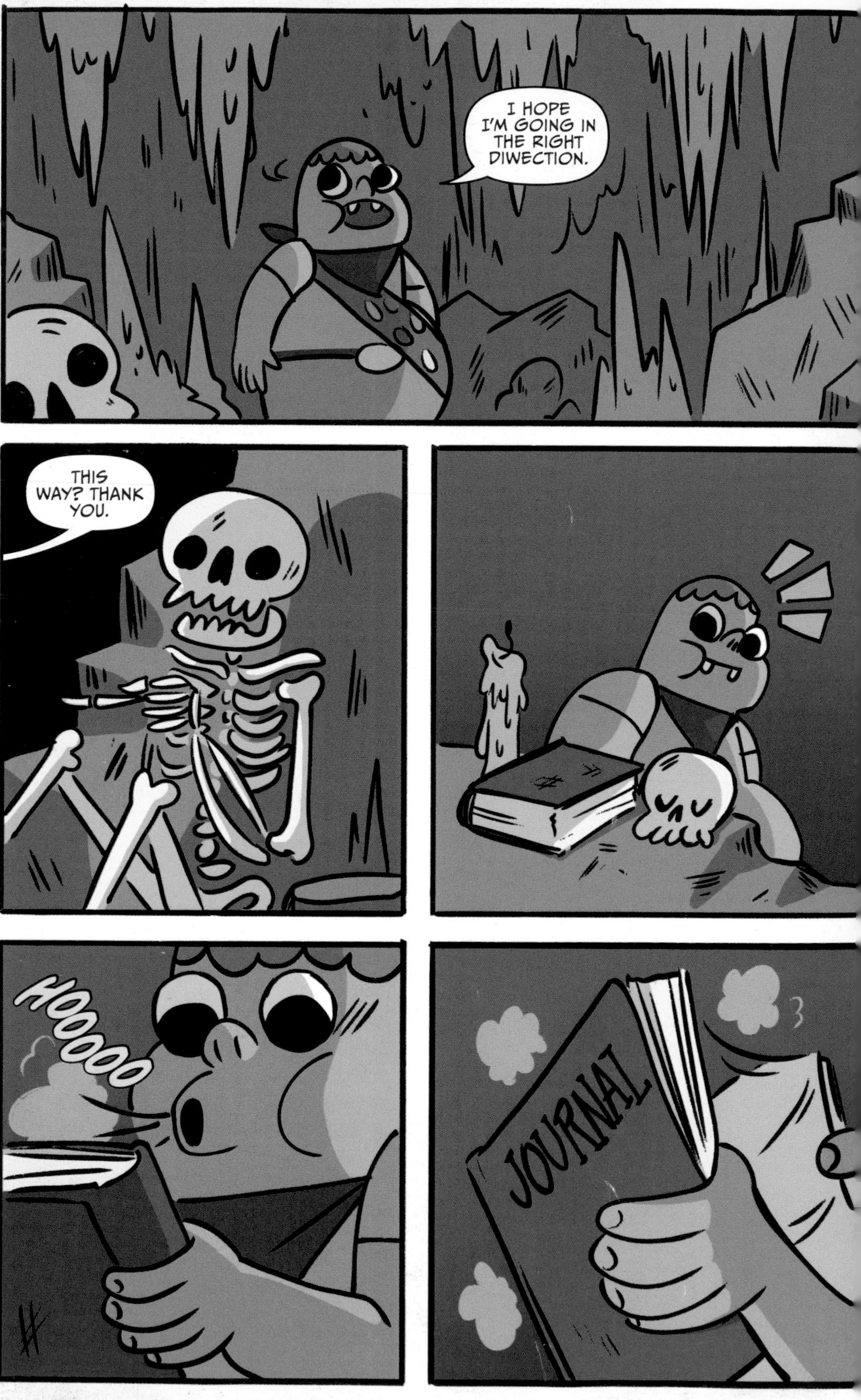
I HOPE I'M GOING IN THE RIGHT DIWECTION.
THIS WAY? THANK YOU.
HOOOOO
JOURNAL

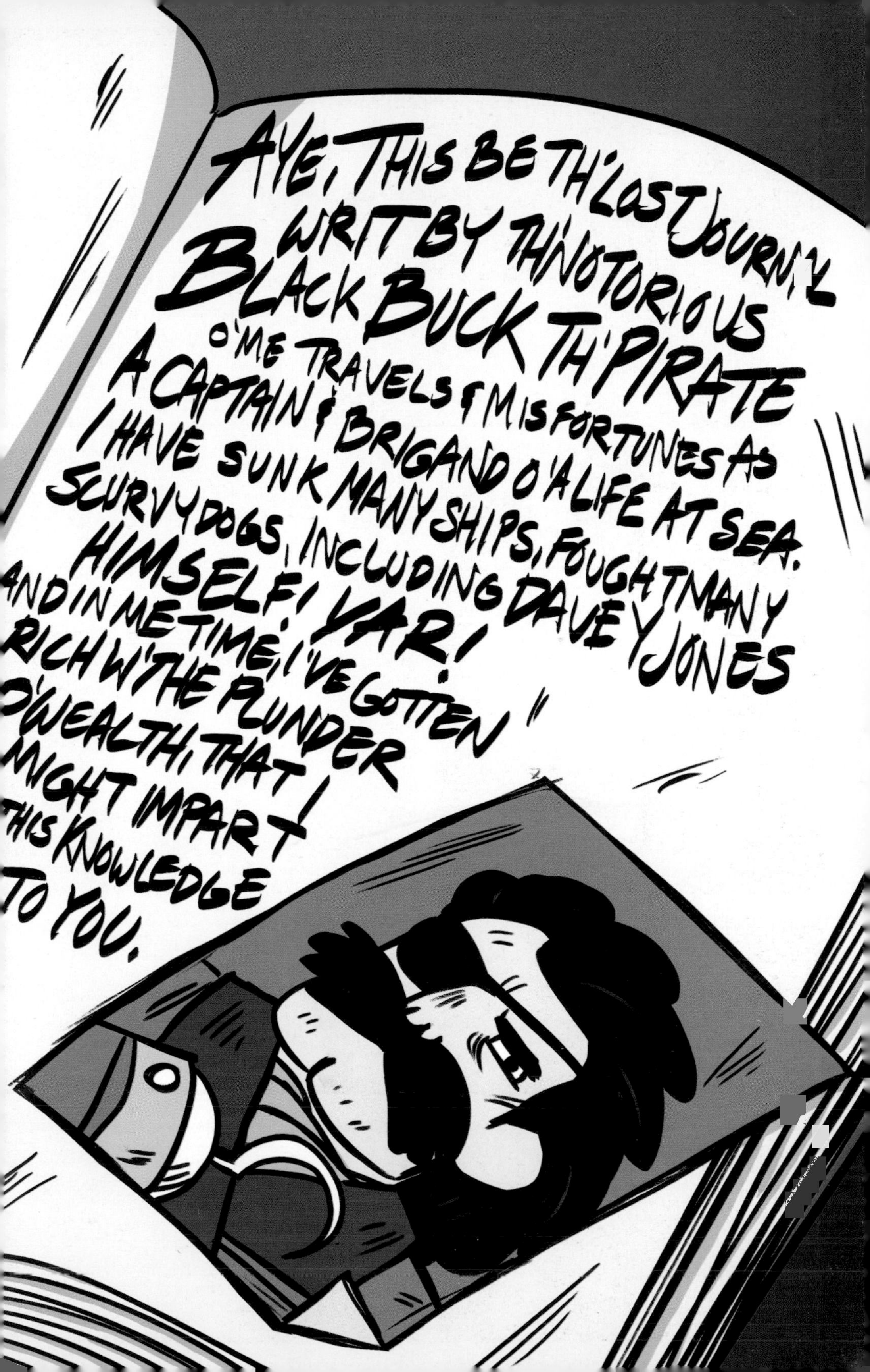
AYE, THIS BE TH' LOST JOURN'L
WRIT BY TH' NOTORIOUS
BLACK BUCK TH' PIRATE
O' ME TRAVELS & MISFORTUNES AS
A CAPTAIN & BRIGAND O' A LIFE AT SEA.
I HAVE SUNK MANY SHIPS, FOUGHT MANY
SCURVY DOGS, INCLUDING DAVEY JONES
HIMSELF! YAR!
AND IN ME TIME, I'VE GOTTEN
RICH W' THE PLUNDER
O' WEALTH, THAT
I MIGHT IMPART
THIS KNOWLEDGE
TO YOU.

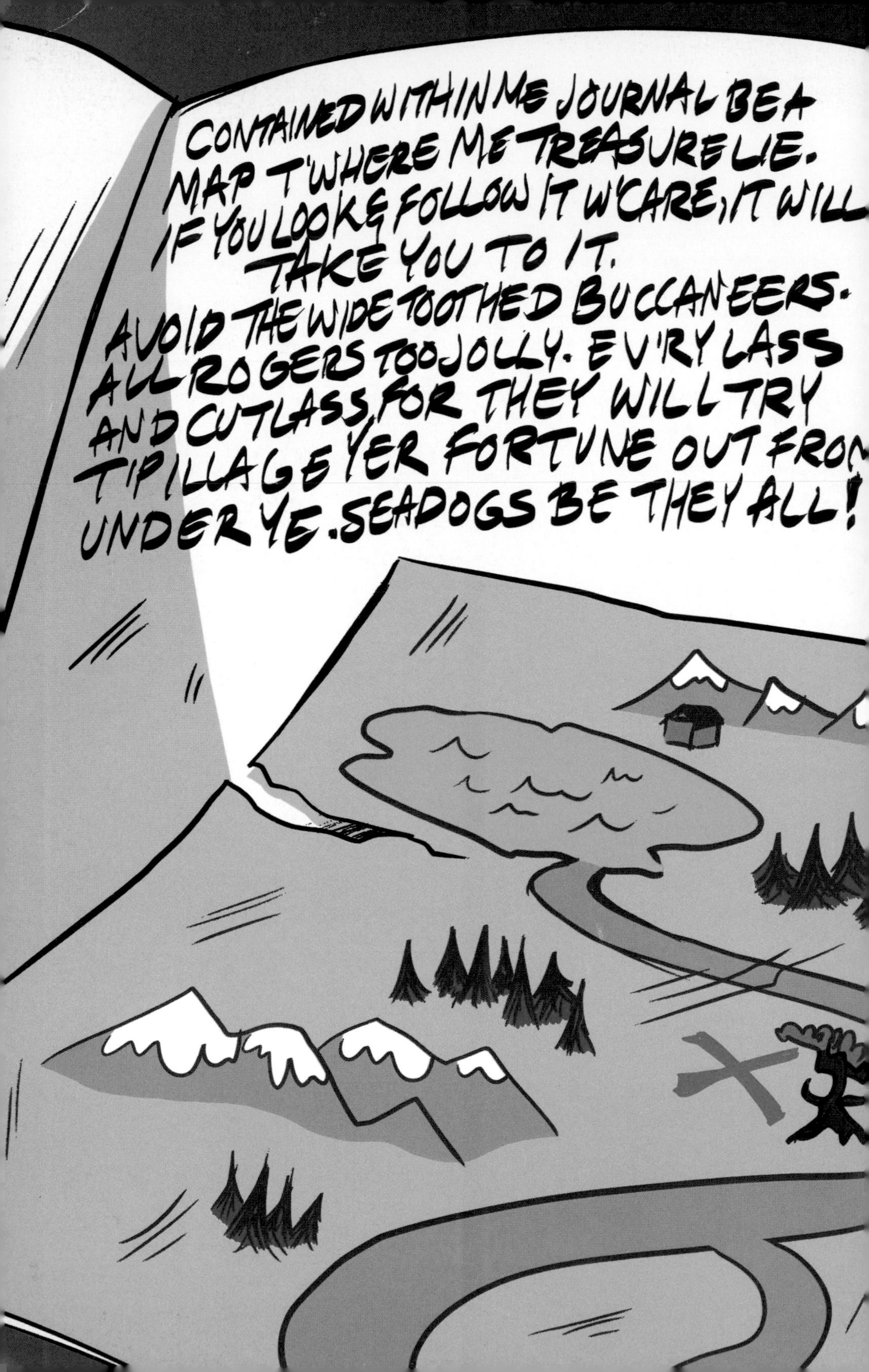
CONTAINED WITHIN ME JOURNAL BE A MAP T'WHERE ME TREASURE LIE. IF YOU LOOK & FOLLOW IT W'CARE, IT WILL TAKE YOU TO IT.
AVOID THE WIDE TOOTHED BUCCANEERS. ALL ROGERS TOO JOLLY. EV'RY LASS AND CUTLASS, FOR THEY WILL TRY TI PILLAGE YER FORTUNE OUT FROM UNDER YE. SEADOGS BE THEY ALL!

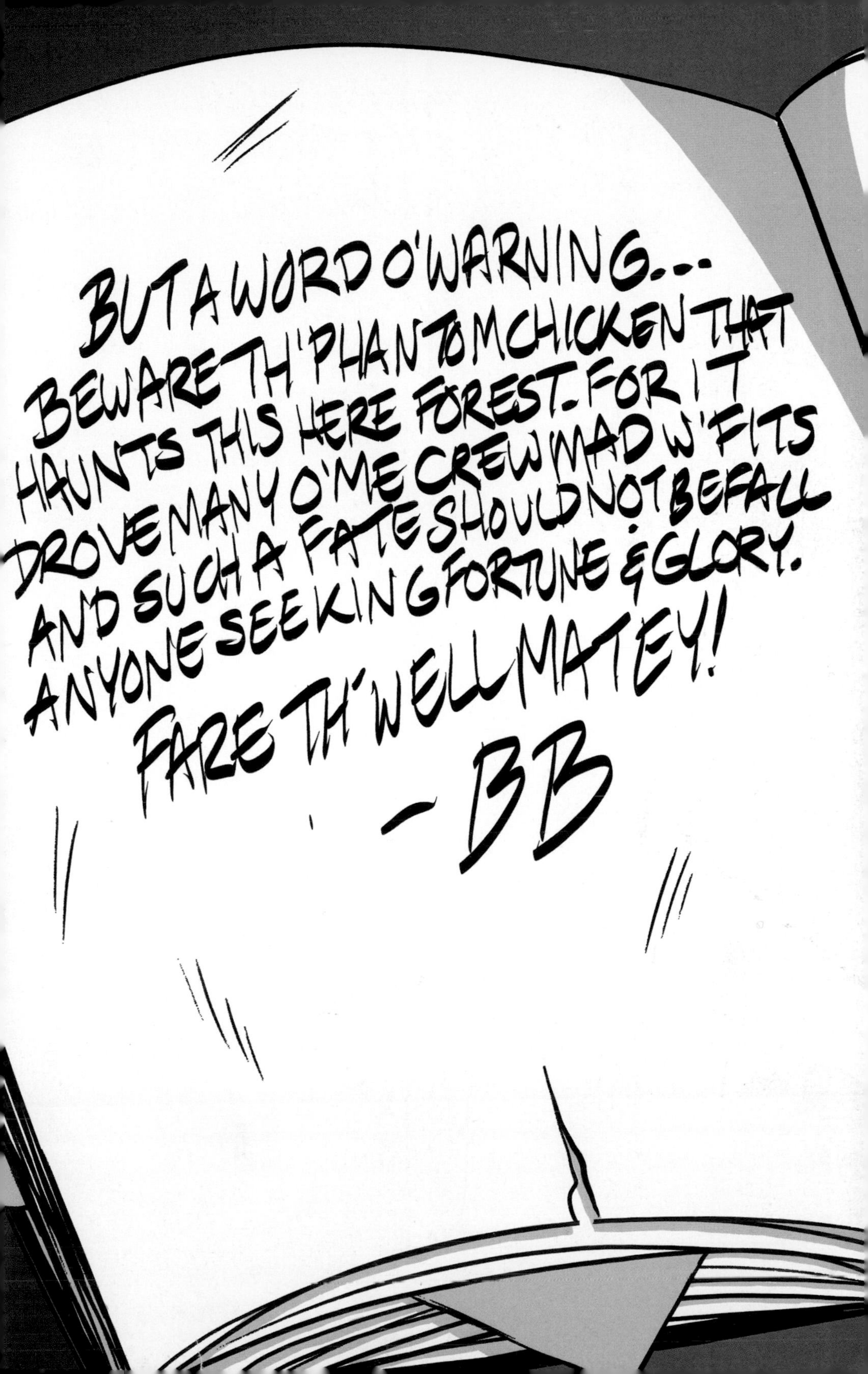
BUT A WORD O' WARNING...
BEWARE TH' PHANTOM CHICKEN THAT HAUNTS THIS HERE FOREST. FOR IT DROVE MANY O' ME CREW MAD W' FITS AND SUCH A FATE SHOULD NOT BEFALL ANYONE SEEKING FORTUNE & GLORY.
FARE TH' WELL MATEY!
-BB

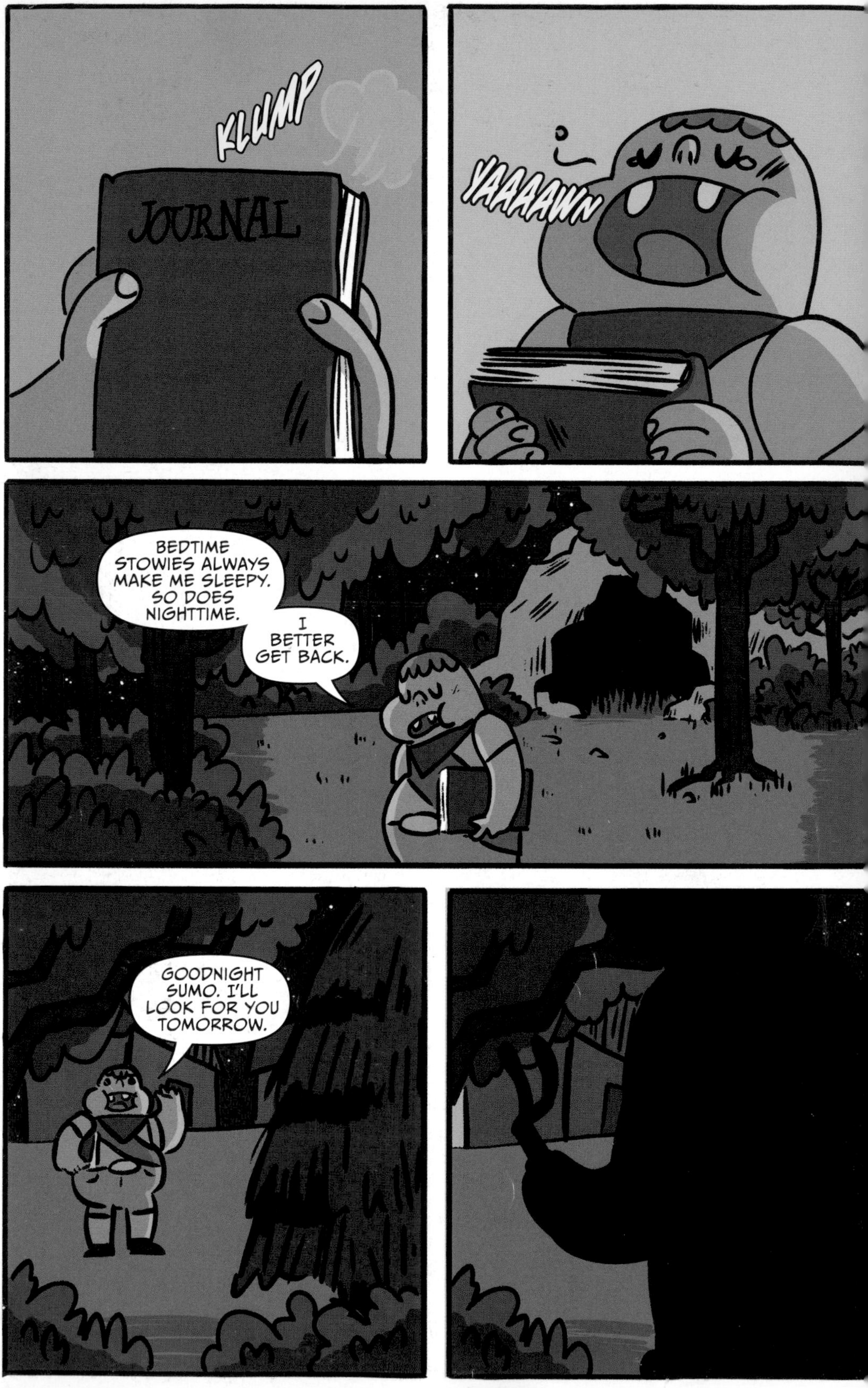
KLUMP
JOURNAL
YAAAAWN
BEDTIME STOWIES ALWAYS MAKE ME SLEEPY. SO DOES NIGHTTIME.
I BETTER GET BACK.
GOODNIGHT SUMO. I'LL LOOK FOR YOU TOMORROW.

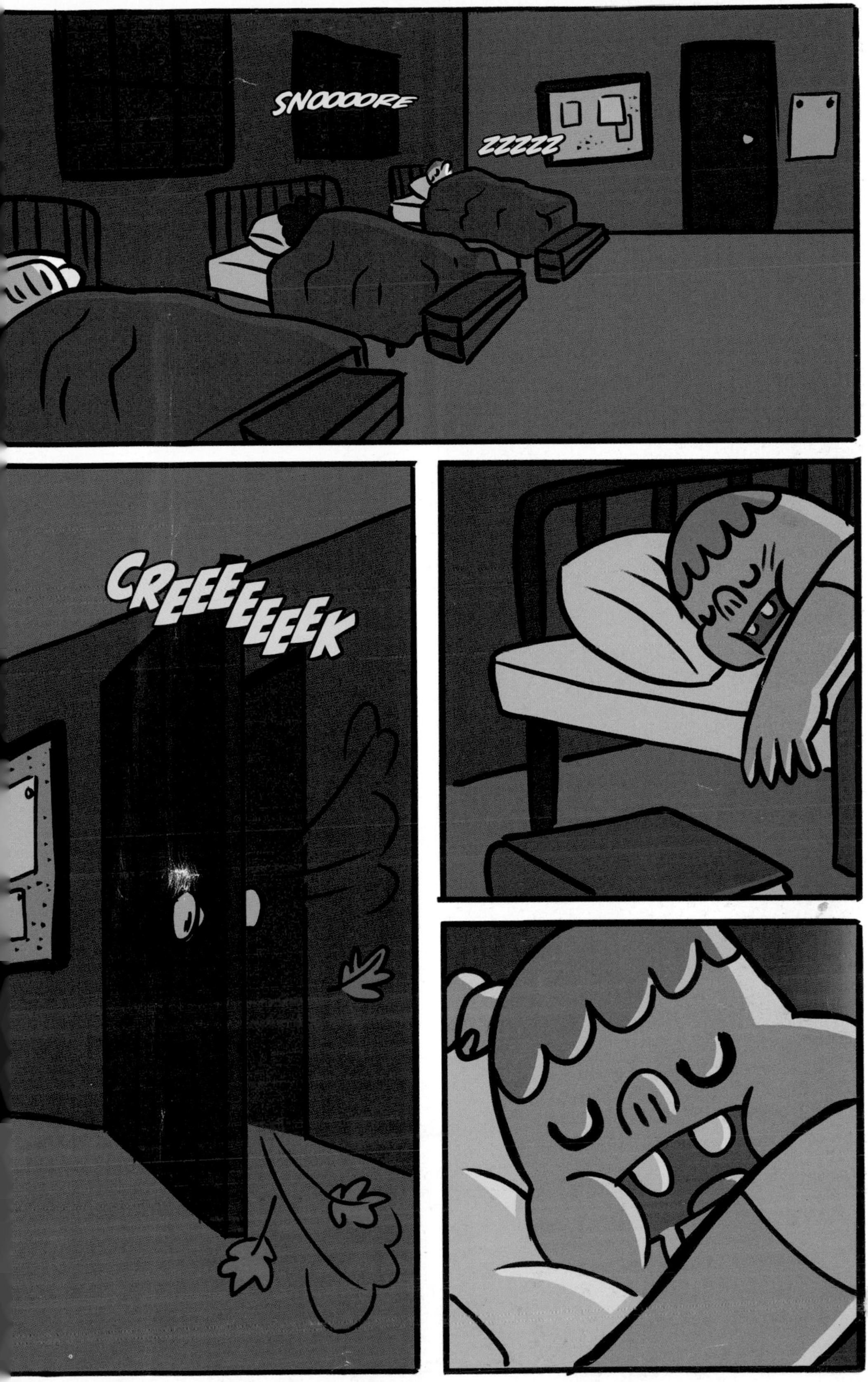
SNOOOORE
ZZZZZ
CREEEEEEEK

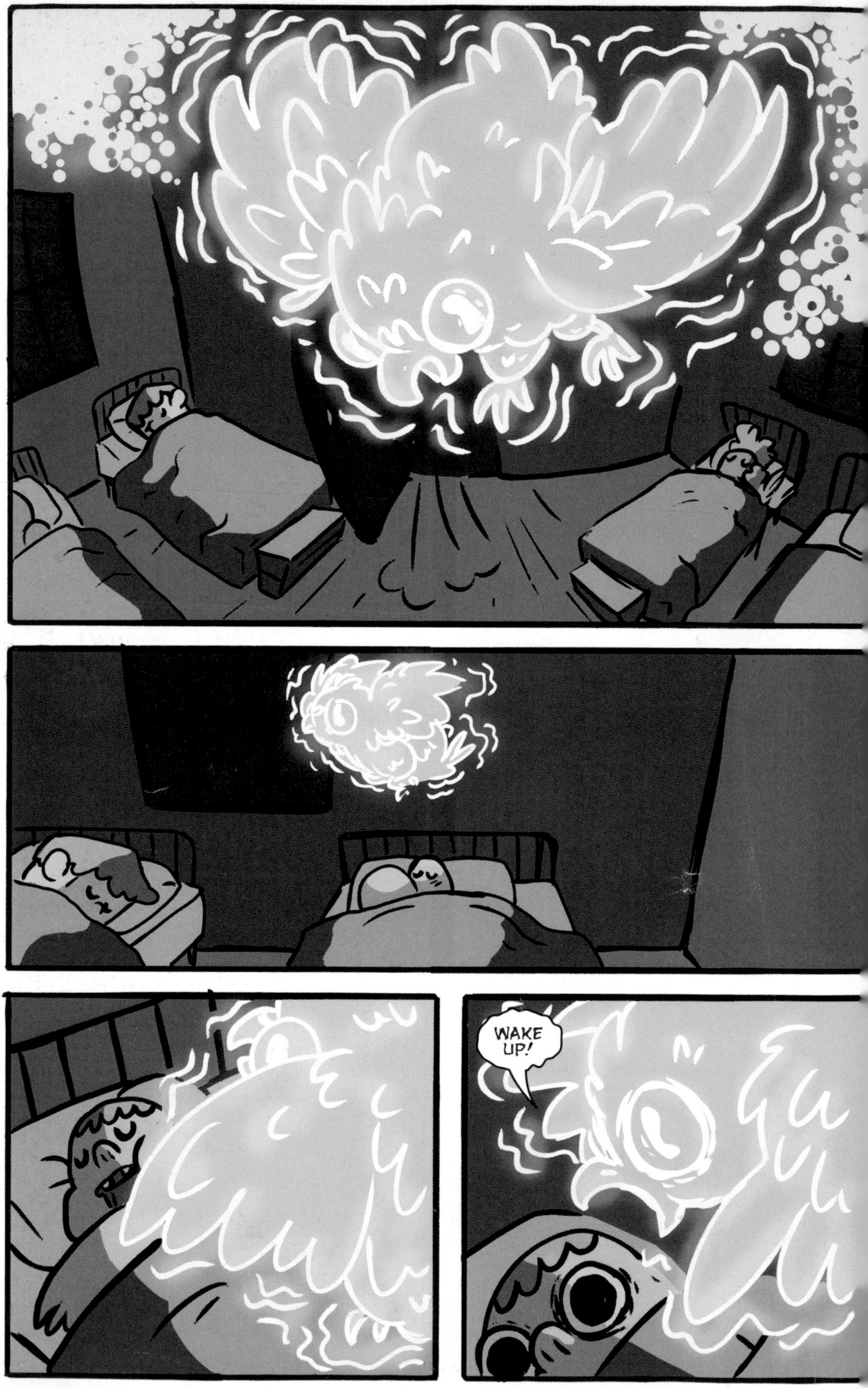
WAKE UP!

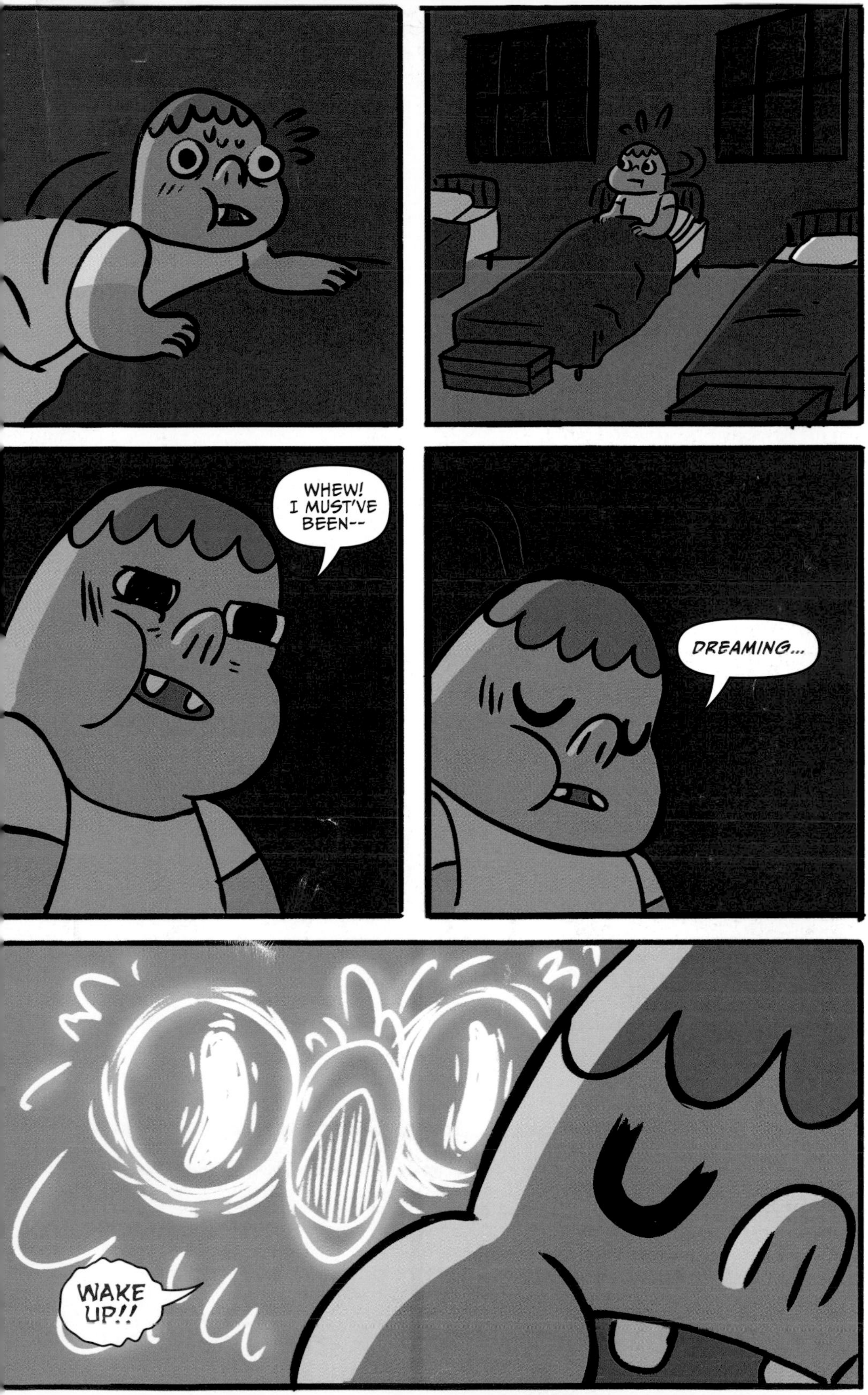
WHEW! I MUST'VE BEEN--
DREAMING...
WAKE UP!!

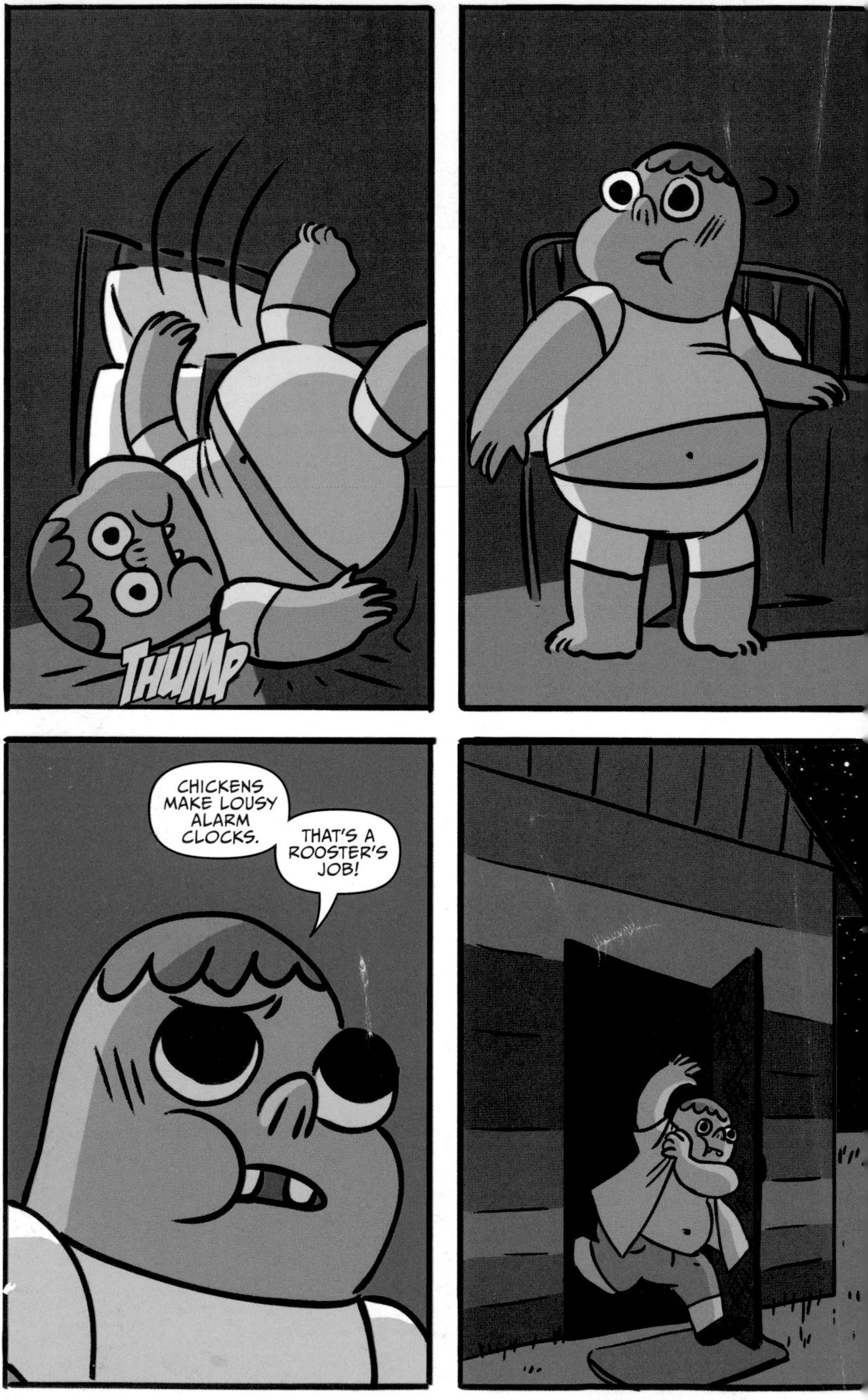
THUMP
CHICKENS MAKE LOUSY ALARM CLOCKS.
THAT'S A ROOSTER'S JOB!

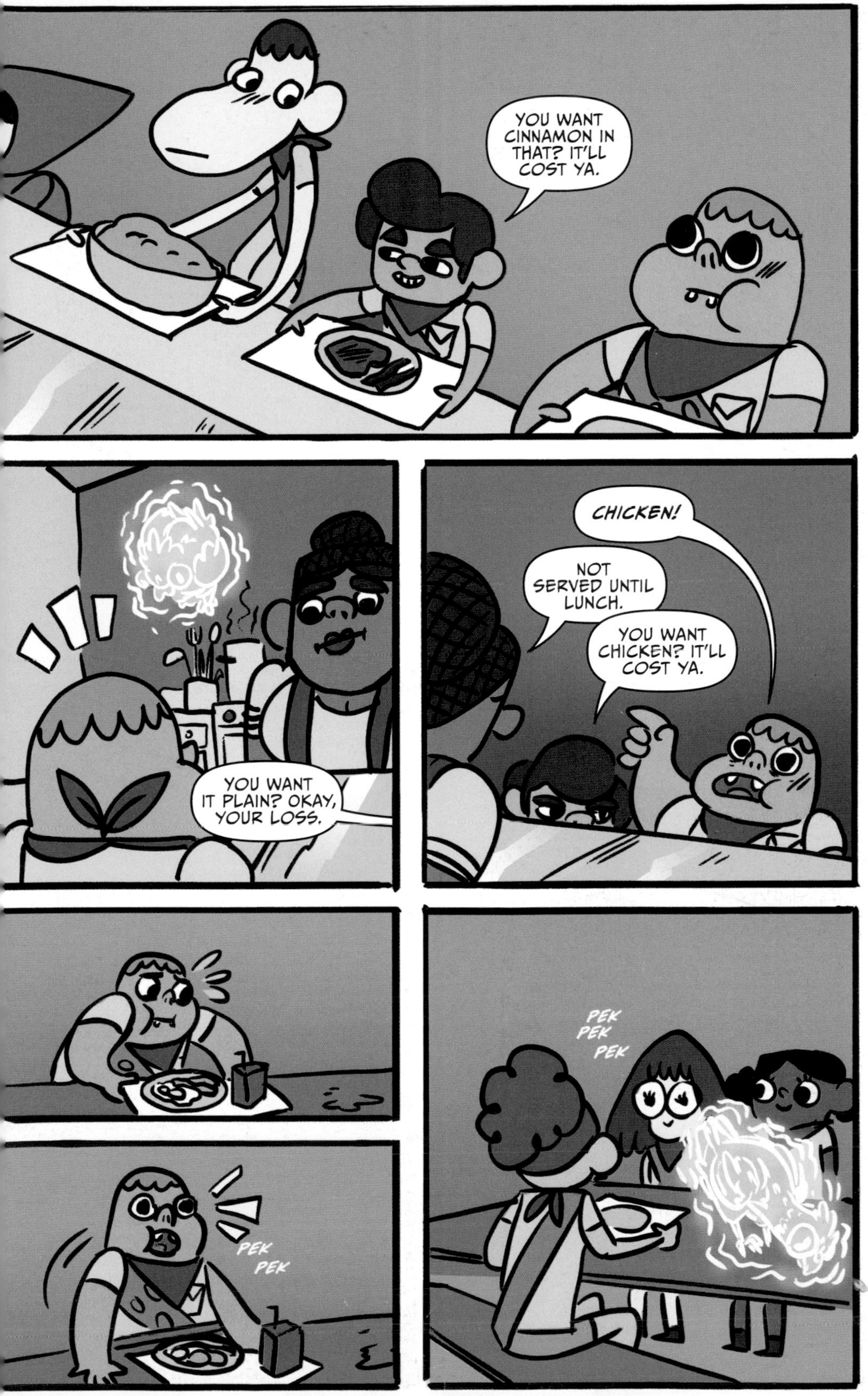
YOU WANT CINNAMON IN THAT? IT'LL COST YA.
YOU WANT IT PLAIN? OKAY, YOUR LOSS.
CHICKEN!
NOT SERVED UNTIL LUNCH.
YOU WANT CHICKEN? IT'LL COST YA.
PEK PEK
PEK PEK PEK

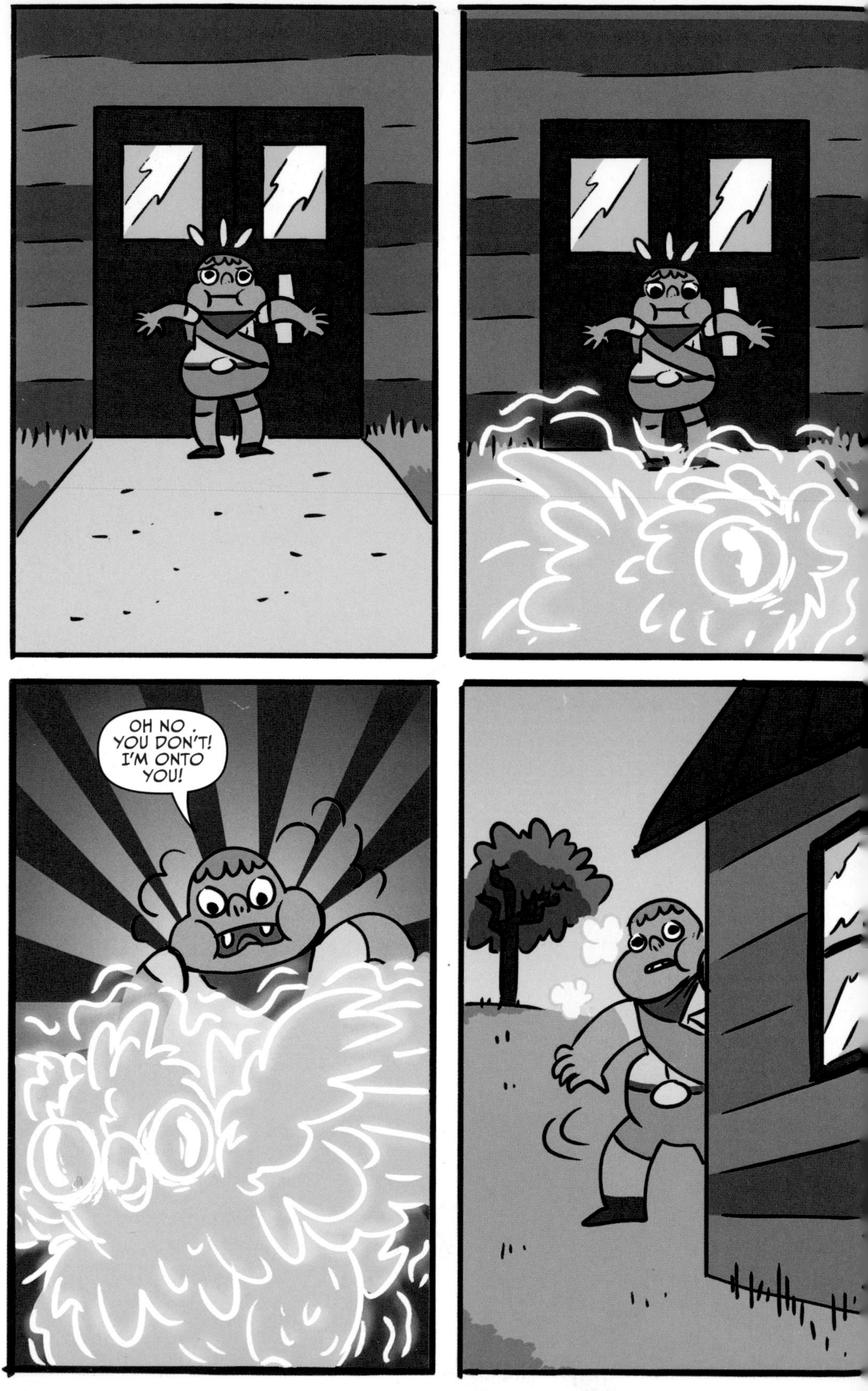
OH NO, YOU DON'T! I'M ONTO YOU!

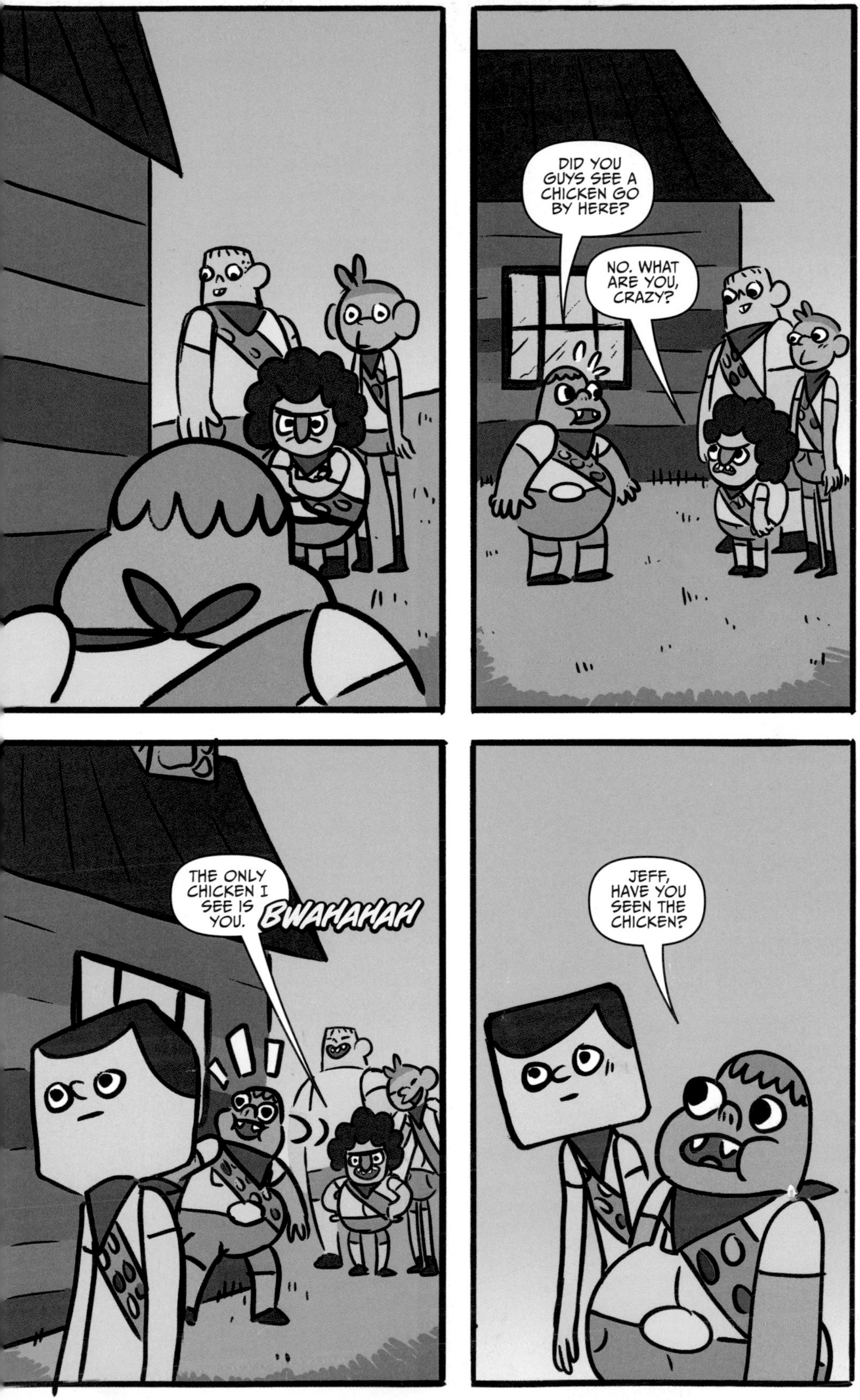
DID YOU GUYS SEE A CHICKEN GO BY HERE?
NO. WHAT ARE YOU, CRAZY?
THE ONLY CHICKEN I SEE IS YOU.
BWAHAHAH
JEFF, HAVE YOU SEEN THE CHICKEN?

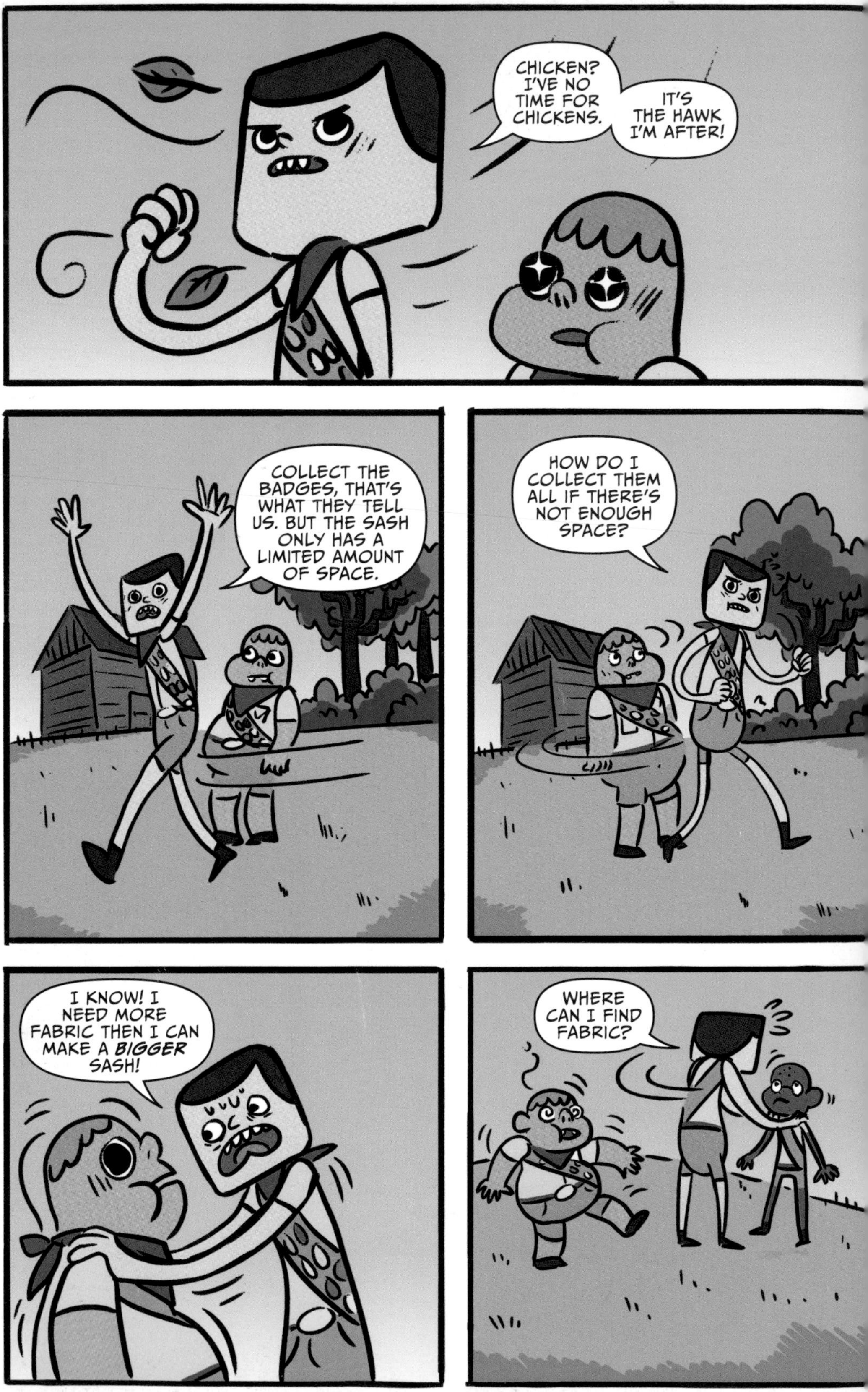
CHICKEN? I'VE NO TIME FOR CHICKENS.
IT'S THE HAWK I'M AFTER!
COLLECT THE BADGES, THAT'S WHAT THEY TELL US. BUT THE SASH ONLY HAS A LIMITED AMOUNT OF SPACE.
HOW DO I COLLECT THEM ALL IF THERE'S NOT ENOUGH SPACE?
I KNOW! I NEED MORE FABRIC THEN I CAN MAKE A *BIGGER* SASH!
WHERE CAN I FIND FABRIC?

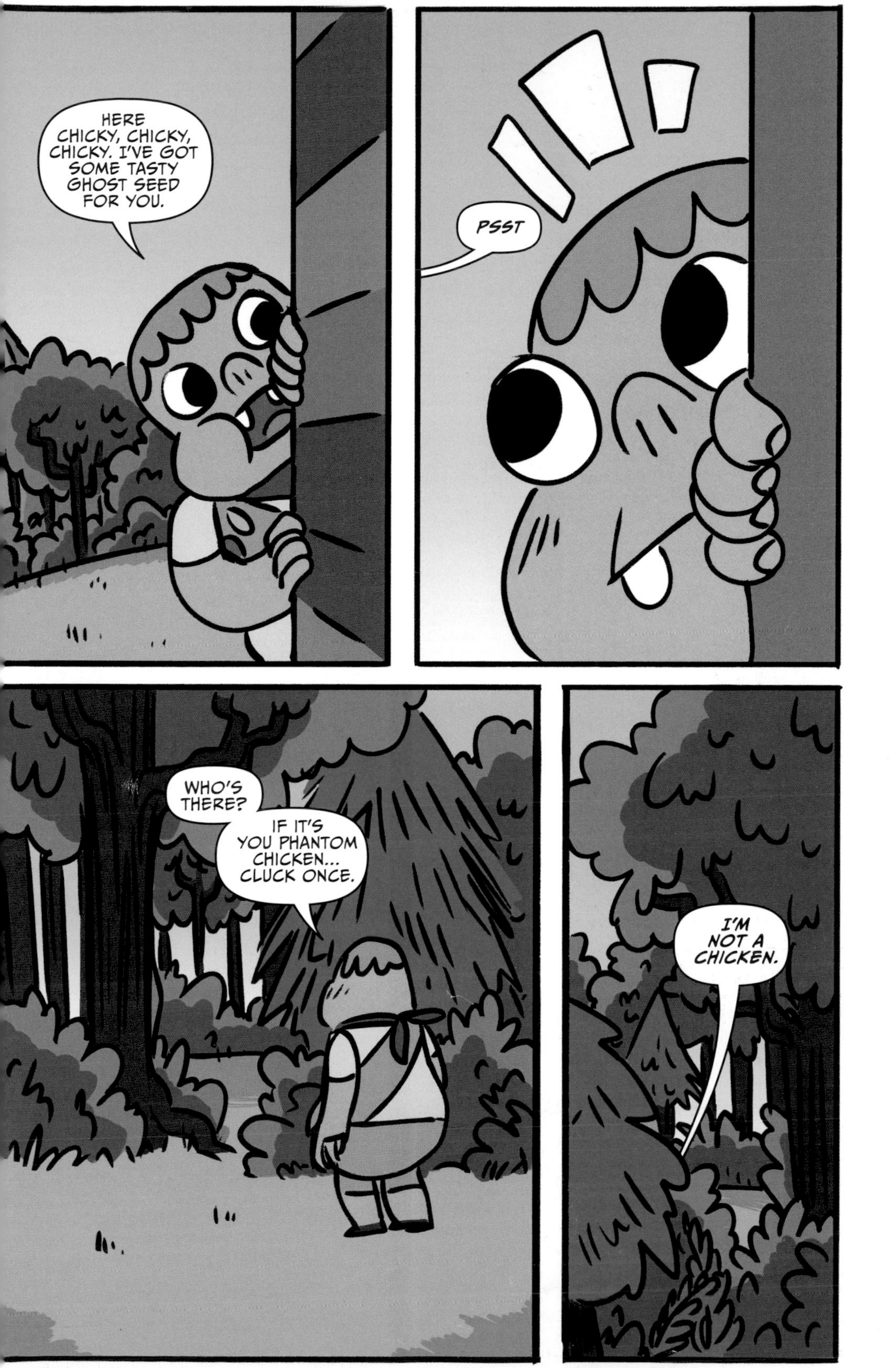
HERE CHICKY, CHICKY, CHICKY. I'VE GOT SOME TASTY GHOST SEED FOR YOU.
PSST
WHO'S THERE?
IF IT'S YOU PHANTOM CHICKEN... CLUCK ONCE.
I'M NOT A CHICKEN.

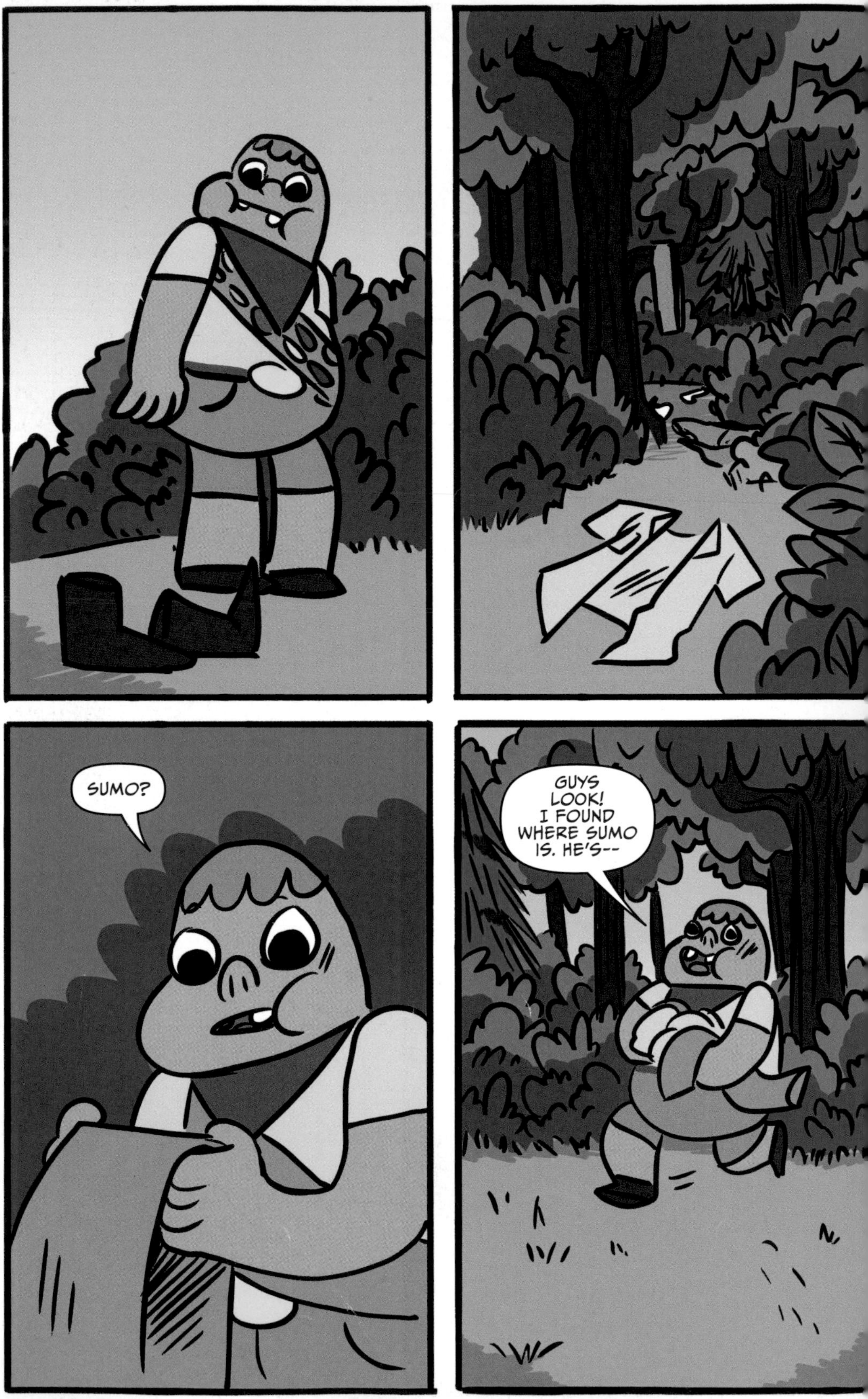
SUMO?
GUYS LOOK! I FOUND WHERE SUMO IS. HE'S--

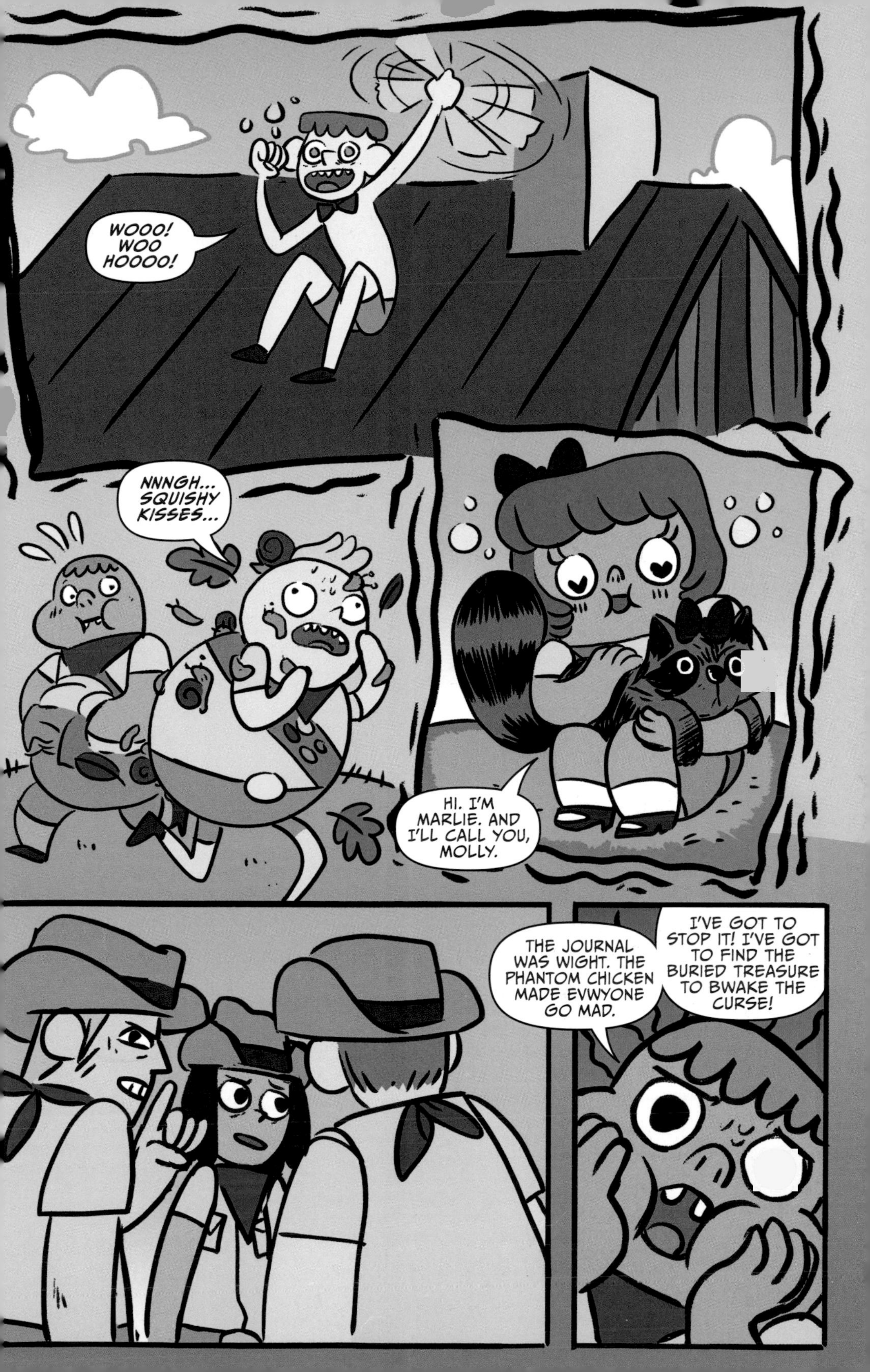
WOOO! WOO HOOOO!
NNNGH... SQUISHY KISSES...
HI. I'M MARLIE. AND I'LL CALL YOU, MOLLY.
THE JOURNAL WAS WIGHT. THE PHANTOM CHICKEN MADE EVWYONE GO MAD.
I'VE GOT TO STOP IT! I'VE GOT TO FIND THE BURIED TREASURE TO BWAKE THE CURSE!

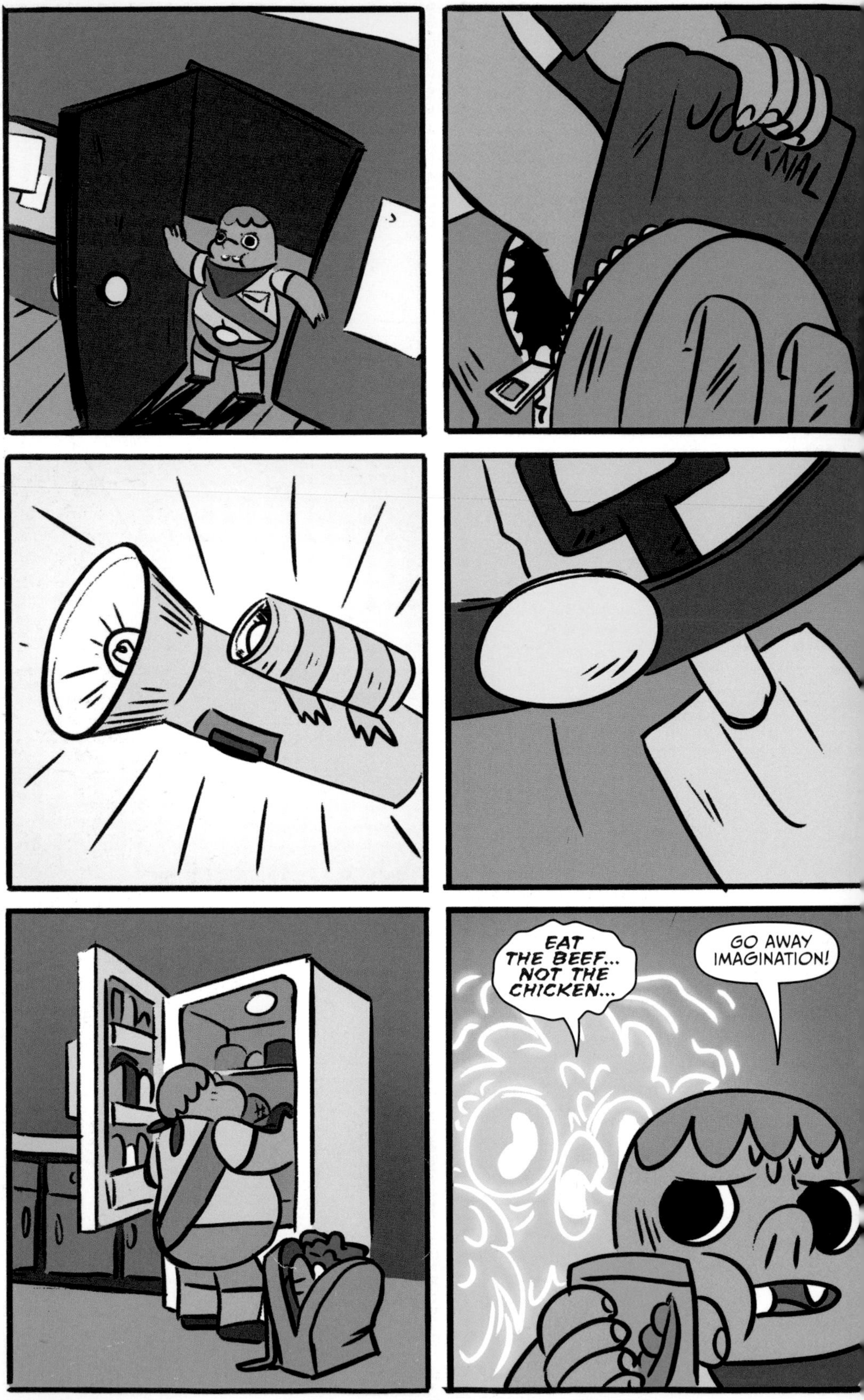
JOURNAL
EAT THE BEEF... NOT THE CHICKEN...
GO AWAY IMAGINATION!

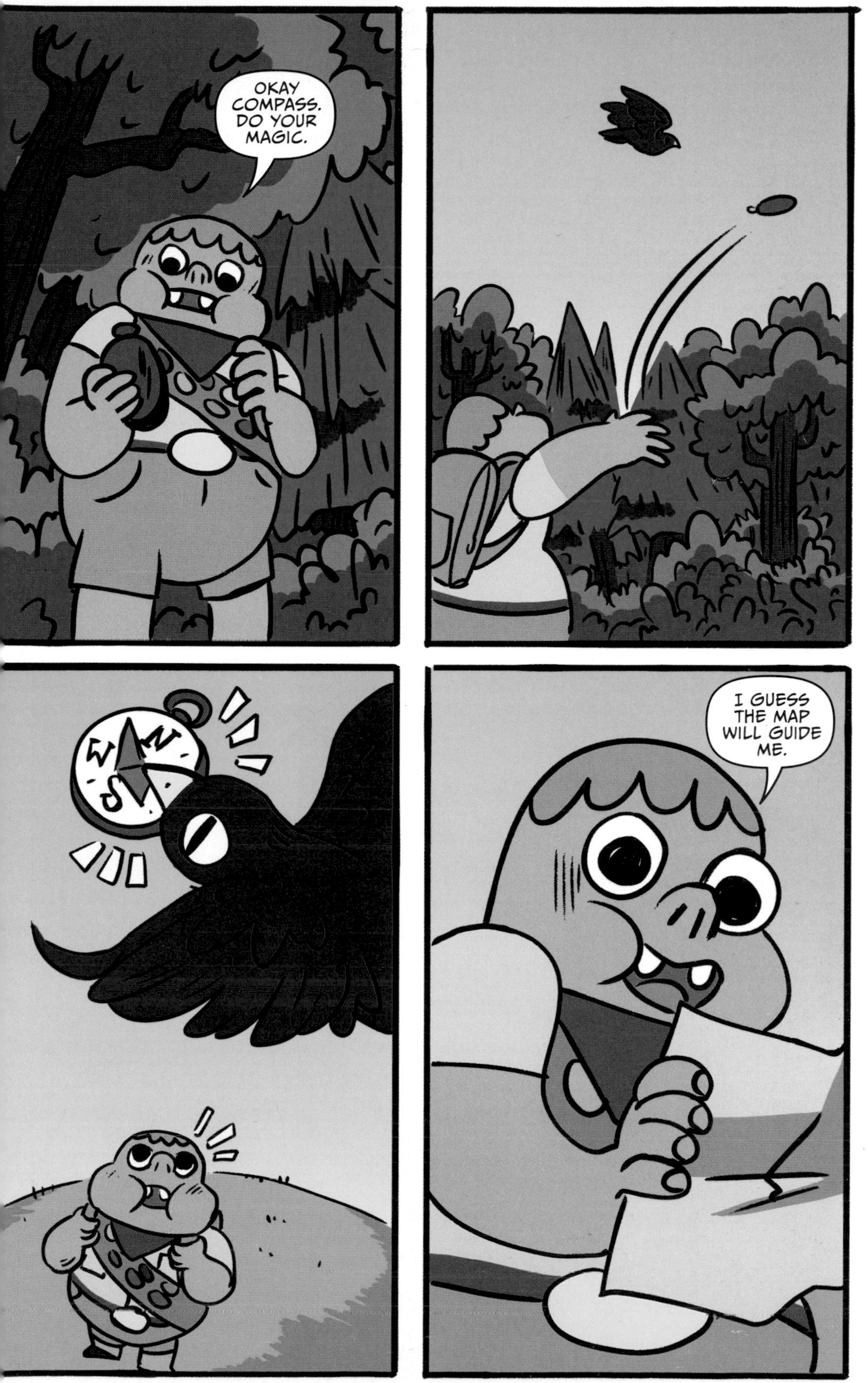
OKAY COMPASS. DO YOUR MAGIC.
N
W
S
I GUESS THE MAP WILL GUIDE ME.

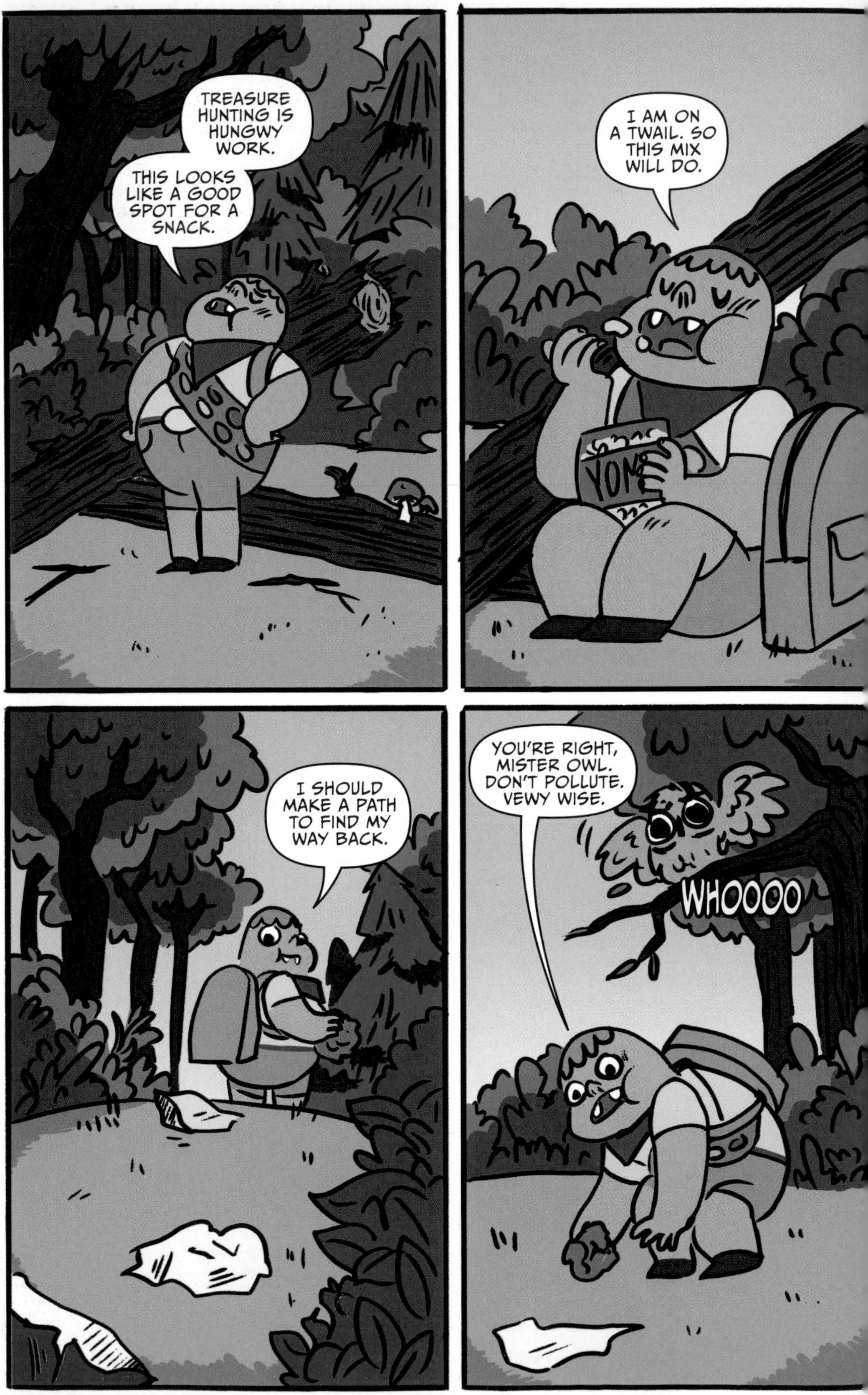
TREASURE HUNTING IS HUNGWY WORK.
THIS LOOKS LIKE A GOOD SPOT FOR A SNACK.
I AM ON A TWAIL. SO THIS MIX WILL DO.
YOM
I SHOULD MAKE A PATH TO FIND MY WAY BACK.
YOU'RE RIGHT, MISTER OWL. DON'T POLLUTE. VEWY WISE.
WHOOOO

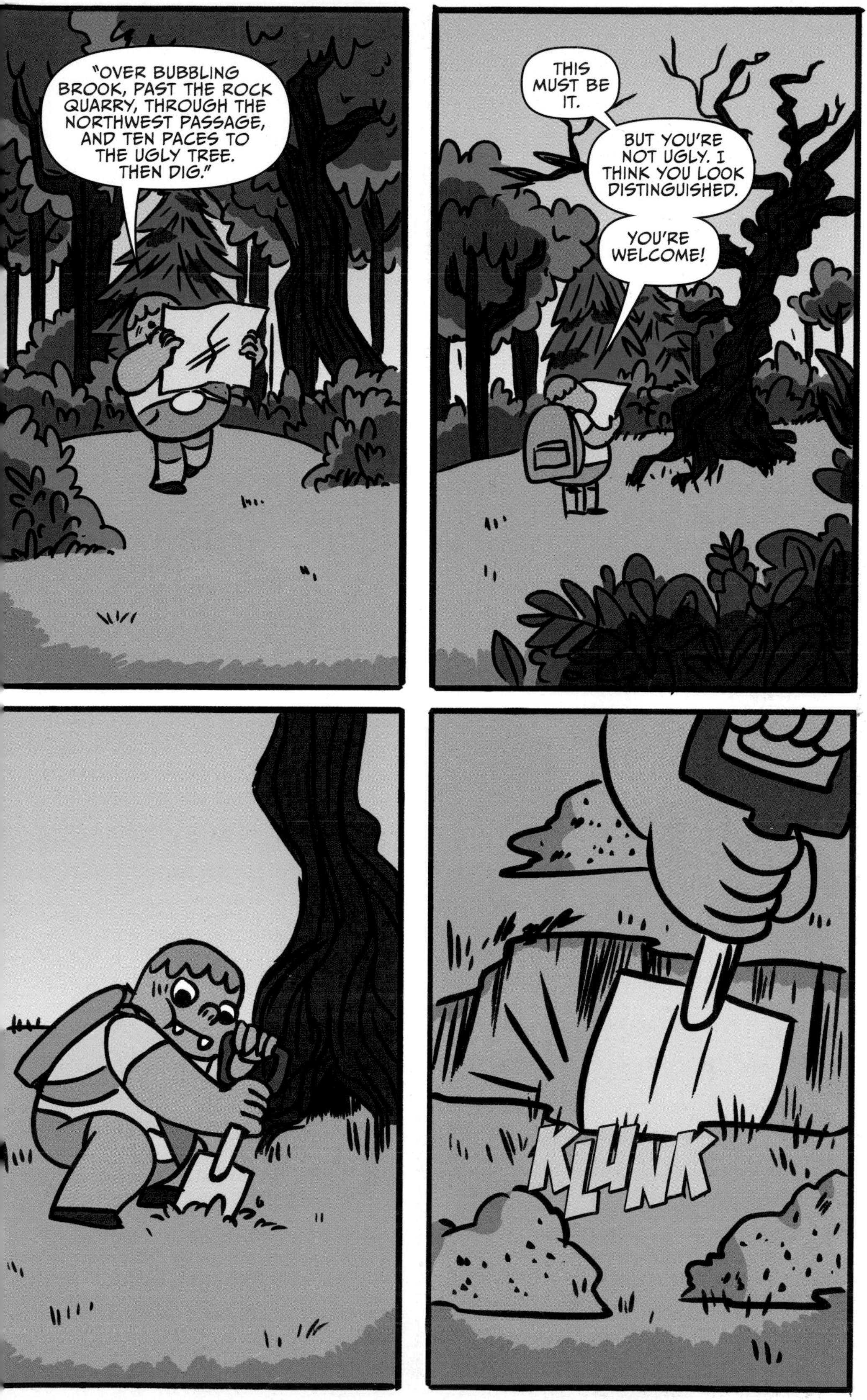
"OVER BUBBLING BROOK, PAST THE ROCK QUARRY, THROUGH THE NORTHWEST PASSAGE, AND TEN PACES TO THE UGLY TREE. THEN DIG."
THIS MUST BE IT.
BUT YOU'RE NOT UGLY. I THINK YOU LOOK DISTINGUISHED.
YOU'RE WELCOME!
KLUNK

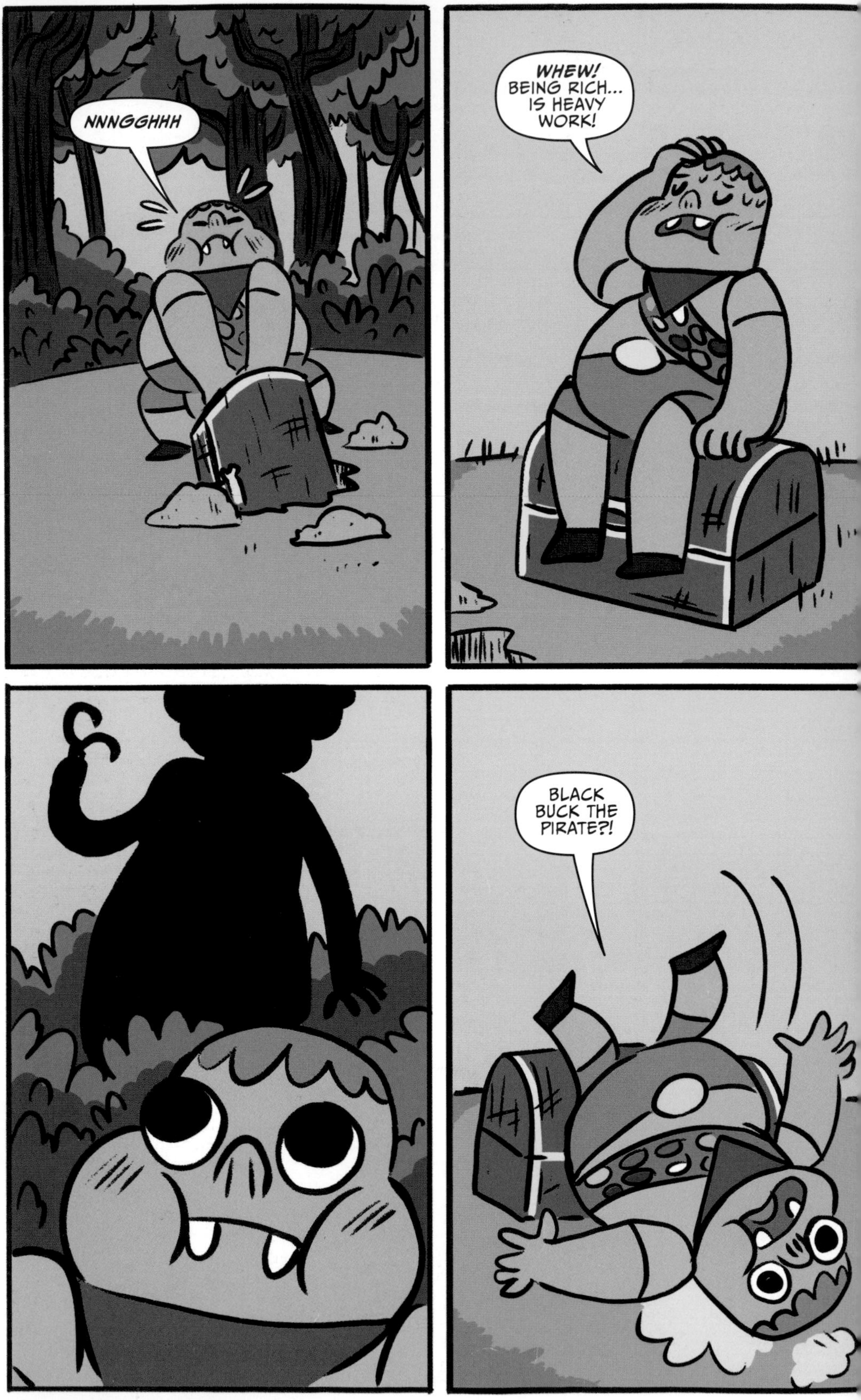
NNNGGHHH
WHEW! BEING RICH... IS HEAVY WORK!
BLACK BUCK THE PIRATE?!

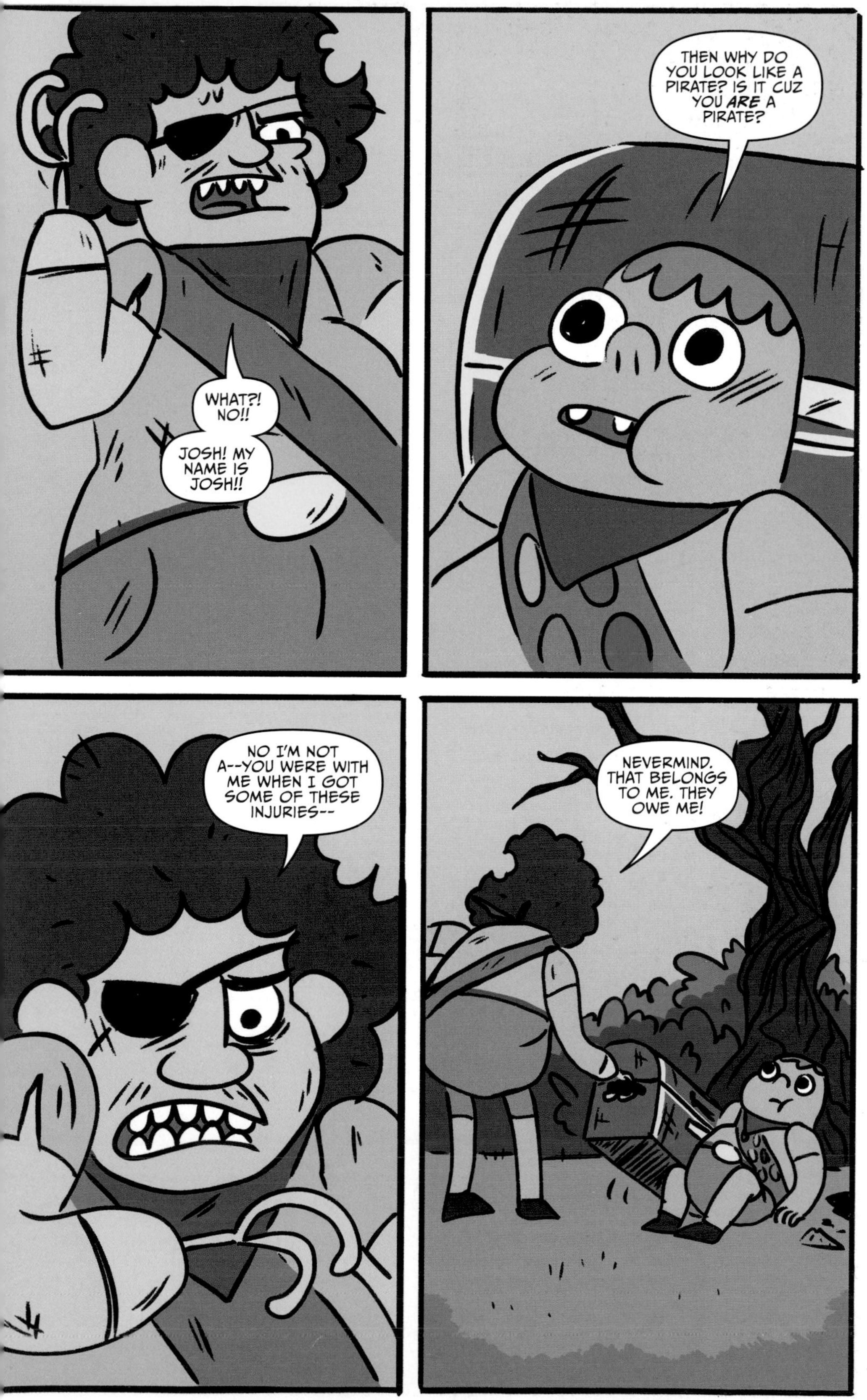
WHAT?! NO!!
JOSH! MY NAME IS JOSH!!
THEN WHY DO YOU LOOK LIKE A PIRATE? IS IT CUZ YOU ARE A PIRATE?
NO I'M NOT A--YOU WERE WITH ME WHEN I GOT SOME OF THESE INJURIES--
NEVERMIND. THAT BELONGS TO ME. THEY OWE ME!

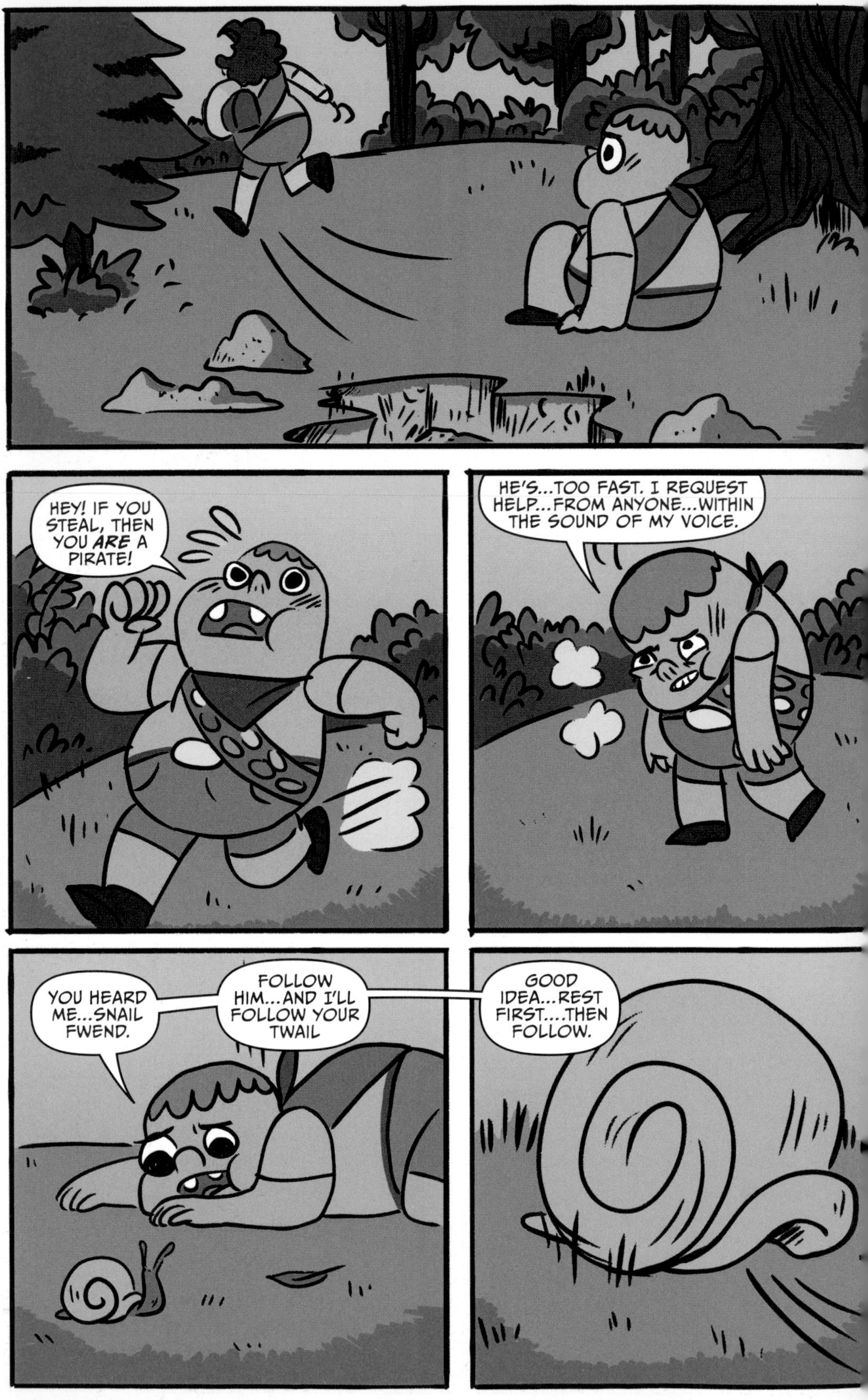
HEY! IF YOU STEAL, THEN YOU *ARE* A PIRATE!
HE'S...TOO FAST. I REQUEST HELP...FROM ANYONE...WITHIN THE SOUND OF MY VOICE.
YOU HEARD ME...SNAIL FWEND.
FOLLOW HIM...AND I'LL FOLLOW YOUR TWAIL
GOOD IDEA...REST FIRST....THEN FOLLOW.

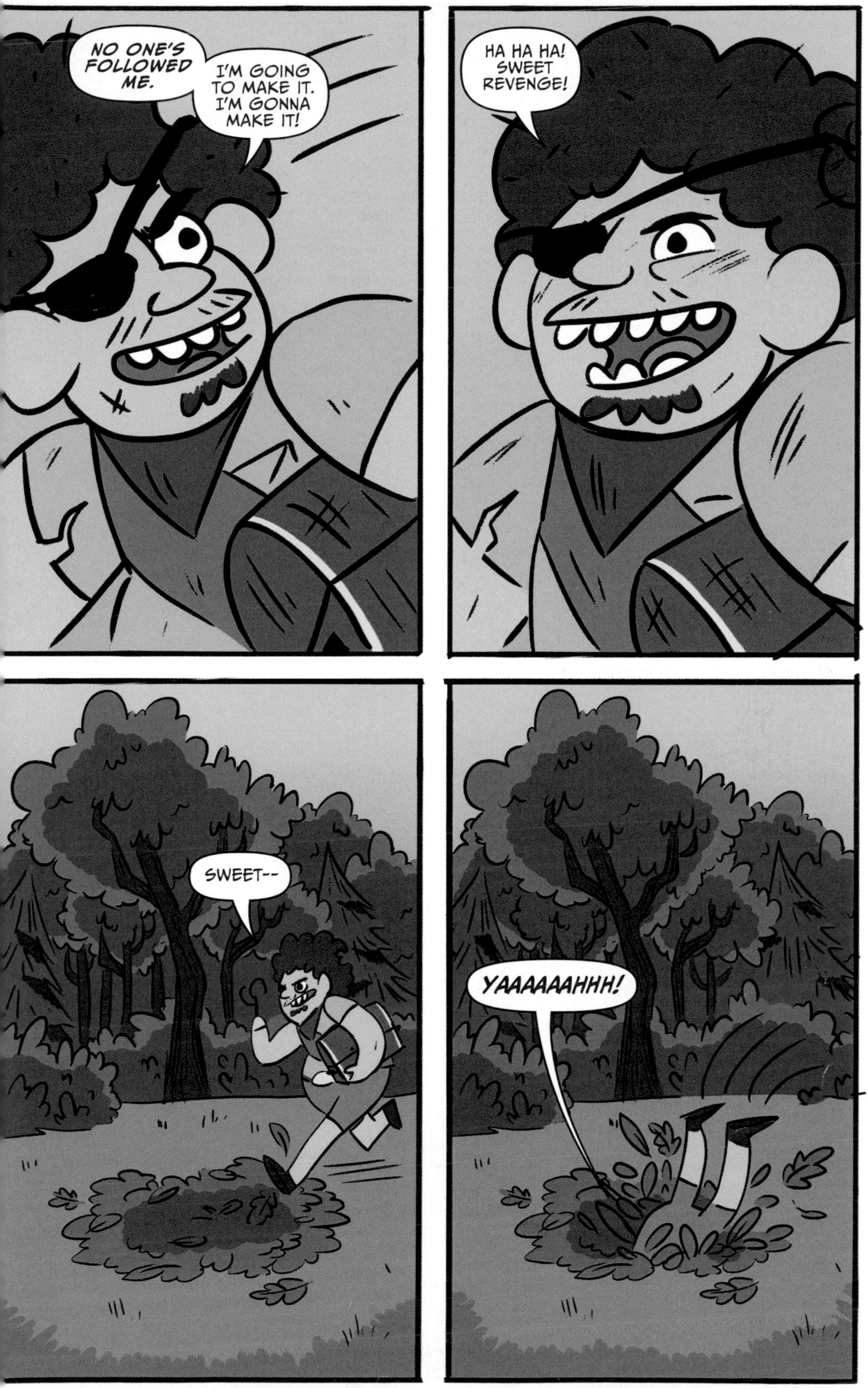
NO ONE'S FOLLOWED ME.
I'M GOING TO MAKE IT. I'M GONNA MAKE IT!
HA HA HA! SWEET REVENGE!
SWEET--
YAAAAAAHHH!

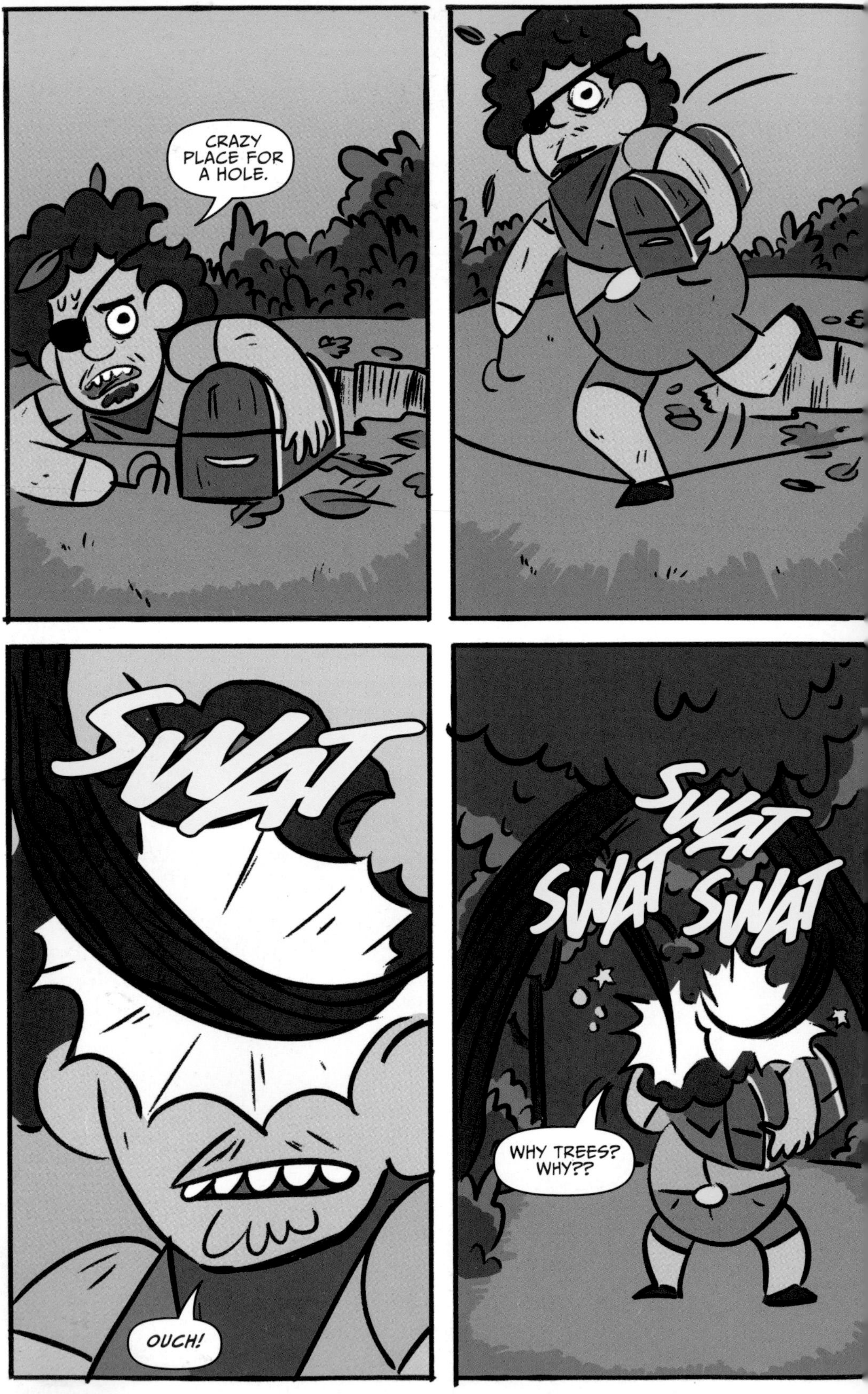
CRAZY PLACE FOR A HOLE.
SWAT
OUCH!
SWAT
SWAT SWAT
WHY TREES? WHY??

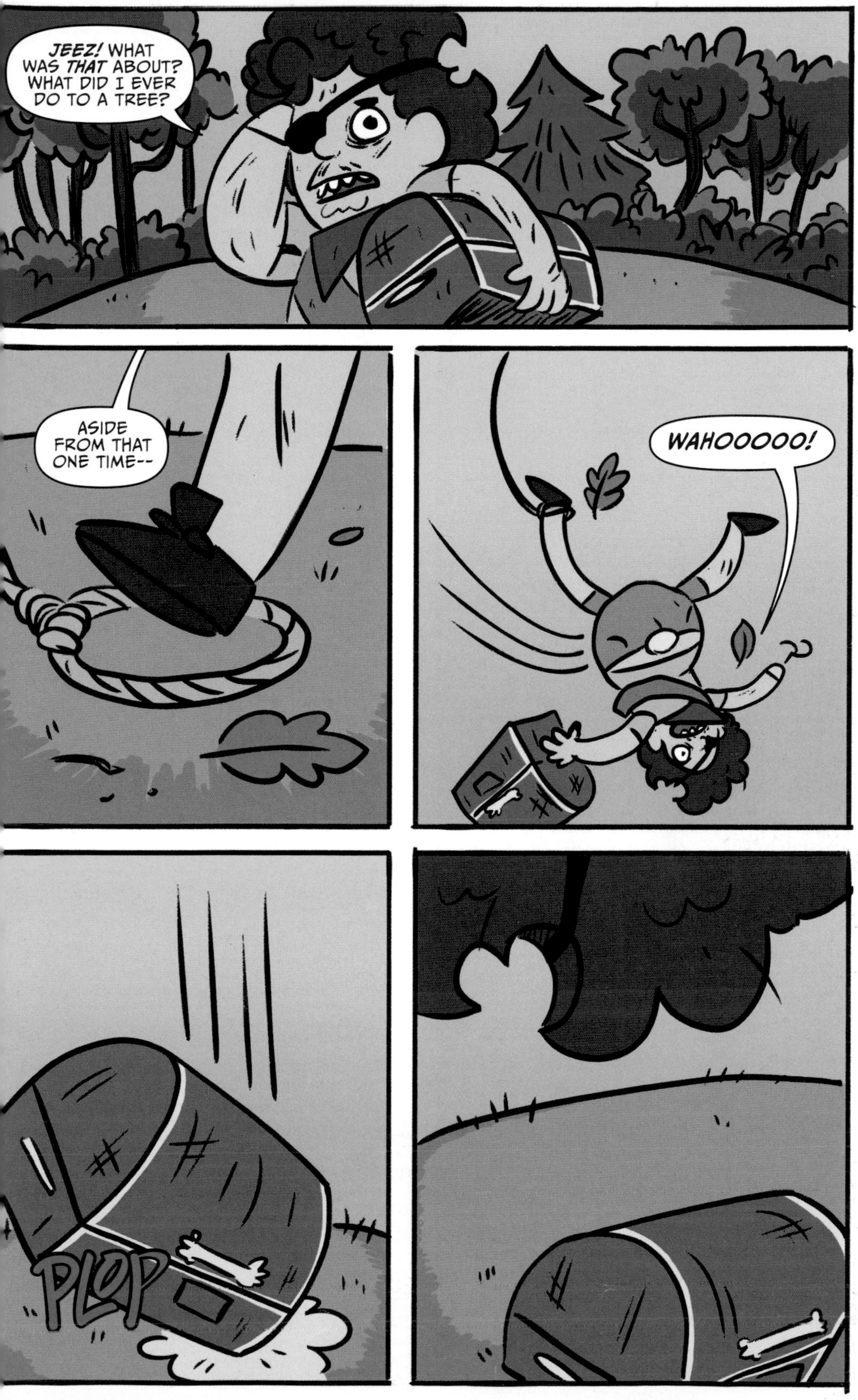
JEEZ! WHAT WAS THAT ABOUT? WHAT DID I EVER DO TO A TREE?
ASIDE FROM THAT ONE TIME--
WAHOOOOO!
PLOP

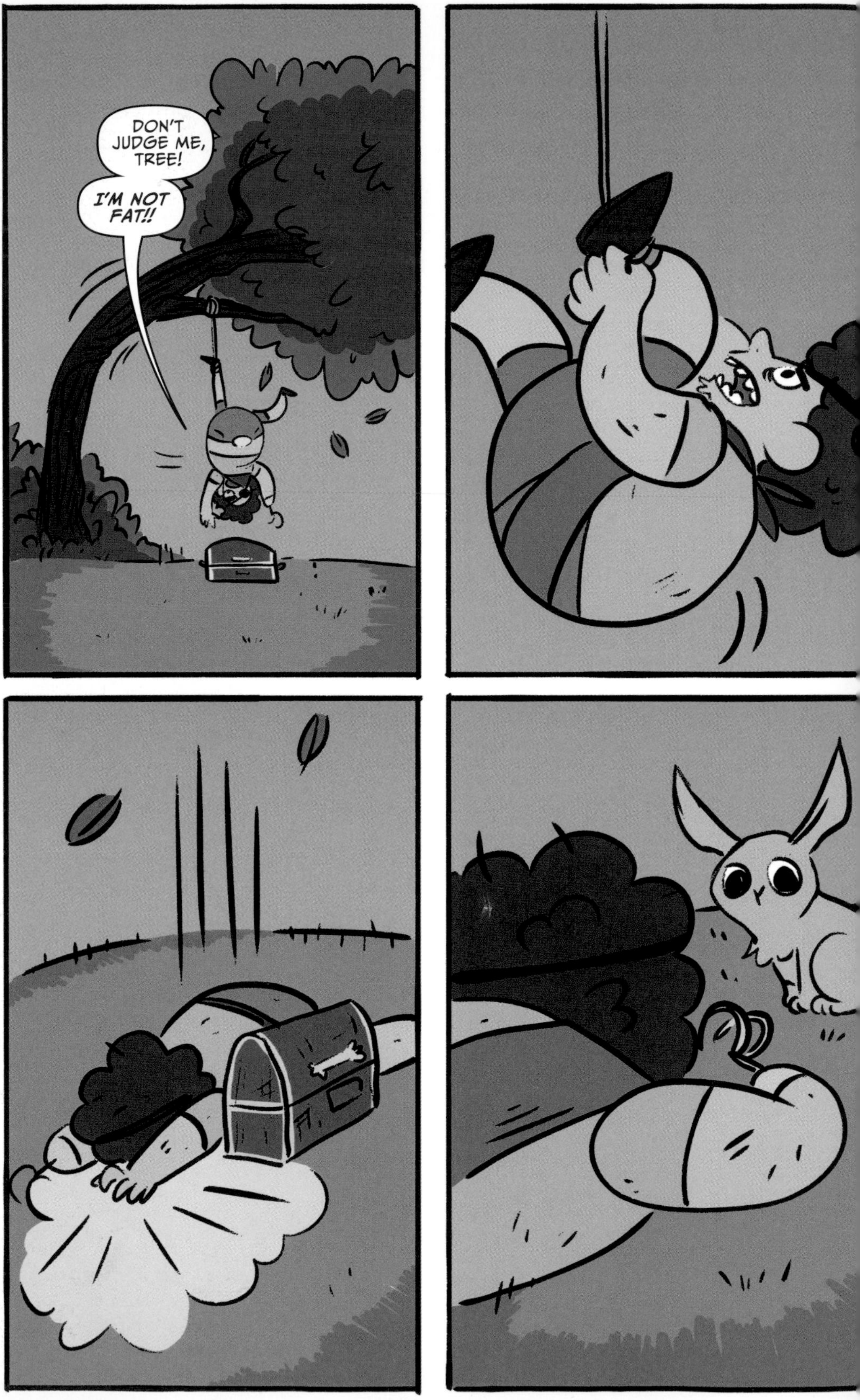
DON'T JUDGE ME, TREE!
I'M NOT FAT!!

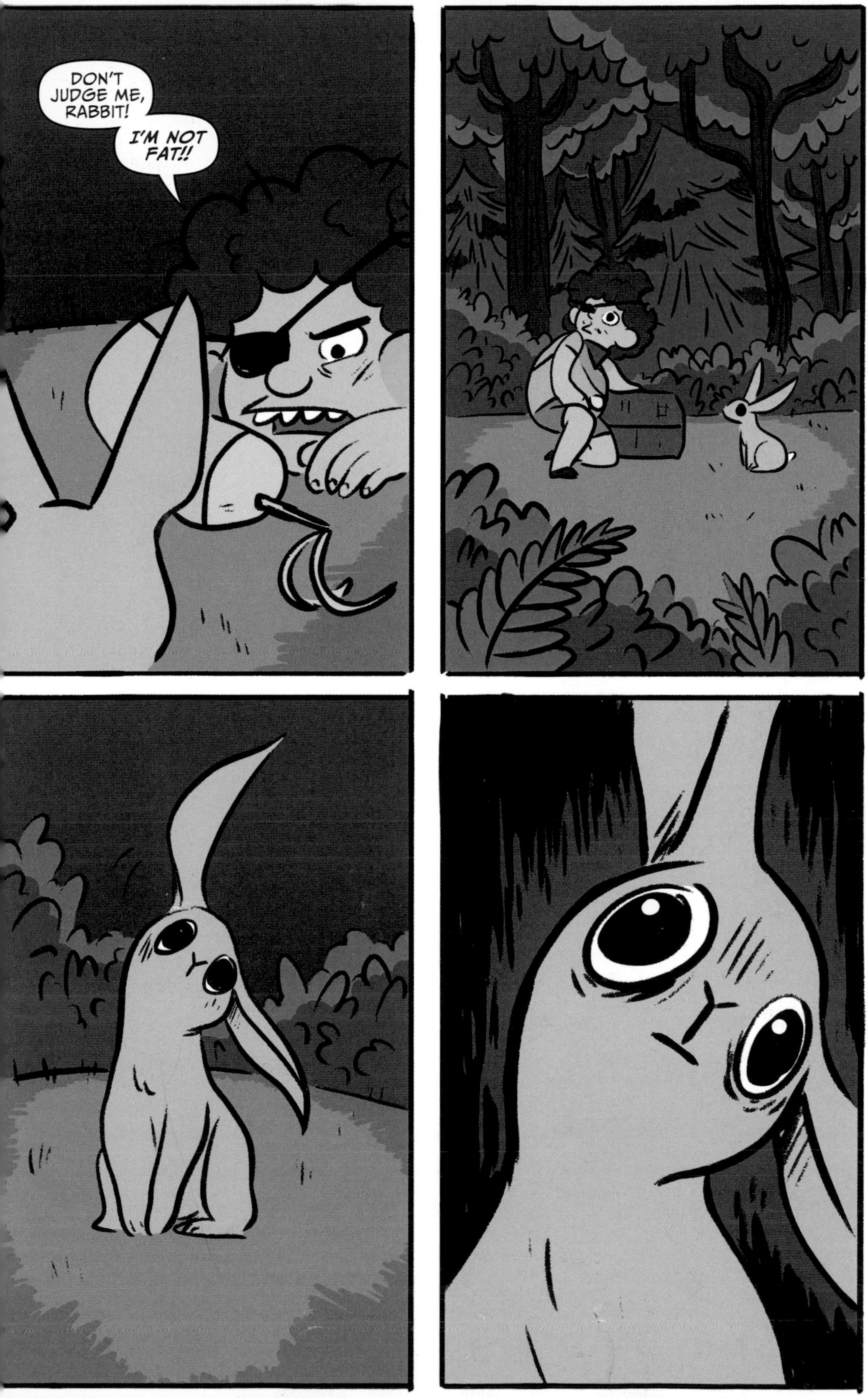
DON'T JUDGE ME, RABBIT!
I'M NOT FAT!!

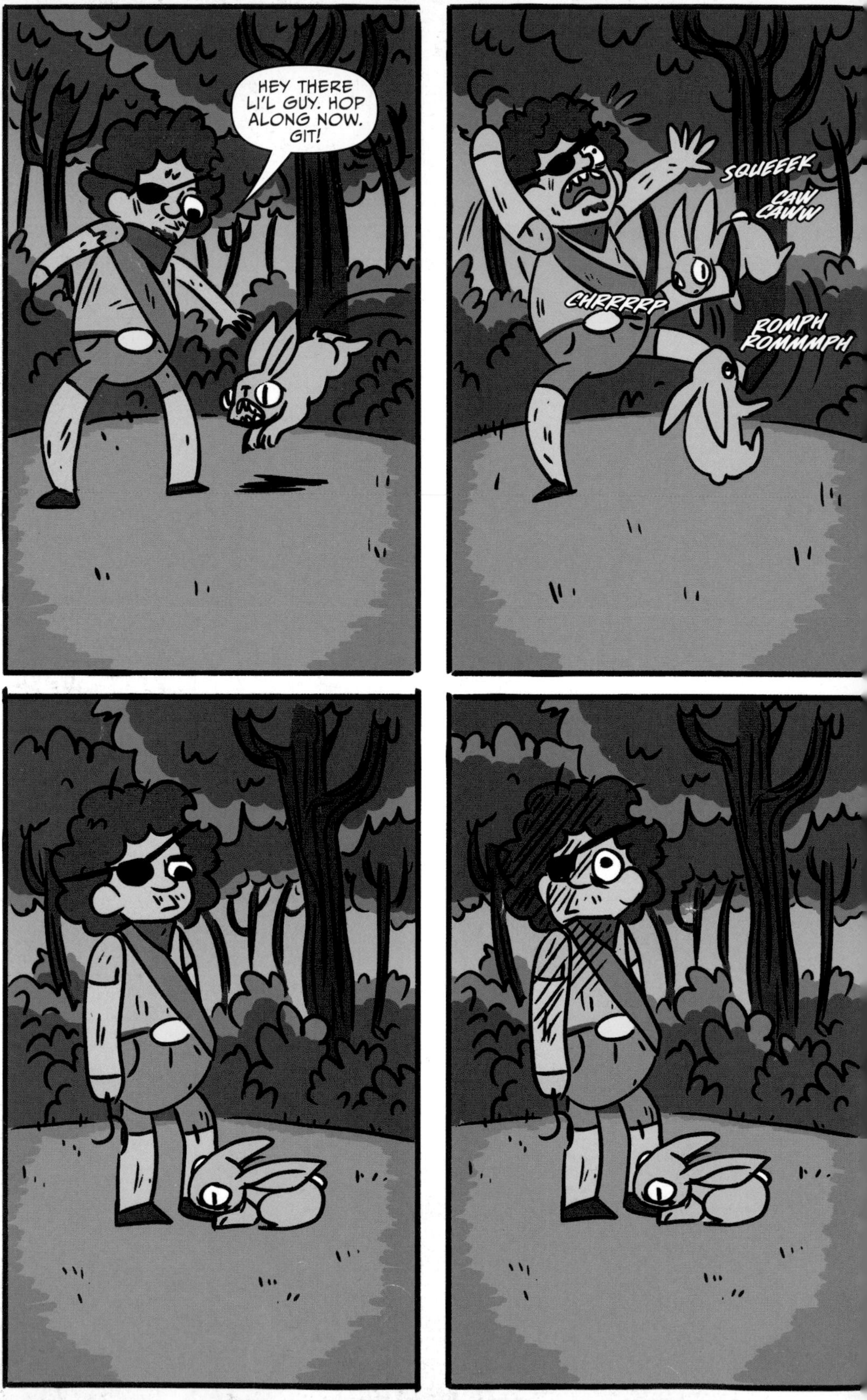
HEY THERE LI'L GUY. HOP ALONG NOW. GIT!
SQUEEEK
CAW CAWW
CHRRRRP
ROMPH ROMMMPH

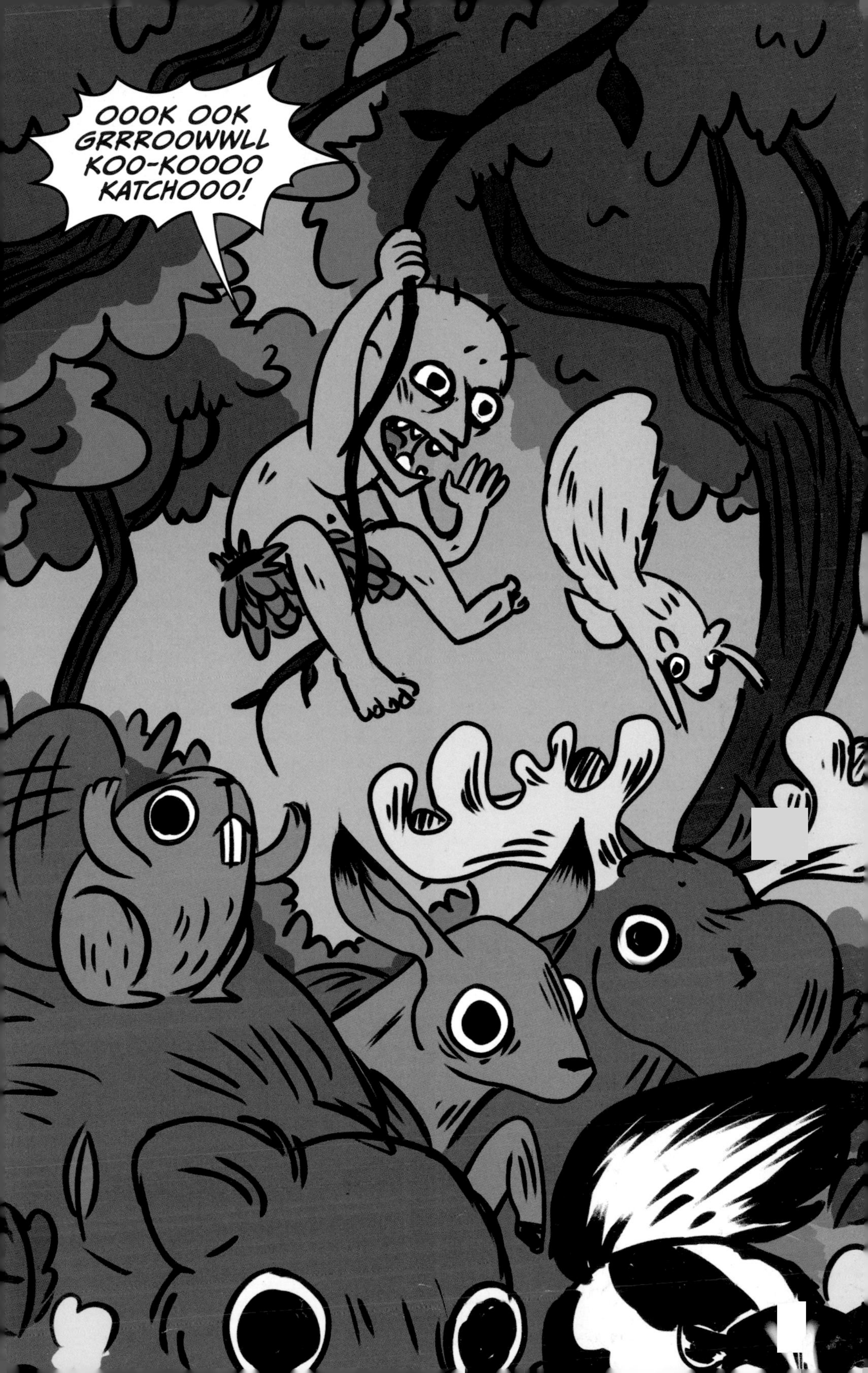
OOOK OOK GRRROOWWLL KOO-KOOOO KATCHOOO!

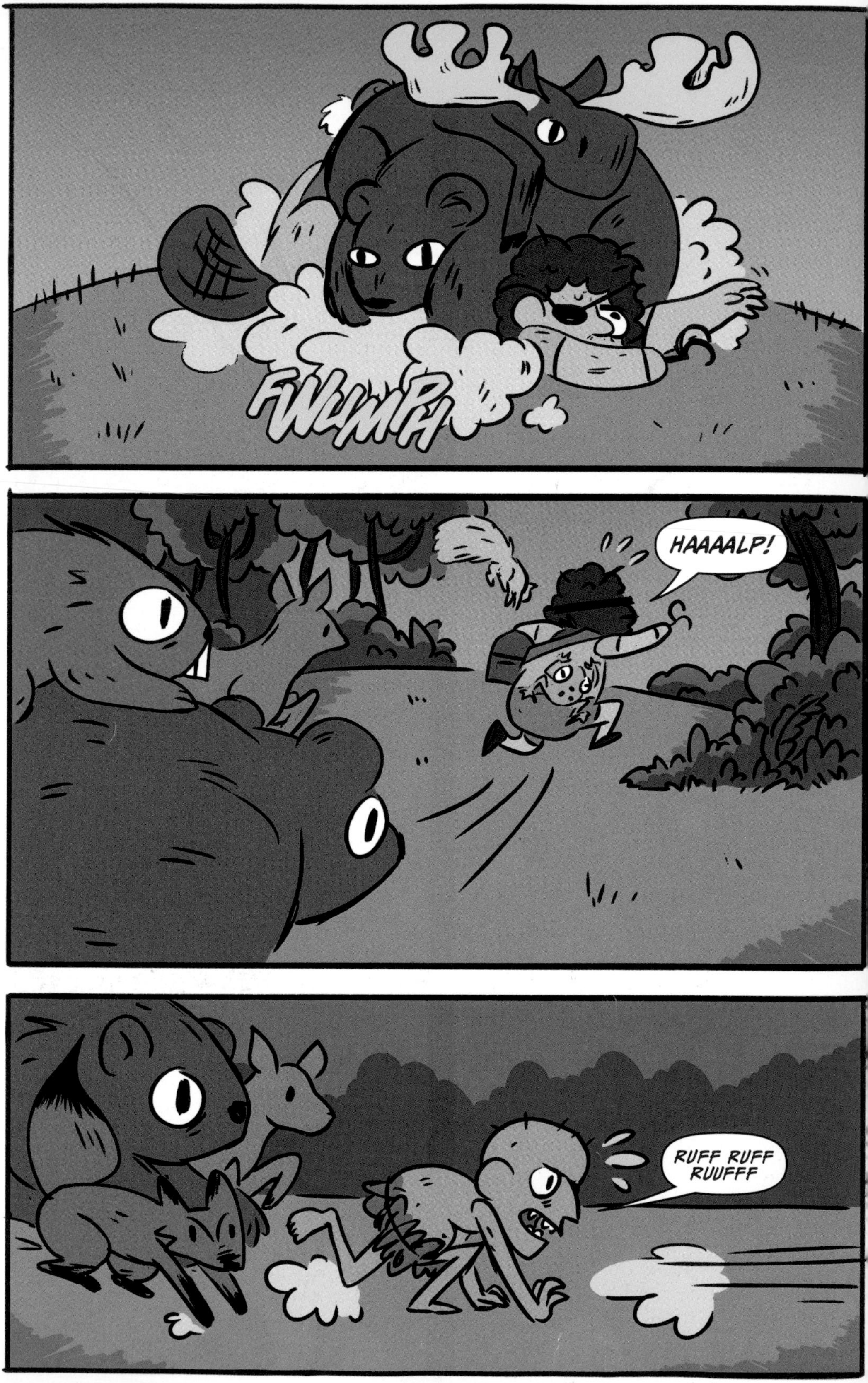
FWUMPH
HAAAALP!
RUFF RUFF RUUFFF

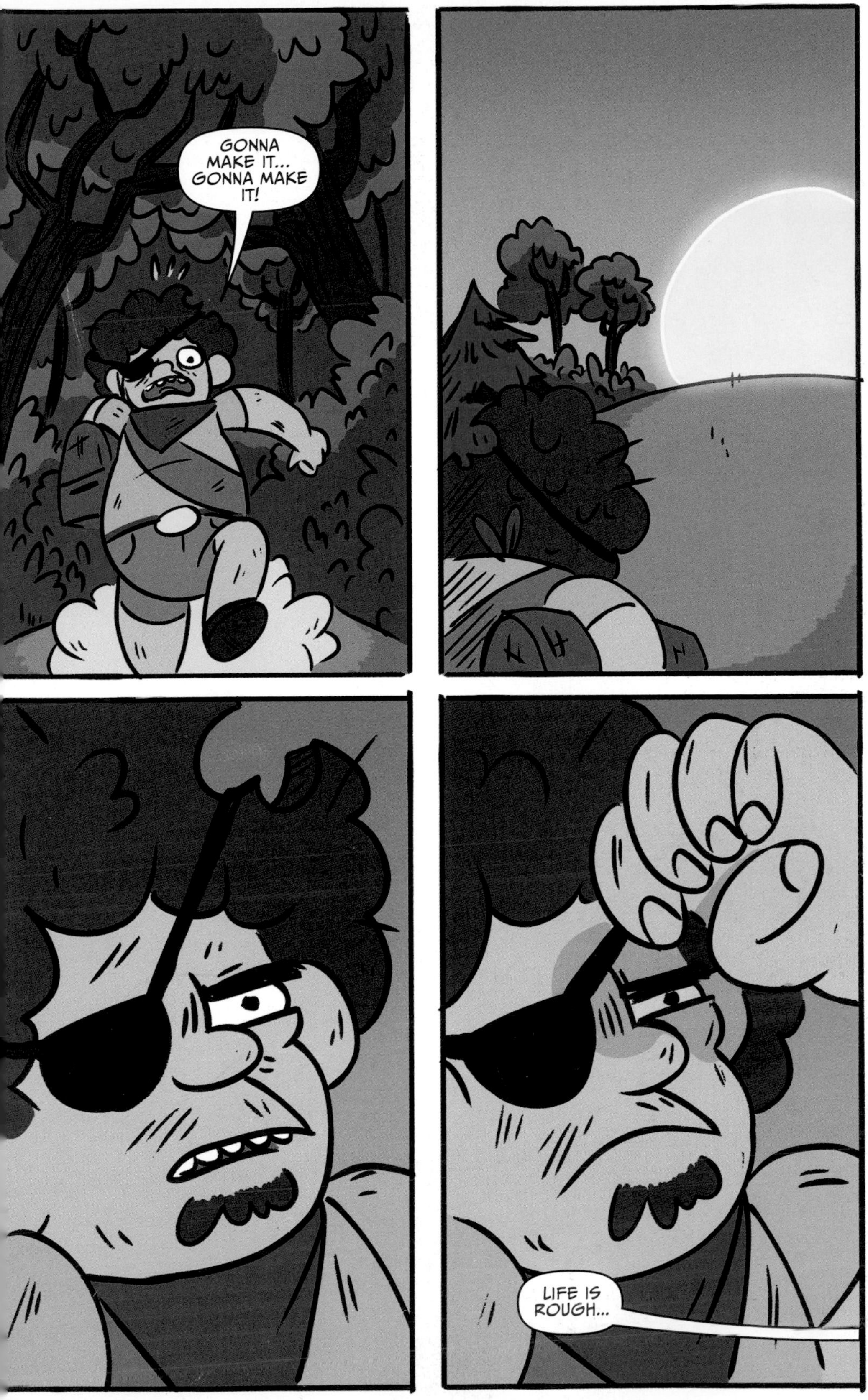
GONNA MAKE IT... GONNA MAKE IT!
LIFE IS ROUGH...

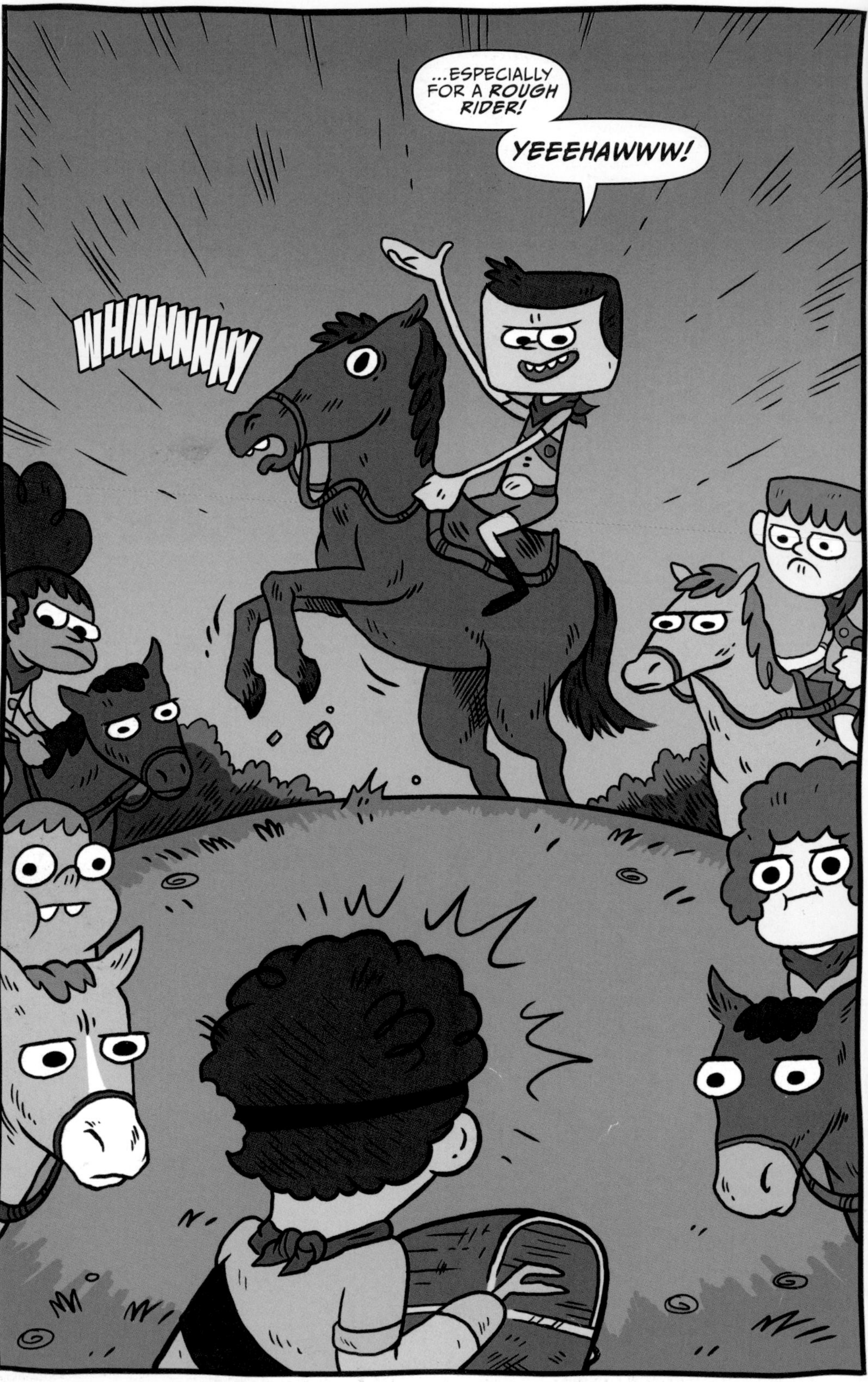
...ESPECIALLY FOR A ROUGH RIDER!
YEEEHAWWW!
WHINNNNNY

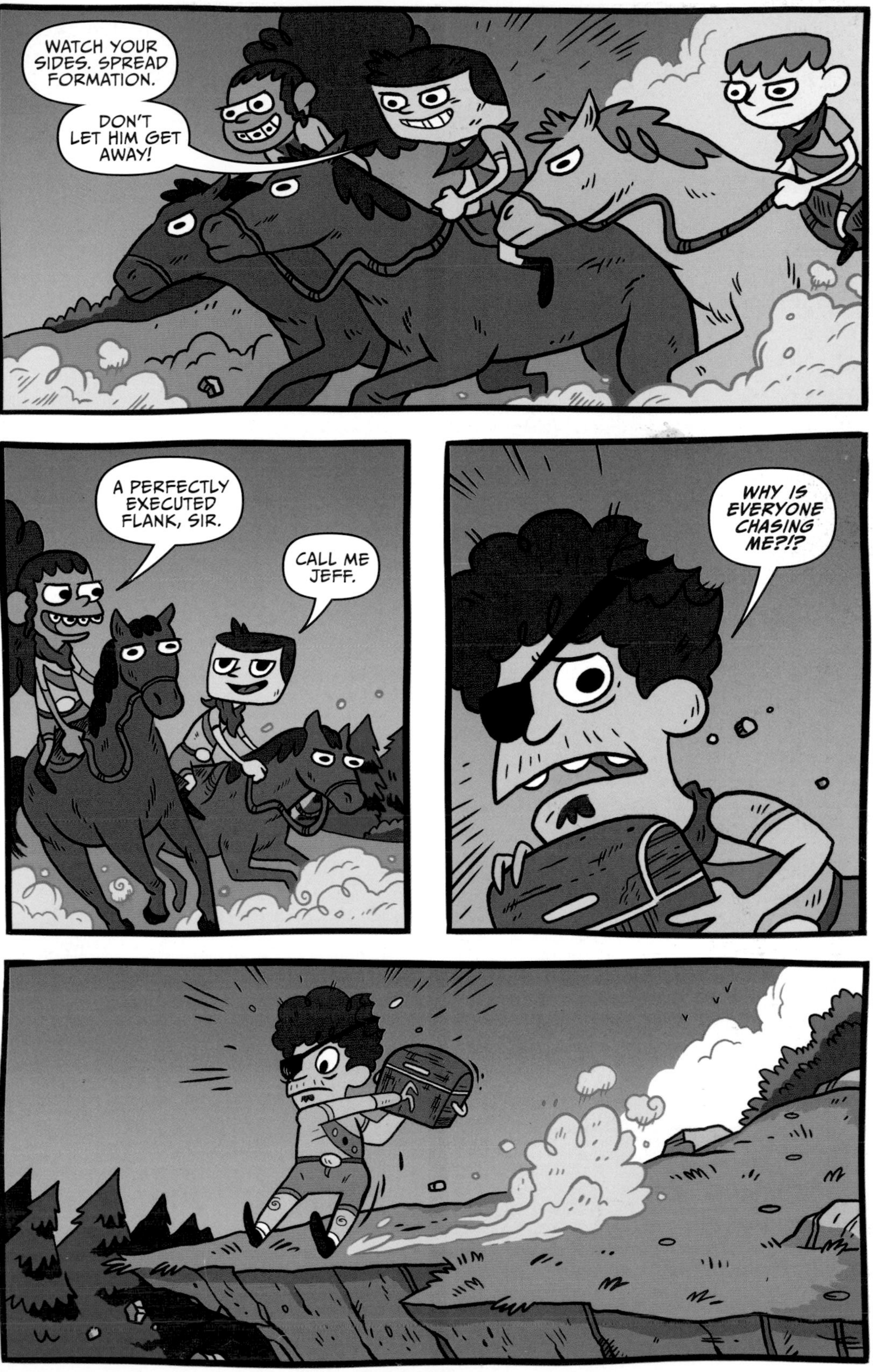
WATCH YOUR SIDES. SPREAD FORMATION.
DON'T LET HIM GET AWAY!
A PERFECTLY EXECUTED FLANK, SIR.
CALL ME JEFF.
WHY IS EVERYONE CHASING ME?!?

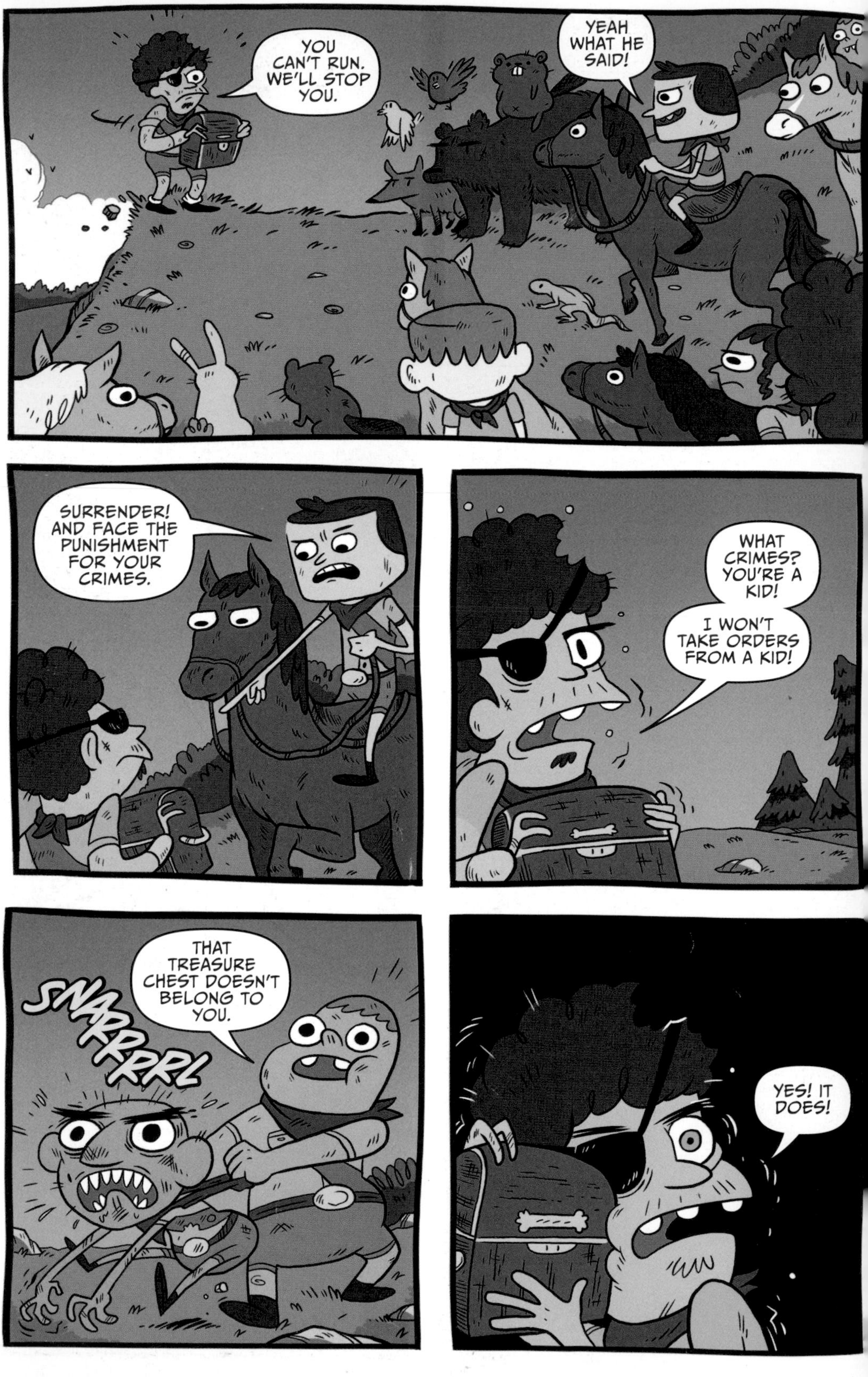
YOU CAN'T RUN. WE'LL STOP YOU.
YEAH WHAT HE SAID!
SURRENDER! AND FACE THE PUNISHMENT FOR YOUR CRIMES.
WHAT CRIMES? YOU'RE A KID!
I WON'T TAKE ORDERS FROM A KID!
THAT TREASURE CHEST DOESN'T BELONG TO YOU.
SNARRRRL
YES! IT DOES!

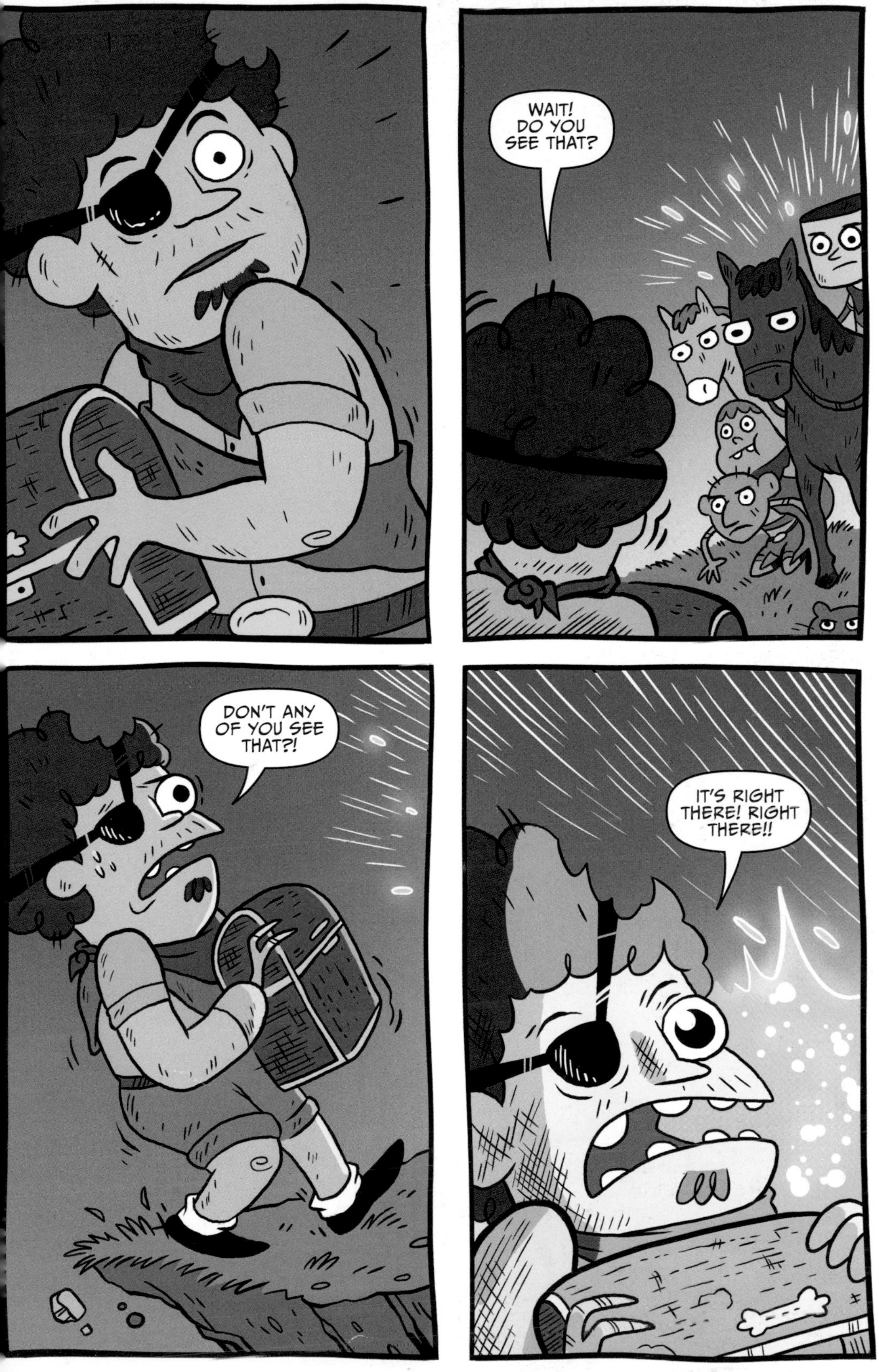
WAIT! DO YOU SEE THAT?
DON'T ANY OF YOU SEE THAT?!
IT'S RIGHT THERE! RIGHT THERE!!

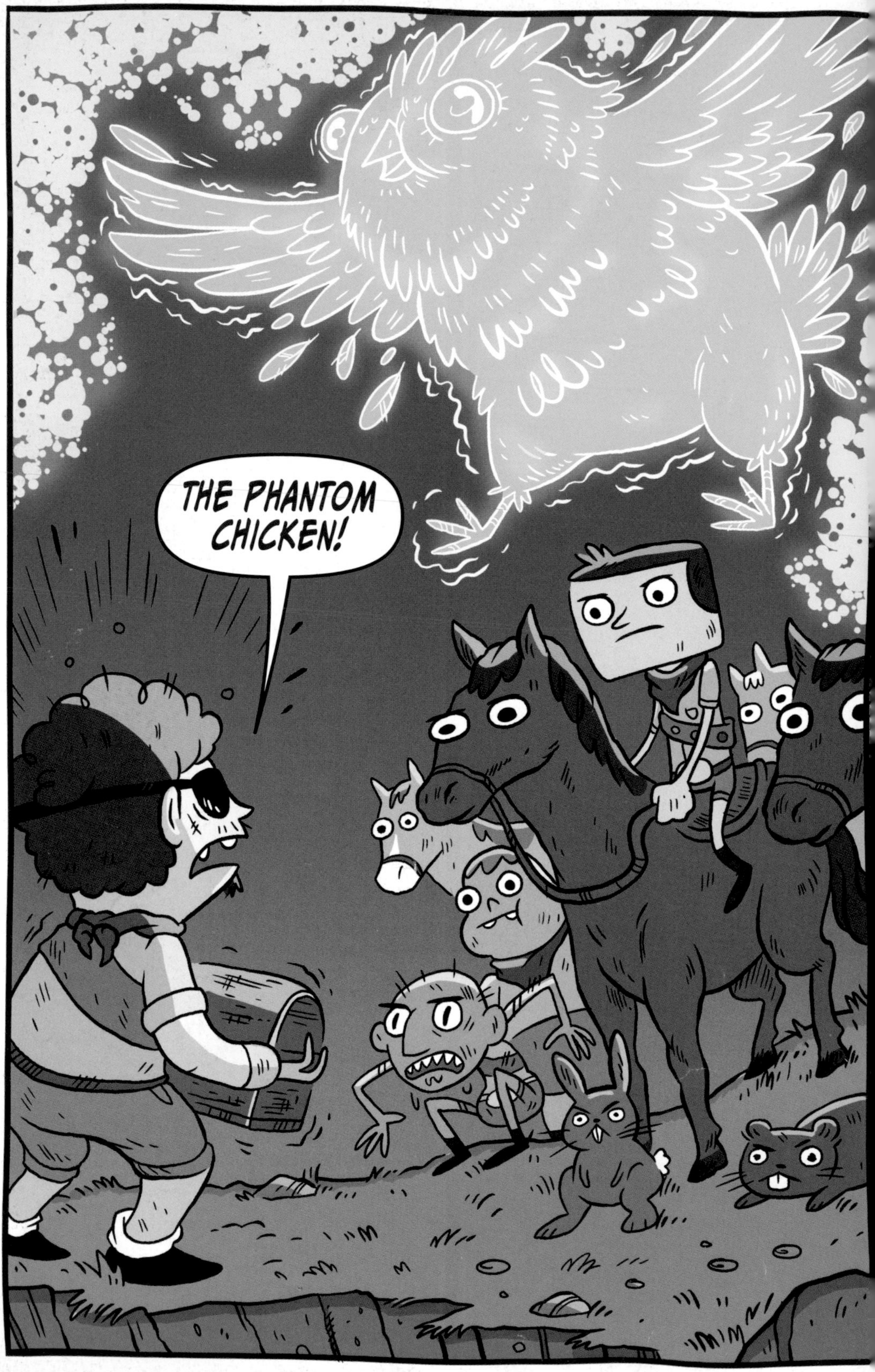
THE PHANTOM CHICKEN!

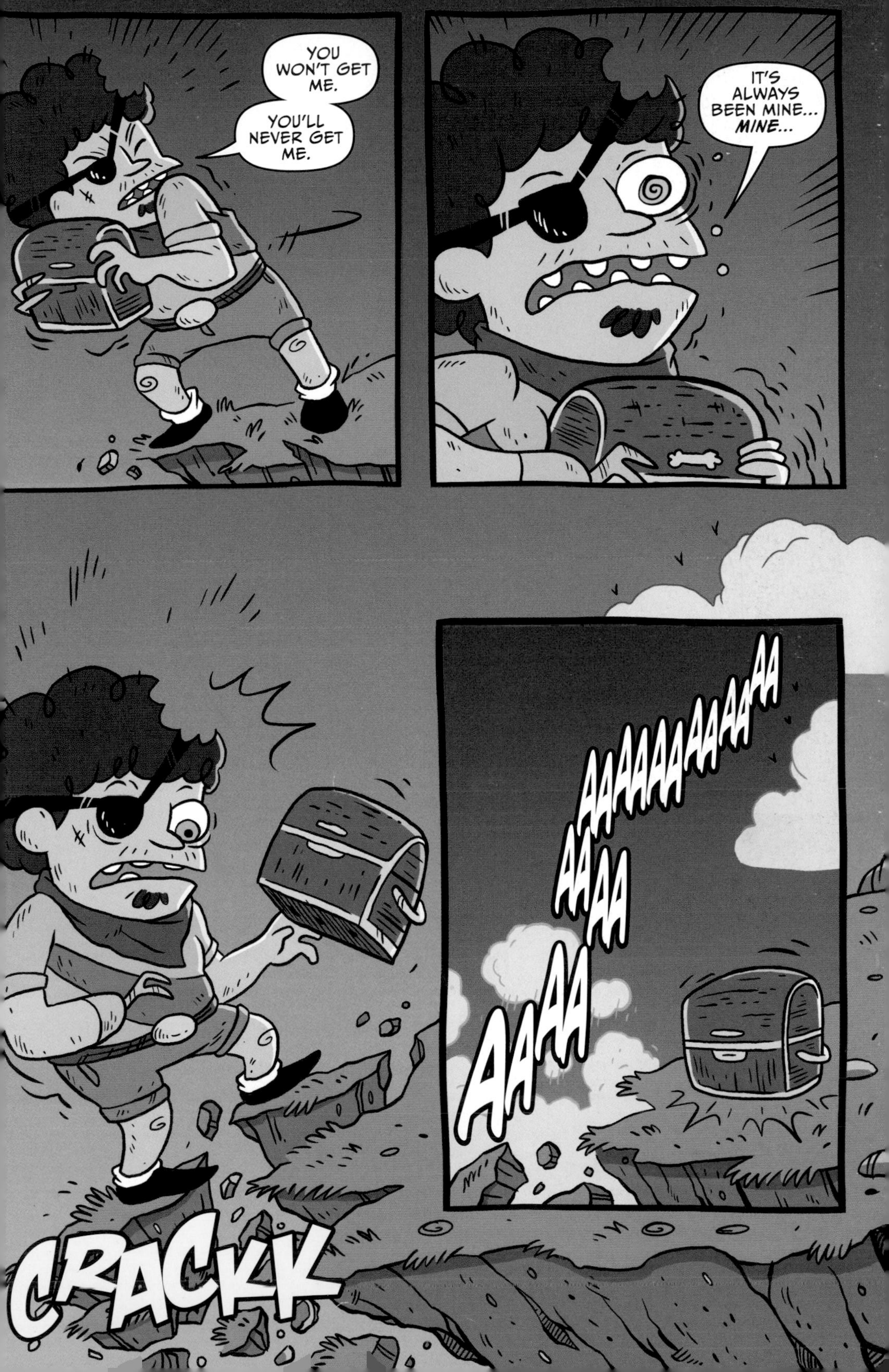
YOU WON'T GET ME.
YOU'LL NEVER GET ME.
IT'S ALWAYS BEEN MINE... *MINE...*
AAAAAAAAAAAAAAAAAAAA
CRACKK

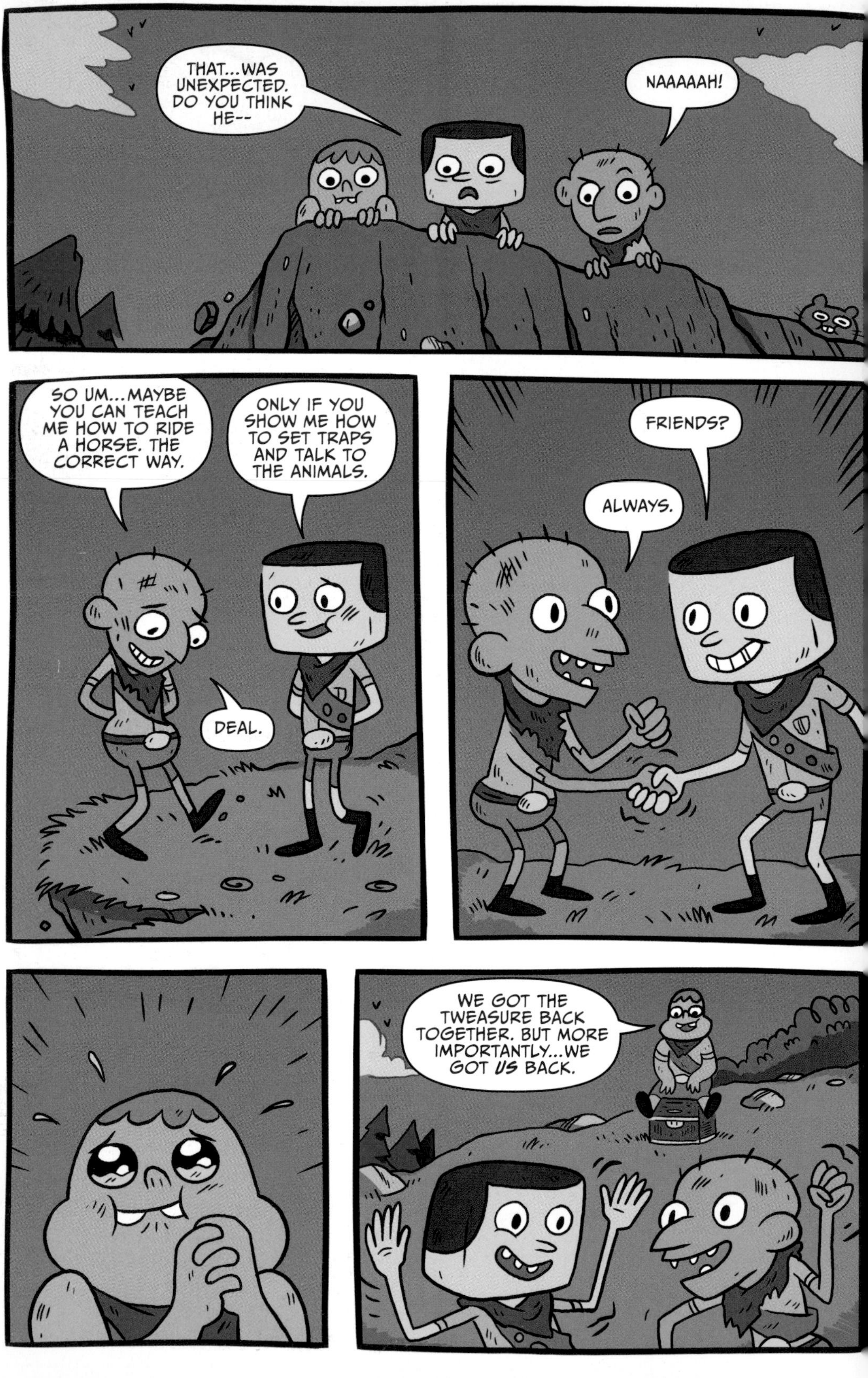
THAT...WAS UNEXPECTED. DO YOU THINK HE--
NAAAAAH!
SO UM...MAYBE YOU CAN TEACH ME HOW TO RIDE A HORSE. THE CORRECT WAY.
ONLY IF YOU SHOW ME HOW TO SET TRAPS AND TALK TO THE ANIMALS.
DEAL.
FRIENDS?
ALWAYS.
WE GOT THE TWEASURE BACK TOGETHER. BUT MORE IMPORTANTLY...WE GOT US BACK.

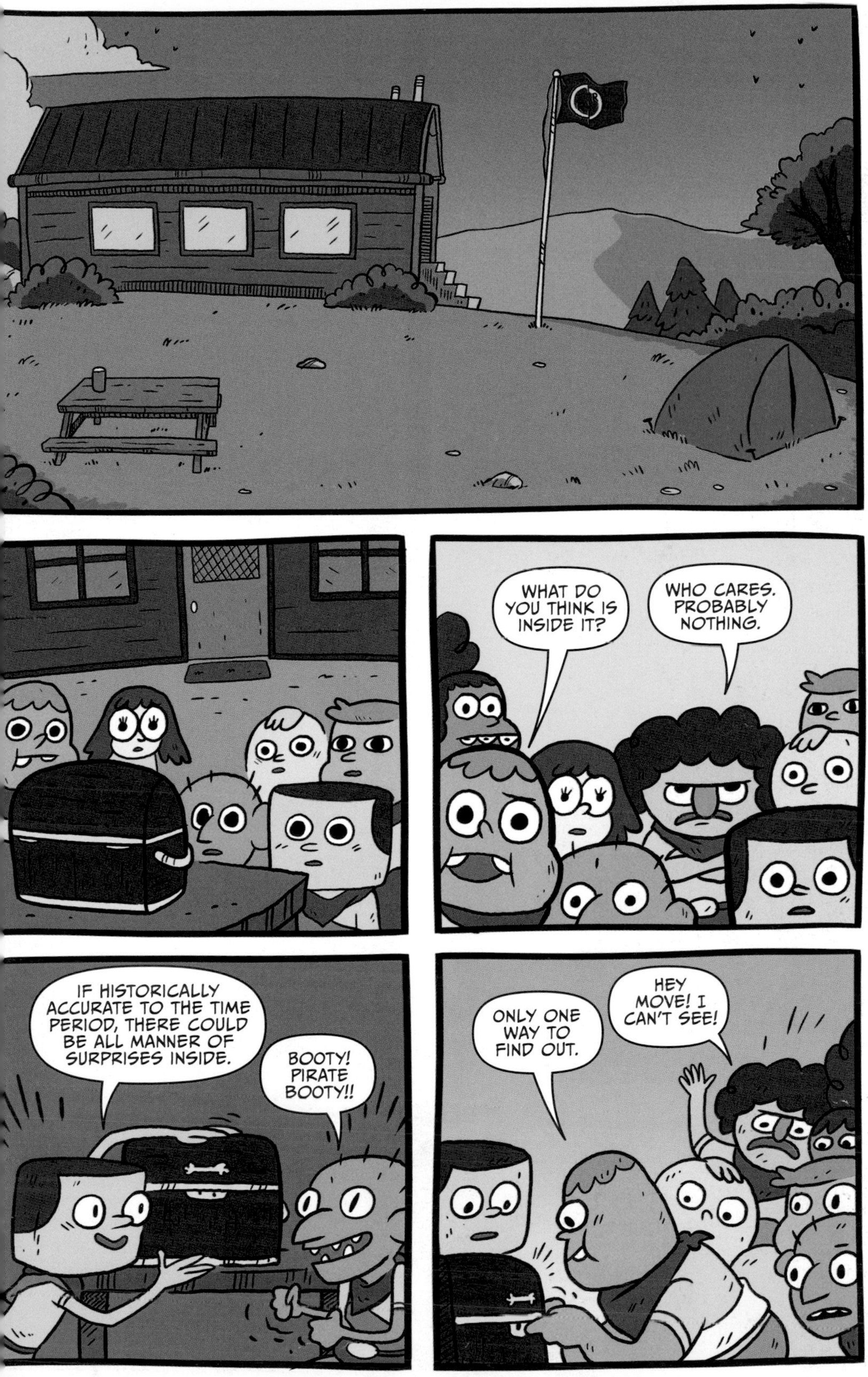
WHAT DO YOU THINK IS INSIDE IT?
WHO CARES. PROBABLY NOTHING.
IF HISTORICALLY ACCURATE TO THE TIME PERIOD, THERE COULD BE ALL MANNER OF SURPRISES INSIDE.
BOOTY! PIRATE BOOTY!!
ONLY ONE WAY TO FIND OUT.
HEY MOVE! I CAN'T SEE!

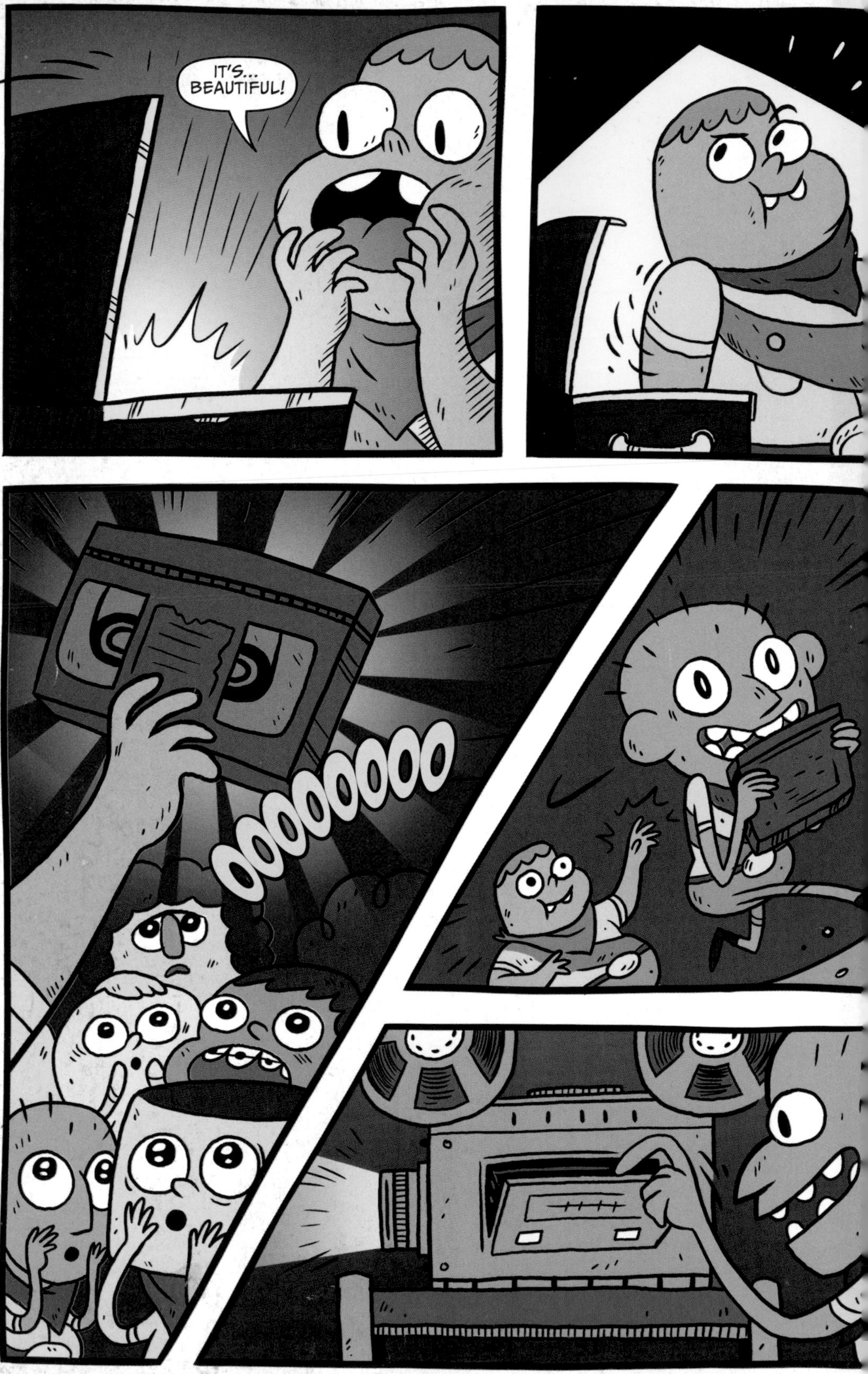
IT'S... BEAUTIFUL!
OOOOOOOOO

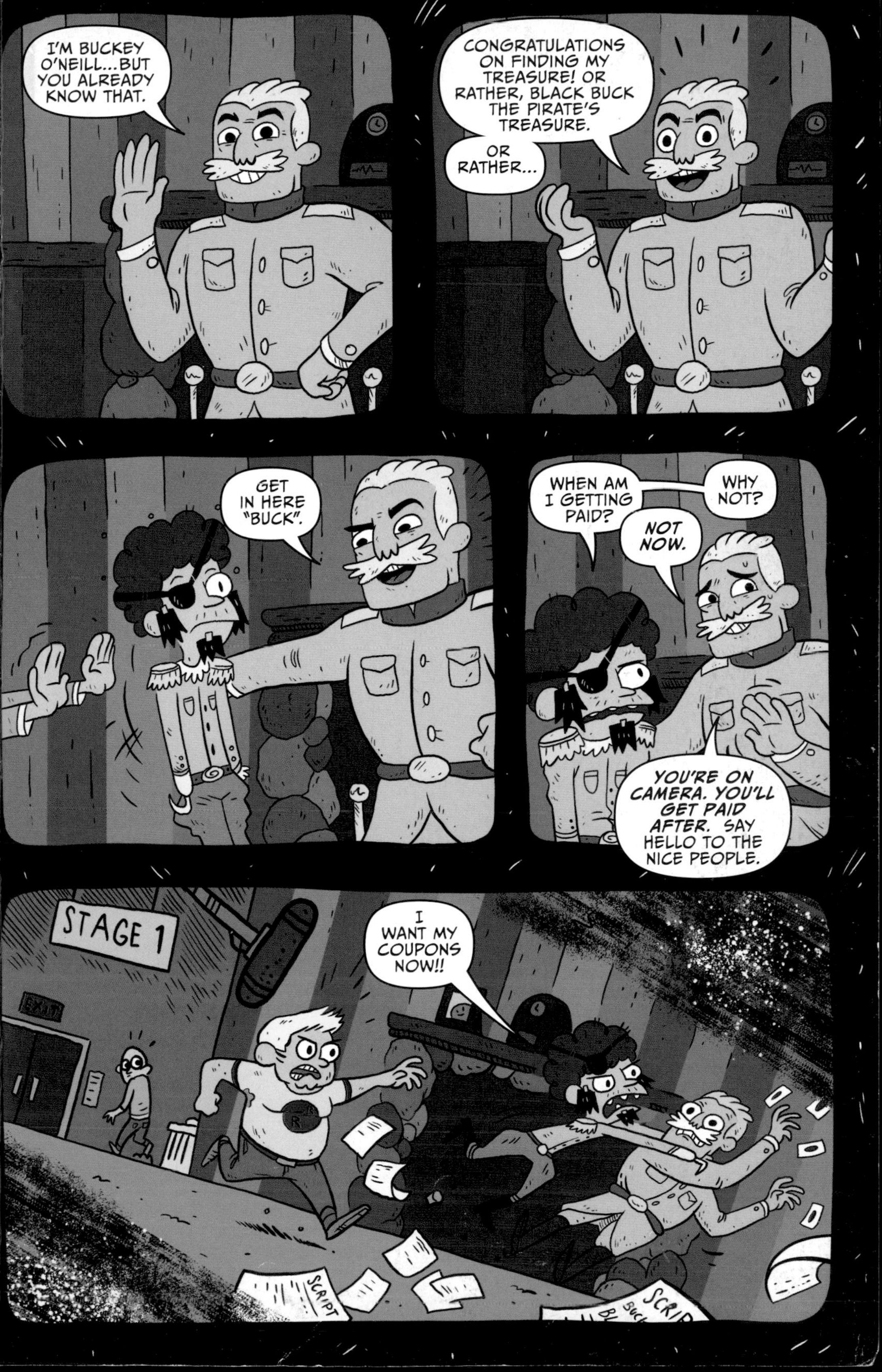
I'M BUCKEY O'NEILL...BUT YOU ALREADY KNOW THAT.
CONGRATULATIONS ON FINDING MY TREASURE! OR RATHER, BLACK BUCK THE PIRATE'S TREASURE.
OR RATHER...
GET IN HERE "BUCK".
WHEN AM I GETTING PAID?
NOT NOW.
WHY NOT?
YOU'RE ON CAMERA. YOU'LL GET PAID AFTER. SAY HELLO TO THE NICE PEOPLE.
STAGE 1
EXIT
I WANT MY COUPONS NOW!!
SCRIPT
SCRIP

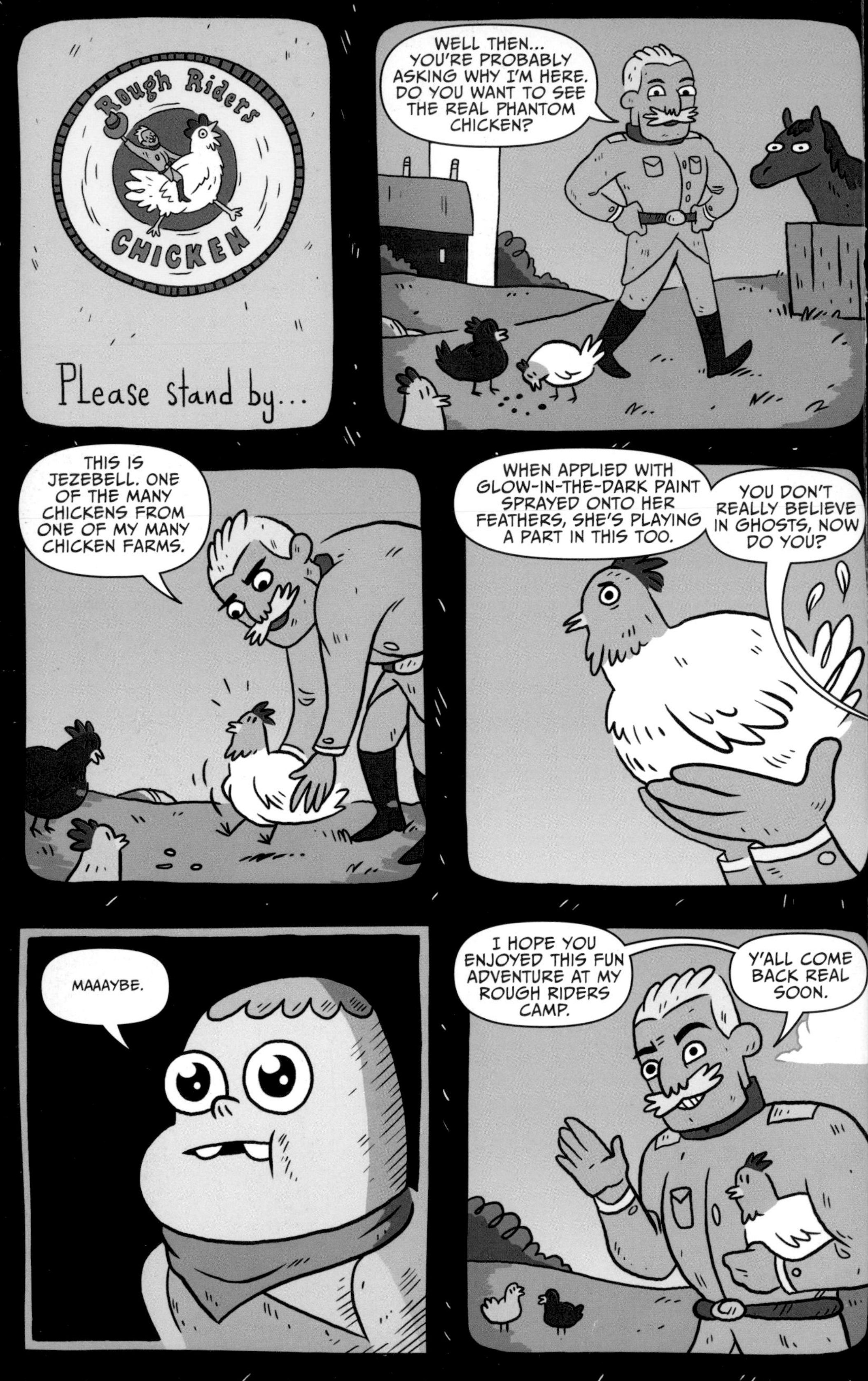
Rough Riders
CHICKEN
Please stand by...
WELL THEN... YOU'RE PROBABLY ASKING WHY I'M HERE. DO YOU WANT TO SEE THE REAL PHANTOM CHICKEN?
THIS IS JEZEBELL. ONE OF THE MANY CHICKENS FROM ONE OF MY MANY CHICKEN FARMS.
WHEN APPLIED WITH GLOW-IN-THE-DARK PAINT SPRAYED ONTO HER FEATHERS, SHE'S PLAYING A PART IN THIS TOO.
YOU DON'T REALLY BELIEVE IN GHOSTS, NOW DO YOU?
MAAAYBE.
I HOPE YOU ENJOYED THIS FUN ADVENTURE AT MY ROUGH RIDERS CAMP.
Y'ALL COME BACK REAL SOON.

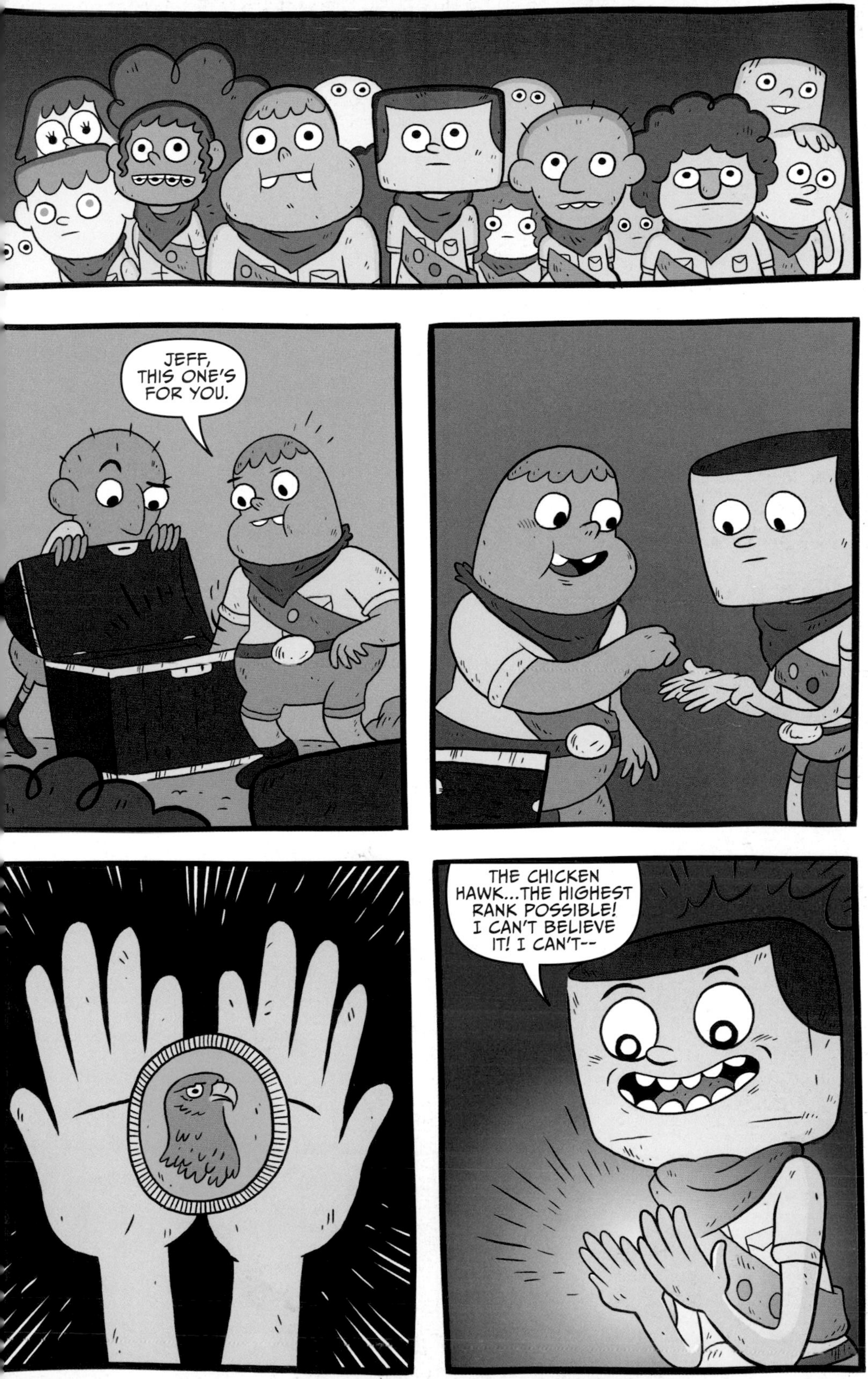
JEFF, THIS ONE'S FOR YOU.
THE CHICKEN HAWK...THE HIGHEST RANK POSSIBLE! I CAN'T BELIEVE IT! I CAN'T--

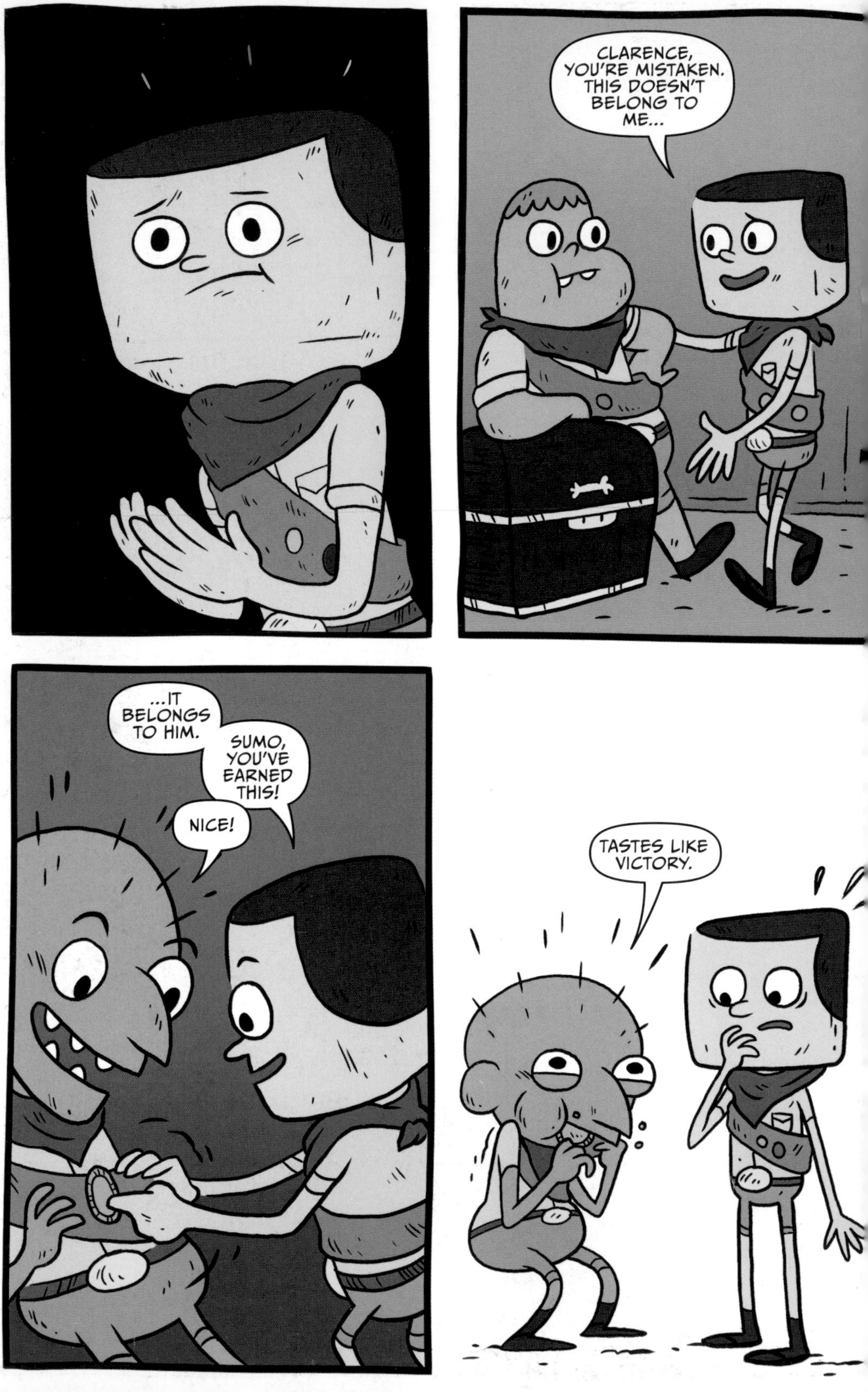
CLARENCE, YOU'RE MISTAKEN. THIS DOESN'T BELONG TO ME...
...IT BELONGS TO HIM.
SUMO, YOU'VE EARNED THIS!
NICE!
TASTES LIKE VICTORY.

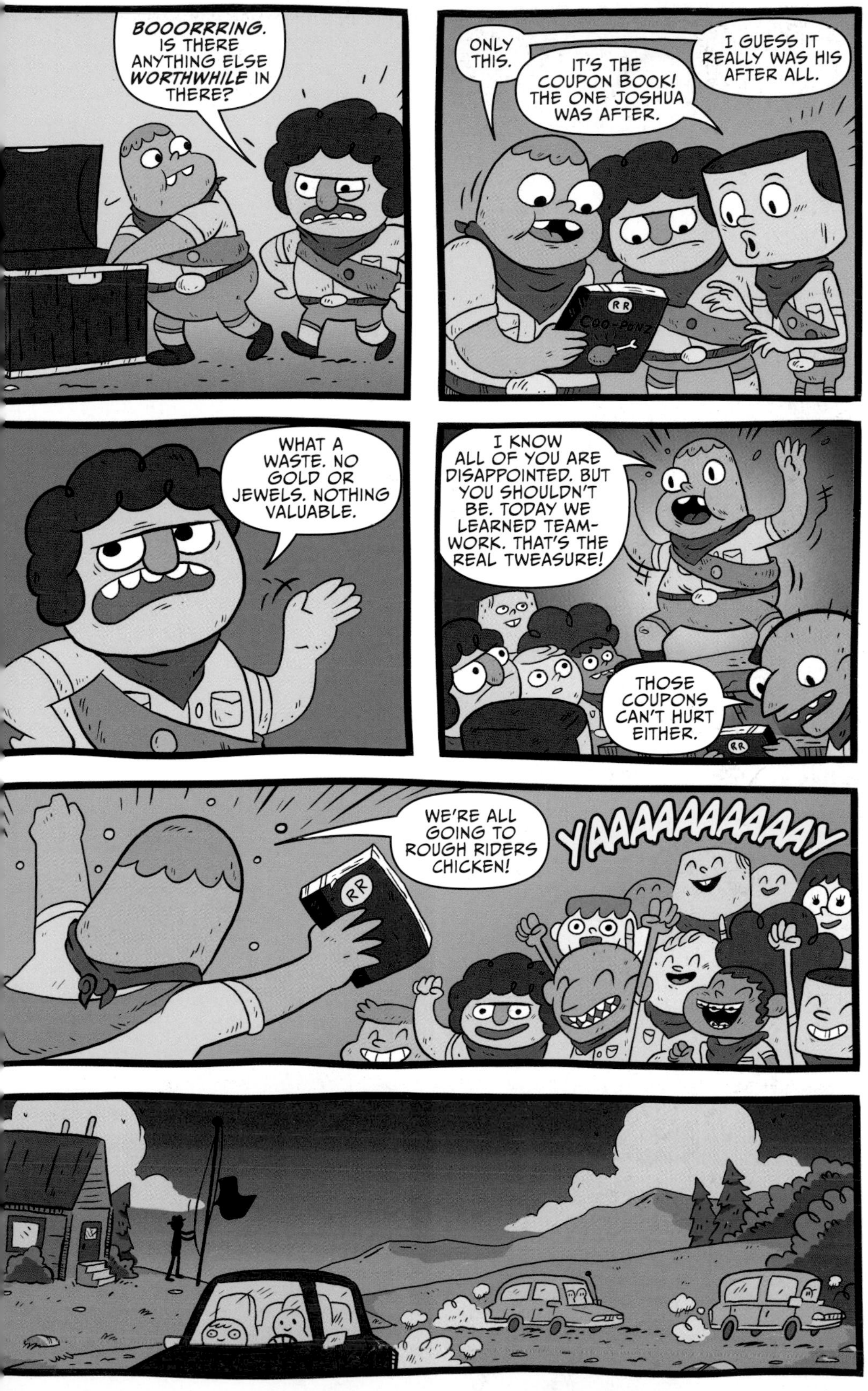

BOOORRRING. IS THERE ANYTHING ELSE WORTHWHILE IN THERE?
ONLY THIS.
IT'S THE COUPON BOOK! THE ONE JOSHUA WAS AFTER.
I GUESS IT REALLY WAS HIS AFTER ALL.
RR
COO-PUNZ
WHAT A WASTE. NO GOLD OR JEWELS. NOTHING VALUABLE.
I KNOW ALL OF YOU ARE DISAPPOINTED. BUT YOU SHOULDN'T BE. TODAY WE LEARNED TEAM-WORK. THAT'S THE REAL TWEASURE!
THOSE COUPONS CAN'T HURT EITHER.
RR
WE'RE ALL GOING TO ROUGH RIDERS CHICKEN!
YAAAAAAAAAAY
RR

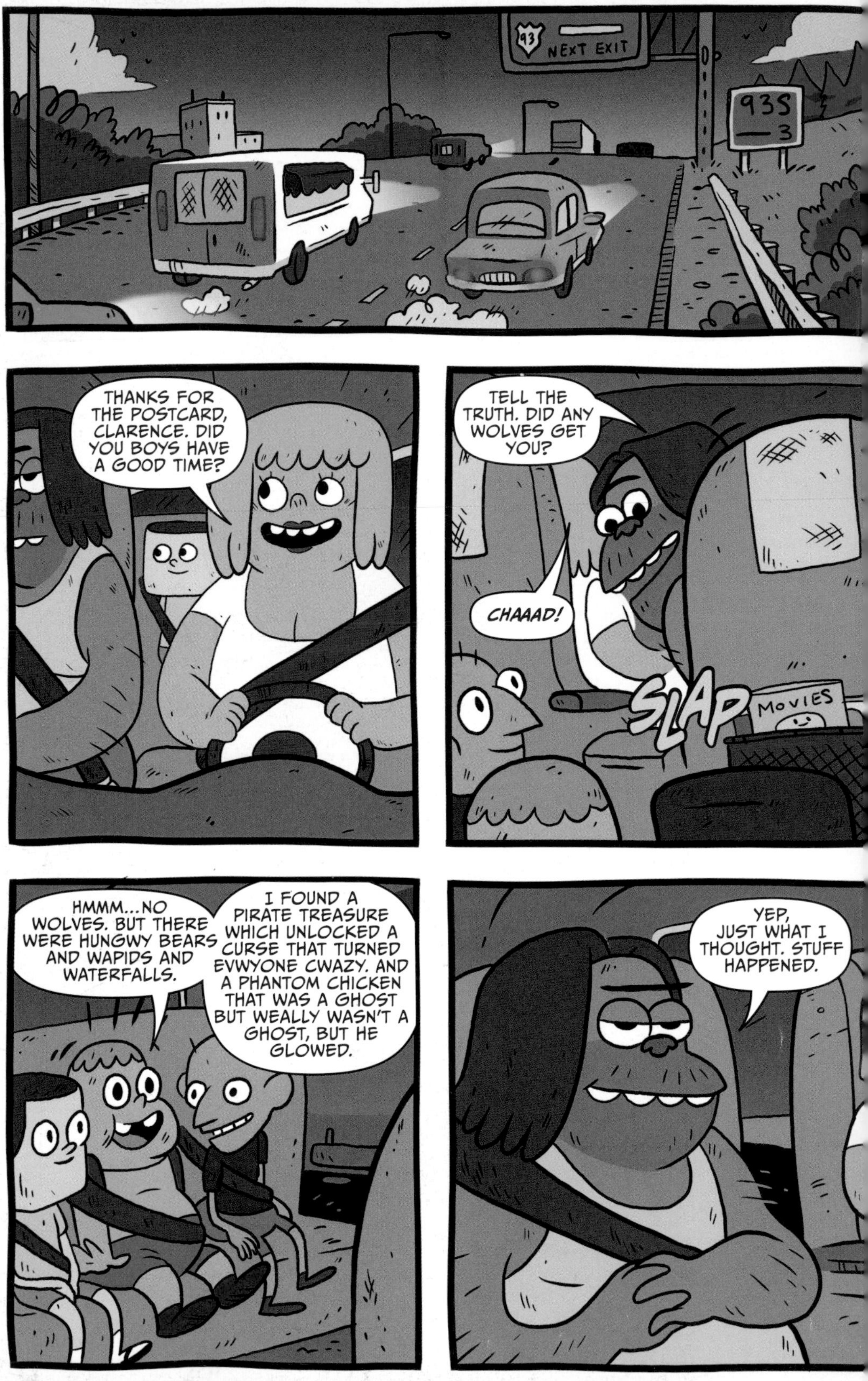
93
NEXT EXIT
935
3
THANKS FOR THE POSTCARD, CLARENCE. DID YOU BOYS HAVE A GOOD TIME?
TELL THE TRUTH. DID ANY WOLVES GET YOU?
CHAAAD!
SLAP
MOVIES
HMMM...NO WOLVES. BUT THERE WERE HUNGWY BEARS AND WAPIDS AND WATERFALLS.
I FOUND A PIRATE TREASURE WHICH UNLOCKED A CURSE THAT TURNED EVWYONE CWAZY. AND A PHANTOM CHICKEN THAT WAS A GHOST BUT WEALLY WASN'T A GHOST, BUT HE GLOWED.
YEP, JUST WHAT I THOUGHT. STUFF HAPPENED.

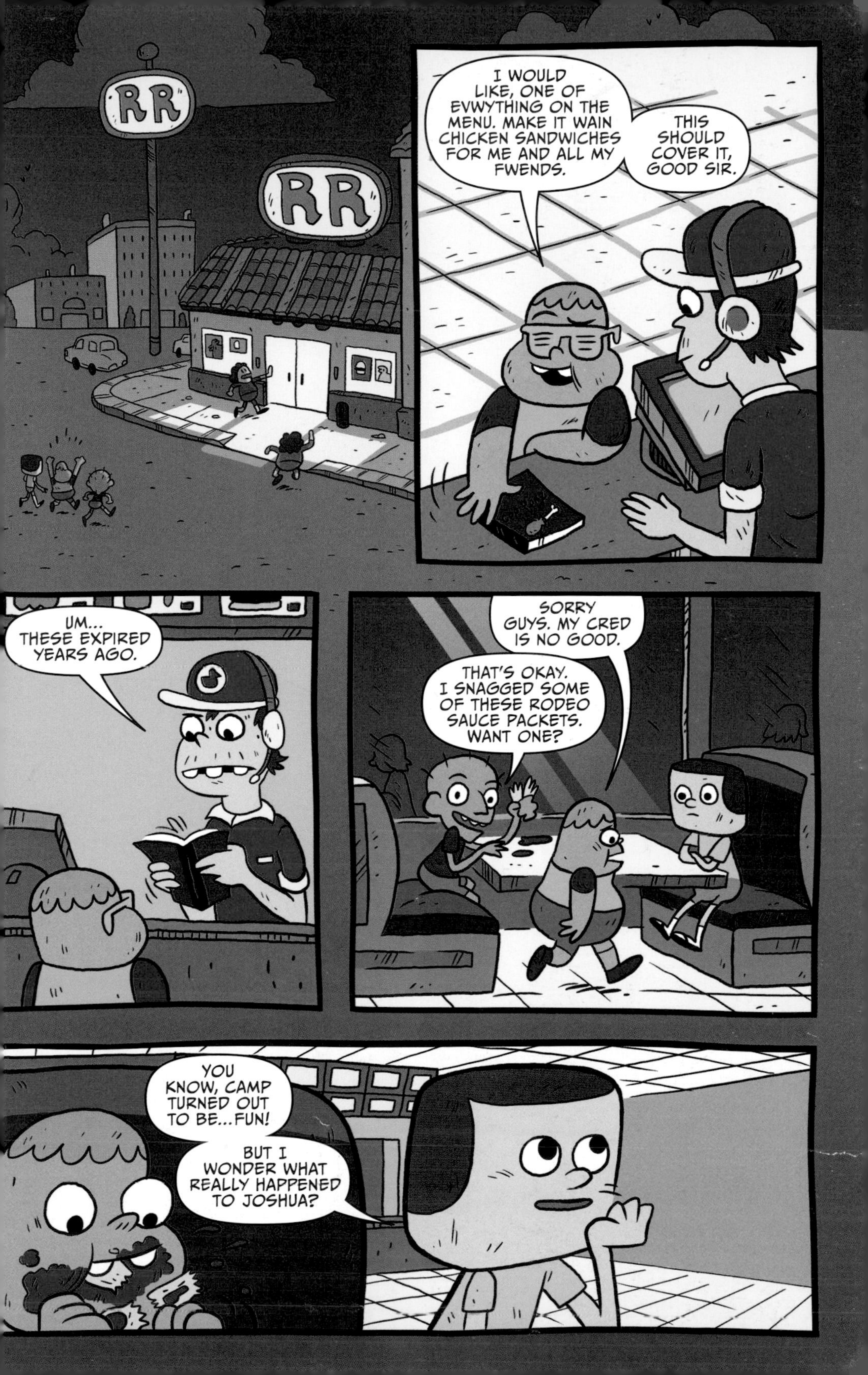
RR
RR
I WOULD LIKE, ONE OF EVWYTHING ON THE MENU. MAKE IT WAIN CHICKEN SANDWICHES FOR ME AND ALL MY FWENDS.
THIS SHOULD COVER IT, GOOD SIR.
UM... THESE EXPIRED YEARS AGO.
SORRY GUYS. MY CRED IS NO GOOD.
THAT'S OKAY. I SNAGGED SOME OF THESE RODEO SAUCE PACKETS. WANT ONE?
YOU KNOW, CAMP TURNED OUT TO BE...FUN!
BUT I WONDER WHAT REALLY HAPPENED TO JOSHUA?

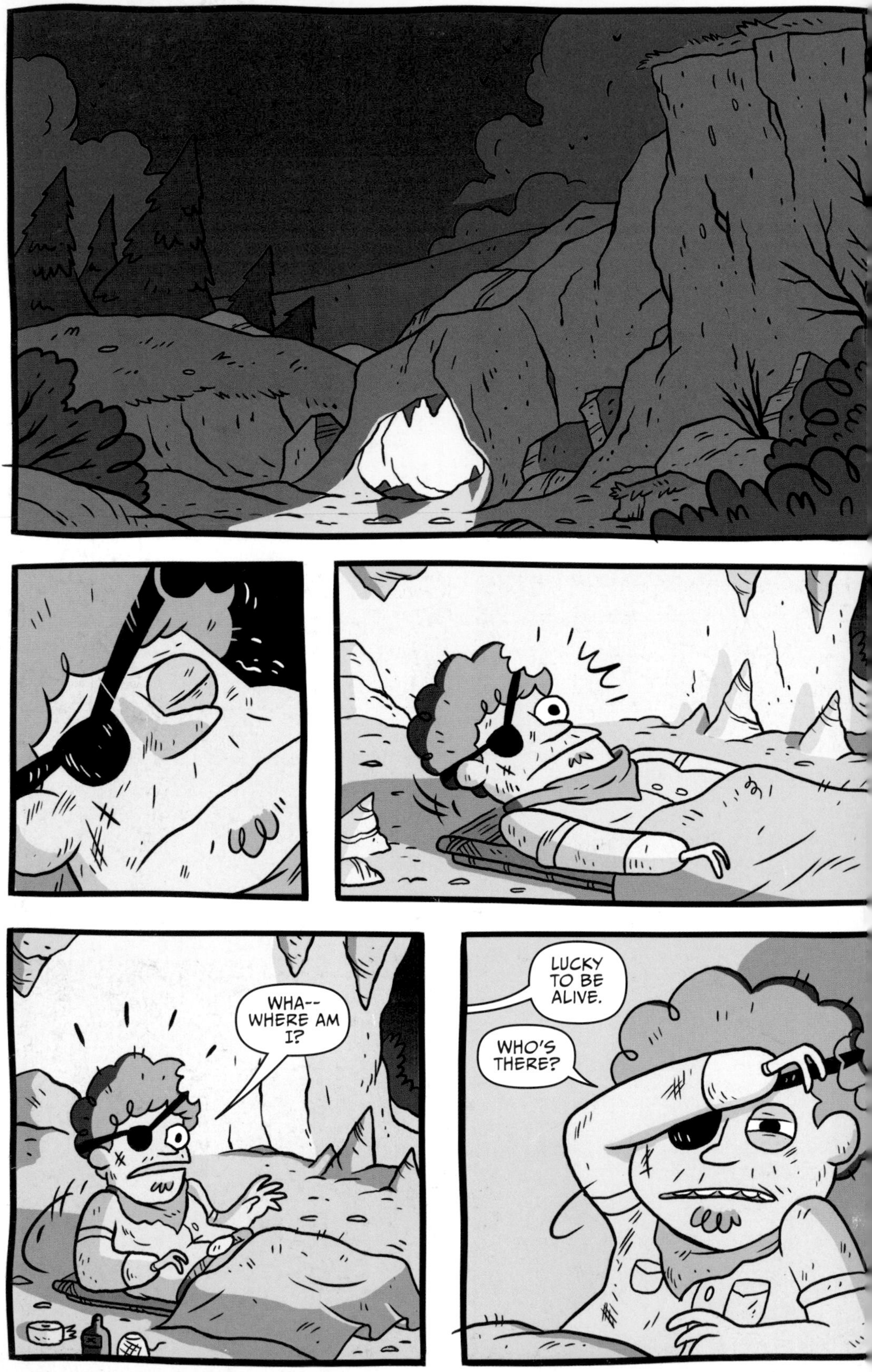
WHA-- WHERE AM I?
LUCKY TO BE ALIVE.
WHO'S THERE?

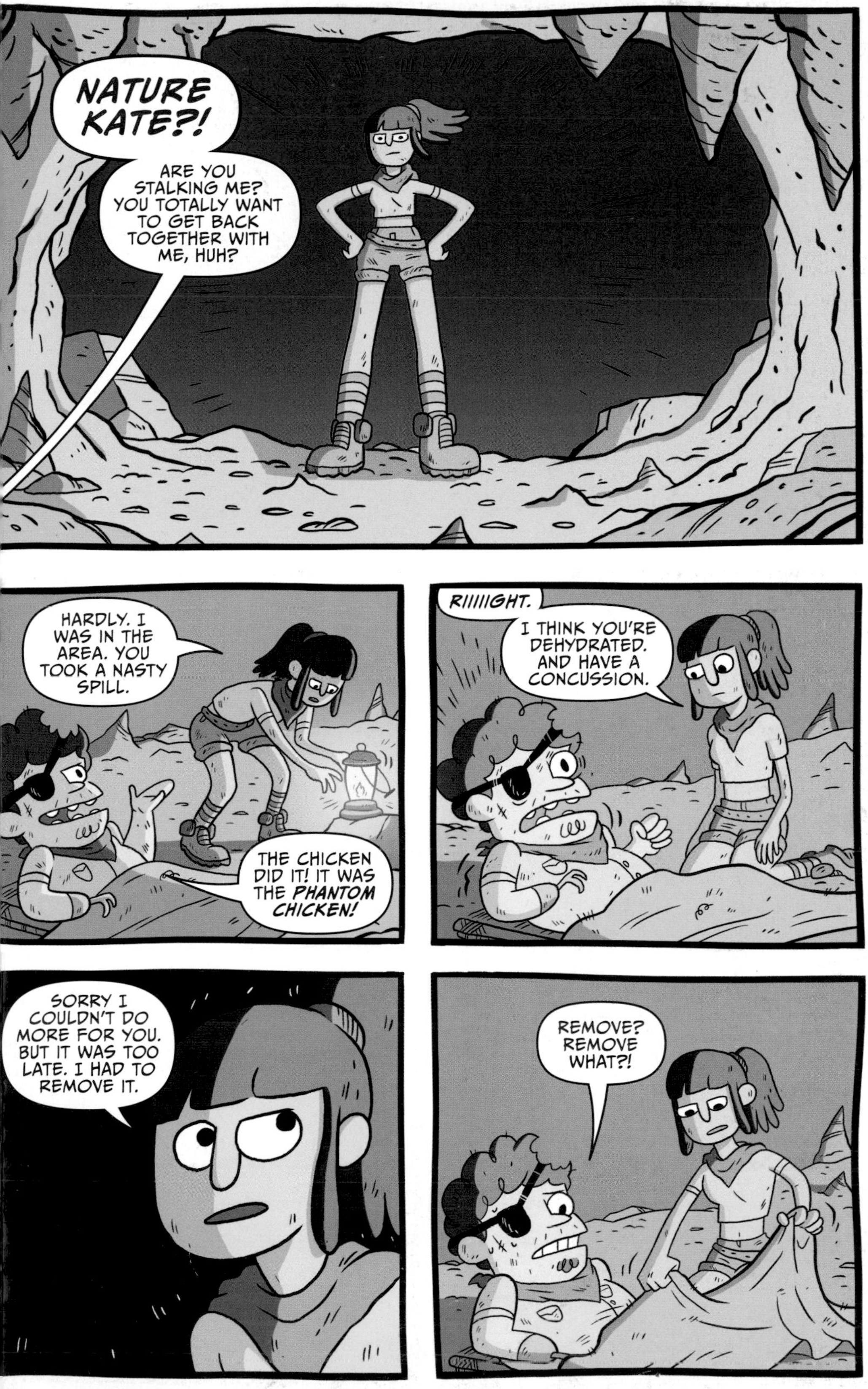
NATURE KATE?!
ARE YOU STALKING ME? YOU TOTALLY WANT TO GET BACK TOGETHER WITH ME, HUH?
HARDLY. I WAS IN THE AREA. YOU TOOK A NASTY SPILL.
THE CHICKEN DID IT! IT WAS THE *PHANTOM CHICKEN!*
RIIIIIGHT.
I THINK YOU'RE DEHYDRATED. AND HAVE A CONCUSSION.
SORRY I COULDN'T DO MORE FOR YOU. BUT IT WAS TOO LATE. I HAD TO REMOVE IT.
REMOVE? REMOVE WHAT?!

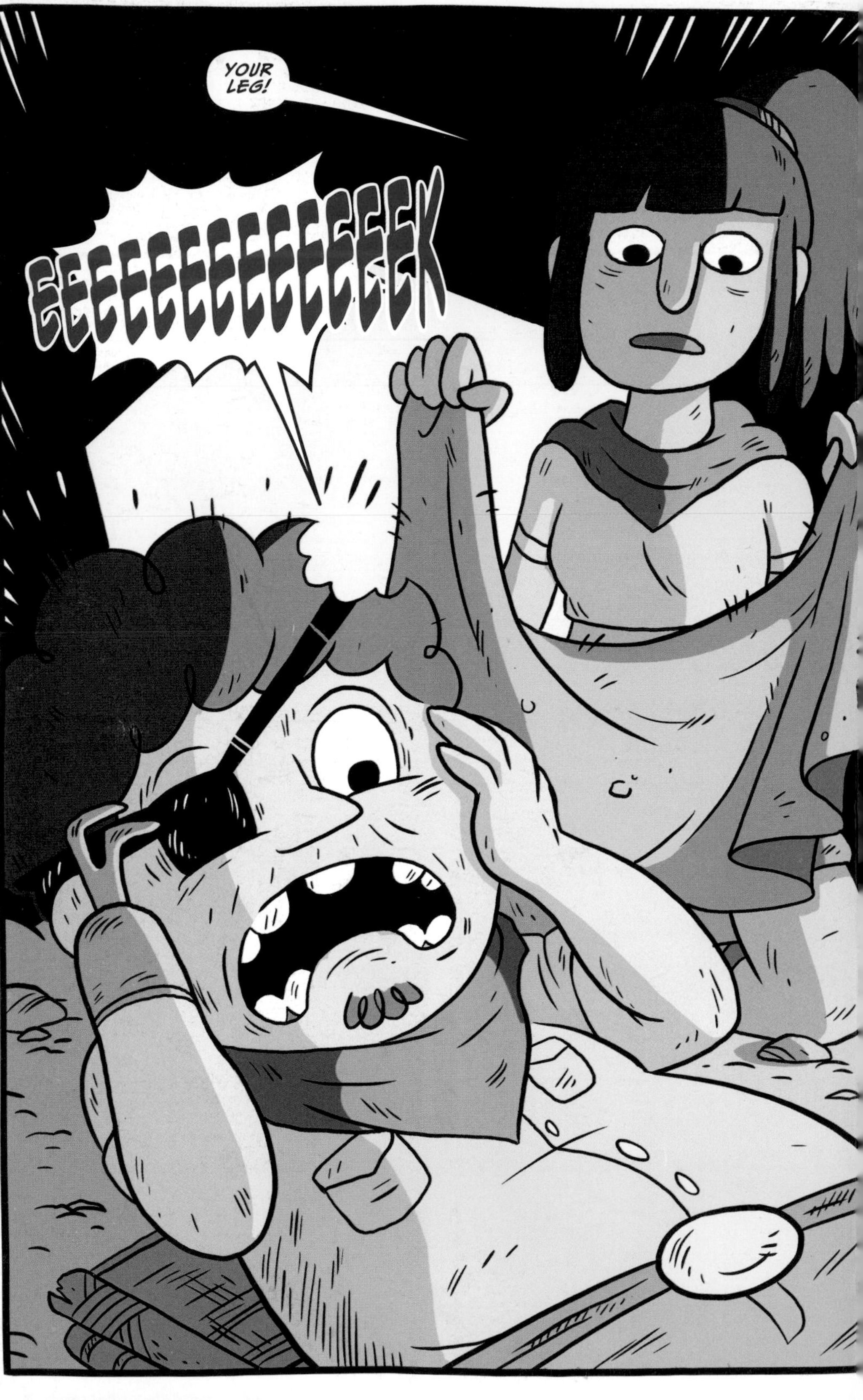
YOUR LEG!
EEEEEEEEEEEEEEK

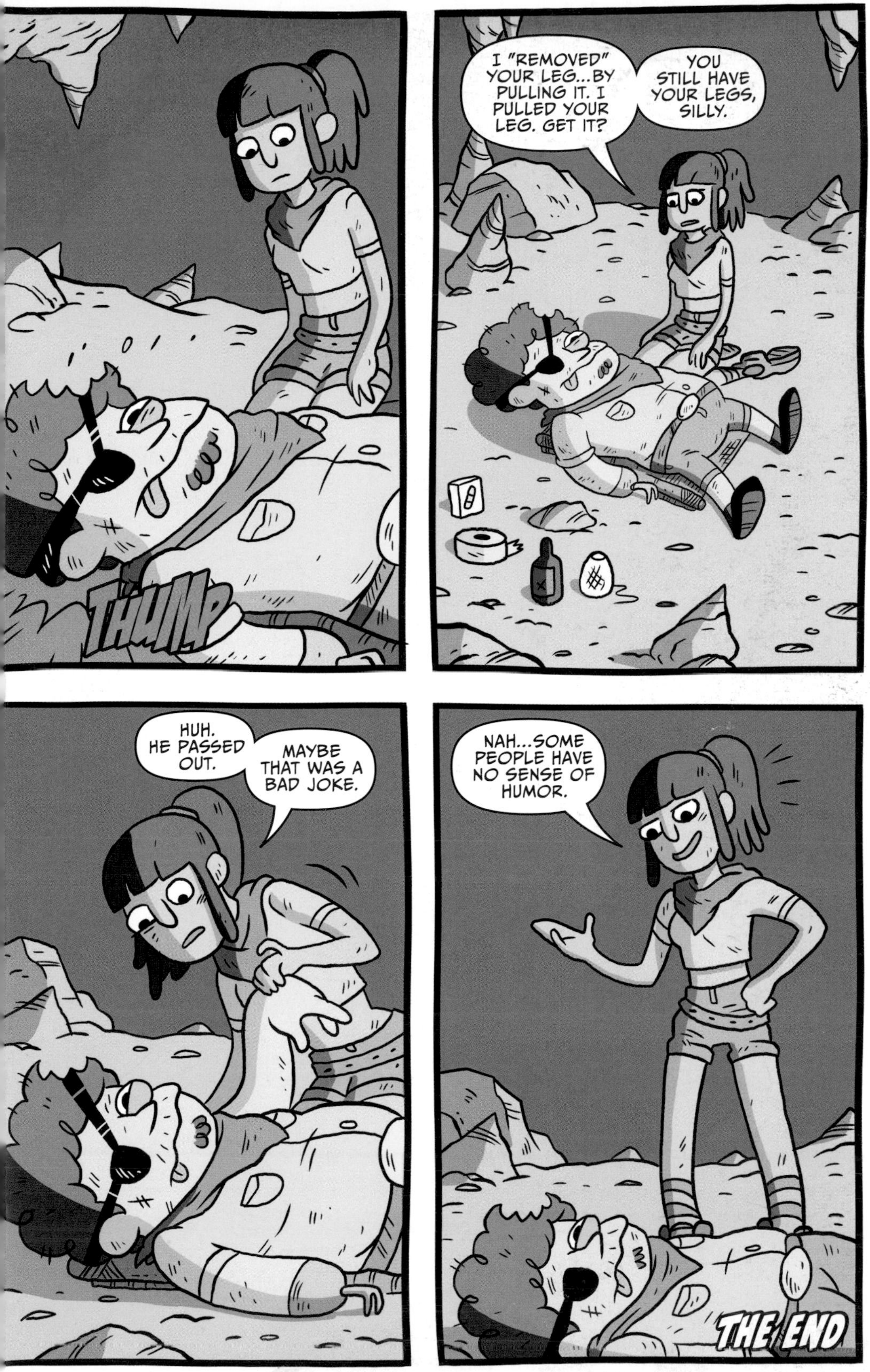
THUMP
I "REMOVED" YOUR LEG...BY PULLING IT. I PULLED YOUR LEG. GET IT?
YOU STILL HAVE YOUR LEGS, SILLY.
HUH. HE PASSED OUT.
MAYBE THAT WAS A BAD JOKE.
NAH...SOME PEOPLE HAVE NO SENSE OF HUMOR.
THE END